ADVANC

DAIRE'S DEVILS

"War is tough, so is writing about it. Danielle Ackley-McPhail's *Daire's Devils* rises to that challenge and comes away triumphant."

David Sherman, Marine and best-selling author
of the *Starfist*, *Demontech*, and *18th Race* series

"A hard-hitting military science fiction with plenty of action, mystery, and intrigue—where do I sign up?!"

Maria V. Snyder, New York Times best-selling author
of the award-winning *Navigating the Stars*

"Plenty of action along with corporate and political intrigue
in the finest tradition of Elizabeth Moon's *Familias Regnant* novels,
with just a dash of Blade Runner-esque mystery
to add a little spice to the mix."

Dayton Ward, Marine and New York Times best-selling author
of *The Last World War* and *Star Trek: Agents of Influence*

"Once again, eSpec Books delivers another thrilling glance
at future military action [...] Ackley-McPhail shows an
acute awareness of military terminology and command structure
[as] the complex, multilayered plot of Daire's Devils unfolds."

Bud Sparhawk, Air Force Veteran, multi-Nebula finalist,
and author of *Shattered Dreams*

DAIRE'S DEVILS

DANIELLE
ACKLEY-McPHAIL

Pennsville, NJ

PUBLISHED BY
AGM Publications
A division of eSpec Books
PO Box 242
Pennsville, NJ 08070
www.especbooks.com

ISBN: 978-1-949691-79-5
ISBN (ebook): 978-1-949691-78-8

Portions of this novel originally published in earlier versions as the following short stories:

"Carbon Copy" in *Space Pirates*, edited by David Lee Summers and published by Flying Pen Press, 2008.
"The Devil You Don't" in *The Stories In Between*, edited by Greg Schauer, et al and published by Fantasist Enterprises, 2010.
"True Colors" in *By Other Means,* edited by Mike McPhail and published by Dark Quest Books, 2011.

Interior Design: Danielle McPhail
www.sidhenadaire.com

Cover Art and Design: Mike McPhail, McP Digital Graphics
Interior Icons: Mike McPhail, McP Digital Graphics

Copyediting: Greg Schauer, John L. French

Dedicated to my good friend, Alf,
for pushing me to finish...

...To James, Anton, and Jorie,
for helping me to polish off the rough edges...

...To Kenny, Lenny, Eddie, Jeff, Victor, Larry, Gustavo (and Myron),
Toni, and Lourdes, for helping me to find my feet in the Alliance...

...But finally, and most important of all,
dedicated to my husband, Mike,
for letting me play in his sandbox.

ACKNOWLEDGMENTS

OTHER THAN FAMILY HISTORY, I HAVE NO PERSONAL EXPERIENCE WITH THE military. I am grateful to my husband, Mike McPhail (Air National Guard), and my friends, Bud Sparhawk (Air Force), Dayton Ward (Marine Corps), and Anton Kukal (Army) for vetting this novel to ensure I made no egregious errors with the elements of my fictional military.

INTRODUCTION

I N 1986 A.D., AT THE ACADEMY OF AERONAUTICS IN NEW YORK, THE ALLIANCE Archives and its Martial Role-Playing Game (All'Arc MRPG), was born to fill a need. Namely, the military members of our Friday night (after-class) gaming group were fed up with the unrealistic combat and encounter systems used by the games we were playing.

At some point, I was challenged by our players (as a design student known for my work with science fiction/military technology) to come up with something *they* could enjoy, that would also be accessible for our younger friends, some of whom were only fourteen at the time. And so it began...

Over the decades of game play, the universe in which the All'Arc is set has changed and evolved (and in a few cases devolved) depending on the players' needs and/or advances in real-world science and technology.

With *Daire's Devils,* it is Danielle's turn to add a new chapter and world-view to this on-going saga; so suit up, the battle is far from over.

Mike McPhail
Creator of the All'Arc MRPG

PROLOGUE

MASTER SERGEANT KEVIN DAIRE PUSHED TO HIS FEET, HIS CHAIR'S METAL base squealing as it slid forcefully back in its anchor track. He slammed his scarred and calloused fist down, rattling the polymer-matrix conference table and overpowering every sound in the war room. Conversations cut off abruptly as most of the room's occupants stilled, those combat-trained poised to act. Everyone pivoted toward him, but he didn't care. Too much was at stake. Too much had been risked... and sacrificed for him to watch it all go down the relief tube now.

"I will *not* dignify this by calling it horseshit." He spoke the words crisp and clear, biting off each one, not even flinching when several ranking brows around the room drew down in stern lines.

"You have to understand what a threat these... um... infiltrators represent," one of the tacticians began. "Once our operative is in place, we can..."

"You are placing one of *my* team in a dangerous position—uninformed, unsupported, and unprepared," he paused, his jaw tightening and his gaze narrowing. "That's a good way to get even a seasoned operative kil...."

Another squeal interrupted him as a second chair slid back in its track.

At the end of the table, General Drovak slowly stood. His hair shone snowy white, and his jawline had gone a little soft with the years. The dark blue eyes glaring the length of the table, however, were plenty hard.

Four stars gleamed on each side of his collar.

"Master sergeant, are you *questioning* orders?"

The silence became a living, quivering thing.

"No, sir," Daire responded, his tone flat. "Just stating my concerns."

"Do you have any doubt that this situation is a threat of the highest order?"

Again, Daire answered, "No, sir."

General Drovak gestured to the aide beside him, who stood and accepted the sheath of papers the general held out, pivoted sharply, and marched the length of the table to deliver them. Though the aide's expression remained neutral, his gaze felt weighted, probing. Daire held it a moment before glancing down at the documents the man held out.

Daire's brow furrowed. There were two sets of orders. Those on top bore his name. When he looked up to meet Drovak's eyes, the general showed no reaction.

"You will issue these orders immediately," the general commanded. "Dismissed."

Resigned, Daire took possession of the papers.

The cluster he was caught in had just got infinitely more fucked.

CHAPTER 1

CORPORAL KATRION ALEXANDER COULD SEE NO STARS.

Well, not from the command deck of the Groom Experimental Complex, anyway. The filter of the protective shielding and the harsh electric glare lighting the compartment rendered anything that would have been visible to her unaided eye imperceptible. Two hundred and seventy degrees of pure, inky black surrounded her. That's why she liked being in space so much lately. It matched her mood.

Like tonight, for instance, brand-new to this post, she'd barely been on the station two hours when the officer of the watch tapped her to cover a shift for someone named Simmons who had reported to sickbay. Kat hadn't even requisitioned her kit from stores yet.

What a classic SNAFU. Everything was off-kilter. Schedules delayed, launch sequences misaligned, posts vacant. With typical military efficiency, everyone's signals had been crossed. Kat had a recall out for the deck crew mistakenly given liberty, but she didn't hold much hope they'd surface. Just as well. She could use the solitude, and one command console operated pretty much like any other in the military. The United Aerospace Command, or AeroCom, favored consistency... in their tech, anyway. Besides, she'd trained in computer infiltration for her military occupational specialty. There wasn't a system in service or development she couldn't run, take apart, or break into.

She was familiarizing herself with this particular setup when a change in the outside ambiance drew her attention.

"Oh, mercy!" She let out an appreciative breath as the ship she'd just cleared for departure came into view directly overhead. If the flight path hadn't crossed a few klicks above her observation dome, she likely wouldn't have seen the ship's movement. The *Cromwell*, a prototype McCormick-class attack vessel built and outfitted right here at the research-and-development end of the station, blended into the texture of space. Her running lights flickered, the only glimmer against the darkness, barely illuminating the matte finish of the hull in microbursts. The black surface's engineered tincture all but absorbed the flashes, further dampened by the almost cellular hatch markings engraved on the ablative hull plating. The ultimate in space camo for ships. AeroCom's systems registered the vessel—they knew what to look for—but, as of yet, no one else could. If it weren't for alert beacons used during conventional flight, the ship would have been a hazard. Shielded against every form of observation short of up-close visual sight, the vessel represented a covert marvel, the prize of any fleet. The trade-off to achieve the equivalent of a sniper ship: the *Cromwell* sacrificed heavier armor for speed, advanced stealth, and weaponry. So, basically, she wasn't any more difficult to disable than her less stealthy counterparts once the adversary knew her coordinates.

Of course... by then, it was theoretically too late.

Ping. Ping.

Kat didn't even twitch as the comm system alert tone sounded through the chamber. That would be Tac Stanton, commander of the *Alexi,* the ship that should have been the next to deploy. Let him stew. She'd encountered him before. Never a pleasant experience. In fact, he seemed to go out of his way to be as difficult as possible, no matter the situation. He should be grateful his ship was getting out of here any time this solar week, given the mess she'd had to sort through when she came on shift.

As the *Cromwell* deployed, Kat's resentment burned raw. She should be on that ship. Instead, they'd stuck her on this station while others... while *her team* went off to patrol the stars.

It made no sense. She had just climbed from the ranks of combat infantry to special ops, only to be notified that she had psych-tested out of her team after only a month. Kat expected that her mother actually had something to do with that ruling. It wouldn't be the first time she'd called in favors to interfere with Kat's "reckless" career choices. Hell, Kat had enlist with AeroCom and journeyed all the way to the Tau Ceti star system just to serve. Not that her efforts had proven completely successful. Kat had more than enough points to have earned her sergeant's stripes but Mother had her papers so tied up in red tape that Kat might be retired before she ranked up. Not that she had any proof of that, beyond past experience...

In any case, for reasons military command wouldn't explain, they had given Kat two options: punch a keypad, or push a broom. Rebelliously, she'd nearly grabbed for the broom. Let them waste years of intensive military training and proven combat experience, right along with her multi-million-dollar transport fee.

Only her honor stood in the way of such retaliation. She had sworn an oath to stand between the common people and the harm they might suffer from not only the Legion but at the hands of pirates and corporations and the faceless, as-yet-undiscovered dangers lurking in space. AeroCom might have forgotten this. Kat could not.

Kat swallowed her bitterness and grudgingly accepted her unsought role of station support staff. She would diligently work every shift she could pull to bring her closer to the day she earned her ticket home. Heck, she hadn't even unpacked her duffle before she clocked in on the roster. She'd still have to stick around until she served her tour, but at least she'd have a ride out of here at the end.

The alert tone sounded once again, somehow seeming more insistent. Again, Kat ignored it. Only an emergency signal obligated Control to respond to hails from vessels waiting in the queue, and this gave no indication of an emergency.

Hands splayed over the keypad—set below flush, into the hip-high console—she entered the final release sequence and sent the *Cromwell* off ahead of schedule with a silent salute. After all, the timetable was already screwed up. The quicker they departed, the sooner she could adjust to her exile. The vessel drifted the proscribed distance before engaging its drive system. From the command deck, her sensors registered the telltale vapors bubbling in the ship's wake as the *Cromwell* initiated its electrogravitic drive envelope.

With her brown eyes burning, she smothered her resentment anew. Her team—the 142nd Mobile Special Operations Team, informally known as Daire's Devils—counted among the vessel's complement of regular troops and special ops teams. Though she had been the newest member of her team, they already felt like family. Being parted from them stung like a betrayal. Whether on her part, theirs, or the bureaucracy's, she couldn't say, but it didn't sit well. Had she rung out of training, no one would have blamed her for knowing her limitations. But to have her superiors determine her—an experienced operative—substandard didn't sit well. To be labeled, out of all those in her team, as unacceptable, and not even know why...

Her fingers clawed the console housing, thankfully in no danger of triggering the recessed keypads. With a deep breath and hard discipline, she forced her bitterness back into its crater and mentally rolled a rock over it. She then turned her focus back to the task at hand.

With the *Cromwell* clear, she began to process the next vessel. This time, she opened the channel as the alert tone persisted.

"You incompetent fool! Can't you follow a deployment schedule?"

Kat's lips tightened into a thin, hard line and her hands fisted reflexively. Her mood darkened even further at the thought of dealing with the notorious Commander Tac Stanton. Pompous ass. They had had dealings with one another when she'd shipped to the Tau Ceti system, and occasionally since then. She would never understand how such a slug had risen to command level.

"A glitch in the deployment systems required minor adjustments to get things back on track, commander," she responded across the open channel in her own carefully neutral tone.

"Glitch?! Station Commander Ghei will—"

Kat cut him off. "The *Alexi's* next in the queue. Is your vessel ready to deploy? If not, I can process the incoming Hirobon transport..."

"Yes!" he snapped out the single word hard and tight, cutting her off. "We are more than ready." Kat's eyes narrowed. Stanton was way too worked up over a simple delay, even for him.

"Commencing pre-deployment scans, now... position your craft for launch," she instructed him as she reviewed the datafeed for anomalies. She noted a small mass registering out near Tagalong, just cresting the planetesimal's horizon. She initiated second-tier scans, but they revealed no recognizable mechanics or transmissions. Density analysis suggested low mineral content and no ferrous deposits. Just a rock... roughly the size—if not the shape—of a good-sized yacht. It fell outside of the scheduled flight path, so she made a note of her observations and beamed a copy of the report to the *Alexi's* flight crew, along with their release codes.

"You are clear to deploy."

She did not linger to watch this vessel. Turning back to her monitors, she started on the next flight plan. She didn't get far. The console in front of her registered an unauthorized communications burst tight-beamed to the station. It ended before she could intercept it through one of the perimeter sensors.

Probably Stanton griping to Ghei because she'd made him wait.

Great. She'd been on-station only a few hours and the first complaint had already been added to her docket.

Kat shrugged off her annoyance. She might not be happy with the turn her career had taken, but she had duties to fulfill and too much honor not to care. Turning back toward the transparent shielding that allowed her a direct visual of her domain, Kat scanned the deep-black oblivion. Toward her distant left, in the direction the *Alexi* had launched, she saw a ghostly glimmer, like the after-image of a camera flash, and nothing else. Had the *Alexi* had enough time to engage its drive and rocket out of range? Kat didn't think so. The older vessel ran with fusion impulse engines.

Something didn't feel right. Kat sequenced a full-system scan, engaging all the remote sensors linked to her console. Reviewing the 'feed as it processed, her every muscle tightened like the steady ripple of a python's coils. She sent a secure quick-burst query to the *Alexi*'s comm and waited for the security-coded confirmation.

The deck comm remained silent.

If her dark brown hair wasn't already bristle-brush short, it would have stood on end. Adrenaline sharp-focused her thoughts in an instant. A growl rumbled in her throat. Her left hand reflexively itched for her gauss rifle, currently locked away in a weapons locker aboard the *Cromwell*, probably already assigned to someone else. Instead, she hit the print button on her console, and the report scrolled out on a thin slice of durable acrylisheet. The hardcopy confirmed her suspicions. Readings showed no sign that the *Alexi* had initiated its drive system. The ship couldn't have moved beyond visual on conventional thrusters. It definitely should still be within hailing range.

"Control to Commander Ghei," she sent out a hail to the station commander. Precious minutes passed with no response. She needed his clearance to initiate High Alert status. "Control to Commander Ghei, please come in, sir," she repeated as she keyed in an urgency code linked to the message.

Still no response. Her internal alarms went into overdrive. On station, there was no time Ghei could call completely his own. Moments of crisis superseded everything. Station commanders were always online, their personal comms bonejacked directly into their jaw, just below the ear, same as ships' captains or elite military squads. Her hand went to the site of her now-deactivated, subdermal comm. She missed the buzzing sensation of someone's words transmitting along her jaw. Sometimes, she thought she felt the faint vibration indicating a live feed, but she attributed that to wishful thinking.

Kat set the hail on auto-replay. Then, uncertain of the commander's status, and faced with a high probability of threat to station security, she snapped into action without command authorization. Flipping open the cap that covered the alert toggle, she notched it to the next level, setting off a klaxon throughout the security zones of the station. No need to panic the civvies... yet.

Not three minutes after the alarm sounded the station's first defense, a wing of Condor-class scout vessels jetted from their hangars like canned air from a hull breach.

"Control to Wing Command, do you copy?"

"Mustang Sally readin' you loud and clear, Control, where we headin'?"

Neither the flatness of the transmission nor the gravity of the situation took the color out of the pilot's irrepressible Texas twang. *Finally, a friendly voice.* And bonus, one likewise from Earth. Kat allowed herself the briefest of smiles and responded, "Spread your wing out in a vector scan of quadrant 0689Alpha looking for unaccounted debris, followed by a deep-space scan from that location targeting the vessel Alexi, ident-code ND-061. Presume hostiles are in the area. Should you make contact with the *Alexi*, secure absolute confirmation of the ship's status. Over."

"Gotcha, Sally off." As they headed for the coordinates she beamed to them, Kat initiated the High Alert protocol.

Her fingers flew over the keypad. First, she punched in the locator sequence keyed to Commander Ghei. A schematic of the station appeared on the monitor before her. The spiraling design corkscrewed around a central maintenance tube, with pairs of directional thrusters running along the coils' outer edges. The Command, or C-deck, in the head, angled out into space to allow Control an unobstructed view of the docking area, the shipyard, and most approach vectors, with auxiliary C-decks at key points along the complex.

Commander Chand Svare Ghei's designation did not register on any coil.

Nervous tension sizzled through Kat. No way Ghei had left the station. From just the short time she'd spent in his presence as she handed over her orders, she recognized him as hardcore and dedicated. She sent a priority-coded message to the head of station security, with a secondary request to search for the commander once they had confirmed the station secure from outside threat.

Extremely uneasy, Kat took the perimeter sensors off standby and set them to full sector scan. One keystroke transformed the transparent observation dome into a split-screen display, allowing her to view the Groom Experimental Complex's total perimeter via the remote sensors while monitoring the constant datafeed. She then initiated the security fields around the station's defense hubs and essential operations. The personnel manning those stations ran through their own checklists. She initiated next-stage High Alert protocols, triggering orders activating all security squads, off-duty and on. Incoming and outgoing ship traffic paused once again—which caused more than a little uproar until Kat turned off the non-station transmissions—and all station personnel were on standby, waiting, as her PawPaw would say, for the shit to hit the fan.

Behind Kat, the hiss of the command deck hatch sent another spike of tension down her spine, mingled with a trickle of relief. *Soon this will all be someone else's headache,* she thought, as she input the final sequence in the security protocol, sending out the ancillary black-box beacon. The beacon would receive low-frequency data pulses mirroring those fed to the station's black-box unit from the external sensors, double-documenting the incident to aid Military Intelligence's Tactical Unit should things go decidedly... not well.

The distinctive sound of the commander's footsteps crossing the deck incinerated any relief Kat had briefly felt. He stopped just behind her and to her right in an overt effort to intimidate. The silence weighed more with each second that passed. Sarge never would have employed such low tactics with someone under his command, especially not for doing their duty. But then, what did she know? Maybe commanding the Devils took a different approach than running a space station.

Shaking off the too-fresh memories of her old team, Kat suppressed the growing impulse to spin and crouch as if an enemy stood at her back. Somehow it didn't seem it would ingratiate her with her new commander. At that thought, her hindbrain scrabbled for her attention as her hand ran across the console in a seemingly idle gesture.

The console still displaying the schematic of the station.

Her throat muscles rippled reflexively beneath her collar, but her expression remained impassive as she glanced down. *What the heck is going on?* A blip representing Commander Ghei should have registered on her monitor, yet Kat's icon remained the only one displayed. In the reflection off the dome, he watched her, a hard glimmer in his gaze. His censure issued a faint, bitter tang wafting from every pore.

"Corporal Alexander, stand down!" Kat stepped back from the console and pivoted to face him, back straight and gaze forward.

"*What...* do you think you're doing?" Ghei demanded, both his tone and expression lethal.

Kat kept her features schooled and her eyes blank as she replied.

"The *Alexi* is gone, sir. She launched, presumably moved beyond visual, and disappeared. Control observed a spatial anomaly, ran prescribed scans." Kat reached for the acrylisheet printout and held it out to him for confirmation. "Scans register no residual vapor trail, indicating the drive unit never engaged, yet the *Alexi* does not appear on any of our sensors. The vessel remains unresponsive to query."

Ghei glanced at the report and then back up. He stared at her a long, awkward moment, almost like a freeze frame, before saying, "That's it?" His expression crackled with disbelief on the surface, but she caught a glimmer of something darker roiling just beneath. "You called High Alert... *without* authorization... for that?!"

"I initiated a priority alert hail, commander. I received no response, despite repeat transmissions. I was unable to summon the *Alexi*... or yourself.

"Sir, station security protocol requires..."

He slashed the air with the blade of his hand. "Enough!

"You initiated High Alert, *without* authorization, because you *missed* a bit of drive vapor?! You anticipated an attack scenario because I didn't respond to a *hail*?" His eyes flashed, and he looked furious enough to send her out to scrub the hull without an MMU. It took an extreme effort for Kat not to flinch. "Did you see an external threat? Was there an explosion?" She shook her head, little more than a sharp twitch. "Was there identifiable debris?"

She set her jaw and met his gaze head-on, keeping her own expression as neutral as she could manage. "As yet unconfirmed, sir, pending the report of the Condor wing deployed."

Commander Ghei drew in a sharp breath. His cheek twitched, and his expression went flat. Every reaction, every comment, prefaced by a subtle hesitation. Beneath her heart's heavy thudding, Kat clearly heard a death rattle... the final moments of her already ailing career ingloriously fading away. At this point, she may well have to walk home.

As they stared each other down, the emergency deck crew popped through the hatch.

"Sakmyster," Commander Ghei called out to one of the new arrivals. "Kill that klaxon. Initiate stand-down and order that bloody wing back to the station." The commander kept his tone controlled as he summarily relieved Kat of her post. "Deck crew, dismissed."

A chorus of "Yessirs" peppered the air as the crew, with the exception of Sakmyster, filed out the hatch.

What the heck is going on? Kat remained at attention as the crew left the C-deck. She kept her eyes forward and slightly out of focus to elude Sak's sympathetic gaze. They'd gone through Basic together the first time Kat tried to join the service, which only made this sting all the worse. She had planned to look him up once she got settled. But then, plans changed.

She found it difficult to keep silent when she heard the clack of the keys as Sak stepped the station down to alert status. As he keyed in the final sequence, he turned to Ghei for further instruction.

"Dismissed."

Sakmyster looked puzzled but did not question the order. Kat caught her breath coming out in short, sharp huffs as he left. She forced herself to a more natural rhythm, though her instincts screamed, *this is wrong!*

With exaggerated care, Ghei laid the report on the console before him. He looked from it to her.

"What were you doing on duty tonight, Alexander?"

She wondered the same thing herself, but it was not her place to question protocol when summoned to duty. "Simmons is down in medbay, sir. The duty officer instructed me to cover his shift."

Ghei looked ready to savage both the hapless Simmons and herself. "And was this cleared with me?"

She kept her expression neutral, though her nerves bug-crawled beneath the surface of her skin. Something bothered her... about his voice... about the situation. She couldn't place it, though. A movement caught her attention. Oddly, his right hand jerked ever so slightly, over and over, as if it plucked at an unseen harp.

"Well?"

Kat pulled her focus away from his hand and back to his face. "I couldn't say, sir. The order came from Lt. Commander Connor."

The commander's jaw went visibly tight, and his hands barely resisted clenching. She felt truly in his crosshairs now, though she could not imagine why. According to protocol, calling High Alert had been justified, given the circumstances, and as for being on the C-deck at all, she was following orders. She remained silent and at attention, her eyes trained straight ahead. Even so, she noted Ghei's gaze flickered slightly to the console displaying the data from the outer quadrants. She watched without watching as his fingers moved to the keypad. He called up the log of her shift. Kat thought he may have paled upon scanning the data.

Ghei left the console, coming to stand in front of her, close. "You are suspended from duty pending a full investigation. You are to report to your quarters and remain there until summoned. Acknowledged?"

Kat wanted to protest, but she'd already crossed too many lines. No doubt, an investigation would absolve her of any misconduct. If anything,

Ghei had acted inappropriately. Something felt very wrong here. If only her team were still around to back her up. Except she had to remind herself they were no longer her team.

"I said, acknowledged?" Ghei's tone sounded one short step from erupting.

"Yessir!"

"Dismissed!"

Kat executed a sharp about-face with all the military precision she could muster, and then strode from the command deck, back erect, chin held high. That pompous ass didn't deserve the oak leaf on his collar.

Ghei's cold blue eyes tracked the woman's movement as she left the room, the hatch hissing closed behind her. He remained still a moment, the sensations washing over him, transitioning from fear to rage to resignation and back again in an unending loop; there were occasional flickers of relief mingled in. He closed his eyes against the emotional onslaught and breathed deep, fighting for control. The fingers of his right hand resumed plucking at the air, seemingly without notice, as he turned back to the console and the printout that would be the death of him if he couldn't find a way to salvage the situation. Everything had been in place. He'd followed instructions implicitly, and yet, whether by design or happenstance, not much more could have gone wrong today.

As if in response to his desperate thoughts, the comm chimed. He glanced over to see a blank viewing screen and an active status light.

"C-deck, Commander Ghei speaking," he responded, though he received no hail.

There was no response.

Ghei's jaw clenched reflexively as he reached out and keyed a code into the system, taking the comm line off automatic record. The moment he did, a familiar symbol appeared on-screen—a stylized cross with all four arms of equal length, like four capital 'T's. A simple enough icon unaffiliated with any group of which he had knowledge. It flashed briefly and then disappeared. "Ghei," he tried again.

"How you managed to fuck things up so royally I will never understand," a voice rife with static sounded over the comm, completely unidentifiable as man, woman, or even human. "Forget about the *Cromwell* for now. I want you to secure her technical specifications and then wipe them from the GEC system. Screw this up, and you won't have to wonder what comes next."

Before he could respond—not that he'd intended to—the status light went inactive. Ghei tensed with the need to strike out, intensified by his inability to do so. His hands were bound, and he'd been dropped in the middle of a mess from which Houdini couldn't escape. His family would be left without even his good name—or his pension—to comfort them. The chill of that realization traveled from the crown of Ghei's head down to his toes. With one short, sharp huff of breath, he turned to the keypad, and his fingers worked like mad trying to isolate the data he'd been ordered to deliver.

Kat made no conscious decision to disobey. Really. She fully intended to return to her quarters, as instructed. But she kept remembering each anomaly that led her to this point. The unmanned stations, the *Alexi* disappearing from the scans, Commander Ghei's lack of response, his code not registering per station protocol. Any one of those would trigger a red flag. But all of them together...? Driven by instinct, Kat headed for the nearest auxiliary C-deck, once again deserted, thanks to Ghei's order to stand down.

En route, she stopped at a security cache and armed herself with a variable-velocity shotgun, a supply of non-lethal riot rounds, and a high-powered taser. Once again, she longed for her gauss rifle. Station-board armaments were a joke compared to special-ops issue.

Kat slipped through the hatch. Using her special-ops training to lockdown the compartment, she disabled the outside access pad. She then moved to the console. Sitting down in front of the keypad with her weapons ready to hand, she tapped into the security protocols and accessed the monitoring system. Within moments, she had real-time close-ups of Ghei and the main console fed to her display, as well as a wide-angle view of the primary C-deck.

At first, she saw nothing on the monitor except an odd symbol, similar to a crusader's cross, only without the extra bits between the arms. For several moments after, the screen remained blank, then the commander's fingers moved over the keys nearly as fast as her own. He accessed duty rosters and security details first. Her personnel jacket flashed on the screen, seeming to remain there infinitely longer than anything else.

When requests for production specs and technical schematics replaced her file in scrolling across the monitor Kat's gut feeling of wrongness increased.

Ghei was after the *Cromwell*.

Kat sent up a prayer of thanks that she'd deployed the ship early. That vessel... in the hands of the wrong party... not good. And the specs and the research data, almost as bad.

Deftly applying her technical training, Kat intercepted Ghei's requests, dispersing them harmlessly in the ether while she tied up his console with error messages and processing loops. It wouldn't stop him, but it bought her some time.

The only way she could think of to remove the data from his reach was to initiate Full Alert. At an experimental complex like Groom, that triggered an automatic wipe of the research databases. An annoyance for the scientists, but all the research data regularly backed up to an off-site server and to the black box, lost to the bad guys, but not anyone else. Much better than having their research fall into the hand of pirates... or worse, rivals. The scientists would certainly agree on that point.

Unfortunately, it took more than flipping a manual toggle to initiate Full Alert.

If she had the codes and clearance, this would have taken a matter of minutes. She didn't. But she didn't need an actual Full Alert. All she needed to do was trigger the protocol that wiped the servers and dumped the data. If she couldn't pull that off, she wasn't worthy of her designation as a computer infiltration specialist.

The computer keys rattled like hail on tarmac as she accessed the system, careful not to trigger any alerts. Groom was a high-security facility, with Ghei the head man in charge. She had no way of telling who else on the station he'd involved. She had to stay below the radar. One by one, she located the necessary codes, identified the protocols, slipped through backdoor channels, the entire time keeping an eye on the monitor for any sudden activity from Ghei. It was slow going, though, and every second she took increased the likelihood of someone noticing what she was up to.

Almost there, she thought. *Come on! Almost there...*

She glanced up, keeping track of Ghei, only to have her gaze collide with his. Ghei glared into the camera. He couldn't know where she was, could he? He'd have to know her location to pull off the same trick...

Then again, true to her luck, he seemed to have figured that out.

With increased urgency, she turned back to her efforts. Not long after, someone tried to open the hatch behind her. When the key sequence didn't work, a thud came at the door, and then another. Unless the person in the corridor had an override, they weren't getting in until she released the lockdown.

"Shit!" she muttered as she gave up being sneaky and plundered the system for the final code she needed. "They couldn't wait five friggin' minutes before they found me, could they!" Her fingers blurred as she raced to initiate the dump. In a matter of seconds, the data would be out of reach of those thieves.

And her console went dead.

"Shit! No!" Her fist came down hard enough to dent the aluminum housing. Had she succeeded? Or had they shut her down before she accomplished her objective? Either way, they had her cornered now.

Somehow, she suspected those in the corridor carried something with a little more kick than a riot gun and a taser. Not for the first time, she wondered why she hadn't opted for the broom...

She took a moment and prepped her pitiful collection of armaments. First calibrating the taser to its highest setting, she then loaded the cartridge and slid the weapon into the cargo pocket on her left leg. Next, she loaded the rifle and secured additional rounds in her right-hand pocket. Once prepared, she moved to the hatch. Beside the door, an intercom corresponded to a speaker on the other side of the bulkhead. Set just above it, a micro-display revealed the commander and two others standing beyond the hatch.

"What do you want, Ghei?" Kat purposely neglected to address him as sir. He'd lost that privilege along with her respect. She released the intercom button and took up the rifle, standing at the ready.

"You've caused me a lot of trouble, Alexander."

Kat tightened her grip on her weapon.

A soft *pop* came as her only warning. She scrambled back, bringing the riot gun to bear as the hatch opened. Two unfamiliar crewmen stood in the hatchway, with Ghei just behind. Before they could take a step, she fired, once, twice. High-velocity suppression rounds slammed each man center mass, sending one of them knocking back into Ghei. The other flew past him. A satisfying *thud* sounded as the man's head impacted with the far bulkhead.

Well, at least one of them wasn't getting up very soon.

She reloaded quickly and had the barrel trained on Ghei before he finished climbing back to his feet. His cohort remained sprawled on the deck, still conscious but gasping for breath. For the moment, a non-threat. Ghei stalked through the hatch and approaching with sure, unwavering steps. Kat let him have it with both barrels. He took one suppression round to the temple, the other square in the throat.

Kat heard a sickening crunch.

"You have got to be kidding me!" she swore as Ghei barely rocked back with the impacts.

Kat had no time to reload. And barely time to drop the weapon. She didn't even have time to grab for the taser. As the commander reached her, Kat pivoted on the ball of her right foot and brought her left leg up in a roundhouse kick aimed at his head. For a surreal moment, it looked as if he would stand there and take it without even a word.

"Nice try, you stupid bitch," Ghei growled, his tone eerily flat, almost as if it came across a comm. His hand intercepted her foot in a crushing grip. The impact jarred her, like slamming into a titanium hull. He shoved her hard off balance. The moment Kat landed on the deck, her face exploded with pain that rivaled that of her foot. Already, she felt her eye swelling.

Her training kicked in, though, and she'd barely impacted before she rolled away, bouncing to her feet, ready to do battle. *What the hell are they feeding station commanders these days, anyway?*

The humor was a bad sign. The black spots dancing before her eyes were another.

Hello, Kittie.

Oh... goodie, the party wouldn't be complete without hearing things, as well. Except... she recognized the voice, and the sensation of it buzzing along her jaw and up into her ear. *Could it be...?* Only one person greeted her that way. Someday, she'd hurt him for it... but probably not today.

Scotch? she subvocalized, hardly daring to believe. Could it really be Technical Sergeant Jackson Daniels, her former comrade-at-arms, the wise-ass of the 142nd, or was she losing it worse than she feared?

There was no response.

Ghei took a swing at her head. She jerked back just enough that he only clipped her jaw.

"Shit!" Kat couldn't hold back the expletive. The spots before her eyes intensified until the entire deck faded to varying degrees of grey.

Shake it off, airman. A different voice came through her comm. It sounded suspiciously like her former team leader, Master Sergeant Kevin Daire.

What the hell's going on, Sarge? she risked subvocalizing again as she dodged the next strike, ducking low and aiming a low side kick at Ghei's knee that should have taken him down. She connected, impacting like a kick to a wall. A solid wall. Another odd crunch sounded, but the man stayed steady. So steady, in fact, he lashed out at her with the leg she hadn't aimed at. He dumped her back to the deck once again.

That quick, Ghei leapt on her, his hands reaching for her throat.

Get your head back into the fight, Sarge growled, ignoring her question. *Your biosensor readings are all over the place. We're nearly there.*

Kat groaned. If her head was any more in this fight it would be splattered all over the deck. She fought Ghei's grip on her throat. Aiming for a disabling blow, she slammed her fist into his groin.

Nothing. Absolutely nothing. It was like the guy had no pain receptors.

The world faded to a uniform grey and rapidly grew darker. Damned if she'd lay down and give up, though. Perhaps physically she didn't have the mass, leverage, or force to break his grip... but there were other means less easily dismissed. Snaking her hand down her left thigh, she drew the taser from her pocket and hit the trigger point-blank into Ghei's chest. A muffled *pop* sounded, followed by crackling and the stench of burning ozone and synthetics as the leads connected, setting the barbs a half an inch deep into the commander's flesh, right through his uniform. His grip spasmed, then tightened, and his body jerked uncontrollably.

Awww! Friggin' Hell! Kat subvocalized. Microseconds later, the charge reached her, and she too began to dance.

Her world went black.

CHAPTER 2

OUT BEYOND TAGALONG, IN A SLEEK CORSAIR SCOUT CRAFT THAT OCCLUDED THE smallest increment of space, Legion Scout Michèle DeVeaux sat patiently at her post, her engines powered down to minimize the risk of discovery. Though she watched her monitors and tracked the activity surrounding the Groom Experimental Complex, her objective was not to spy. Today, if all went as planned, she was to play courier.

Of course, surely any intel gathered would not go amiss. Not that much opportunity had presented itself. Nestled in a compartment just large enough for her to reach her various controls, her vessel built for speed and not conquest, DeVeaux bore witness as two ships departed. The first, barely visible to technical or optical means, had to be the *Cromwell*. The other easily tracked by her systems bore ident-code ND-061. The *Alexi*.

Her expression drew down in a very Gallic moue of distaste. Even by the twisted sense of honor she'd been raised under, the captain of that vessel, and a good portion of his crew, held no honor at all. Her hand darted to her console, redirecting the external sensors on her aft housing and initiating a recording sequence as the rogue vessel accelerated, firing on the one preceding it. A brief and uneven battle ensued, leaving the *Alexi* adrift—intact but disabled—and the *Cromwell* a swiftly vanishing pinpoint of light. She diverted a message sent from the *Cromwell* to the GEC reporting the incident and requesting the apprehension and detention of the *Alexi*'s crew. As distasteful as she found the aggressors, they nominally served the same side. Likewise, they could not turn coat against the Legion if they were not caught.

DeVeaux started to transmit the incident to her superiors when her Corsair shimmied violently. The sensation felt similar to being ensnared by the drive wake of a much larger vessel, yet the alerts remained silent, and nothing registered on her sensors. The scout froze like a mouse, desperate not to be seen, instinct overcoming commonsense. Brief blips on her sensors seemed to indicate weapons' fire—presumably from the *Alexi*—but against what? Her gaze remained riveted on the monitor before her.

She could see nothing at first until suddenly, the heavens flared like a bright plasma arc. By the time her vision cleared and readings went back to normal, the *Alexi* had ceased to be.

Michèle DeVeaux remained still for a very long time.

Then, moving slowly, as if something out there still watched and, in any way, could possibly see her, she ran diagnostics to ensure her vessel remained operational. Whatever had destroyed the *Alexi* had been highly localized. Not even her sensors had been impacted. In fact, they continued to record the sector previously containing the *Alexi*. A check of the sensor readings and recordings shed no additional light. One moment, the *Alexi* had been adrift. The next, a flash brighter than the sun, and not even a trace of debris remained.

She entered her personal observations on the occurrence into the logs, then returned her attention to the monitor displaying the Groom facility, noting the increase in traffic in the surrounding sector as what seemed like every craft available zipped and hovered like hornets protecting a disturbed nest. Had the station's sensors picked up what had happened to the *Alexi*? She had received no transmission to abort, but clearly, the GEC stood on high alert. With a deep sigh, she prepared to retreat.

Only...

She detected a signal transmitting from the complex, tantalizingly dense but not aimed toward her receptors. Try as she might, she could only intercept the smallest fragment, enough to know the content was encrypted. Enough to expect this was their objective, frustratingly out of reach.

"*Merde,*" she muttered to herself. Her sensors could not detect whatever had received the package, only the general direction where the beam had been focused.

With carefully controlled pulses of her engine, she slowly made her way toward the receptor she could not see. When she reached what she calculated was the right region, she used her targeting lasers to try to light up what she expected was a black-box buoy, only to have a proximity warning sound sharp and shrill in the tiny cocoon of cabin space surrounding her. Cursing with a bit more passion, she shut down the lasers and lowered any other sign of power usage even further as an AeroCom transport flew by. Once it moved clear, DeVeaux tight-beamed a brief encrypted message in the direction of the research complex, on a private channel:

The operative has failed. Must retreat. Clean up the mess.

A tiny sensor on her console lit, confirming receipt of the message. For the briefest instant, she powered up her engines to full speed, then cut them off again, risking the sudden energy flare in lieu of a low but clear drive signature leaving a trail. With masterful skill, DeVeaux glided away on the momentum, unnoticed, as the hornets made a beeline for where she had been.

Two sets of eyes watched the secondary monitors intently, one steel-grey, the other hazel, darkened to bronze. They scarcely shifted away. The biometrics had them the most concerned. Even hardened soldiers gave off certain indicators during tense situations, but the readings on the biometric screen spiked a bit more than that.

"We're not going to get there in time, are we?" Scotch asked, his jaw white-edged.

"As near enough to make no difference, Daniels," Sergeant Daire answered. "She's had the same training your sorry ass had. *Twice.* She'll hold her own until we get there."

And yet, he hovered just as close over Scotch's shoulder as Scotch did over the console.

"Campbell!" The yell came from both throats as alerts started sounding in conjunction with a series of hard spikes on the screen. Suddenly, biometrics cut out. They didn't flatline. They just stopped displaying altogether. Scotch didn't want to consider what that might mean. "Campbell!" he bellowed once more. He fell silent as Sarge's hand came to grip his shoulder. Hard.

"Sir?" the pilot responded from the drive compartment, as calm as if he were just taking them through maneuvers.

"You get us to that facility, stat, even if it means redlining every gauge," Sarge ordered as his hand anchored Scotch to his chair. "And you, Daniels... you work that system and get me all the intel you can over her 'jack."

Technically, bonejacks weren't supposed to work that way. Special Ops teams didn't bother much with technicalities. Scotch tweaked the settings for all he was worth within recommended tolerances but retrieved only silence. Cursing vehemently, he tried again, this time ignoring the instruction manual. Still nothing.

"Damnit! Come on, Kittie!" he snapped and tried a combination of settings not mentioned in any manual anywhere. Silence. A sharp sizzle, as from an arcing circuit. And then he heard it...

Thump, thump. Silence. *Thump, thump.* Silence. *Thump, thump...* then, barely audible, *"Shiiiit..."* followed by a long, low groan.

Scotch grinned up at his team leader.

Sprawled out on the auxiliary command deck of the Groom Experimental Complex, Corporal Katrion Alexander finally saw stars. She didn't mind so much at the moment. It meant she couldn't possibly stare at the smoking mass less than a meter away from her. That was *not* how a taser was supposed to work. Through her mental haze, she tried not to wonder what happened or why the air reeked of ozone and fried synthetics instead of scorched flesh. She didn't know how long she'd been out, but her muscles still twitched here and there.

"Hey, Sarge," she croaked aloud after manually toggling her comm. "If I break a transport, they take it out of my pay packet, yeah?"

Silence hummed over the 'jack a moment, then in a cautious tone, Daire answered, *Um... yeah...*

How much you reckon they'll dock me for wrecking a commander?

Scotch laughed, and so did Sarge, producing an interesting jangle along her jaw.

Sarge answered first. *I think we can let this one pass, Alexander. Just don't make a habit of it.*

Kittie... for this one, they might just give you a medal! Scotch chimed in.

Oh, goody... some fruit salad to clutter my chest... I'd settle for reinstatement to the Devils. Kat held her breath. It was only post-engagement banter, but her comment couldn't be more fervent.

You were never really off the rosters, corporal, but let's hold that for debriefing. We have a situation to wrap up.

Relief would have floored her if she weren't already down. *Yes, sir!*

Taking a few deep breaths to settle her emotions and compartmentalize the aches, she hauled herself to her feet and turned her focus back to getting the Devils on board. She never once looked at the crumpled heap still on the ground, though she did note that his cohorts had fled.

Scotch, what's your location? she asked

Dockside, in visual range and closing, he responded.

Kat did some quick logistical calculations. Automatically, she visualized the station's layout from her earlier scan for Ghei: The primary C-deck lay in the head. The auxiliary C-deck she occupied fell about mid-station. R&D and the aft C-deck resided in the tail toward Tagalong.

Do you have access to the station schematics?

It's been on screen for the last hour, Scotch answered. *I could draw you a picture if I had a crayon.*

I'm heading for the primary C-deck, Kat reported. *You can infiltrate the complex via the maintenance tube, outward-end of the station, just past the first coil. Comm me when you're in position, and I'll key the outer access hatch for your entry.*

Roger, Sarge responded. *Now get moving, airman.*

"Ah, crap!" Kat cursed as her diminished vision caused her to misjudge the hatch, clipping it with her right shoulder as she exited the aux. C-deck. "As if I didn't have enough bruises."

Ignoring the pain and the occasional random spasms, she double-timed it back to the primary C-deck.

"What took you so long?" Kat grumbled, annoyance she didn't really feel coloring her tone. Damn, if it wasn't great to be back with her team. Even if she and Scotch headed to clean up a corpse she'd rather not think about too closely. Sarge remained holed up with the chief of security on the main C-deck sorting out the rest of the mess.

"After we disabled the *Alexi*, it took us a while to turn around and get back in range."

She stopped dead and turned to face Scotch. "The *Alexi*?!"

"Yeah, seems Stanton thought the pay grade for pirate captain was better than what he drew as an AeroCom commander."

Kat laughed, but after the initial shock, she wasn't paying too much attention to what Scotch said. They neared the auxiliary C-deck, and while this wasn't her first kill, it had unsettled her more than any other.

"That's why you were here, according to Sarge," Scotch continued. "MI knew something was up and needed someone on the inside that wouldn't be suspected. 'Course, no one planned on the shit hitting the fan this soon. MI assumed they would have time to brief you on the QT... the asses. That's how come your 'jack was still live. You saved our butts by launching us early, by the way; else the ambush would have gone down different."

As what he said sank in, Kat had to fight back some justifiable aggravation. Some warning would have been nice. Still, it wasn't Scotch's fault. She'd love to take it up with Sarge, though, without a doubt. Of course, it didn't work that way in the military. Kat put it from her mind, burying her annoyance, instead wondering what in the world happened to the *Alexi* if the *Cromwell* had only disabled it. Before she could ask, they reached the aux. command deck.

Kat sighed. Time to clean up her mess.

At the hatch, she hung back, letting Scotch precede her into the compartment. Her breathing grew erratic, and the edges of her vision started to haze. She had to steel herself to enter. This should not have been a kill, and the way it went down left her rattled.

"Come on, Kat," Scotch said from the hatch, his hand reaching out to gently grip her shoulder. "Trust me, you need to see this."

The understanding moment of connection ended with Scotch's very next breath.

"Besides, how many times have each of us dreamed of zapping an idiot officer? You just earned yourself some serious cred."

Kat growled and smacked his arm, pushing past him onto the command deck. She didn't want to do this, but orders were orders. She'd just as soon get it done quickly.

Scotch laughed and came to stand beside her as she stared down at what remained of Ghei. Neither one of them spoke for a long, taut moment.

"What the *hell*?!" Kat finally exploded.

"Damn, woman, I know we're the Devils, but is that all you can ever say?"

With not one nerve left to get on, Kat grabbed Scotch by the collar and yanked him down. "What. Is. That?"

"Don't know what those that came up with them named them, but Sarge calls them composites." Scotch squatted beside the... remains. Kat joined him. He continued, "They're pretty damn good, you have to admit... too good. Near as the engineers can figure, the frame is a carbon fiber/ organic matrix composite. Strong as all get-out. Hard to detect unless you know what to look for. We don't yet... this being only the second one we've... secured.

"You can't see them, but this muddy fluid leaking out, that's full of nanites. Thanks to you, fried nanites." He caught her eye and grinned a wicked grin. Kat had to smile back, as shaken as she was.

"These little buggers are packed under the synthskin. They're linked to an operator located somewhere nearby... in this case, likely the real Ghei, seeing as there was no difference in voice to give this one away..." Kat thought of the unidentified mass she'd registered out by Tagalong when all of this started. If whoever was behind this could make something synthetic look and act like a man, maybe they could make a ship look like a rock. Anyway, she pulled her attention back to Scotch, who'd continued talking.

"The operator works the nanites by remote, some kind of surface-mapping algorithm or psionic receptor interface or who knows what. As far as we can tell, what this guy 'saw' the operator saw, and any reactions the composite showed transmitted real-time through the interface and was pretty much instantaneously mimicked by the nanites so..."

She must have looked as if she didn't give a damn about the particulars because Scotch stopped explaining the tech. Kat just shook her head, feeling more and more like she'd slipped dimensions or something because this wasn't any kind of reality she understood.

"Anyway," Scotch looked over at her, "betcha the FCC never anticipated this."

Kat looked at him sidewise as he stood up beside her.

"FCC?" She didn't have any energy to puzzle out where he was going with this.

"The Federal Communications Commission..."

"I know who they are, Scotch," she growled. "I just don't know what your point is."

He grinned like the irrepressible imp that he was, on or off the battle-field, and nudged the semi-melted husk on the ground with the toe of his boot. "Why, they have strict regulations against pirate copies."

Kat seriously reconsidered her decision not to hurt him.

CHAPTER 3

CAPTAIN JOHN CRYSON, THE MOST RECENT IN A LONG LINE OF LEGIONNAIRES going back to his many times' great grandfather, leaned over the computer display in his quarters aboard the star carrier *Destrier,* feeling every one of his forty-three years. He would swear he could sense his brown hair turn grey as the footage of yet another setback played across his monitor.

His gaze did not waver as he repeatedly watched the recording of the *Alexi's* destruction, tight-beamed to him as it happened by the Legion scout assigned to that sector. He didn't particularly care about the *Alexi* or her incompetent crew—they'd earned their end—but their failure burned in his gut. Stanton had been a fool. Their orders had been to capture the *Cromwell.* Then to take control of the flagship and its crew, aided by Legion operatives already aboard. The plan's only possibility for success was for the *Alexi* to wait poised and ready ahead of the vessel's known flight path.

Which, thanks to some fuck up by the station command staff, did not happen.

No matter. They had other plans in motion.

One bright note. At a point in the footage, Cryson caught a glimpse of what he believed was the prize he sought. Just barely visible for an instant before the image flared and the *Alexi* vanished as if it had never been—making it clear what made the *Cromwell* the most coveted ship in anyone's fleet.

After all... this was war... and those with the best toys won.

Cryson planned to win, and he would need every advantage to do so, for he fought not just opposition but history. Events that unfolded before he was born represented a constant threat to his future. It did not matter that the Utopia Mandate—outdated legislation banning the transportation and possession of lethal weaponry—and its unanticipated role in the Battle for Demeter now held little relevance to anyone other than historians. It meant everything to those whose lives had been forever shaped by their progenitors' involvement. Cryson raised his eyes to an ancient standard hung with care on the bulkhead: it bore the icon of a winged fist holding an upright dagger. That icon, or rather the group it represented, had a checkered past, particularly in its later years. Most pertinent to Cryson, decades ago, one crucial defection overturned French rule of the stellar colony on Demeter and forever branded the Legion as renegades... and they hadn't even gotten to keep the prize.

To make up for that, they'd been enthusiastically living up to the appellation ever since.

It came down to a matter of survival. Really, they had little choice: it was and always would be the Legion against the universe. John Cryson and his fellow Legionnaires had sworn to reclaim Demeter, the jewel of the Tau Ceti star system, by any means necessary. Which brought things back to the best toys. The *Cromwell* topped everyone's wish list, but it would fly Legion colors before another standard month passed. The ship and the strategic advantage it represented were vital to the survival of his forces... not to mention their success.

He'd just hit replay yet another time when the comm unit by his elbow chimed. With a growl, he canceled the program and initiated the comm.

"Cryson, go."

The screen before him filled with a familiar face, delicate features dominated by large, impassive eyes. Yuki-Ko. Poster child for the Hirobon Omni Corporation Empire. At one time, one of their most prominent astro-nautical designers before she took more of a public post at the helm of the corporation. She wore a suit of muted grey silk with an oriental collar. Her creamy alabaster skin could have been carved from frosted ice and the short, straight black hair bracketing her face gleamed with echoes of heart's-blood red. She spoke in calm tones built upon a frame of steel, her Asian inflection doing nothing to soften the words. "Captain Cryson, you will desist in your efforts upon the McCormick-class vessel, *Cromwell*."

How did she do it? Simultaneously, polite and cutthroat. Without moving a muscle in her face or varying one tone in her voice, the bitch managed to convey extreme displeasure and an overt threat. Cryson laughed and shook his head, unable to help but feel some respect for the woman's skill... and her balls. Not that it would make a difference in his activities.

"Or?" he asked, lifting his right eyebrow just to see a touch of anger spark deep in her gaze. He didn't bother wondering how she knew he had designs on the *Cromwell*, but it did make him curious. The right side of his mouth came up in an almost-grin, somewhat masking the fact that his teeth were clenched. At the same time, he activated one of his pet programs, a virtual ghosting engine that kept tabs on the competition; all the deep connections none of his rivals wanted made public knowledge, all the covert deals strategically executed. With a few well-chosen keywords, he narrowed his search until he found what he looked for: Imperial Aeronautics was in the process of acquiring Carmichael Research Institute, one of the firms with research labs on the Groom Experimental Complex, which meant *Hirobon* planned to go after the specs for the McCormick design, rather than the vessel itself. But then, they had greater resources to manufacture such things, not to mention less of a time constraint.

Cryson's eyes narrowed as Yuki-Ko inclined her head the slightest degree in *faux* respect before speaking. "*Shyobai aw sensoo mitai na mono-desu.*"

A consummate corporate warrior, she cut the connection before he could respond. Cryson didn't require a translator program to interpret her warning. Like any good soldier, he made a point of knowing his adversaries.

Business is war. The battle cry of Hirobon and their independent Ronin mercenaries—loyal warriors who worked outside of Hirobon's official governance to advance the parent company's interests. John Cryson knew better... war was business, one the Legion literally fought to make profitable.

He could not allow Hirobon or any of its holdings to seed the field with stolen technologies based on the *Cromwell*. The Legion would lose any advantage to be gained in securing the ship the moment that became widespread. In lieu of the ship, he needed not only to obtain the data but also to prevent Hirobon's efforts. His gaze intent and his face now devoid of expression, Cryson called up an encrypted comm line courtesy of his contact with the Teutonic Knights and pinged his key operative aboard the *Cromwell*.

Alexi engaged and destroyed, he sent. *Fall back to the secondary plan. Make all effort to secure design specs.*

He received a response almost immediately.

Acknowledged. Stand by for urgent sitrep.

Cryson sat forward as those words scrolled across his screen, a frisson of unease skating down his back. He watched as a dense data-pack transmitted to his console. Rather than extract the clearly extensive report, he sent, *What happened?*

Ghei-synthetic discovered and neutralized. AeroCom in possession of the remains. Please advise.

Damn it! Cryson had argued against the use of synthetic operatives, certain the technology held too much risk to justify the expense when men and women could be inserted just as easily. He had been overruled. His superiors and their allies had believed the potential worth the risk to have key, highly ranked personnel replaced with undetectable copies. Now, not only had they lost the tech but the enemy had been alerted.

At least his superiors had been right in one regard. Captured synthetics betrayed no secrets. Small comfort in light of the loss.

Please advise, the operative repeated.

Primary objective: Eliminate any evidence that may point to the Legion, Cryson instructed. *Secondary objective: Remain alert for an opportunity to secure the design specs. Tertiary objective: Collect any intel that will advance our cause. End.*

Acknowledged, the operative responded but did not disengage.

Cryson waited, slowly leaning forward as another message appeared on his console.

Strategic operatives are in place aboard the Cromwell. *Do you wish us to take the ship?*

The temptation hung heavy in the air. Cryson's fingers flexed, eager to type yes, but he resisted. *Do not engage,* he responded with reluctance. *The risk is too high. The* Alexi's *attack has put AeroCom on alert. Hold for now until instructed.*

Acknowledged. But again, the operative did not disengage. *Love you, Daddy. End.*

In the privacy of his quarters, Cryson laughed out loud at his daughter's impertinence. What a treasure. Other fathers had 'kittens,' he had a mole. An operative raised and trained under the auspices of the AeroCom forces with absolutely no traceable connection to the Legion. Even Hirobon had no clue of her existence.

Cryson relaxed against kid-soft leather dyed the red of Imperial Japan, taking great satisfaction in that symbolic act. It was, after all, a command chair salvaged from the wreckage of the first Hirobon vessel he'd ever destroyed.

Well, he thought, *let the battle begin.*

At the ping of an incoming message, Cryson straightened and turned back to his monitor. No image came through, only visual noise, followed by the symbol of the Knights. Smothering a curse, Cryson engaged the comm.

"Cryson here. Go."

"How do you propose to mitigate this disaster?"

Cryson grunted beneath his breath, working to contain his annoyance before he spoke. He did not recognize the voice. Any communication with the Teutonic Knights was always masked, or encrypted, or filtered in some way. Paranoid bastards. It didn't matter who spoke. Cryson had been given strict orders to cooperate with their allies. That didn't mean he would sacrifice Legion interests... or shoulder the blame for the failure of the Knights' synthetics.

"Unless you put a maker's mark on your *creation*, there is nothing to tie the remains to either of us," Cryson finally answered, as contained as he could manage. "And you said that a defunct unit would tell them nothing, not even how they are controlled, so what's the problem?"

"The synthetics are a finite resource, as are those who can operate them. Do not waste them before we obtain what we are after. Or you and the Legion will bear the responsibility and the expense."

"You haven't even told us what you are after," Cryson snarled, his teeth clenched. "How are we supposed to deliver?"

"What you do not know, you cannot reveal." Though the voice was disguised, the contempt was not. "We will provide the relevant details as they are needed. For now, you are to desist in your efforts to secure the *Cromwell* and get the synthetics into place so we can test their effectiveness. We will worry about the endgame."

Clean-up went quick and quiet. From the ranks of the Devils, only three other members had joined the retrieval op. Warrant Officer Armand Campbell remained aboard the transport, which orbited the GEC at the ready for rapid departure, and Sergeants Christine Dalton and Oren Truitt coordinated with security to glean any possible evidence from the station commander's quarters and office. Scotch took care of the composite, bagging it up and shipping it off to Intelligence on the fastest AeroCom courier on the station, along with a full report. Sarge was still smoothing things over with the corporate heads, who didn't know which to freak out about more: the fact that they'd been infiltrated, or that their data had nearly been compromised. Kat, in the meantime, had orders to retrieve her kit and turn in her station ID.

Kat found locating her bunk tricky. She'd only been in her quarters for all of half an hour before she'd been tagged for duty. By the time she found her way, every inch of her ached, and her vision swam in and out of focus. Palming the hatch open, she lowered herself to the bunk.

Just a second. All she needed was a second.

Her duffle still rested by the door, never unpacked, so it wasn't like she didn't have a little extra time. And crap, did she hurt. Bad enough that she would have left everything behind if she *had* needed to pack. For the first time in her life, she wished her mother was here. Kat's battered body could use some of the pampering and fussing that would normally annoy her no end. Or at least a narc-patch to annihilate the pain. Hell, go for broke and slip her some "Combat." She wasn't even sure if she would care, no matter the health risks the compound carried. Of course, all of this did smack of whining, something no Alexander was prone to.

What could she say... it had been a rough day.

Almost her last, even. Perhaps moving across the galaxy and leaving her loved ones behind hadn't been her best decision. A grimace cracked across Kat's face, followed swiftly by a wince as her jaw and the right side of her face protested. Her thoughts lingered on her family.

Her mother, Laine Alexander, served as a corporate representative to Congress, refined, delicate, and crackerjack sharp. Not only did she not understand Kat or her career choices, Mother actively hindered them, leaving things strained between her and Kat.

Now PawPaw... there wasn't anyone in the world that understood her better than him. Clark Matisse could not have been more different than his upscale daughter-turned-politician. A retired soldier ranching in South Dakota, Kat's grandfather was no doubt responsible for every earthy, straightforward bit of spunk that had gotten Kat this far in the military. (Of course, there was currently a doubt in her mind as to how well she'd represented.) Gnarled and weather-beaten by years of hard work, Paw-Paw was as tough as an old piece of shoe leather, showing a bit of wear but with plenty of use left in his hide. Kat hoped that she was still as good at kicking around at his age. Hell, at this point, she hoped to make it to his age.

A sudden sob raked through her. If she'd died, she would have taken a third of her family with her. Kat's father, Henri Alexander, had died shortly after her birth. Himself a corporate representative to Congress, he'd fallen victim to union protesters worked into a frenzy by failed negotiations on a key proposal. In a show of uncharacteristic determination and run-away support from both the sympathy voters and political intriguists—who frankly had seen her as both a pushover and a diversion—the widowed Laine had assumed his seat and commenced with turning the political arena on its ear. At times, Kat definitely felt proud of her mother.

Unchecked tears continued to trickle down her cheeks.

Maybe now wasn't the best time to think about distant loved ones. Before Kat could drop completely into a good jag, a chime sounded as someone accessed her door panel. Struggling upright, she managed to prop herself up on her elbows just as Sarge came through the hatch. He took one look at her face, reached into his pocket, and drew out a military-issue handkerchief. With an ease she could almost have hated him for, he squatted beside her bunk and carefully wiped at her battered, tear-stained face.

Mortified, Kat closed her eyes and fought for the strength to regain control.

"Buck up, airman," Sarge spoke quietly. "Any fight you walk away from is a good one."

She growled, and some heretofore unknown reserve of energy rose to the surface. "Scotch is the wise-ass, Sarge. Best you leave it that way." With almost no wincing, she swung her feet to the deck and leaned against the bulkhead as Sarge chuckled and moved to the lone straight-backed chair that took up a third of the space in her quarters.

"You ready to talk?" he asked, giving the impression he would have tilted the chair back on two legs if it hadn't been bolted to the deck.

Her jaw bunched enough to make her wince, and any remaining tears dried fast. "Why? Can you tell me that?" She already knew the answer, but she couldn't *not* ask.

Daire's head shook slowly. "Sorry, Alexander. Not here, not now. But you can believe the way they handled this was under my objection."

She watched him through narrowed eyes a moment, then nodded her acceptance of those facts. Anything else was irrelevant to the current situation. Besides, his eyes held understanding with a promise couched beneath. Kat had enough patience to wait until he made good on that.

"Anything else?" he asked.

Kat carefully shook her head.

Sarge nodded, then held her gaze. "I've contacted General Drovak, the one responsible for assigning you here, and reported the attempts on the *Cromwell* and the GEC. He agrees the situation is more volatile than anticipated. He's on his way, with reinforcements." Sarge paused as if waiting for her to respond, but given how she felt, Kat decided it wiser to reserve comment. When she remained silent, he grunted and rose to his feet.

Snagging her duffle with one hand and her forearm with the other, he hauled both of them up. "Come on... let's get you out of this shithole."

Out in the void, with the Groom facility no more than a point of light, Lieutenant Anton Petrov came about, sighted on his target, and powered up the fore laser banks. The maintenance pod hadn't any true armaments, though, as with most AeroCom craft, the design could be easily reconfigured if needed. Unfortunately, doing so would have been an immediate red flag if anyone noticed him making the modifications. He could not risk drawing attention to his activities, which meant all he had were the lasers used to clear debris from the pod's flight path.

For a moment, he considered the rock before him, about the size of an antique Volkswagen. It scarcely seemed an issue, but clean-up was clean-up, and many a man throughout history had hung from a loose end. Not him. The three frontal lasers came to bear on the "debris," slicing it open to its hollow core.

Before he could destroy it completely, an alarm pinged on his console. Another vessel approached, and he could not afford to be intercepted. He came about and headed back toward the station. The wreckage he left behind worried him, but the important part had been dealt with. Whatever remained was unlikely to register as anything but debris to the approaching ship. Anton didn't watch as oxygen vapor and biological matter misted the vacuum of space, too busy reversing trajectory and wiping his trail, both physical and electronic.

Scotch had brought Kat her gauss rifle. She could have kissed him for it, only Command frowned on such behavior among the ranks, even though it wasn't expressly forbidden. Instead, she sat at rest in the back of the troop transport, the gauss across her knees and her hand clutching the barrel as if it might disappear.

"Hmm... what's that old phrase?" Scotch commented from the other side of the transport. "Oh yeah... 'you can have my rifle when you pry it from my cold, dead fingers.'"

"Don't tempt me, Scotch," Kat snapped back, only half teasing, still raw from her short reassignment, not to mention the near-fatal encounter that ended that exile. Her eyes locked with those of the good-natured wise-ass, and a muscle in her jaw twitched. She was overreacting, but knowing didn't help. She felt raw in a way not even her first combat engagement had left her. She *personally* wanted to confront the real Ghei, or whoever was behind the piracy she'd very nearly failed to avert... or survive. She wanted to share with them how much she... appreciated what they'd put her through.

"Kat," came the quiet command from the drive compartment, "stand down."

The strap of her rifle trembled from the tension of her grip, causing the metal coupling to tap against the weapon. Sarge had noticed; Kat hadn't. On the bench across from her, Scotch and the others looked concerned. She drew a deep breath and allowed her lids to drift down over eyes that burned. She struggled to regain control. Sarge was right. Scotch was a part of her team, one of the airmen who protected her back. He didn't deserve to have her frustration taken out on him, even if he didn't always know when to leave well enough alone. Drawing another deep breath, Kat forced her eyes to remain closed, her fingers to relax their grip. Better to use this time to rest up. Who knew what they would be up against once they reached the *Cromwell* and went in pursuit of the pirate vessel?

"Stow your weapon and strap in, Alexander," Sarge ordered from the front of the transport. "We're about to drop out of drive."

Kat's eyes snapped open. She didn't argue, not that she would have—her recent encounter with the composite posing as Station Commander Ghei to the contrary, she actually respected authority—but she sensed the shift in the engines. The last thing she wanted was to end up drifting loose about the cabin. Double-checking to make sure the gauss was properly powered down and the safety engaged, she opened the weapons locker beneath the bench and strapped the rifle down. With the locker once more secured, she engaged her safety harness and braced herself for the pending braking maneuver. Not for the first time, she wished the transport had viewing portals. After the day she'd had... just *one* day... she could use the affirmation of watching the *Cromwell* come into sight.

Rather than stare at Truitt, who sat directly across from her, she closed her eyes again and sat there, breathing slow and deep, visualizing her new objective. Once they joined the rest of their team, all resources would hunt down the camouflaged pirate vessel. She tensed, thinking of her encounter with the composite. The phantom *crunch* of his windpipe still taunted her, as did the stench of fried nanites and flash-melted synthskin. Nothing worked her over as much as the sight of him coming after her, despite the fact he should have been dead on the ground.

She opened her eyes to find Truitt still staring at her, an indecipherable expression on his face. When their eyes connected, he smiled and gave a little wink. She heard the others call him True, but she didn't know if that was just a shortening of his name or if it had some other relevance.

"Brace for docking," Sarge warned them as the *Cromwell* deployed the magnetic grapple that guided their transport into the docking collar. Turning her gaze to the back of the transport, Kat thrilled at the *thud* of impact on the hull plate and finally relaxed... *okay, marginally relaxed*... at the initial jerk of the mechanism reeling them in.

Home might be light-years away, but the *Cromwell* did a good imitation for now.

Kat bit back a groan as she bent to retrieve her rifle from the weapons locker. Now safely within the fold, as it were, she allowed herself to acknowledge the aftereffects of her encounter. She ached all over, and her swollen right eye throbbed in time with her pulse, but her left foot hurt worst of all. It was definitely wrenched from when composite Ghei had intercepted her roundhouse kick and planted her face into the deck, but at least she could put her weight on it without screaming. Of course, she did her best to keep all but the most obvious injuries from Sarge's attention. The last thing she needed was to be slapped with restricted duty. Not now... not when they were going after the sons of bitches responsible for this.

Sarge moved past her toward the rear hatch, his hand briefly resting on her shoulder, getting her attention. She straightened and turned toward him, slinging her rifle out of the way across her back. They lingered alone in the crew compartment, the others having moved through the hatch. "Scotch and I are the only ones on the *Cromwell* that are aware of the nature of your reassignment. It needs to stay that way a while, understood?"

Kat's gut burned as she fought the impulse to ask why, then she nodded.

Sarge nodded back, his intent grey gaze pinning her. "Debriefing in five hours, airman."

"Yes, Sarge," Kat responded. She watched a moment while he stopped near the rear cargo locker, peering inside before clicking it closed and locking it with his personal code.

The lock mechanism looked odd, like no design she knew, mixing a physical and electronic component—and cracking locks was a sub-skill of her MOS. Some heavy-duty security, and it hadn't been there before they'd dropped her off at the GEC.

Now, what is that about? A part of her itched to figure it out, just for the challenge. The rest of her just wanted to get off her feet.

She'd find out in time. Or not. At the moment, she didn't really care which. She just wanted Sarge to move on so she could make her way off the transport without him noticing it took a bit more effort than it should. Before he went through the open airlock leading to the hatch, he turned back to her. "Campbell noticed some anomalies in the computer systems during docking. I need you to check it out after debriefing."

"I can..." she started, thinking she could get it out of the way now and take her mind off the grilling to come. She didn't get that far.

He shook his head. "*After* the debriefing," he repeated, his expression unyielding. "For now, I suggest you get some rest."

Okay, not like she could argue or even particularly wanted to. "Yes, Sarge."

She gathered up the rest of her gear and slowly followed after Scotch and the handful of others from their team who had come to retrieve her, careful to keep her weight balanced mostly on her right leg without betraying herself by limping. As she cleared the hatch, her right hand reached out and caressed the squad icon newly painted on the transport's hull, just this side of the docking collar. A stylized grinning devil head emerging from a ball of flames. She didn't have to look for a signature to know that Scotch was the artist. Next to the painting, he had stenciled the name *Teufel* in big, bold letters. Apparently, the transport had been christened while she'd been gone. If she weren't so tired, she would have laughed: *Teufel* meant "devil" in German. Both the name and the art proclaimed for all and sundry that this troop transport belonged to Daire's Devils... well, as much as any military-issue resources belonged to a particular team. *Who said tagging had gone out of fashion in the twenty-first century?*

Beneath the art, someone had bolted a metal plaque. In two columns, listed by Squad, the names and ranks of all the Devils had been etched in bold strokes:

Team Leader: Master Sergeant Kevin Daire

Alpha Squad
Warrant Officer Armand Campbell
Technical Sergeant Jackson 'Scotch' Daniels
Staff Sergeant Suzanne 'St. Sue' Brockmann
Sergeant Christine Dalton
Sergeant Jamal Kramer
Sergeant Thomas 'Tivo' Vee

Sergeant Oren 'True' Truitt
Corporal Katrion 'HellKat' Alexander

Beta Squad
Warrant Officer Miki 'Blade' Mata
Technical Sergeant Zack 'Zaga' Asturrizaga
Sergeant Ivan 'Pecker' Kopecky
Sergeant Kamilla Danzer
Sergeant James Hemry
Sergeant Isaac 'Ike' Hand
Sergeant Danny 'Truck' Mack
Sergeant Ken 'Colonel' O'Connor

Kat gasped and ran her fingers over her name. To see herself listed there as if she'd never been gone told her more than anything she was back where she belonged. It also made her more determined than ever to stay there. As much as she just wanted to forget the hours she'd spent away, there was no chance of that with the scheduled debriefing, endless questions designed to call up every possible detail of the ordeal, burning them into her memory for all time.

Still, it beat the alternative.

She stood there a moment as the others left the bay. Once they were gone, Kat made her way across the hangar to the corridor, walking as normal as she could, but much more... leisurely than she would have preferred. She had no clue how to get back to her bunk. It would have been helpful to follow the others there, but she didn't want anyone to notice she was having issues.

Pausing as she reached the hallway, she tried to get her bearings, except she hadn't been anywhere long enough to form them. Noticing a comm console on the opposing wall, she stepped up and keyed in for basic information access.

As she worked the keypad, she slumped against the internal bulkhead, taking the weight off her injured ankle. She couldn't help but sigh. A few keystrokes called up the ship's schematic. The vessel was huge. Twenty-five decks, hundreds of corridors. Even with the whole aft section on the map greyed out, indicating areas mothballed until the *Cromwell* took on more crew, the scale overwhelmed her.

A pulsing marker indicated her current location.

Tapping in the designation for the Devils' barracks, she groaned as a line linked the two locations, changing color to denote each transverse between different levels of the ship. Just looking at the distance exhausted her. There was a more direct route via a nearby troop-transport lift, but using that for anything short of combat deployment carried a stiff penalty and a permanent mark in your record. Kat was almost tempted. Her other option was to turn around and sack out on the *Teufel*. Only someone would notice.

"Hey now, no need to prop up the walls... This is AeroCom's state-of-the-art flagship. It'll stay up just fine all on its own."

Kat jerked upright. Pain shot up her leg as she settled her weight back onto her injured ankle. Spying a fellow Devil behind her, she sucked in a breath through clenched teeth and tried her best to turn it into a smile.

"Welcome back, HellKat."

"Hey, Brockmann," Kat greeted her teammate after getting control of the pain. "The cleaning crew seems to have swept up my trail of breadcrumbs. Just getting an idea how to get back to quarters..."

Staff Sergeant Suzanne Brockmann grinned back at her. "And here I was going to ask if you wanted to go dancing."

Her tone was teasing, but Kat felt herself go pale at the thought.

Brockmann didn't miss it. "Hey... you okay?"

"Just wiped." Kat managed half a grin before it slid from her face, and she slumped back against the wall. "Actually... I'm dead on my feet here. I will take a solid week of your duty shifts if you can get me back to my bunk."

She held her breath as she waited for Brockmann to answer. Other than Scotch and Sarge, Kat didn't know any of the Devils all that well yet.

With a sympathetic look, Brockmann tilted her head in the opposite direction Kat would have gone. "Come on, this time's a freebie," her fellow Devil answered with a grin. "Did you eat yet?"

Kat had started to follow but stopped abruptly. Damn, if she could remember her last meal. As she shook her head, her stomach grumbled.

Brockmann chuckled and tugged her gently forward as if to get her started again. "Let's get some calories into you first, or you'll feel even worse when you wake up." Kat didn't have the energy to argue. She just followed as Brockmann turned at a side corridor and led her down a few levels to a compartment designated auxiliary mess AQ-08. Inside, a few bolted-in booths lined the left-hand bulkhead, and the military equivalent of an efficiency kitchenette lined the right: Heater unit, cryo unit, and racks of ration packs.

"The General Mess has actual prepped meals, but it's also two levels up and a klick away, closer toward the command deck."

With a groan, Kat shook her head. "At this moment, I'll take a rat pack over even one of PawPaw's ribeyes."

At that, Brockmann groaned. "Oh man, I don't know about that... what I wouldn't give for honest-to-goodness beef. All they've got up here is 'stank' meat."

If she'd had the energy, Kat would have agreed, though tank meat—vat-grown protein—wasn't as bad as Brockmann made it out to be. In flavor, anyway. Texture was a whole other matter. But what else could you expect from protein cells that hadn't ever seen the inside of a cow? There was only so much science could do when growing meat without a face... or any of the other biological aspects that set hoof-grown beef apart.

Kat must have zoned a moment because the next she knew, Brockmann pushed her down into a booth. "Sit. I'll be right back with something easy to eat." She moved off before Kat focused enough to even respond, let alone protest.

Before Brockmann came back, the hatch opened, and a few airmen tumbled in, their color a little high and their voices loud enough that Kat winced. If she had to guess, she'd say they'd been drinking. Only one of them was a Devil. She didn't remember his name. Hell, she was lucky she recognized his face at this point, as tired as she was.

"Hey! We got our noob back!" he half-hollered as he dropped into the booth across from her. There was something about how he said it that wasn't as jovial as he made it seem.

Talk about obnoxious, Kat thought as she slumped against the wall and rubbed her forehead, which had begun to throb.

"Get real, Kopecky. You're just glad she's back because she's the only one newer than you," Brockmann said as she returned to the table, setting down a plate of stew-like goop in front of Kat. "Besides, Scotch says she's got more points than you and I put together."

Sergeant Ivan Kopecky's expression got a little ugly at Brockmann's push-back. "Yeah, St. Sue? Then why's she stuck as a lowly corporal?"

Kat couldn't resist that one. "An act of Congress," she muttered as she spooned food into her mouth.

His laugh could have been compared to a donkey's... if Kat didn't have so much respect for donkeys.

"Good excuse!" Kopecky nudged the guy sitting next to him and winked. Kat just kept eating, not bothering to explain. Her issues with her mother weren't any of his business. Good thing she wasn't interested in how her food tasted. She shoveled the goop into her mouth just to be done. All she wanted was to get out of there and into her bunk.

Brockmann, however, seemed to have had enough. "Watch it, Pecker... she made it through basic twice. You barely made it the once..." she growled, smacking the drunk-ass fool across the back of the head. "Now get back to barracks and sleep your stupid off before you find yourself assigned extra duty."

Kopecky looked like he intended to protest, but his friends hustled him out the hatch.

When they were gone, Brockmann settled on the bench across from her.

"Slow down before you make yourself sick."

"Who's to say the food won't anyway?" Kat quipped. The meal wasn't the worst she'd ever had, but it wasn't far off.

Brockmann just shook her head, then nodded in the direction of the disappeared drunks. "Don't take Kopecky seriously. He had some buddies on the *Alexi*. His head's not in a good place right now."

Kat nodded and kept working on her food. This time so she didn't have to respond. She wasn't sure how she felt about what Brockmann said. Many airmen aboard the *Alexi* had lost their lives, but from what Sarge told Kat, they had done so while violating their oaths. How many of them had been complicit, though? Or had they even been aware of the attempted piracy? She set her spoon down and had to swallow hard not to lose what she'd just eaten as flashbacks from her encounter with Ghei ambushed her. Closing her eyes and drawing a deep breath, she fought them back, then slid to the edge of her bench.

"If we don't get going, I'm likely to fall asleep in the goop," she muttered, nodding toward her half-eaten meal. Brockmann followed her lead, sliding out of her bench and gently clasping Kat's shoulder before disposing of the tray and moving past to open the hatch.

"Hey, Brockmann," Kat asked, slanting her companion a side look with half a grin. Comfortable enough to ask a question she'd never dared ask before. "Why do you all call him Pecker?"

Brockmann grinned back. "Because Ko-peck-y can be a real dick sometimes, but he's one of ours, and we love him, so we gave him a handle to remind him not to be *that* guy."

"And why'd he call you St. Sue?"

The grin faded from Brockmann's face, and her gaze went pensive. For a moment, Kat didn't think she was going to answer. Then a peaceful, almost-smile replaced the grin.

"I pray for those that fall. Some of the others find that... confusing."

Kat's brow furrowed. "Why?"

"I pray for all of them. Even those I've ended." Brockmann paused a moment before correcting herself. "Especially those I've ended."

On that sobering thought, they made the rest of their way to the barracks in companionable silence.

Her current mission complete, DeVeaux returned to Demeter, dropping her Corsair scout craft low and fast into the troposphere to avoid detection. She nearly buzzed the towering treetops as she glided toward the Legion's most recent covert base, an abandoned AeroCom facility tucked in the 'skirt' of a nearby mountain, hidden in one of its deep folds. They had been entrenched at this location quite a while now, which made her nervous. The more they came and went, the greater the likelihood someone would discover their position. This base was a bit more protected than most, but that didn't mean it couldn't be compromised. She was tired of uprooting and establishing new bases. Not today, and not because of her.

Using as little power as possible and relying on her senses, she dipped and banked among the trees' upper reaches until she came to a scar in the canopy left by a powerful lightning strike. The gap marked her entry point. Legion foot soldiers had scaled the boles of these giants to strategically widen the opening, burning away the signs of their effort to blend with the natural damage. As the canopy closed above her, she switched her gimbaled engines to VTOL position and used her maneuvering jets to propel her forward to the improvised landing pad just large enough for her craft. Deveaux did not relax until her landing gear touched down. From a hut tucked among the massive tree roots, the ground crew came forward to help her climb free of the cockpit. Others scurried to move the compact craft into a makeshift 'hangar' camouflaged among the forest's towering root system.

"Merci," she murmured as she left her flight gear in their keeping and headed for the tree line and the path leading to the main structure. Deveaux stopped behind the foremost row of trees and scanned the area both visually and electronically before proceeding. Nothing. She left the trees' shelter and made her way carefully up the base of the mountain. Out

of necessity, the path remained rough and unmanicured, making for a treacherous walk if one weren't careful. Finally, she reached the sheltered nook containing a neglected compound that appeared to have been a testing facility at one time. For what, she could not say. The place had been stripped, and whatever had caused it to be abandoned had fried most of the wiring. Deveaux pondered the scorch marks on the cobbles and the light stanchions, as she always did, but continued on, eager to report and be done with it so she could rest.

She entered the building into a large atrium area converted to work-space, desks running down the side to her left, a reception area backed by a row of enclosed cubicles to her right. Part of her wondered who had funded the refit. Certainly not the Legion. They didn't have the resources for something of this scale. Or rather... what resources they did have wouldn't have gone into outfitting offices. Like many things she had noticed at this outpost, DeVeaux told herself it wasn't her concern. Pondering such could be dangerous.

Approaching the reception area, she stood at attention before Sergeant Cole, the officer on watch.

"Scout DeVeaux reporting."

"Welcome back, DeVeaux. Your commanding officer?" Cole asked, following protocol, though he already knew from countless missions before.

"Captain Cryson, aboard the *Destrier*."

The OOW made a notation on the tablet before him, and a tech port on the desk spit out an activation chit. Handing it to her, he pointed toward the cubicles at his back. "The second terminal to my right has been cleared and encryption engaged. Use that code to connect," he instructed, nodding toward the chit.

DeVeaux pivoted and headed for the indicated cubicle. Though she was in Legion territory, she scanned the immediate area with caution. The building seemed relatively empty... or at least this area did. A few of what appeared to be civilian staff worked at the desks across the large open space. They wore fatigues but without Legion markings. DeVeaux did notice what appeared to be a cross-like symbol on their right collar. One looked up at her, expression almost challenging, but after a moment, he turned his attention back to his work. The side by the cubicles stood empty save the reception desk where Sergeant Cole sat.

Turning to the indicated cubicle, DeVeaux presented the chit to the security lock affixed to the outside. The lock gave an audible *click*. She opened the door and entered. As she closed herself in the lock reengaged.

A subtle hum filled the compartment. Putting it from her mind, she sat before the terminal and keyed in her identcode. Almost immediately, the comm connected her to Cryson as if he'd been waiting. Maybe she imagined it, but he seemed to brace himself as if he had given up on expecting anything other than bad news.

"Scout DeVeaux, report."

"Yes, sir," she responded, wishing she weren't about to meet his expectations. "Our efforts on the Groom Facility have been discovered, the Ghei-synthetic both exposed and neutralized." He did not swear, but distinct white lines appeared around Cryson's mouth as his muscles tightened at her news.

"I am aware of the situation. Anything else?"

"No, sir."

Slowly he shook his head, briefly looking away and then back to her. "Dismissed, Scout DeVeaux. Consider yourself on leave until contacted with your next assignment."

"Thank you, sir." DeVeaux disconnected and left the cubicle, returning the chit to the officer on watch before taking the elevator one level down, where a portion of what had been research labs had been converted to open-plan barracks, aptly similar to a homeless shelter or hospital ward. There were levels even lower than this one still used for research or development of some kind, but she did not concern herself with those. What she did not know she could not betray.

There were no assigned bunks. Those in residence sacked out where they could, ready to pull up stakes and head out at the slightest warning. DeVeaux tucked herself in a corner, out of the way, but still close to the exit. Sliding in earbuds and shielding her eyes, she fell asleep to a soothing instrumental, more than ready to leave the world of intrigue and conquest behind.

CHAPTER 4

MUSTANG" SALLY TANNER, AEROCOM PILOT AND LIEUTENANT IN THE ALLIED martial forces, roamed the corridors of the GEC in a faded set of old fatigues and walking shoes, her tight, sandy curls darkened by sweat to the color of toffee. She wasn't one for limits or restricted movement. Goodness only knew how she'd ended up in space where those two concepts ruled ninety-nine percent of her time. But she'd been unable to resist the vastness of the other one percent. To pacify her need for great expanses when she wasn't in the cockpit or EVA, she power-walked the halls for her exercise rather than hitting the workout room the way the rest of the station's complement did. Yes, still just as closed in, but Groom was a massive complex. It took several hours to span the spiraled station's length, or at least the unrestricted sections. For a gal from Texas, that wasn't near big enough, but she couldn't get much better out here without an environment suit.

Twenty-five feet ahead of her stood the security door to the research area. Time to decide whether to hump it back to her quarters or take the lift down. All the excitement about the fake Ghei and that special-ops team and everything had Sally pretty keyed up. Ignoring the transport hatch, she pivoted around to head back by foot when a muffled *bang* and a sudden acrid odor stayed her steps. She turned her head, trying to pinpoint the source. Before she could isolate it, the deck plates beneath her shuddered to the side and back again. She found herself wedged against the bulkhead, her ears ringing and her vision greying out when two more explosions shook the complex. Loud bangs that sent her heart into overdrive. She tried to scoot up the wall, but her body just trembled and jerked, remaining crumpled on the deck.

Emergency lighting came on as the main power cut out. In the dark moment between the two, the shape of a man came through the security door, lean and wiry, vaguely familiar... and somehow wrong, his movements unnatural. The darkness hid his features. She didn't know what detail set off her instincts, but her mind had latched on to something.

The form came closer, moving into the glow of a muted red emergency light. Just barely, she could make out the sharp blade of a nose and a distinctive brow drawn low. *Petrov?* She thought it was one of the transport pilots she occasionally socialized with, but she couldn't be sure. If only her eyes would focus enough to tell. Sally tried to activate her wrist comm as he came closer, his legs lifting in hard jerks as if his feet were shod in marble.

Before she managed to coordinate her hands, a fourth, more distant explosion shook the station. A high-pitched whistling sound filled the corridor, and the pressure changed. Atmosphere drew past her like a stiff breeze, picking up speed. Sally gasped and again tried to rise, but the deck beneath her continued to shake with increased violence. Her hand slipped and the bulkhead again impacted hard with the side of her head. Her vision swam as the figure reached down for her.

Grey deepened to black.

If Yuki-ko had learned anything over years of standing silent and attentive at her father's side, it was this: *If you cannot gain what you wish by direct acquisition, do so by strategy.* From the remote comfort of her public office aboard Hirobon's interstellar headquarters—circling just beyond Demeter's sphere of influence—she engineered the take-over of Carmichael Research Institute, which would gain Hirobon access to the Groom facility. But such... mergers... were not completed quickly or cleanly. The final stages had begun, but further action was required to ensure success.

The plans for AeroCom's flagship could not be had at any price, but Yuki-ko could undermine their advantage, eating away at its foundation until what she desired fell into her hands. Though the vessel's details were classified, careful sifting of the manifests of goods delivered to the Groom Experimental Facility had narrowed down the components that had gone into the *Cromwell*'s construction and which corporations had supplied them.

She knew such details were not enough to satisfy her father, but it did give her somewhere to start. Eventually, they would secure the *Cromwell*'s schematics. When they did so, she would prove her worthiness, presenting her father with controlling shares in those businesses already conversant with the necessary parts to replicate AeroCom's state-of-the-art flagship.

Not that Hirobon had any need for such a vessel. There was power, however, in being the corporation able to provide such products of interest. And Yuki-ko had been taught to value power above all else.

Welcome to debriefing hell.

Kat had expected a standard debriefing, herself and the rescue team members hashing over the details for Sarge and perhaps the unit XO. She was wrong.

Apparently, the nightmare wasn't over.

From those involved in the incident, only she, Scotch, and Sergeant Daire were present. They stood before the resident top brass of Military Command. Colonel James Corbin headed up the review board, Kat wasn't familiar with the other officers, and no one bothered to introduce them. It felt more like an interrogation than a debriefing. They had been here for over an hour now, just questioning Sarge and Scotch.

"Corporal Alexander, please relate your account of the events that took place on the Groom facility," Colonel Corbin instructed.

Kat took one measured step forward from where she stood at parade rest beside her commander and Scotch. Stopping ramrod straight, she saluted. At a gesture from the board, she resumed parade rest. "Yes, sir. At 2200 universal standard time, I disembarked from the transport for reassignment to the Groom Experimental Complex. I delivered my orders to Station Commander Ghei and was assigned quarters. At 2325, I was called to duty by Lt. Commander Connor."

"You were assigned duty less than two hours on station?" The question came from the stern-faced captain on the end, his stylus tapping a steady tattoo on the datascreen set into the table in front of him.

"Yes, sir. The normal shift crew had mistakenly been given leave, and the crewman I was covering had been admitted to medbay."

"Continue."

Kat recounted how she had found things in disarray, with the shift understaffed and duty schedules misaligned. The one woman on the board, a major, frowned as Kat admitted to deploying the *Cromwell* out of sequence, even though her actions had kept the flagship out of the pirates' hands.

Kat felt her jaw tighten. What did they want? It wasn't as if they'd disclosed the facts to her before using her to infiltrate the situation. The inquisition continued with her accounting that the *Alexi* had gone missing, and how the station commander had been unresponsive to her priority hails. She detailed her actions, from the unsanctioned High Alert to deploying the auxiliary black box. When she reached the point of her encounter with what she had presumed was Commander Ghei, the members of the board shifted forward, interest bright in their eyes.

"What first betrayed the fact that the individual you faced was not the commander?"

"When I called up the schematic of the complex and ran a scan, his presence did not register on the station. When he arrived on the command deck, the scan was still active, yet there was no trace of his presence on the monitor, indicating he was missing his identchip."

"You did not consider this might have been a system malfunction similar to the disruption in the duty assignments or the deployment schedules?"

"That was my first assessment, sir. However, his actions throughout the encounter raised several doubts in my mind."

"And how did you respond to these doubts?"

What is this shit? How much longer is this going to take? Her foot throbbed in a steady beat—her face pulsed in time with it until she wanted to scream at the board for being heartless, suspicious bastards. As the questioning went on, the ache of her injuries ramped up until she just wanted to get the hell out.

"I sought confirmation of my suspicions, checking the system for file access and using the auxiliary command deck to initiate remote observation of Commander Ghei."

"So," Colonel Corbin said, "you opted to investigate your commanding officer rather than report your suspicions, is that correct?" She heard overt censure in his voice.

Kat fought the impulse to snarl, keeping her tone neutral. "A scan of the computer systems seemed to substantiate my concerns. My remote observation of Ghei further supported my assessment that he intended to steal the schematics for the *Cromwell*. With no way to determine who among the crew might be involved in the piracy, I judged it expedient to safeguard the system data before taking any further action."

"What did you observe that you assumed was of an illicit nature?"

"Ghei received an encoded message from an unknown party right before he started his attempt to access the data. There was no visual, just an icon of an equal-armed cross capped at the ends, like a 'T.' Immediately after, he started going after the data."

More than one member of the review board frowned, and they murmured among themselves a moment. Kat presumed they fussed because her neutrality slipped as she mentioned Ghei's name, as well as the notable omission of his rank. By contrast, they hardly reacted at all to her previous admission of independent initiative and the use of her military-funded training as a computer specialist for the unsanctioned observation of a superior. She had no doubt that they disapproved. Why she couldn't say. Hadn't she accomplished what they'd intended? Or had she? It wasn't so easy to keep in mind that not everyone knew why she'd been on Groom. Kat tried to bury her annoyance deep, with limited success. Still, some glimmer of her thoughts must have slipped past her guard because every brow before her drew down in a scowl.

A familiar vibration went through Kat's jaw. *Lose the attitude, Alexander,* Sarge murmured over his bonejack in a tone as cold and sharp as ice-coated razorblades.

Kat drew herself up to attention despite the fact they'd been given leave to stand at rest. Without a word, the others followed suit. They remained that way for another half hour. As the board continued to grill her the questions shifted more to what she could tell them of the composite's function and performance than the actual sequence of events that had exposed and subsequently destroyed the imposter.

She told them as much as she could remember in explicit detail, but something nagged at her. Some flicker just out of reach. It wasn't something big or obvious. She'd gone over all of that. Kat frowned and closed her eyes a moment, replaying memories she would just as soon forget, from Ghei's unexpected appearance to his equally unexpected demise.

"There may be one more thing..." Kat hesitated, unable to capture the elusive memory. Her head throbbed more the longer she tried.

Colonel Corbin's frown intensified. "Well?"

"I'm sorry, sir, I can't quite remember."

For several long heartbeats, Corbin did not react. Kat resisted the impulse to shift her weight off her throbbing foot, but not as hard as she resisted the smartass desire to ask if there was anything else. And again, that foxtail flicker of memory, only this time giving her enough of a glimpse for her to remember. The pauses... the hesitations. It had seemed like Ghei had been just a touch out of synch.

Kat opened her mouth to share the intel when Corbin interjected.

"Be sure to get back to us when you do. Now, if you are through wasting our time?"

Kat's back stiffened at his dry sarcasm. Closing her mouth, she nodded and took a step back beside her teammates. It would keep until she told Sarge later because Kat would be damned if she told Corbin anything now.

"With all due respect, Sarge," Kat said in a tight voice, her eyes locked on the back of her commander's head, "what the hell was *that* about?"

He didn't answer. He didn't stop or even turn. He didn't tear her a new one like she deserved. For that, she counted herself lucky. Stretching her stride despite the pain shooting through her foot, she followed him down the corridor and back toward the docking bay and the systems check he'd ordered earlier. Beside her, Scotch easily kept pace, a gleefully amused look on his face as he glanced from her to Sarge, clearly waiting for one of them to give. Before Kat could catch up, the crewman on duty hailed them. His name tape read 'TIPMAN.'

The man wore a determined expression, but not for long. "Sir..."

The look Sarge gave him cut the private off, the man's throat bobbing as he swallowed whatever he'd been about to say.

"We're here to check out a systems malfunction on our troop transport," Sarge said. "Keep your crew out of our way so we can get the job done and get down to the business of some R&R."

The poor crewman seemed thrown, freezing momentarily, before responding, "Yes, sir." The only thing about him with any starch left was his uniform. Newbie.

Sarge didn't hang around for anything more before turning sharply and continuing to the berth where the *Teufel* was docked. Scotch and Kat were no more than a step behind him. Kat felt micro tremors course down her back. Stress. Fatigue. A limp had crept into her stride. She'd already been on edge *before* spending hours under the lights. She needed rest, but barring that, some action would do. Something told her to get ready for the latter. Tivo, the team tech, or Campbell, their primary pilot, usually vetted the transport. On rare occasions, she'd even done it herself, but never Sarge.

As they neared the shuttle, Kat automatically scanned the docking bay, making a mental note of the cameras and other security measures. She expected no trouble, but it never hurt to know what safeguards were in place. They were all pretty standard, but one of the alarms sounded, polluting the air with a high-pitched squeal. Kat noticed a clear absence of any hangar personnel in the immediate vicinity, though she could see crew members at work across the bay. Impressive, that. She didn't know what the alarm meant, but she wished she'd had it ninety minutes ago, seeing how effectively it cleared the area.

"How come they haven't done anything about the klaxon?" she wondered aloud, looking around for the source of the screeching. "What is it, anyway?"

Scotch laughed, and Sarge shot her a predatory grin. Neither said a word as they did a visual scan of the bay. The laughter cut off like it had never been, and the familiar gleam of a combat operative entered Scotch's gaze.

"All clear, Sarge."

The master sergeant punched a code into the hatch keypad.

With a curse, Kat locked her hands over her ears, the sudden movement throwing her off balance, settling more of her weight on her injured foot. Instant nausea gripped her.

"What the *fuck!*"

Similar cries echoed from across the cavernous bay as the hatch swung open. The unmuffled sound coming from inside assaulted everyone's hearing. Kat swayed as the high-pitched noise shot her equilibrium to hell. Only Scotch's arm bracing her kept her from landing on the deck. Sarge disappeared inside, and the sound cut off abruptly. Kat remembered the unusual lock he had secured when they'd left the transport earlier. *Was that the source of the sound? Or was this the malfunction Campbell had recorded?*

"Inside," Sarge called from the belly of the craft. "Now."

Kat found herself back on the bench she'd vacated almost nine hours earlier. Her ears still buzzed, and all her aches had ramped up even worse. She groaned as Sarge handed Scotch the field medkit. Within seconds, he had stripped off both her left boot and sock and extracted a pressure bandage from one of the pack's external pouches. None too gently, he slapped a transdermal patch on her ankle before snapping the seal on the bandage to activate the chemical coolant that would further reduce the swelling in her foot. He then encased her damaged foot and loosened her boot sufficiently to slip over the bandage. Lastly, he rubbed a bit of anti-inflammatory cream on the swelling around her eye and along her jaw.

She clenched her teeth and fought not to scream.

"You *ever* pull something like that again, and I'll have you off my team so fast the ink won't have time to dry before you're gone. For real."

"Yes, Sarge." Her error wasn't in being injured but in not disclosing her injuries; in combat, that could get a teammate killed or blow an op. She should have known better. She *did* know better. She'd just let recent events get her head twisted around. Scotch patted her good leg approvingly before pushing to his feet and stowing the medkit back in its compartment.

Kat moved to follow, but Sarge held up his hand. "I'm not done, corporal."

Settling back in her seat, Kat went cold clear to her bones. She held her breath as he continued, certain her career was over for good. "Let me be eminently clear. You are not to withhold vital intel or disregard orders to act on your own. Should I become aware of another such occurrence, you will face disciplinary action. There are procedures in place for such situations, and you are to follow the chain of command, am I understood?"

"Yes, sir," Kat responded, her mouth so dry the words nearly stuck in her throat. She then winced. Technically, she'd already withheld intel again. Before that could come back and bite her in the ass, she spoke up. "Sarge, I remember... That other detail about pseudo-Ghei. It was almost like his reactions were time-delayed. Not long... a matter of seconds, but enough it stood out."

Sarge gave a sharp nod

"I'll let Command know."

He then turned to the storage locker Kat had noticed him checking earlier. As he swung the hatch open, she gasped and found herself beside him before she'd realized she'd moved. Though she'd never personally set eyes on the unit, she recognized the auxiliary black box from her training. The Groom facility's ABB, according to the etching on the pure black unit. *Thank you, Sakmyster!* she sent the thought winging in the direction of the GEC and the former comrade who had trusted her judgment enough to flaunt pseudo-Ghei's orders. The rescue team must have intercepted it when they'd come to get her.

She could feel the shit-eating grin spread across her face as she looked up and met the eyes of her commander and her teammate.

"We've got him!"

With eager hands, she reached for the unit, only to have Sarge step in her way.

"*That* was them not trusting you."

Kat blinked. Gave her head a shake. Opened her mouth to ask what the heck he was going on about. Then it registered. He'd answered her earlier question.

"*That* was them trying to determine if you had a grudge... or a conflict of interest...."

She remained silent, her jaw clenched shut, breathing deep and getting her temper in hand.

"Well, airman," he asked, "do you?"

A few more deep breaths. Really deep. She focused hard on not buckling beneath Sarge's continued stare. "I guess that depends, sir."

"On?"

"If they are on our side or the pirates'."

He gave a slow nod and stepped aside.

With care, she drew the battered microsatellite—or microsat—from the locker. "Did we do that?" she asked, running her hand over the burn scoring and hefty dent down the left side.

"They take that kind of stuff out of our budget when we don't play nice," Scotch said from the back of the transport. "Must have been our pirate, though how he knew it was there and why he didn't just haul it in and dump it somewhere else, I couldn't tell ya."

Kat grunted and continued to examine the unit. It was important to make sure she didn't wipe the core in her attempt to access the information they were after. The external access was all but obliterated. She would have to crack the case. "Hey, Scotch. Grab my kit, will you?"

The tools landed on the bench beside her. Carefully, she turned the unit over to access the bottom. The tech team that had designed this particular ABB model allowed quick-and-dirty access methods that would not endanger the internal circuits. Taking out her microtorch, she cut away the base along the designated markings indicating her safety zone. She switched off the torch with the final burn and set it aside to lift the battered housing away. As she suspected, the primary ports were useless, but there were several more inside for just such situations as this. Again, she wondered what had done such damage. Even as far back as the late 1990s, black boxes were known for being nearly indestructible, and the technology had only improved. This unit was top of the line, evidenced by the receivers being still operational despite the abuse to the shell. And yet, someone had clearly tried their best to turn it into plasma.

Powering up her tablet computer—a specialist's unit, with more bells and whistles than a hero's parade—Kat networked the systems and did a hard burn of the data. Her field computer was made for such things, and yet the transfer took forever. The ABB held an impressive amount of data.

"Almost done?" Sarge looked on edge. "We have only so long before they wonder what we're doing in here."

"Sorry, Sarge. There's a lot more here than I expected."

Finally, the dump completed. Not soon enough, though. From the front of the transport, the comm squawked.

Kat stole a moment to scan the data anyway, searching for Ghei's last coordinates before powering down. The comm squawked again, and Sarge cursed, giving Kat a look. Quicker than spit, she disconnected her machine.

He took the tablet from her and stowed it in the locker where he'd kept the microsat. She watched him a moment, then turned her attention to the gutted ABB in front of her. She had no idea what to do with it. As she tried to figure that out, a hand came into her field of view. It held a timed charge. Armed.

"Take it," Sarge said. "Slip it among the circuits and weld the housing back together. We'll launch it from the rocket shaft. If they ever find any of it, they won't recognize it from any other bit of debris."

Kat did as ordered. When she finished, Scotch slapped a separator charge on one end for propulsion and jettisoned the evidence.

The comm squawked again, and Sarge moved to respond.

"Sergeant Daire. Go ahead."

There was a pause, then a crackle. "Master sergeant, deck crew reports rocket fire from your vessel. Explain."

Everyone tensed even further. They all recognized Colonel Corbin's voice.

"Sorry, sir," Sarge said, his tone calm and completely reasonable. "My tech noticed some computer anomalies at docking. My specialist was attempting to correct the matter when a system glitch fired off the launch tube."

"A technician will be down immediately to check it out."

"Thank you, sir. That will not be necessary." Sarge didn't even flinch. "The issue has been resolved. My specialist is finishing her report now, complete with diagnostics."

Kat swore she could hear the officer's teeth grinding in frustration, but if so, his voice didn't betray it. "Very well. Have a copy sent to my office."

"Yes, sir. You'll have it in five minutes."

The comm went dead.

"Well?" Sarge turned to Kat expectantly. "That gives you four minutes to fake something convincing. Start with that incident docking with the *McKay* a month ago. It's similar enough."

Kat moved to the transport's computer banks. Her fingers pelted the keys like driving rain, already halfway to the *McKay* data. She tweaked here, copied there, pulled diagnostics from the last overhaul, and doctored the digital timestamp. With seconds to spare, Kat had a brand-new report with nary an electronic footprint out of place. Behind her, Scotch let out a long whistle. Sarge just turned and headed for the back of the transport. "Send it," he called over his shoulder as he stowed the gear and secured the locker, rekeying his code.

"Sarge," Kat called to him.

He stopped and looked over his shoulder but didn't say a thing.

"We *did* get him."

Sarge responded with one of his patented nods before he looked away, inspecting the transport interior to ensure nothing had been overlooked that might betray them. His inspection finished, he waited by the open hatch for the two of them to join him. Just beyond his shoulder, Kat could see that several dock personnel had moved strategically closer to the transport. She started to toggle her bonejack off standby, preparing to use the subdermal comm to warn Sarge. Before she could do so, she caught the seemingly random movement of his hand.

He ordered her down using one of the field combat gestures specific to the Devils. She resisted the urge to look around to see why he felt the area was unsecure. Yeah, something was up, but as long as Sarge was already aware, she would stand down and wait for his cue.

Sarge issued the next order aloud. "Tech Sergeant Daniels, the team's timing was a bit off on the last op. Schedule a live-fire exercise for 0700 UST."

"Yes, sir," Scotch said and headed off across the docking bay to inform the team and log the exercise with official channels.

Kat experienced a surge of adrenaline that flushed the fatigue from her system. Sarge's words said one thing, his hands another. They were going wheels-up in the morning to use one of Scotch's favorite antique phrases. Alpha Squad was being deployed, not the entire team. And at 0400 universal standard time, not 0700.

Curious. She had to wonder why Sarge distrusted the *Cromwell*'s crew... and the command staff.

She took a step forward and winced, forgetting to be careful with her wrapped ankle. She held her breath and caught Sarge's eye, just waiting for him to ground her. They stood with their gazes locked for a long, silent moment before Sarge gave a subtle nod. "Go rest up, Alexander. You have an exercise to run in the morning."

Kat's breath escaped on a grin. "Yes, sir!" Her energetic salute made him growl, but it was balanced by the understanding in his gaze. He turned and headed off, leaving her to make her way to quarters with some dignity.

As the corporal limped across the docking bay, Private Tipman watched her leave before retreating to a supply compartment, his demeanor no longer awkward or timid. Nominally, he prepared for inspection, straightening supplies, counting inventory, cleaning up the shelves. But as he moved about the compartment adjusting things with purposeful intent, a faint hum, more felt than heard, filled the space, replacing the muffled noise coming from the active bay. Behind him, the hatch opened as someone entered, and the din briefly flared full force. Tipman waited until the hatch closed and the outside sounds vanished once more before speaking.

"The Legion's efforts draw too much attention. If they continue to go after the *Cromwell* this aggressively, they could derail our whole operation. You will instruct them to desist, or we will withdraw our support." He looked over his shoulder with a pointed stare, waiting for the man to nod.

"They have been told. I will reinforce those instructions."

"Good. Now, what is the ETA of our objective?"

The officer frowned. "The *Venture* is scheduled to arrive in three days. He is confirmed aboard."

"Excellent. We must secure the Ty'Pherrein with all haste. He is the key to perfecting the synthetics."

"What's wrong with the handlers we already have?"

Tipman rounded on the man. "Those we have are flawed... of mixed parentage, not pure specimens. They function, but as you yourself reported, imperfectly. We are missing some key component only present in a full Ty'Pherrein. This is our best opportunity to obtain one."

"Like he's going to cooperate once you abduct him."

"We have no need of his cooperation. We have developed a compound to ensure his participation."

The officer's lip curled in distaste, and disagreement made him bold. "All this will do is draw AeroCom's attention. How is that worth it? Your synthetics already work well enough no one else has been able to tell the difference. Why risk it?"

Turning fully around and giving up his pretense of preparing for inspection, Tipman pinned the man with a glare. "Are you questioning your orders?"

"No, sir," the officer answered, his stance rigid.

"Good, because we have gone to great effort for the express purpose of obtaining this pure specimen."

"But if we draw the wrong attention, more than just the operation will be derailed."

Tipman turned his back on the man, hiding his annoyance. "That is not your concern," he said as he lifted the inspection log off a nearby hook and held it out to his 'superior,' ending the discussion.

CHAPTER 5

CHIMES MURMURED IN THE BACKGROUND, INTERWOVEN WITH THE SOUND OF water lightly dancing down upon smooth, rounded stones. The chamber walls seemed brushed by the gentle flicker of candlelight, though no open flame appeared in evidence. The scent of fresh ginger tea redolent with orange wafted from a demitasse cradled in a delicate china saucer on the desk. The overall impression was of serene elegance.

Yuki-ko scarcely noticed the calculated effect, her attention riveted upon the seemingly ageless gentleman behind the desk, his satin-smooth pate lowered as he read the dispatch displayed upon his monitor. She made no sound, nor did the tall, lean-muscled man subservient behind her. She waited, head bowed, lashes lowered, and in silence, for their leader's edict. Though outwardly submissive, she peered through the fringe of her lashes, alert and aware. After a long moment, he raised a seamless face and considered them both with ancient, jade-green eyes. He did not speak as his right hand came up to stroke the elegant soul patch below his lip, which ended at a narrowed point just above his chin. A familiar gesture. She tensed and straightened her spine even further as his eyes narrowed almost imperceptibly.

With inherent grace, he stood, smoothing the lines of his formal tunic as he did so. "You were told to secure the technical specifications for the McCormick-class vessel," he said in Japanese, breaking the tense silence, the words somehow both harsh and beautiful.

"*Hai*," Yuki-Ko and her subordinate both answered, respectful.

Casually stepping from behind his desk, the man moved toward a section of the chamber that felt more war room than Zen garden. He stopped before a partial schematic superimposed over a digital image of the *Cromwell* taken early on at the Groom shipyard before the vessel had been commissioned. A few items of gathered intelligence hung beside it, arranged neatly on the magnetic surface of the wall. Fortunes—both political and financial—could be made several times over if Hirobon succeeded in securing the details on how to reproduce—and conquer—the McCormick design's many advantages.

A chill coursed through Yuki-ko as his intent gaze moved from her to the mostly blank wall and back again. She longed to swallow but dared not though acid bloomed in her throat.

"And yet I have just been informed that Legion saboteurs have hit the Groom Complex, their servers and back-up servers destroyed." He waited expectantly, chin forward and head just barely tilted. The only sound was the jingle of chimes, in harmony with the enclosed rock fountain but at odds with the tension swiftly overtaking the room.

Yuki-ko paled but did not speak. She had not been given leave.

"Have you already secured what I require?" her superior continued, the words dangerously soft.

"Imperial Aeronautics has attained the Carmichael Research Institute, a firm with labs on the complex. Our people are in transit to replace key staff. Expected arrival is early next week..."

"That would be a no, then?" he interrupted.

She nodded sharply, eyes remaining lowered.

"This is unacceptable," the man said. "You have missed your best opportunity to secure the information, and Hirobon has lost face in the eyes of both our clients and our enemies."

She could not hold back a gasp at his harsh tone, her expressionless façade slipping ever so slightly. As several strides brought the man to stand directly before them, she and her subordinate went to their knees.

The elder's hand snapped out. The impact of skin against skin broke the serenity of the chamber. Though her head jerked to the side with the force of the blow, she did not whimper or flinch.

"You will make this right, Yuki-ko," he snapped, then he pivoted and left the room.

She answered anyway.

"Yes, father."

Thanks to Brockmann, Kat not only knew her way back to the barracks, but she knew the quickest route. Even with her bandaged ankle, it only took her fifteen minutes, and three of those were spent waiting for the lift. By the time Scotch made it back from logging the exercise, Kat lounged in the common area with her legs propped on a low table sipping at a couple ounces of dark rum to which she had added a splash or two of PawPaw's homemade ginger ale. The rum had cost her two vice credits, but after the day she'd had—hell, longer than that—it was worth it.

Scotch tried to snag her glass on his way to his bunk, and she flat-out slapped his hand away.

"Aww... isn't that cute," he quipped. "Kittie Kat's learned to slap fight." Playfully, he swiped back.

"Don't even try it..." she growled, smothering a giggle as his comment and actions brought up memories of Merry and Kismet, two cats she'd had growing up. They used to fake slap fight each other all the time, trying to get someone to get up and give them whatever they wanted. Kat, however, had no intention of giving Scotch her drink. "Get your own... assuming you have any v.c.'s left..."

He just grinned and headed for his bunk to change. Kat's gaze followed him of its own accord. She giggled at the little shrug he made to swipe his embedded identchip past the sensor to open the hatch. Anyone else could just walk past, and the door would open—if it was their assigned bunk—but Scotch stood a bit too tall and beefy, his chip higher than the sensor. An annoyance for him, but amusing for her... Of course, that could be the influence of the rum.

As soon as he disappeared inside, she went back to watching Brockmann, Campbell, True, and Tivo—Sergeant Thomas Vee—over by where they held team meetings, play makeshift pool on a 'table' made from the top of a cargo container they had bungee-strapped to the conference table, six tumblers someone had liberated from the mess, and a pad made from a heck of a lot of low-friction tape in place of felt. Kat had no clue where they'd gotten the regulation balls from, but they'd repurposed the carbon-fiber rods they used to clean their rifles as cues.

Kat laughed as True made a show of setting up a complicated shot only to scratch most impressively.

"That's another one!" Kat crowed as she picked up the tablet she'd tucked by her side. She'd written the players' names across the top of the screen, surrounded by the odd doodle or ten of that equal-armed cross, just because she couldn't get it out of her head. Using the stylus, she added a mark beneath True's name. The marks represented vice credits lost. One for missing a called shot, three for losing a round. So far, True was down five credits to everyone else's one or two. St. Sue hadn't lost a one, trouncing them all.

"Aw! Come on!" True groaned, hamming it up and giving Kat a broad wink, then flat-out proceeded to lie. Though her perception fuzzed, she had the uncomfortable realization that he might be flirting. "Campbell bumped the table!"

At his claim, Campbell bowed, then raised his 'cue' like a sword, his stance reminiscent of a sword kata rather than a traditional fencing position, revealing some serious martial arts training. Kat found that rather interesting. With a first name like Armand, she would have expected him to be more comfortable with an épée in his hand—or maybe a claymore, given the name Campbell—but not a katana. Not that he held any one of the three, but Kat had no difficulty imagining the latter blade in place of the carbon fiber rod.

"I must defend my honor!"

Good thing this is in fun, Kat thought. *Or True would be in some serious trouble.*

The others scrambled out of the way as Campbell slashed and flowed and spun, while True waved his rod wildly to block his opponent's more precise strikes. Hemry called out some damned good fencing advice to True, which the cutup blithefully ignored. The rest of the team cheered from the sidelines, wagering amongst themselves as the combatants fought from one end of the common room to the other and back again, their rods clacking with each contact. Even in jest, Campbell showed considerably more technique than his opponent, reflecting a definite Asian influence. Kat laughed so hard she nearly spilled her drink until Scotch reached out and rescued it. She hadn't even realized he'd come back and sat down next to her.

Her laughter trailed off as he stole the smallest of sips, his eyes locked on hers the entire time. He ran the tip of his tongue over his lip as he handed back the glass with a much subtler wink than Truitt's. For some reason, she swallowed hard, forgetting all about the hijinks going on around them.

This time Scotch rescued her before she even realized she was at risk, reaching out to block those goofing off before they tumbled backward over her legs.

"Okay! That's enough fooling around," he called out, an edge peeking out beneath his good-natured drawl. "Finish your drinks and hit the sack. That live-fire exercise will come earlier than you expect tomorrow."

Everyone groaned, but they quickly complied, the makeshift pool table broken down and tucked away as the airmen headed to their bunks. Kat finished her drink quicker than she would have liked, barely even realizing it as the tip of her tongue swiped across her lip.

As she, too, moved to comply, Scotch called out, "Hey, your tablet."

Kat turned to retrieve it, but Scotch didn't let go, instead scanning the screen. He looked back up at her, his gaze so intent she felt touched. "Is this the symbol you saw on Ghei's screen?"

The change between flirty-and-fun Scotch and seriously-intent Scotch chased away a bit of Kat's indulgent buzz—though she did have to admit to a pleasant flutter in her belly that she wasn't going to consider too closely. Dragging her focus back to the conversation, Kat nodded.

"You see this again—anywhere—you tell Sarge or me, understood?"

"Why?"

Scotch gave her a pointed look but didn't resort to saying 'because I said so.'

"This is the symbol of a shadow organization called the Teutonic Knights, a group of highly intelligent individuals that like to think of themselves as political influencers. Only they care less about the politics and more about their own power."

Kat frowned. "I've never heard of them."

"Not too many people have outside of the upper echelons. They aren't interested in drawing anyone's notice. They'd much rather be the masters behind the puppets. But trust me, if they are involved, things are about to get very complicated."

"You mean, like... more complicated than they already are?"

At Scotch's nod, Kat really regretted having already downed the rest of her drink.

Cryson wove his way through the crush of activity spread out across the docking bay as the crew shifted goods to make room for those newly arrived. The resultant noise rang loud enough to make him long for the silence of vacuum. He resisted the urge to stop up his ears as he steadily made his way toward the recently filled berth, too impatient to wait in his quarters for her passenger. His objective had just exited the causeway linking the *Destrier* to the docked shuttle, *Flechette*.

"Anton," the Legion captain called out as he raised his hand to draw the man's eye. Something about the lieutenant's expression as their gazes connected set off a warning flash in the back of Cryson's brain. He kept his features neutral and gestured toward the relative quiet of the dockmaster's empty office, altering his own path in that direction. It took several more minutes of dodging before he made it across the deck. Anton reached the office first, so Cryson closed the hatch behind him.

"Well?"

The Legionnaire grimaced.

Cryson commandeered the dockmaster's chair, motioning Lieutenant Anton Petrov toward a shipping crate, the only other perch in the room. "Tell me what I'm not going to be happy about first," Cryson said, figuring to give the man a starting point. Instead, Anton looked hesitant, as if that hadn't narrowed his options at all.

Damn! How much had gone wrong? Cryson wondered.

Anton drew a bag from over his shoulder and held it out. Cryson accepted it, peering inside to find a dump drive, an external memory source about the size of a big man's fist, with a storage capacity of fifty zettabytes, enough to store five times the data found in the research facility's computers combined.

"I'm not a tech, sir. I can't tell you what I retrieved, but it is safe to say that any data housed at the GEC has been irrevocably lost other than what's on there. Anyone that wants to score the McCormick-class technical plans will have to find their way into the heart of AeroCom to get it."

Cryson let out a long, hard breath. They had scored a solid hit against Hirobon. "So, where's the part I'm not going to like?"

"Someone saw me."

An understandable risk, easily dealt with. Clearly, nothing major if Petrov had escaped to rendezvous with the *Destrier*. At least... one would assume. Only, Cryson sensed more remained unspoken.

"And?"

The faint smell of stress seeped into the space as Petrov flexed his fingers into fists and out again. The rasp of his flight suit against the cargo crate set Cryson's nerves on edge. Or maybe that was just his well-honed instincts.

"*And?*" he repeated, his brow drawing tight as he eyed the man.

"I knew her, captain," Anton started, his voice carefully neutral.

As soon as he heard the word 'her,' Cryson knew they had reached the actual part he wouldn't like. He sat back and locked the lieutenant with a hard glare, head tilted slightly in expectation as he waited to hear that a witness had been left behind still breathing.

"She's in the *Flechette*'s auxiliary cabin," the man spoke softly. "She needs a medic."

"A medic?!" Cryson snapped. "All she should need about now is a casket!"

Anton's jaw bulged and flexed as he clearly restrained a knee-jerk comment. "Sally's not just a nice person, captain. She's decent folk. There aren't enough of them around out there. She didn't do anything but end up in the wrong corridor at the wrong time."

"So, you should have knocked her out and left her behind, not brought her along like some stray cat."

Something about the Legionnaire's expression gave him away. Cryson went still, his face like etched steel as he made a leap of logic. "She was already unconscious, wasn't she?" Anton flinched. "Damn it, Petrov! What were you thinking? It's not like she's just going to forget what happened!"

"The explosion ruptured the hull. She was trapped in the section that was depressurizing. If I'd left her there, I might as well have killed her..."

"Like you should have to begin with, you think?"

Anton wisely didn't respond.

Cryson sighed hard as the space behind his left eye began to pulse. "It's done. Come on, let's go take care of your new *pet*."

"Quit dawdling, Kittie, and get your tail in here."

"Oh, cram it, Rotgut," Kat snarled at Scotch as she slipped past him and moved into the belly of the transport. Though she would never admit it, he was the reason she was late. Between his little mind trips and their exercise today, her head had been so twisted around she'd barely slept.

The rest of Alpha Squad was already in place: Brockmann Tivo, and Dalton sat on one side of the crew compartment, with Scotch, Kramer, and Truitt on the other. The only ones missing were Sarge and Campbell, their pilot. Joining her squad, she passed the load compartment, which was crammed with gear, including what looked to be a full complement of pulse cannons. Someone had been busy. Without a word, she settled onto the bench next to Brockmann and, in short order, reassembled her gauss rifle, checking and rechecking each connection before running a quick systems diagnostic, finding everything in working order. She had hated breaking it down (a soldier wanted a gun if cornered, not a club) but carrying the weapon through the corridors would have drawn attention.

She sat there, gripping the rifle, telling herself to relax and rest up. Of course, the more time that passed waiting for Sarge to come through the hatch, the more Kat got a bad feeling. She didn't even try to rest up. Instead, she gave her gear a thorough inspection, ensuring everything was accounted for and stowed appropriately. The whole time, she tried to shrug off her apprehension with marginal success.

The others sat back, reasonably relaxed and bullshitting, but she sat ramrod straight on her bench, gauss across her knees and her eyes locked on the back of the transport, hardly aware of the sound of her sling hardware rattling against her rifle as she absently tugged the strap with her finger.

"Stow your weapon, Alexander," Sarge said when he finally came through the hatch. Campbell entered the transport behind him as Kat complied. The pilot locked down the hatch and the airlock before joining Sarge at the front of the transport. Their expressions were hard and focused as they settled in at the drive console and flew through the start-up sequence. The comm squawked, and Sarge shot a look and a gesture back toward the waiting team. All eyes focused on him, and none missed the message: *Quiet. ID-Dark.*

Kat let out a sharp breath, which earned her a hard scowl. She lowered her head in acknowledgment and worked to regulate her breathing even as she pressed hard against the bone behind her right ear. Official channels would deny it, but special ops teams could deactivate their identchips. Those in the crew compartment did so, as ordered.

"Transport 62-Delta; identify yourself, pilot."

"Warrant Officer Armand Campbell speaking."

"Identchip scan confirmed. One passenger registered. Identify."

"Master Sergeant Kevin Daire present and reporting." Sarge's voice remained cool, with just a normal shade of impatience.

"Acknowledged and confirmed. Are you prepared for launch, pilot?"

"That is an affirmative, Control. The *Teufel* is ready for launch."

Launch Command made no comment or acknowledgment of the given name of their craft, merely continuing with protocol: "Please confirm the purpose and duration of your flight."

Sarge placed a hand on Campbell's shoulder, silencing him. "Sergeant Daire speaking. We are embarking on a test flight to confirm systems are fully operational prior to scheduled live-fire exercise. Planned flight duration is two and a half standard hours."

"Thank you, master sergeant, you are cleared for launch."

Kat and the rest of the squad strapped in before the docking collar released and the tether disengaged. Until the thrusters took them out of range of the *Cromwell,* their drive engines would remain off-line, leaving them without gravity. The squad settled in for the wait. Handhelds came out, conversations continued, eyes closed, and peace—or at least quiet—

reigned. Until Sarge cleared his throat, that is. Everything but the transport stopped as Sarge turned his chair about to face his team.

"We have a situation."

The last eyes opened, and the men and women of the 142nd Mobile Special Operations Team straightened, their attention riveted on Sarge, who looked grave.

"Command has informed me of an attack on the GEC. Someone hit the developmental labs responsible for the McCormick-class designs causing considerable damage to the facility. The command areas remain functional, but the research labs are wrecked. Casualties include sixty-seven injured, ten dead, and five unaccounted for."

Kat gritted her teeth at the revelation. In fact, she might even have growled, given the covert glances she received from the entire squad. She ignored them. There were at least two people at the GEC she cared about, but if Sarge had those details, he didn't share them. As much as Kat wanted to ask, she restrained herself and focused on the briefing.

Sarge went on as if unaware of the reactions. "The details of our assignment," and here his gaze settled on Kat as he gave a brief nod of concession before continuing, "have not previously been disclosed to you.

"There is a reason we were assigned to the *Cromwell*. It is suspected that the ranks in this quadrant have been infiltrated at all levels, and key personnel have been subverted or replaced by composites. Apparently, they have targeted the flagship. Several attempts have already been made, including the multiple events at the GEC."

"The piracy must stop. The terrorist activity must stop. Space is dangerous enough without the addition of human threats. We are Military Command's countermeasure. As such, we report directly to General Drovak and no other. Needless to say, this is a covert assignment. The *Cromwell* command staff has not been informed. Our standing orders are first to observe the crew, reporting on potentially seditious acts. Beta Squad has drawn this duty. Our second objective: to actively pursue and halt pirate activity in this quadrant. That is where you come in. Thanks to Corporal Alexander, we have a fresh lead on one of the subversives. As a result, this is a fact-finding/intercept mission. The intel we secure could be the break we need to neutralize this particular threat."

With that, he unbuckled his harness and floated up to the nearest tether bar. He hauled himself hand over hand to the other end of the transport. At the storage locker, he used his handhold's leverage to muscle his legs down to where he could slide his feet into the bootdocks built into the deck. Kat watched as Sarge released the lock. He opened the locker and withdrew her computer kit. Slinging the strap securely over his shoulder, he closed the door and disengaged from the docks, then hauled himself back toward the drive compartment.

"You ready for some satisfaction, Alexander?"

She accepted her kit when he stopped in front of her, but she didn't really need it. They were returning to the GEC, or the surrounding sectors, anyway. Her computer held the data, but Kat had already memorized the last known coordinates of Ghei's vessel. She rattled them off from memory and even the frequency at which he'd been transmitting.

"Impressive," Sarge replied in a dead-flat tone. "Now power that thing up to verify, and then determine what other useful data we've retrieved." He returned to the drive compartment without waiting for a response.

Yeah, so showing off wasn't her best idea. Kat deployed the tablet computer, slipped the zero-g tether over her wrist, and sat back with the system firmly in her grip. Start-up flashed by before she could blink. Opening the microsat data file, Kat quick-scanned what she'd downloaded.

"Oh shit!"

Heads turned at her outburst.

"Report, corporal."

"Coordinates confirmed, sir." Even to her own ears, her voice sounded stunned as she rattled off the information she'd provided earlier. *I did it,* she thought. *I friggin' did it! Ghei and his goons weren't quick enough!* A crow of laughter escaped her.

"And?" Impatience edged Sarge's voice.

"Sarge," she managed in a semi-normal tone, looking up to meet his stern gaze. "We are in possession of the collective data from the research facility... *All* of it."

The transport jinked ever so slightly as even Campbell shot a look in her direction at that pronouncement. He quickly turned away, correcting course and evening out their trajectory.

Kat hardly noticed. Satisfaction flooded her, bursting forth in a broad grin. Before her last encounter with Ghei, she had attempted to initiate a Full Alert, which would have dumped the station's research databases to the secure black box while wiping the primary servers, thus removing the prize from the pirates' reach. Ghei's people had crashed the system before she could tell whether she'd succeeded. Well, they'd failed to thwart her. Out of habit, Kat fished an exabyte drive from her kit and plugged it into the port on her tablet. The first thing she had learned in her MOS was the importance of creating backups. She copied the files and started the transfer while still reviewing the data, not trying to read it but allowing the pattern to imprint on her memory as she had been trained to do. This data was vital, both to the researchers who created it and to Command. But beyond that, the intel gathered by the station's sensors could represent the only evidence they had against the pirates.

"Alexander," Sarge said, his tone still less than patient. "How about seeing if there's any intel on there of immediate use?"

She cringed and turned her gaze back to the tablet. "There are several other drive signatures recorded, sir. It's a long shot, but they might be useful in identifying and tracking the pirates." She didn't hold out much hope for that, but a soldier learned to use any advantage that came to hand.

"Safe perimeter reached," Campbell cut in. "Setting course and engaging drive."

The Devils didn't expect anything to still be there. They headed to the coordinates to pick up the trail of Ghei's vessel. Originally, Kat had taken it for an asteroid—as the pirates had clearly intended—back when she'd still been on the command deck of the Groom facility. The ABB hadn't been fooled. It had picked up traces of the drive signature, the unique particle trail left by the ship's engines. They could use that to track him. It wasn't a precise method, but they could come close with formulas for calculating drift. Of course, they had a way to go, with not very much in between. That didn't dissuade Kat from linking the signal from the external cameras so that it ran the feed on her tablet. She'd always hated not seeing where she was going, whether on a dirt road in a car or across the galaxy in a transport.

There wasn't anything to see for the longest time. Under drive, the cameras caught only the bright blue glow of passing space punctuated by random white pulses caused by the proximity of something of sufficient mass to minutely affect the electrogravitic drive envelope. There wasn't a whole heck of a lot out here to worry about, and if they did come across something, proximity alerts gave them plenty of warning. Kat settled back and let the changing light patterns mesmerize her. She wasn't asleep, but it was the next best thing to it. Her muscles took advantage of the distraction, relaxing until she slouched against the bulkhead, eyes still fixed on her computer. She barely noticed the engines modulate for deceleration as they came out of drive—until the light patterns deepened and strobed wildly.

"Watch out!" An alert on the drive console went off moments after her shout.

"Campbell, evasive maneuvers!" Sarge snapped out the order as he helped man the controls. "Clear trajectory, two degrees port."

A particularly virulent curse rose from the cockpit as they barely missed the burnt-out hulk. Eyes still riveted, Kat hit record on her system, catching every frame as the external cameras tracked the wreckage into which they'd nearly plowed. There would have been no coming back from that. It wasn't huge, but it was dense, according to the data scrolling across the bottom of her screen.

The rock-ship drifted there like a recently fissured geode. The rock exterior encased a compact craft smaller than one of the escape pods, the standard model that had earned the epitaph "The Can" for good reason. What Kat saw on her screen looked barely bigger than a cryosleep tank... with none of the amenities. The camera panned some more as they passed the obstacle.

Kat gasped, and her grip on her computer white-knuckled. From over her shoulder, she heard choruses of "Damn!" and not a few gulps before Sarge's voice cut through it all.

"Enough!" he barked. "Break it up."

Kat bit back a more vehement "Damn" of her own. She felt cheated. "I was wrong. Someone else got him."

"Corporal Alexander... disconnect that system link."

Crap.

"Yes, sir."

Her breath hissed out short and shallow as she broke the connection, unable to look away from the final image recorded: two-thirds of an environmental suit still strapped into a conchair.

"Shake it off, airman, and close that file," Sarge's voice echoed faintly above her.

"I was wrong..." she murmured again, her finger jabbing the power-down button.

"Maybe... we'll have to see," Sarge said. He then turned toward the rest of the squad. "Scotch, Brockmann... suit up for retrieval. I want anything you can find that may tell us something, including the remains, stat.

"Stow your gear and snap to, Alexander. We have a refit to execute."

Kat looked back to the rear of the transport. Scotch and Brockmann climbed into top-end versions of the standard MMU, streamlined and built for combat or recon. Brockmann carried a retrieval pack that included a cryogenic body bag similar in principle to the coolant bandage strapped around Kat's damaged ankle. She glanced at the rest of the squad as they maneuvered expertly in freefall, hauling gear from the load compartment, deploying combat armament, and retrofitting the transport. Showing no evidence of the goof-off he'd been last night, Truitt helped Tivo detach the tension cap from the two-stage weapons port, on the starboard side—transports might not have a call for more than the lasers and basic rockets used to clear debris from their flight path, but in AeroCom, every vessel was designed to be retrofitted in the field to meet combat needs. The tech slid in a cannon auto-mount, jacked it into the system, and replaced the tension cap, maintaining the transport's environmental integrity. A brief jolt and a mechanical *whir* sounded as the external seal retracted on reconnect.

"The starboard cannons are online and ready, Sarge," Tivo said. Dalton, the team's weapons specialist, reported similarly for port and aft cannons.

"Campbell, activate weapons control," Sarge said. "We may not see trouble, but all of you will damn well be ready for it, am I understood?"

"Yessir!" the squad responded collectively as they completed the refit.

Kat was still harnessed in, tablet in hand. "Sarge, put me on the retrieval squad."

He glanced down and gave her a hard stare. She couldn't blame him. As the team's newest member, she didn't have all her clearances yet. "You are not yet rated for zero-g combat."

"All due respect, sir," Kat said, "they aren't rated for invasive data retrieval." She held up her computer. "If there's a computer core, it has to be extracted, not just yanked out. It's the only way we have a chance of retrieving anything more than physical intel."

Sarge didn't look convinced. "Sure this isn't personal?" It was one of those not-questions.

She went for bald-faced honesty. "Does it matter, sir? Because I could lie..."

That drew a quirk of Sarge's upper lip, if not an actual smile. Just then, Scotch drifted up from behind. "It's good, Sarge, let her come... we could use a mule to haul the gear."

Kat restrained herself from giving her teammate a sour look... or a non-regulation salute. Scotch angled a smirk her way—surely knowing the direction of her thoughts—but his gaze remained solid, steady, and serious. Despite his wisecracks, she had no doubt he had her back. They waited in patient silence for Sarge's ruling. Okay, not so patient, at least for Kat, but she made sure she *appeared* patient, which was the important bit.

"Double-time it, Alexander," Sarge said by way of approval, "before our drive-wake propels the derelict out of range. We don't have fuel to waste coming about."

By the time he closed his mouth on the last word, Kat already had her harness disengaged, retrieved her rifle, and propelled herself toward the equipment lockers and her MMU, tablet still in hand and her gauss drifting behind her from its strap. She lost a few moments temporarily securing both, but still, she suspected she broke several suit-up records. Maybe she imagined it, or maybe Sarge really was chuckling behind her, hard to say, as she lowered her helmet over her head. Taking her microtorch out of her kit, she attached it to the utility mount on the back of her left gauntlet, then withdrew her tablet once more and linked it to the PacsComp built into her helmet so she could access its functions if needed. She then zipped the computer back into its compartment. Finished. She activated her bonejack and switched it to the squad band before positioning herself by the airlock.

"Ready for deployment, sir."

Sarge had returned to the drive compartment. Only Scotch and Brockmann stood there watching her, 20mm recoilless rifles slung over their shoulders and amusement clear in their expressions despite the obstruction of their helmets. She could almost read their thoughts: *Noob.*

So be it. She just didn't want Sarge changing his mind. Brockmann propelled herself past Kat to the airlock, her movements deft and efficient despite the zero-g environment. Scotch stopped in front of Kat and held out the tether. She reflexively accepted it, not even thinking about what was on the other end.

Looking down, she sighed.

"I wasn't joking about the gear, corporal," Scotch's words buzzed along her jaw. In his other hand, he held a pulse pistol. "Stow your weapon. Sarge is right. You haven't been cleared for zero-g combat."

"Only because my mommy hasn't signed my permission slip," Kat grumbled back, only partially successful in turning bitter resentment into a lighthearted joke.

Scotch just gave her a wry smile and handed her the pistol, which she slid into an external thigh pocket. "This is for personal protection only," he instructed. "Should it come down to an encounter, do not initiate engagement. Duck and cover or haul ass back to the transport with what we came for. Brockmann and I will take care of the offensive while you secure the intel." Then he grinned. "You do realize this is all academic, right? Not like there's anything out there for anyone to hide behind."

That took the sting out of the rest of what he had said.

This was a covert assignment. If it came down to it, the higher-ups would claim no knowledge of the mission rather than raise the subversives' suspicions. End result: Alpha Squad members had written off their careers already if things went bad. Of course, just in case they weren't hung out to dry over this, violating regs in a conflict situation could ground her or even ensure Kat never rated for zero-g combat. Not much of a future in special ops after that.

Yeah, with that as perspective, she was fine playing mule.

"Get your asses out there and get this done," Sarge snapped over their squad frequency, "before some trigger-happy command crew over at Groom mistakes us for more pirates."

CHAPTER 6

THE GLOBULES WOKE HER. TINY FLOATING SPHERES BRUSHED HER SKIN, bursting like time-delay raindrops. Each rupture released the scent of spilt blood. In an atavistic response, Sally flailed away from the smell or tried to, anyway. Her limbs moved too freely, as if the grav generators had glitched. All she managed was to burst a bunch more bubbles. Well, that and wake a wide ribbon of pain down the right side of her head. The pressure behind her skull spiked, driving her back into unconsciousness.

The next time Sally woke, she remained as still as possible, letting awareness return at its own speed rather than chasing it away. Lying still gave her some time to figure out what was what. Or try to, anyway...

She lay strapped down somewhere in absolute darkness. Not restrained, but locked down for flight, secured for safety. There was something wrong with that but damned if Sally could put a finger to it just then. She had a feeling she should remember something, except her brain wouldn't cooperate. Heck, she was lucky she knew her own name. Who the hell strapped her to a hard bunk, and why? Not like the GEC was going anywhere.

Something had knocked out the lighting, or it would have come on the moment she'd moved. Even the emergency lighting appeared out, though she had a vague recollection of it initially being engaged. She wasn't sure she was ready to deal with whatever had caused that.

As she puzzled things through, yet another bead of blood collided with her face, the fluid clinging as it splattered. More than just the lights were out if things were floating. She had little doubt the blood was hers, given the pain lancing through her skull.

Even as she realized her situation, a jolt shook the compartment, followed by a steady increase of pressure. The familiar sensation focused her thoughts. She'd experienced it repeatedly over the last two years during many a shuttle docking. She wasn't on the GEC anymore.

That cleared her mind like a jolt. Survival instincts kicked in. A surge of adrenaline put a sharp edge on the darkness. Carefully, she brought up her arms, going for the clasp on the strap holding her down. It rested in the middle of her chest. She had no problem reaching it, but the angle made it tricky to undo. She made her third try when the compartment's pressure abruptly equalized, leaving her feeling slightly leaden.

As the lights came up, her eyes squeezed tight against the brightness. Her body tensed, hands instinctively fisting quite uselessly, given her current position. She forced them to relax at her sides and lay still as two sets of footsteps entered the cabin. Her ears tracked the sound as an unfamiliar voice spoke.

"What the hell am I supposed to do, recruit her?"

"If she was the type you could, I likely wouldn't have thought twice about leaving her behind."

Petrov. The second voice was definitely Petrov. Maybe he didn't realize how that sounded, or maybe he didn't care. Either way, his words both flattered and riled her up. From the sharp huff of breath, whoever he spoke with was less than amused himself.

"If I were you, I'd shut up about now and go get that medic before I make sure the matter is moot." Beneath his anger, Sally recognized a sense of friendship that precluded any offense. At his order, Petrov moved off, and Sally heard the hollow *thunk* of a hatch closing.

Silence followed. The light remained too bright for her to crack her eyes enough to look out through her lashes. A fact she suspected had more to do with the injury to her head than anything else. Leaving them closed, she strained to catch any sound that would alert her to the man's movement. All she heard was his muttering.

"Decent folk, huh? Hot piece of tail is more like it." One of them didn't know Petrov well but damned if she knew which. She couldn't help but grumble at that admission.

The man laughed. "Awake, are you?"

Sally refused to answer as she heard him walk across the deck and open a compartment. More steps, and then a man's worth of weight settled on the edge of the bunk. The overwhelming smell of isopropyl alcohol stung her nose as a piece of damp gauze swept over her left arm below the half sleeve of her fatigues before moving to her neck and then up to her face, making her flinch as he reached her right temple. She gritted her teeth and wanted to snarl but wouldn't give him the satisfaction. He chuckled again and patted her arm as he stood and moved away in the direction of the hatch, calling out behind him, "Don't worry, I'll most likely kill you in the morning."

The absurdity of the classic movie reference—particularly coming from what she could only presume was an actual pirate—startled a laugh out of her. That laugh ended in a gasp as her head imploded with the pain.

Cryson got out of there as quickly as he could. Though he was furious at Anton, he could almost understand the man's sentimental response to the woman. She clearly had looks. More importantly, she had strength and courage, traits those in the Legion respected. That didn't make her any less of a problem. Hell, it likely made her more of one.

He'd reached the end of the causeway when Anton came striding back through with a medic trailing behind him. Stopping and spreading his stance until he blocked their path, Cryson waited for them to stop themselves. "You patch her up, then she's for Detention. No giving her the run of the ship, no confinement to your quarters or wherever the hell you thought you'd put her. Get her into lockup until I figure out what to do with her."

Anton opened his mouth to protest. Before he spoke one word, Cryson's fist connected with his jaw. The Legionnaire kept to his feet, but his upper body jarred back and to the left, impacting the plasti-steel plate sheathing the causeway's interior. Anton straightened, his hands relaxed at his side.

"Any questions?" Cryson asked, his voice low and even and colder than a dead star. His eyes didn't leave Anton's. The Legionnaire straightened and stood at attention, face expressionless as he returned his captain's stare.

They stood that way long and silent until the medic cleared his throat impatiently.

"No, sir," Anton answered, the words garbled only slightly, though the side of his face had already begun to darken and swell. "Thank you, sir."

Cryson moved past him without speaking. He never should have left his office. Not that the woman would have been any less of a problem, but at least then he wouldn't have to contend with the memory of her tumbled blonde curls and the faint sprinkling of freckle across her nose.

Or the cold, harsh reality that at some point he might have to make good on his casual threat.

Just returning from the GEC after inspecting the damage to the Carmichael Research labs, Yuki-ko drifted above the Hirobon facility in her personal craft, the *Hachisunohana,* waiting for docking clearance. Like all Hirobon direct holdings, this was an interstellar space station, answerable to no planetary power or government, much like international waters operated back on Earth.

Ruled only by profit—and Hirobon—the facility saw much traffic as a place where... delicate... negotiations could be carried out with minimal interference. For a price, of course. In strategic orbit around Tau Ceti Three—the planet known as Demeter—such opportunities were plentiful as many parties maneuvered for control in one manner or another.

Resigned to the wait ahead of her, Yuki-ko tilted her command chair to a more comfortable angle and dimmed the cabin lights. Settling into the chair's contoured grip, she took in the distant stars stretched before her. They seemed to shimmer and wink against the obsidian darkness as the drive envelope keeping her in steady orbit created a faux atmospheric effect. The peace and solitude eased her tension. For the moment, she turned her thoughts from her rather costly failure and merely contemplated the universe.

No problem had the power to loom against such a backdrop. Not even the mess at the GEC.

With a few taps on the controls built into her armrests, soothing reed music filled the drive compartment. Yuki-ko relaxed into the grips of this private solitude—in a craft of her own design—and allowed herself to dream of a life among the stars, not tangled in business but with the freedom of exploration.

New stars, new species, new vistas.

Discoveries to be studied and learned from, rather than assessed for their financial potential and exploited in the name of profit and honor. Tension reached out from deep within to snare her once more. With rigid control, she forced even those thoughts from her mind, but the moment was lost.

Even as she purged her worries, a chime sounded from her console.

"Chikushou!"—son of a bitch!— Yuki-ko swore, indulging her annoyance in the seclusion of her private craft as she never would on the station. She sat up and retrieved a message from one of her Ronin—an agent embedded with an AeroCom special operations team assigned to the *Cromwell.* The communication appeared text-based rather than verbal. Excitement coiled in her belly... or perhaps more tension. She found it difficult to tell anymore.

As the decoded words scrolled across her monitor, she gasped and leaned forward even more.

<<Research data from the GEC not lost. Black box retrieved by Aero-Com vessel, intel within reach. Will notify you once it has been secured.>>

On a hopeful whisper, Yuki-ko breathed, *"Chikushô!"* Oh, shit!

CHAPTER 7

KAT'S NERVES TWITCHED AS SHE HAULED THE RECOVERY KIT. NOT THE easiest thing to drag around. It kind of resembled one of those shower kits with all the individual zipped compartments that unrolled flat so you could access everything or bundle it up compact for storage... only monster-sized. Bulky as sin and a pain in the ass to maneuver (clearly, the designers had not considered the dimensions of the various hatches it would have to go through), but better than losing several years' pay replacing tools lost to the vacuum of space.

When she finally managed to exit the transport, Kat had her first eyes-on view of the rock-ship. The rest of the retrieval team, already halfway there, put the shattered mass into perspective. Compared to the vessel she'd just left, it was a toy. The inside had to have had just barely enough room for Ghei to move around, with some storage for necessities. She could not conceive that it was ever meant for manned space travel.

Scotch and Brockmann confirmed her suspicions as they reached the derelict ahead of her. *Damn!* Scotch's response came drawn out and stunned. *Sarge,* he called over the squad band, *this man was* not *here willingly.*

Kat came up behind him and grudgingly concurred. It pissed her off, leaving her conflicted in her hatred. A closer look inside the pod revealed two things: the body was restrained, not secured, and the vessel had been welded shut. Whether the remains strapped to the conchair were Ghei or not, whoever it was, he was a victim not a collaborator.

Get to work on that system, Kittie, Scotch said as Brockmann grabbed the retrieval gear from Kat and scrambled over the jagged lip. The woman lost no time transferring the remains to the cryobag and scouring the inside of the compartment for anything that would aid them in their pursuit. Kat didn't know what disturbed her more: the pirates' ruthlessness or the detached manner in which her squadmate performed her task.

Come on! Scotch snapped, drawing Kat out of her thoughts. *You have a job to do, so do it. I'm not too comfortable with our asses hanging out here.*

Kat found no convenient jack-in port this time. Not because the pirates were tricky, but because of their brutality. Her search for the primary systems didn't turn up much. Literally. No navigation system. No drive computer. Nothing but life support, communications, and some modified gear she couldn't identify—likely something to do with the composite's remote operation. This was no ship. It was a coffin. *Drop 'em and leave 'em* was the catchphrase here. Kat's stomach turned violently. Even if the real Ghei had been a willing participant, he didn't deserve this end. No one did. Which kind of robbed her of her focus. Having a face to hate made it easier to get a handle on things. Ghei had been a known quantity. Now, the enemy remained unidentified, which gave them the edge. That really pissed her off.

She turned her mind back to the task at hand. Without any kind of port for infiltration, it would take too long to hack in manually. Her air supply would deplete well before she finished, assuming external forces didn't interfere first. She powered up the microtorch she'd attached to her gauntlet, physically extracted what computer systems there were, and slid them into her kit.

Crawling out from where she'd completed the extraction, Kat bumped into the conchair. She flinched and turned, her mind still seeing the partial remains. Reality interjected, though. At eye level, she now saw the bottom edge of the conchair arm. The foam padding was shredded. Not clawed or torn, but little bits picked out quite purposefully. In an instant of epiphany, the memory of Ghei's plucking fingers came to mind. Kat understood now that he'd tried to leave them—or someone, anyway—intel. A name? Hard to say. The letters had been picked out by feel. The first one might be a 'C,' or maybe an 'L,' and the last was definitely an 'N,' but those in between all ran together in haphazard plucks. Maybe someone back on the *Cromwell* could decipher them using a digital scan.

Using the sensors on her helmet, Kat snapped an image of Ghei's message and the chair itself direct to her tablet for later review, just in case. Quickly, she scanned the interior of the rock-ship and the remains of the chair from all sides, maneuvering to stay out of her teammates' way. With her task complete, she pushed off before remembering she was also there to play mule. Kat pivoted back.

Hey, Scotch... The rest of her words drifted off as the section of space past his shoulder came into view. *Ah, hell! Company on your six.*

Scotch cursed, and Kat faintly heard him mutter about vipers in the nest. Someone on the inside had to have given them away. Was it someone on the *Cromwell*? Or one of their own men? Kat mirrored Scotch's curse. But now was not the time to dwell on betrayal. There were pirates to fight.

Scotch and Brockmann carefully fired their jets for a controlled turn toward the incoming threat. Both of them brought to bear their recoilless rifles, though what good the weapons would be against an attacking frigate, Kat couldn't imagine. Of course, how pathetic did that make her when she looked down to spy the pulse pistol Scotch had given her in her grip? Remembering her orders, she shoved it back into the pocket she'd drawn it from and turned to secured the gear.

Leave it and get back to the ship! Scotch ordered.

Hell no! I can't afford the replacement charge.

I said get out of here! he growled. *We'll grab the gear.*

Kat wanted to argue, but she knew she wouldn't win and distracting those with the weapons to defend them put everyone at risk. She took mere seconds to secure her tablet and abandoned the rest, as ordered. Then, with a blast of her thrusters, she jetted toward the Teufel's airlock even before Sarge's command to retreat came over the band.

Sound doesn't travel in space. No atmosphere, nothing for it to bounce off. It was a false cliché, though, that no one could hear you scream. There's plenty enough atmosphere in a helmet and lots of enclosed surfaces that made the sound seem to go on forever. Kat's head rocked with the sound traveling along her bonejack as one of her team screamed. She didn't have time to spin around before the side of the *Teufel* lit up with the colors of hell until it briefly looked made of flame. The blast came from behind her as the pirates took out the derelict. The explosion's shock wave sent Kat tumbling. End over end, catching brief glimpses of the fierce, quickly exhausted blaze as unused air tanks in the derelict ruptured in the blast. The dying embers silhouetted the large, limp form of one of her squadmates.

The sight hit her like a board to the gut. Kat told herself it was Brockmann. After all, the cryobag still floated nearby. The moment she thought that guilt almost crippled her as badly as the fear that she was wrong. Not that losing Brockmann was any better, just easier to take than picturing a world without Scotch. But... maybe they were only wounded. Kat fired her jets to counteract her uncontrolled spin. She went flying toward the wreckage forgetting such things as orders and intel and pirate ships with pulse cannons.

Back to that transport, corporal! The voice was familiar, if not the tone. *Now!*

She didn't sob. She wouldn't sob. Soldiers didn't, you know.

(Yeah. Another lie.)

Where you at, you sonofabitch? A western twang crept into her voice as she snipped at Scotch. Her temper had always carried echoes of her PawPaw, though this time it was heavy with relief.

On your 4 o'clock, get your tail to the transport. We have to get out of here.

Brock...

She's gone! Brockmann's gone! Now move you're ass, corporal! Scotch barked. *I've got her and the sorry piece of shit we came out here for.*

Kat wanted to argue, only her training—and her relief—kicked in.

It took one jet to spin her and both to send her on her way. The left jet gave a little sputter, and an early warning light blinked on in the rim of her visor. Her powerpack ran low. Shouldn't be an issue less than twenty meters from the airlock. Of course, by the time she faced the transport, it was too late. The attacking vessel spewed pirates with heavier armaments than anything she had. Several broke off in an attempt to relieve her and Scotch of their burdens and likely their lives. The others took potshots at the *Teufel*, pinning the rest of Alpha Squad on board. The unmarked frigate came around, firing warning shots that shook the transport. Their flight path would bring them in close like they planned to grapple onto the hull. The *Teufel* just managed to keep them at bay using the thermal rockets. Kat waited for the transport's engines to fire up in a strategic retreat that would take the rest of the squad away from the risk of capture. That would signal the end for the retrieval squad and the mission objective, but she couldn't believe Sarge would sacrifice the team for just two men. She wouldn't even expect him to.

Only, with a *whoosh* and a light cloud of venting atmosphere, the airlock opened. Tivo, Dalton, and Truitt, the three best shots on the team, appeared in positions of cover around the open iris. Each of them had a short-order 50-cal. in their hands and a secondary weapon slung over their shoulders. They methodically picked off the pirates. Even so, one of the unfriendlies closed in on Kat's position, despite the fire team's cover fire. There were just too many for the three of them to take out.

Kat deployed her pulse pistol and fired. Nothing happened, and the pirate drew closer, his weapon trained on her head. Her breath quickened, and acid burned her throat. *Not like this, dammit!*

From the direction of the *Teufel*, Kat spied a flash of weapons fire as Truitt noticed her predicament. The pirate's body jerked with the impact, the rounds traveling straight through the environmental suit. Blood and atmosphere formed a cloud around the slowly twisting remains.

Kat shuddered and returned the malfunctioning pistol to her pocket. *Better you than me.*

With the rest of the pirates occupied, she glanced toward Scotch. As her eyes settled on her teammate, she wanted to call out, to warn him there was a pirate closing in from behind, but even that wouldn't be in time.

No way in hell! Kat fired her jets full thrust with a grit of her teeth and barely a glance at her powerpack warning light. Her pulse pistol was useless, but her gaze locked on the microtorch still affixed to her gauntlet. She had one chance. The enemy's attention was completely fixed on his target. He had no clue his buddies hadn't dealt with her. Minute adjustments of her body posture shifted her trajectory until she aimed straight at the pirate's head. She powered up the 'torch and gladly burned the last of her reserves.

Impact. A jolt and a *pop*, a brief swirling cloud as the pirate's suit vented atmosphere, and more of that screaming—this time from Kat—as the momentum sent her tumbling against the inertia of her victim's body, her arm locked in place, the gauntlet scorched and her wrist throbbing.

She screamed again as her wrist bent back against her weight as much as the gauntlet allowed, saved only from a break by the suit's rigid structure and the fact that the torch tip finally cut itself free. Scotch's voice rippled along her jaw, *Damn, HellKat...* His arm locked around her waist and drew her down as he gave a short burst of his jets to cancel her spin. *Remind me not to piss you off!* Relief filled his voice, as well as a new level of respect.

Kat laughed, a tinge of hysteria dancing around its edges. *I haven't killed you yet, so you're probably safe...*

The joke fell flat, tripped up by a confusing hodgepodge of uncomfortable emotions. Groaning, she tried to use her jets to back away. They sputtered, and she noted the warning light had transitioned to red. She was tapped and trapped. Looking anywhere but at him, she noticed the rest of the Devils had come out to play, even now forcing the pirates back.

Come on, Kittie, time to go home, Scotch murmured, tucking her tighter against him as he went full thrusters toward the *Teufel*.

Wait! She fought against him, though what she thought that would accomplish with her powerpack spent, she didn't know. *Brockmann... and the...*

Before she could protest further, Truitt zipped past and headed back with their comrade's remains and their objective. Dalton followed behind, hauling the toolkit. The damned fucking toolkit. Deep in the pit of her mind, Kat had to wonder if her hanging back had gotten Brockmann killed.

St. Sue... Kat murmured, her throat closing tight. Softly, barely even subvocally, she began to recite the only pray she knew straight through, not having been raised in any formal church beyond the open plains. *Now I lay me down to sleep, I pray the Lord... Sue's soul to keep. And if she should... die... before... she wakes, I pray the Lord her soul to take.*

Just as softly, Scotch murmured, *Amen.*

That startled Kat. She'd forgotten for a moment that she wasn't alone in her own head. Scotch tightened his grip. Kat wasn't a hundred percent sure he meant only to keep them from spinning at her sudden jerk. Though she found comfort in that, inside, she seethed, not at him, but the enemy. And a bit at herself.

Other than Scotch, Brockmann had been her first real friend on the team. Though they'd all signed on knowing they might well be called to the ultimate sacrifice, Kat raged inside. Even if this did put them one solid step closer to pinning the bastards down, it was scarcely worth the loss of a teammate, let alone a friend. More than ever, Kat wanted to get a bit of her own back against the pirates.

But make no mistake, she was no saint and would waste not a thought or a prayer on any of *them* that fell.

Not this time, though. A scan of the zone showed that everyone else had already fallen back to the transport. Kat gave up and settled in for the ride, trying not to resent Scotch's looking out for her. That's what teammates did. Guilt gripped her heart a little tighter at that thought.

They'd nearly reached the shuttle when a warning came across her bonejack. *To your 3 o'clock, stat!* Scotch dodged to the right, sending them spinning. The fire team must have missed one. The heat of the laser blast they'd barely evaded bubbled the surface of Kat's visor while her curses blistered the inside. Her stomach spun as Scotch corrected and slammed them past the airlock iris, right into the internal hatch. *Go! Go! Go!* he barked as the airlock closed practically on the tips of their boots.

As the chamber filled with atmosphere, they shed their helmets but remained suited. With an intensity she'd never seen before, Scotch turned her toward him and searched her over, quickly calming as he found her hale and whole. The same could not be said for Brockmann or Ghei. Kat averted her eyes from the two cryobags taking up the deck in the load compartment, the toolkit beside them. Propelling themselves through the hatch and to the open bench by the drive compartment, she and Scotch settled side by side.

"Strap in!" Sarge bellowed. "Tivo, take the conn and get those cannons ready to fire."

The *Teufel* shuddered, and warning alarms went off. From the sound of it, the pirates were bouncing chaff rounds off their hull. More useless intimidation. The pirates wanted something, or they would already have turned the *Teufel* into a cloud of vented gas and debris. The transport's pulse cannons whined and popped. More detonations just off their battered hull.

This game of tag grew old.

The pirates must have thought so as well because the impacts struck more aggressively, like they risked more to disable the AeroCom transport... or make sure no one else could get their hands on it and whatever item of interest it held. Like, say... the derelict's computer cores or the information from the research station.

A glance at Sarge's face told Kat he considered the same thing. And—given the frigate had more drive force than the transport, the *Teufel* could dodge but just couldn't keep out of range of the more powerful vessel.

"Campbell, ready the thermal rockets. Tivo, charge the pulse cannons and hold fire. Engage on my mark. Target their engines. Disabling shots only," Sarge issued the orders in a sharp, clipped tone. "I have the conn." He brought the transport in hard and fast despite the continued fire from the pirate vessel. Capitalizing on the smaller craft's greater maneuverability, he brought the *Teufel* arcing along the pirates' starboard side and pulled ahead, giving Campbell and Tivo a clear firing solution from all ports.

"Game over," Sarge growled. "All weapons, fire!"

They were too close. Shots meant to shut down the engines instead hit the core. As the frigate exploded, the resulting shockwave shook the *Teufel* hard enough to knock those in back to the deck if they hadn't been strapped in. Alerts went off as they took some collateral damage. No one inside cared. Rarely did they get to avenge their dead so swiftly and thoroughly.

Gotcha! Kat thought. The rest of the squad cheered as Campbell took over the helm and aimed them for the *Cromwell*'s coordinates.

"Better get some rest, Kittie Kat," Scotch murmured, pressing his hand to her cheek. She rested her head on his shoulder. Kat wasn't sure which startled her more, the fact that he'd touched her or that she'd instinctively leaned against him afterward. She was about to jerk upright in protest when he said, "We still have that live-fire exercise when we get back."

"You mean... we're not for the brig once we dock?"

Scotch chuckled. "Shh. Don't even think it. Sarge has us covered. There's a covert training op registered by those who cut our orders. It'll have come down channels by now, with all the proper timestamps."

Kat swallowed hard and looked up to meet his eye. "And Brockmann? What do we tell them about her?"

His expression grew solemn. "The truth. A pirate ambush. She'll not be the first airman to fall during training. Now settle in and get some rest already. He's not gonna take it easy on any of us after this. There's too much at stake."

Gripped by doubt, Kat had to ask. Over his private frequency she murmured, *Was it because of me? Did we lose her because of me?*

What? No! Why would you think that?

I took too long to get out of there...

Kat felt Scotch shake his head.

The only ones responsible for Brockmann's death are the fuckers we just took out.

She wanted to believe him, but the doubt lingered... the guilt lingered. What if he'd only told her what he felt she needed to hear? What if he was just looking out for a teammate in another way? Kat twisted around and looked up at him needing to see if he believed what he expected her to believe.

His expression held nothing but conviction. With a solemn nod, she lay her head back against his shoulder. Dutifully, she attempted to shut off her thoughts and let herself relax. Still, the tension bubbled up and out of her like a Tourette's outburst. "I wanted Ghei!"

Scotch grunted and pressed his cheek against her head. She ignored the hint and went on.

"Now I have no clue who's responsible, dammit!"

He chuckled and reached up, gently rubbing her ear and against the pressure point behind it. The returning tension drained out of her, and the world started to dim.

"Better the devil you know..." she heard him murmur in agreement before she drifted off.

"What do you mean, they found the remains?" Cryson asked his tone dropping low and tight as he spoke over the comm, his gaze darting over toward Petrov, who waited to report. The Legionnaire gave a credible approximation of a Gallic shrug for someone who wasn't French. Cryson glared, then spoke to Commander Stahn, on the other end of the comm. "Deal with it. Retrieve any intel and bring it back to the base. We'll sort the details out later. Just make sure they can't make any connection to the Legion." He disengaged the comm, slowly turning to his lieutenant, who waited to be debriefed.

"I'd completed the primary mission when I was interrupted by a vessel heading for the GEC," Anton said, answering the unasked question. "With only the lasers, there was no time to break the vessel up completely."

There was nothing Cryson could say. The soldier had properly followed his training. Maintaining cover always superseded covert mission objectives.

Of course, this time, that directive might just backfire. Should the planetary community connect the Legion to recent events, their efforts would have done more to set back their cause than to advance it.

Cryson stood and turned to Petrov. The debriefing could wait. They had more important matters to deal with. "Time for a council, lieutenant. We need to come up with a new plan. I want all officers in the war room in half an hour."

"Yes, sir." Petrov turned and hurried from the compartment to sound the general call.

As Cryson watched him go, the captain's expression hardened. Sloppy. His grandfather always held that informality led to insubordination, which—unchecked—led to insurrection. Cryson had been taught that there was one thing an officer could never be to his men: a friend. And yet, he'd still managed to grow too comfortable among those serving under him, Petrov in particular. Time to re-establish the chain of command before he lost control of it.

Grimacing, he turned back to the comm to report to his superiors.

With a groan, Kat jerked upright as the *Teufel* thunked against the airlock. Docking connected with magnetic clamps and air *whooshed* as the seal pressurized. She frowned, wondering where Scotch had gone and why he hadn't wakened her. The other Devils climbed to their feet, making preparations to depart, everyone except Brockmann, whose body lay out of sight in the load compartment.

The team moved slowly as combat fatigue weighed them down. Kat tried to rise, hindered by the full weight of her powered-down EVA suit. There certainly were worse things than falling asleep sitting in an MMU, but she didn't really give a crap about any of those things right now. Not when her body screamed with the effort to shift the heavy suit without the aid of the built-in servos.

Servos that would not engage without the helmet locked into place to complete the circuit to activate them. It hadn't been a problem when she was hyped up on adrenaline, but her body had tightened up as she slept, the endorphin rush from the battle a fleeting memory.

Cursing beneath her breath, Kat muscled through the pain and forced herself to her feet. Slowly, methodically, she went through the process of removing her suit, all of her focus locked on the task to filter out the sounds of the corpsmen collecting Brockmann and Ghei from the load compartment. Kat marginally succeeded.

By the time she brought her encased arm up to undo the final fittings that would free her from her protective prison, the corpsmen were gone. Also, by then, sweat coated Kat's limbs, and the silent snarl on her face warned the others away before her last raw nerve snapped. Well, most of them, anyway.

When she looked up, she discovered Kopecky standing nearby, waiting.

"Hey," she greeted him as she laid the suit as neat as she could across the bench for the hangar crew to maintenance, trying to sound as if she weren't wrestling a maelstrom of rage and guilt and grief over the mission.

Not that she fooled anyone.

One look at Kopecky's eyes told her he fought the same internal battle. He gave her something between a grimace and a grin. "Hey."

When he said nothing further, she shook her head and turned away, grabbing her gauss rifle and gear from beneath her seat. By the time she turned to leave, he'd moved into her path. The faintest of tics beneath his right eye betrayed his nervousness. Nothing else did.

"What?" Kat snapped, too bone-weary and on edge to suppress her annoyance. She needed to get out of there. She needed to get to a safe space where she could shut down and process. The longer she stood here, the more she felt ready to fly out of control.

Kopecky winced, his head dropping and turning to the side in reaction before coming back up again. "Listen, Kat, I just wanted... needed to apologize. I was out of line the other night. I was messed up about what happened with the *Alexi,* and I took it out on you." He shifted in discomfort again, falling silent as one of the team left the crew compartment and moved past them to leave. "You didn't deserve that, and I didn't really mean it. I just wanted you to know. I'm sorry."

Kat felt like such an asshole. "Don't worry about it, Pecker. Apology accepted."

"Cool." He grinned, though his gaze didn't look any less tormented. Kat imagined she looked much the same. The aftereffects of combat... and loss did that. Haunted a soldier and filled them with the need to retreat behind protective walls, even as it pushed them to mend bridges or make some kind of connection, to reinforce that they survived... this time.

She waited expectantly, but he still didn't move. "Um, are we done?"

The awkwardness returned, but only briefly as he scrambled out of her way. "Thanks," she called over her shoulder, not sticking around to hear a fresh new apology. She was too beat for niceties, even after sleeping the whole way back.

Most of the team had already left the transport by the time Kat pushed through the load compartment to the docking ring hatch. She heard someone knocking around... restoring the transport to... um... factory settings, but she wasn't about to dawdle and get roped into helping. Saluting as she passed their irreverent squad icon before quickly averting her eyes from the roster plaque beneath it, Kat slung her gear over her shoulder and dropped her head down as she headed for the exit to the docking bay. She wanted a solid ten hours in her bunk before she had to deal with any of the ramifications of that day. Or anything else, for that matter.

"Oh! Hey, Kat!"

Inwardly, she groaned.

Kat turned to find Oren Truitt scrambling from the transport to catch up to her, like one of PawPaw's pups, hope eclipsing the uncertainty in his gaze. Internally, she sighed. Outwardly, she raised her hand to show she'd heard him and waited as patiently as she could manage as he jogged to where she stood, a thousand-watt smile on his face. True had been watching her like a kid on his first crush for a while now.

"Thanks for stopping," he stammered, his face pinking up a bit as he fidgeted. "Um... I have to finish helping put the transport in order, but... um..."

Kat tried not to flinch. If she had to guess, True's core impulse after combat was to connect. "No problem. What did you want?"

If he pinked before, he turned bright red at her question, clear to the tips of his ears. "Um, well... Would you have dinner with me tonight? In the Mess? They're serving beef stroganoff, and it ain't half bad." He finished with that last bit on a hopeful uptick, like that might entice her. And given the state of chow on most military vessels Kat had served on, she could understand that, but there was no way Truitt wasn't walking away disappointed.

"Listen, I appreciate the offer... but..."

Before she even finished, Truitt winced, the light in his gaze dimming. "No... no... don't say it. Just give me a chance." He gave her an earnest look. "Just once. One meal...?" He made a clear effort to put on the charm but did not elicit the hoped-for response. "I can honestly promise that I'll always be True."

Now Kat winced. That was bad.

"A true friend," she said gently, putting emphasis on the friend.

His expression crumbled, but he straightened his shoulders and pasted on a mere echo of his earlier smile. "No... no problem," he mumbled, avoiding her direct gaze.

"I'm sorry..." she started, but before things could grow anymore awkward—or maybe not—a sharp whistle sounded from the direction of the *Teufel*. They both turned to look, only to discover Scotch glowering at them from the transport hatch, a frown weighing down his lips as his gaze moved back and forth between the two of them like he caught them doing something wrong. Kat cocked her hip and glared back at him, starting to wonder what bug crawled up his butt.

"Sergeant Truitt," Scotch barked, ignoring Kat's annoyance completely. "Front and center! Social hour is over. We have detailing to complete, airman."

True snapped to attention, all awkwardness falling away, though disappointment still dimmed his gaze. "Yes, sir!" With a wave of farewell in Kat's direction, he hurried back to the transport.

Irritated by the self-satisfied smirk Scotch didn't bother to hide, Kat flipped him off before wheeling around to leave. While it wasn't unusual for him to be a wiseass, it was completely out of character for him to be a straight-up ass.

What was that about? Scotch groused over her private frequency as she left the bay.

Nothing. Nothing at all, you... bully, Kat snapped back subvocally. Then she stalked away, half-determined to change her mind and tell True yes the next time she saw him, just to be contrary. She wouldn't. That wouldn't be fair to Truitt, no matter how much it would serve Scotch right.

All she cared about now was not stopping for anything else until her head hit her pillow.

Maybe I was the one that died in the attack, and this is hell, Kat thought as she entered the barracks. The moment she came through the hatch, Sarge motioned her over to the section of the common room set up for team meetings. The impressive array of machinery on the table in front of him showed he had requisitioned some data-transfer equipment on the way back to the barracks.

Longingly, she looked toward the compartment housing her bunk as she wended her way across the room, maneuvering around piles of gear, carefully stacked weapons, and weary airmen that hadn't made it past the—and she used the term loosely—comfy chairs. Kat leaned her rifle against the nearby wall but kept her bag close. Clearly, she was going to need the contents. As much as she desperately wanted to rest, it was better to get through this now than stretch things out by stowing her kit first.

"Have a seat, Alexander," Sarge said, gesturing to the one in front of the equipment.

"Thank you, sir," Kat said, strictly out of politeness, and with little sincerity. Sarge didn't even blink.

"You have the intel? All of it?"

She nodded and pulled out both her tablet and the computer core she'd extracted from the derelict.

"Very good. I need you to copy those files for encryption, then burn a backup as well."

She felt a twinge of guilt over the copy already in her pocket. With every-thing that had happened, there had been no opportunity to mention it.

Before she could say something, a thought arose. Why hadn't they just turned everything over to Command or MI? True, it was questionable who they could trust aboard the *Cromwell*, or they wouldn't have gone through all of this to begin with, but surely someone should be sifting this data so they could clean up the ranks and stop these pirates. Of course, none of that concerned Kat. She'd been given an order, and she was expected to follow it.

"Any time, airman," Sarge prompted, tapping the table in front of her.

Kat jerked, so weary she must have shut down for a moment. Her nostrils flared as the scent of honest-to-God coffee wafted past. Then, by some miracle, Dalton set a full mug down beside her. Before Kat could say thank you, Sarge cleared his throat, and Dalton moved off, disappearing into their bunkroom.

Allowing herself just a sip to jumpstart her brain, Kat went to work consolidating the data. A frown tugged at her lips. The data seemed off. Not that she had had a lot of time to review it on the transport, but part of her training involved retaining patterns in the code for later evaluation. The data didn't match up with her memory. But who could have changed it? When would they have had the chance? She started to say something, but some instinct in her hindbrain said no, and she closed her mouth again, wondering if she was just that exhausted. Right now, it felt like gravity alone could defeat her.

The feeling wouldn't get any better until she hit her bunk, and she couldn't do that until she finished. Well, after a trip to the ion shower, anyway. And that wasn't happening until the files were burned. Sighing, she forced her focus back to the task. Once she isolated and organized the data, Sarge leaned over and entered an encryption code. When he stepped back, Kat created two copies. As her commander watched, she deleted the data from her tablet computer and cleared her cache, then reformatted that sector of the drive.

"Thank you, Corporal Alexander," Sarge murmured, his tone solemn and subdued. "Dismissed."

Kat sat there and finished her coffee just to have enough energy to shower and climb into her bunk. She watched Sarge collect the files and the salvaged computer core and disappear into his quarters. Of its own accord, her free hand slid into her pocket and fingered the exabyte drive. She had copied the data out of habit. It was a part of her training; always make a backup. Now other instincts kicked in. Telling her to keep that backup close. Telling her she needed to check that drive in the morning.

Kat had a feeling she wouldn't like what she found.

CHAPTER 8

THERE WAS NO STATELY PROCESSION TO THE AIRLOCK. NO POMP AND circumstance as the hatch opened. Brockmann's body wasn't set adrift in the vastness of space to echo the dignity of an ancient warrior's burial at sea.

No.

She had been taken away in a body bag the moment the *Teufel* docked. By the time the 142nd Mobile SOT mustered later that day in the barracks common room for debriefing, a corpsman had arrived, presenting Sarge with a one-inch, compressed-carbon cube and a bag of effects. All that remained of Staff Sergeant Suzanne Brockmann, Special Ops, one more offense credited against the pirates that had invaded the sector.

Kat felt her hands flex, accompanied by a familiar itch in her fingers. That could have been her reduced to a geometric shape. Almost was... *twice*.

She must have moved without realizing she had. Beside her, Scotch cleared his throat and stepped between her and her pile of gear, staged and ready, like everyone else's, for the officially scheduled, slightly post-poned exercise. Well, more accurately, between her and her gauss rifle.

"Down, Kittie, down," he murmured, his hazel eyes capturing her gaze. "Ain't no pirates here." Something about his expression made her wonder if he believed that.

Kat growled. She seemed to be doing that a lot lately.

She and the rest of the team snapped to attention as Sergeant Daire accepted the remains from the corpsman, ignoring the bag of effects. Turning his back on the man, Sarge cradled the cube embedded with Brockmann's identchip in his left hand and drew his combat knife with his right. He then bowed his head. The team gathered around and followed suit. No one spoke a word aloud as each of them bid farewell to their fallen comrade. Nor as, one by one, each of them stepped forward and, with their blades, scratched a line into the smooth, shiny surface of her compressed remains below the etching of her name and rank. Each of them maintained silence as they fell back to form a loose half-circle around their commander once they completed their part. Sarge looked up and met each of their gazes. Without glancing away from them, he raised his knife and etched his own line, bisecting those left by the team.

Each line segment on the cube represented a solemn oath that the remaining pirates would be brought down. That Brockmann would have vengeance.

Only then did Scotch step forward to secure her personal effects from the still-waiting corpsman. Unlike Kat, Brockmann had no family to send material belongings back to, even if the military were willing to foot the bill. Whatever that small, compact bag held, along with anything in her quarters, would be shared out among the team according to need. The rest would be held in reserve or given where it would best serve.

The corpsman turned to leave.

"Wait." Sarge motioned for Kat and Scotch to step forward. She suppressed a flinch and came to attention in front of him. "Alexander, Daniels... accompany Corpsman Kane back to medbay to be cleared for return to duty."

Shit. Kat had been expecting that. They were with Brockmann when the pirates took her out. A muscle in Kat's jaw twitched as flashes of her last psych evaluation pulsed through her memory. It didn't matter that it had been staged. She hadn't known that at the time. Her breath came a little faster, and she fought it back to a normal pace. Told herself this was just routine. A physical assessment. Others had been wounded in the ambush, but they sustained only superficial damage and had been handled by the field medic, whereas she had been banged up from her previous encounter with the pirates.

"Alexander..." Sarge's tone carried both reassurance and a warning as he nudged her along. She resisted at first as she struggled with conflicting senses of justice and anger.

Her jaw worked a few moments before she got out the words. "Scotch was right. Ghei wasn't there voluntarily. I don't know if he had family or not, but could the Devils maybe do something for them if he did?" They kept funds aside for stuff like that, taking care of those left behind when there was a chance Command would dust them off. Whatever Ghei may or may not have been, no one's family deserved that.

Sarge stared at her a moment. Long enough, she felt her skin twitch. Then, with a faint smile, he nodded.

Not completely happy with the answer—after all, Ghei had still controlled the composite that had attacked her, whether he had a choice in it or not—

Kat ran a hand over her dark brown, regulation-length bristle of hair and shook off her nerves. Accepting the inevitable, she followed Scotch and Kane to the lift.

Behind her, Sarge addressed the rest of the team. "Command has called a general inspection for 1700 hours. Use this time to get your bunks in order." His voice held an edge that had Kat glancing over her shoulder in time to see him tighten his fist around Brockmann's cube and about-face. In silence, he returned to his chamber to secure their fallen.

Master Sergeant Kevin Daire knelt on the floor of his quarters. He'd been there ten minutes just staring at the beat-up footlocker that, for now, was his; loathing to open the thing. With little exception, it held all his worldly goods. And evidence of his shame. He pushed that thought away hard.

The footlocker also held the tribute box.

For the first time this tour, he needed to bring it out.

He shot a look at the shiny black cube sitting nearby on his compact desk, and his teeth clenched. *Better never than late,* he thought.

Straightening his spine, he turned his attention back to the locker. Reaching out, he pushed up the lid. Inside were his personal effects: a battered white Bible (a pocket-sized New Testament, including the Psalms, like a child received at their first communion), three paper letters (old and worn), and his son's bear with all the stuffing removed (the only way Command would authorize its presence in his kit).

It felt somewhat fitting that he housed the tribute box with this shrine to his past.

First, he drew out the Bible, then the six-inch-by-nine-inch aluminum tribute box. The flattened bear crackled as the hand holding the box brushed against it, causing him to flinch.

Unlike him, most of the team had someone waiting for their return, one way or another. For those that didn't, they resided in his keeping, honored for their sacrifice. Kevin settled back on his heels, the box before him on the deck. One hand reached out for Brockmann's cube. The other took up the Bible, which opened readily to Psalms 23. With a bowed head, murmuring the familiar passage in a voice heavy with mixed emotion, Daire paid private tribute to the fallen before interring the cube among those already in the box. Kissing the Bible, he returned everything to its place, closed the footlocker, then rose, his eyes moist in the privacy of his quarters. Death might be a reality of war, but he couldn't help feeling he'd failed another. He couldn't help but feel like a hypocrite.

Before he could wallow in that particular recrimination, the squad band chimed.

Sarge? Dalton's voice prickled up his jaw to sound deep in his ear.

Go ahead.

Do you have a moment? she asked. *I've noticed something I'm not sure about.*

Kevin glanced at the digital display hardwired over the hatch leaving his quarters. 1650 hours. *It will have to wait, sergeant...*

My concerns are legion, sir.

He froze both at Dalton's interruption and her wording. Silently, fervently, he cursed at the use of the code phrase he'd been given to recognize his handler. He could have gladly gone on forever without hearing that, particularly from someone he had trusted. Guilt surged through his gut. *I'm sorry. We have inspection in ten. I can meet with you after. In the meantime, I suggest you make sure your bunk is in order.*

Yes, sir. Something about her tone stirred his combat instincts. Worry... frustration... concern? Tension of some sort ran tight beneath her response. He couldn't quite pinpoint it. The sensation put him on alert, but against what?

Don't worry. Come see me after and we'll talk, Kevin told her, silently cursing Colonel Corbin and his bullshit inspection.

The war room aboard the *Destrier* was stark and bright, the table and those seated at it equally utilitarian. Soldiers packed the chamber, seasoned veterans, all. A bit more mercenary perhaps, than their AeroCom counterparts, but soldiers just the same. Seated were his senior officers, their attention locked on the updated intel flashing across the central monitor. Flanking the room were the junior officers, equally attentive as they stood back against the walls awaiting orders. The room smelled of stale coffee and sweat. The comms had been switched off to prevent interruption. Other than Cryson's voice, the only sound was the *scritch* of his aide's stylus making notes on a datapad.

The glaring, industrial light did nothing to soften the men's expressions as Cryson detailed their failed efforts at claiming the *Cromwell* followed by Hirobon's attempts to steal the technology out from under them. He withheld nothing, not even the presence of their 'guest' or Anton's role in recent events. He needed informed input from men aware of all the pieces in the game.

"We've headed off Hirobon for the time being," Cryson concluded. "Now we need to come up with a strategy for getting hold of that ship. Not only is it state-of-the-art in both camouflage and weaponry, but I have confirmation *Cromwell* is field-testing AeroCom's top-secret advanced hyperdrive system.

"That system, gentlemen, is capable of getting us from Tau Ceti to the Sol system in *five* days... with no one capable of tracking the flight." He paused to gaze at each man's face as that fact penetrated their brains. All previous hyperdrive systems averaged twenty-one days at best for the same journey. "With that combined technology..."

The hatch opened with a bang, cutting off Cryson's last comment. He glared toward the disturbance. The young ensign currently assigned comm duty as a runner stood framed by the hatch collar. His face appeared bloodlessly pale.

That didn't bode well for Cryson's mood. This mission continued to spiral into a clusterfuck. He looked back up at the ensign and met eyes both wide and shocky. The soldier's breathing held a decided hitch. Cryson gestured to one of the junior officers to escort the unsteady man into the chamber and then a seat. Another came forward with a bulb of water.

Cryson waited until the man accepted it and emptied half the bulb. "Report, ensign."

"*Viper's* been destroyed, sir. No survivors."

The uproar at his words drowned out anything else the messenger might have said. The destruction of a frigate and its crew was no small loss. The Legion didn't have the same resources corporate or government entities did. Cryson let the raging go on a moment as he assessed the reactions of those in the room. Outrage and loss were the most common. No one was suicidal enough to look satisfied, but several faces appeared neutral enough to send up flags. They might just be internalizing. Then again, they might not.

Scowling, Cryson made note.

"Quiet!" he called out over the din, waiting for the men to settle and sit down before turning back to the ensign. "Tell us what you know."

"Commander Stahn took out a crew of thirty after an AeroCom vessel nosing around near the remains of the comet craft. They engaged the enemy but were unable to intercept the intel. They then fired on the transport directly, attempting to disable it and secure the evidence. That is where the transmitted logs end." The ensign paused to draw on the bulb. "We sent out a scout to investigate. All they found was wreckage and remains. It was confirmed the *Viper*. The enemy craft had already departed."

"Did the logs mention the other vessel's identification code?"

The messenger nodded. "AeroCom vessel 62-Delta. The *Viper*'s captain also noted someone had painted a devil on the craft and the word '*Teufel*.'"

Cryson grimaced and filed those details away, relief warring with loss as discipline began to break down around him. His daughter might have been on that craft. And *Viper* would have destroyed it if *Teufel* hadn't struck first. He shoved that thought away, his guilt tangled with his relief.

Questions started firing around the room as, in their outrage, his men forgot protocol—never their strong point to begin with. Two questions stood out: *How did AeroCom know where to look?* This is what most of the men demanded to know. Cryson could think of two possible answers to that but kept the information to himself for now. The other question was spoken only once, and it silenced everyone in the room: *Why was there anything there for them to find?*

Many hostile gazes locked on Lieutenant Anton Petrov. Some held doubt and distrust. Others (from those with friends and family aboard the *Viper*) promised retribution. Cryson had to act before there was bloodshed among the ranks.

He motioned two of his security officers forward and turned toward Anton. "Lieutenant Anton Petrov, you are hereby relieved, charged with dereliction of duty, consigned to Detention until an Inquiry has been completed. You will remain there until you have been acquitted or until such time as you are sentenced. You will have no communication with any crew member on this vessel unless supervised, and you will have no access to any communication system, internal or external, until such time as it has been deemed you are not a threat. Do you understand?"

His lieutenant came to his feet, disbelief clear on his face. His mouth opened and then closed again, and his body tensed as if there were any chance he could fight or flee. He wasn't stupid, though. Once he got his initial impulses under control, his eyes darkened with betrayal, but he did not resist as security personnel flanked him, drew him around, and escorted him from the room. Cryson watched him go, not sure himself if any guilt lay hidden there, but fully confident Petrov wouldn't have survived leaving the room any other way. When the hatch closed, Cryson turned back toward the gathered men. His eyes locked on his security chief.

"Go. Take a team and search his quarters. I need to know if there is any further cause for concern."

"Yes, sir," the man responded as he too left the room.

The others on the council stiffened as Cryson gave the order, and an uneasy murmur circulated among the members of the war council, but no one raised an objection. He sensed outrage and approval with undercurrents of unease. Time to take a closer look at those under his command, but first to address the matter at hand.

"Settle down," he ordered and then brought the focus back to the council. "What we need is a way to force the *Cromwell* to come to us..."

CHAPTER 9

THIRTY MINUTES IN THE PSYCH CHAIR, AND KAT FELT READY TO BITE something. It didn't matter that they gave her the short-form evaluation; it still put her on edge. She apparently hid it well, though, and didn't set off any red flags. Once the counselor signed off on her jacket, Kat shunted over to medbay proper. There they gave her a noxious cream to deal with the last of the swelling around her blackened eye and a shot in her wrenched ankle that hurt ten times worse than the original injury for all of thirty seconds, after which she felt nothing. The damage remained—a lingering reminder of her first engagement with the pirates—but the pressure bandage the med-tech put back on her took care of that. Then, finally, she received authorization to return to duty.

Poor Scotch. Kat could still hear him arguing with the counselors as she left medbay to head back to the barracks. As a first-hand witness to Brockmann's termination, Command wanted Scotch to submit to a full psych evaluation before reinstating him to active status. Scotch made it clear he considered that bullshit. Kat chuckled as he suggested they submit to a self-administered rectal probe.

She chuckled and moved quickly toward the lift, not hanging around to see which near-immovable force triumphed. Better to make herself scarce before someone stopped to wonder how her brainpan was doing after finding half of Ghei—former commander and maybe pirate—floating in space.

Toggling on her bonejack, Kat couldn't resist a parting jab. *Come on, Scotch, ten minutes on the couch, and the shrink will have you visualizing cute little puppies and white sandy beaches. It'll be fun!*

Scotch tossed an off-color suggestion her way.

Talk about torture, he went on when she didn't spar back in kind. *I'm allergic to dogs, and the only beaches in this sector come with an atmosphere that would dissolve the flesh off human bones in thirty seconds. I'll have to pass. The torment would be too much to take... I might crack, and then where would we be? Now get the hell out of my head, so I can deal with these quacks!*

Kat laughed as she switched the comm off and made her escape.

She hadn't known that about the beaches... not really her thing. Give her a dusty trail over sandy dunes any day. Although....

As she entered the lift, she forced away unexpected thoughts of Scotch lounging on the sand somewhere toasting his buns, instead turning her attention to the data they'd retrieved from the Groom microsat, fingers fidgeting with the exabyte drive she'd carried in her pocket like a talisman ever since they returned from the encounter with the pirates.

Sarge had secured the encrypted files in a lockbox in his quarters until General Drovak arrived, while she and Scotch had taken the backup, along with the rest of the stuff they'd retrieved from the pirate derelict before Brockmann fell, and hidden them in a shielded compartment located near the *Teufel's* engine reactor where a scan, visual or otherwise, would not detect their presence. Only Sarge, Scotch, and their unit commander, General Drovak, knew where to find the intel.

Kat didn't even want to think about trying to crack the code. Fortunately, that wasn't her job. Sarge had instructions to turn the material over to the general or one of his agents as soon as possible. The whole situation had Kat nervous, though. With evidence that the crew assigned to the *Cromwell* may have been compromised, they couldn't know who to trust outside of their own team.

Kat shut down that thought and focused on getting back to the barracks. She looked up as the decks ticked by. The lights fluxed and the car slowed. For a moment, she thought she was screwed; she didn't have much time left to get her bunk in order before the inspection. She half-expected a jerk and the *thunk* of the lift coming to an abrupt halt in the shaft, but the lift continued to descend. With a hiss, the doors opened. Kat exited the lift and trudged down to the common room she had left less than an hour earlier. If not for the neat stacks of gear, she would have thought the team had left without them. The base of her neck tingled, and her eyes narrowed. Short of lights out, the barracks were never this quiet. There was always someone kicking around.

She sniffed. Something foreign had made it past the air scrubbers. The remnants were faint, an acrid bite deep in her throat. Call her paranoid, but with talk of pirates and compromised security and subversives being bandied around, instinct screamed at her to get the hell out. But what if something had happened, and members of her team needed help? It took an effort to hold her breath until she reached her gear. For a moment, her vision greyed. She outright had to force her fingers to flex and loosen as she paused by her own pile of equipment. She grabbed her breather and jerked it over her eyes, nose, and mouth until the thick gasket settled snug against her skin. As soon as it did, she purged her lungs and took several rapid gulps of regulated air and blew them out just as quickly to clear any residual. She then settled into slow, even breaths and picked up her rifle.

Kat should have felt silly, but she didn't. Paranoid came to mind... but she hoped the mask's filters were enough to combat whatever contaminated the air. As she continued into the compartment, she held her rifle at the ready.

That alone made her feel better.

"Hey, Sarge..." she called out, the words only slightly muffled. Her breath came a little faster, and she forced it back. It took some effort to concentrate as she scanned the empty compartment. Before her lay the area designated the common room, where the team spent most of their downtime. Directly to her left lay the compartment housing the hygiene facilities. To her right, Sarge's personal quarters. Beyond that, there was a simple polymer table and vidscreen for planning sessions and formal meetings, situated in the common room's far-right corner. Over on the far left, what passed for a private mess... mess being the operative word. Between the two points, butt-up against the far bulkhead, lay the crew quarters, five identical compartments side by side. All the hatches were closed, except one. Kat angled left and headed toward the compartment on the end with deck-eating strides. "Yo, anyone there...?" she called out.

Silence.

Kat moved closer, swaying as her breathing picked up again as if she starved for oxygen. The acrid odor seemed to intensify rather than fade away. A curse made it halfway to her lips before she lost track of it. Lightheaded, she braced herself against the open hatch. Her body swayed again, and her head dropped forward of its own accord.

For a split second, she saw an out-flung wrist, mottled clear around with bruising, caught between the hatch and the frame. The pattern of the discoloration—near black where the arm rested against the deck—disturbed Kat, but she couldn't focus on why. She leaned forward to push the door panel into its retraction slot to reveal Dalton, the Devils' weapons specialist. Kat frowned at the compression marks on the woman's face as if she'd worn a breather recently. Kat leaned forward to check for a pulse, but it wasn't one of her strengths.

What was Dalton even doing here? These weren't their quarters.

Kat tried to remember whose quarters they *were*. She quickly scanned the compartment, identical to the one she shared with Dalton and two others. No-frills, industrial. Two bunks to a side—top and bottom—with room for two footlockers beneath the bottom bunks. Along the back were storage lockers for equipment. Her brow furrowed as she spied other bodies on the deck. It looked like Tivo, Kopecky, and True, sprawled as if they all passed out in the middle of preparing for inspection. One more... who was missing? She struggled to recall, but her thoughts kept swimming.

Kat stepped over Dalton to investigate. As she did so, she caught movement from the corner of her eye. A man's hand reached over her shoulder, snagging her mask and tugging it off. She heard a faint hiss as the gasket seal parted from her skin, and the earlier odor intensified, more concentrated in the close quarters.

Out of instinct, she pulled away, trying to pivot to engage only to slump to the deck as an unknown chemical agent took effect. From where she lay, she spied Dalton's breather half under one of the bunks. She also saw the corner of a tablet computer.

Her computer.

Before Kat could react, a swirl of darkening colors drew her down into the black.

The air seemed to shimmer as an armored figure stepped over the bodies now blocking the hatch, the chameleon circuit blurring any defined lines and obscuring all identifiable features. However, it could not compensate for the movement. Heading to the bunk on the left, they squatted down and pulled Kat's tablet computer from where someone had hidden it beneath. Then, without a glance at the bodies strewn about, the figure vacated the compartment, their steps sure and unhesitant. They moved to the compartment two over from the first, not even slowing as they approached with swift steps. The sensor light to the right of the hatch flashed red, then suddenly flickered to green. The hatch slid open. Quickly pulling a footlocker from beneath the right bunk, they set down the computer prominently in sight. Lifting the lid with one gloved hand, they typed a few keys, then lowered the lid, leaving everything in place as they left the compartment, moving with purpose.

"Time to change your damn name, you pain in the ass," a familiar voice grumbled over Kat as someone gave her a sharp shake. "Before you use up all nine lives. Come on, Kittie... Atten-hut!"

Kat grumbled back and shoved at the hands lifting her semi-vertical.

"Yeah, you go ahead and fight, g'on, give me what-for," he went on. "Just do it with your damn eyes open."

She cracked her lids just enough to recognize medbay's familiar walls and Scotch's pale, taut features as he leaned over her. At his back, a med-tech and a corpsman tried to get around his muscular frame to separate them. Her eyes opened yet further, and she waved the men off. Scotch's grip loosened until most of her body came once again in contact with the bed, but he didn't let go. Kat could almost swear she heard a relieved sigh as his eyes closed on whatever expression they held. She didn't speak until the others had moved outside of the curtains that had been drawn to give her a measure of privacy from the other cots.

"What happened?"

Scotch looked up and met her gaze, his eyes dark. The muscles in his jaw twitched. When he spoke, it was low and through his teeth. "I was hoping you could tell me. We've been infiltrated. Not just the *Cromwell*... but the Devils. A sleeping agent was introduced to the barracks wing... a time-release gas grenade hidden in the central duct. The atmospheric sensors were disabled. Someone set up induction fans to force the fumes into every compartment in the wing. Had to be done from the inside." His grip tightened on her shoulders once more until she winced in discomfort.

"He's gone. Sarge is gone."

At his words, Kat gasped, flashbacks of Brockmann's death turning the news into a one-two punch. If not for Scotch's grip on her, Kat would have curled in a ball. Grief and rage and confusion darted around inside her like a rat trapped in a cage. Sarge couldn't be gone, not in such a senseless way. Her team commander, her friend... no, family. Actually, after what they'd been through, closer than family, which said a *lot*. Damn, if only her thoughts would stop swimming.

"Somebody took him," Scotch went on, his tone dangerous and low as he bent his head close to hers. "His quarters have been ransacked, and the lockbox is gone. They took him, and we have to get him back."

His words arrowed past the faint buzzing still in her ears. Her head whipped up, and this time Kat snarled.

If Scotch hadn't leaned in, he would have been safe.

But he did.

Instead of continuing to resist his grip, Kat used it to her advantage. She drew back and slammed her forehead into his. He didn't see it coming. Of course, she wasn't so pissed that she didn't pull back a bit at the end. No sense in knocking out the only person absolutely certain not to have sold out to the pirates.

"Aw! Fuck!" Scotch swore. "Go'dammit!"

"You bastard," she snapped back at him. "You had me thinking he was *dead!*"

Medbay personnel came scrambling through the gap in the curtain before she and Scotch could truly get into it. They were smart this time. They'd sent in men with some muscle. Not that they needed it. Scotch looked more than ready to get out of striking range.

"Tech sergeant, you have to leave now."

"Oh, save it, we both are," Kat cut in as she swung her legs off of the bed. She brought up the hand not bracing her and brushed the sore spot forming on her forehead. She fought off a trace of dizziness and ignored the corpsmen's protests. The men fell silent, though, as she marched through medbay, her backside playing peek-a-boo in a classic hospital gown that hadn't changed one wit throughout medical history, at least not in the military sector. Her lips twitched in a faint smile as she heard the "damn" breathed behind her in what sounded like Scotch's voice. Not that she cared who else saw—being in the military quickly stripped away any sense of body-consciousness—but rather than distract those going about their duties, Kat snagged a second gown from a nearby pile, shrugging into it like a robe.

On her way out, she noted only seven members of the 142nd present in medbay, other than Scotch and herself. "Where are the rest?" she called back over her shoulder.

"Those that have recovered were relocated to alternate crew quarters for now." Scotch raised his voice to be heard. Kat smirked as he caught up with her halfway to the lift. He carried her neatly folded fatigues under one arm.

"You know, I could have you up on charges for striking a superior officer."

"Ranking, maybe..." she drawled, with hints of her PawPaw's voice seeping into her tone. Scotch pouted in response and rubbed at the faint red spot on his forehead.

"Anyway," Kat went on, "we don't have time for that bullshit. Sarge is out there somewhere waiting on us."

The pout vanished.

They headed to the barracks in silence. Once in the lift, Kat watched closely as the levels changed. Again, several decks before the barracks, the lights fluxed, and the car slowed. Her eyes narrowed. Reaching out, she depressed the button to stop the lift and then sent it back two levels. Once it got there, she sent it to their original floor once more.

What? Scotch asked, watching her closely.

She said nothing but waited. Again, the lift fluxed precisely at the point it had before. Kat resisted the impulse to dart her gaze about the close compartment as she finally responded in the same manner. *The lift did that earlier too. And now it's done it twice again. As PawPaw likes to say: once is chance, twice is coincidence... three times is by design. Someone wanted to know when company was coming.*

Scotch grunted and nodded in agreement as the lift stopped at their level.

When the doors hissed open, Kat found herself greeted by security personnel with riot guns poised to fire. She tensed and stopped absolutely still. What she wouldn't give for her gauss... or at least her fatigues.

"Scotch?"

He stepped forward, and the guards slung their weapons and fell back to parade rest. Apparently, he had clearance. With a nod at the men, Scotch moved past them into the corridor, heading for the barracks. Glancing warily at the grinning security detail, Kat followed. As she passed their position, she was glad she'd thought to cover her back. She already felt naked enough without her weapon.

"You could have warned me," she hissed once they were well away from the guards.

Scotch merely put on a suffering look and ran his free hand over his forehead once more. Neither of them said another word until they cleared the hatch to their quarters and Kat found herself staring down the barrels of two more riot guns, held by security waiting within the common room.

"Jerk," Kat murmured in Scotch's direction as she broke away, heading for the compartment she shared with Dalton, Sergeant Kamilla Danzer, and Warrant Officer Miki Mata, Beta Squad's pilot. The hatch slid open in response to her identchip.

Right away, Kat noticed her footlocker in the aisle between the bunks with her tablet computer sitting neatly on top, neither stowed as they should have been. At first, she thought, *good thing I wiped the data when we got back*; followed by, *who the hell had known it had been there to begin with?* A third part of her hindbrain twitched as if neither one of the first two thoughts had a clue, but Kat couldn't remember why. She swore and moved to inspect the computer. Suddenly, Scotch intercepted her before she could lay a hand on the protective cover.

"I taught you better than that, corporal," he growled.

She froze instantly, not used to Scotch really pulling rank. Of course, she couldn't argue. Her lack of caution was both sloppy and foolish. Good way to get more people killed. Good way to end up cubed. "Sorry."

"Get dressed," Scotch ordered, holding out her fatigues, and abruptly he left the compartment. As soon as the hatch closed, Kat stripped off the double set of gowns and drew the military-issue tee shirt and navy-blue fatigues on over her skivvies. She'd sheathed her combat knife on her hip and was just sliding a shipboot carefully over her pressure bandage when Scotch returned. He carried a cluster of odd items: nitrile gloves, a pouch of talc, what looked like an industrial hand wipe, and a thick, chunky flashlight. A face shield perched on his head, and he wore a set of high-tech protective goggles. Though Kat hadn't seen Scotch utilize these skills before, he was the team's demolitions expert. Kat watched in fascination as he set the items down in a neat, orderly row, pulled on the gloves, and drew the shield down over his face. He then motioned her back.

First, he picked up the powder and sprinkled it over the tablet cover. The stuff revealed nothing but the unblemished surface of the casing. "Kill the lights," he ordered in that non-Scotch tone.

Kat complied. When she turned, he raised the squat light and trained it over the computer, clicking through several settings, the light altering with each one. Blacklight. Normal light. Ultraviolet. Supernova. And a few she didn't even have a made-up name for. It felt almost ritualistic, only fast. Click. Trail the light over the laptop in the ceremonial pattern. Trail the beam along the thin gap between the bottom of the tablet and the top of the locker. Click. Repeat. "Lights," he ordered.

"Sir, yes, sir!"

"No signs of a tripwire or other trigger, no evidence of foreign contaminants," he murmured as he ignored her wiseass attitude and gently ran his gloved hands over the tablet in a final check. Then, confident the unit wasn't rigged to blow, Scotch motioned her forward. Kat moved closer and watched as he flipped open the protective cover.

Upon seeing the screen, Kat swore loud enough that one of the guards opened the hatch and peered in.

"Tech sergeant?" The man's tone sounded tense, and his gaze went from her to Scotch, who had subtly shifted until the guard didn't have a line of sight on the tablet.

"Sorry," Kat answered for him. "Bumped my foot..." Tugging up on her uniform leg, she bared the bandage on her left ankle. The guard just stared at her, a long look down to her ankle and up again, less like he doubted her, more like he remembered the earlier view. She allowed steel to infiltrate her gaze. "Thanks, we're good."

Scotch didn't need to give her a look for her to know she'd annoyed him. "Thank you, airman. You can return to your post." It wasn't like the guy could argue. Scotch outranked him too. Kat resisted the urge to peer through the hatch to confirm the guard had moved back across the room. "Low profile, Alexander," Scotch muttered beneath his breath. "Try to remember we like not being noticed right now."

"What are they even doing inside," she hissed back. "Shouldn't they be guarding the hatch?"

"Command is keeping the incident quiet for now," Scotch explained, saying nothing more as he turned back to the tablet.

And bit back a curse of his own.

Their perp had left the log-in window open. Someone had typed the words "BRING EVERYTHING" in the user id field. Vague enough, but Kat understood the message. The bad guys wanted the data, not just the specs on the *Cromwell*—which they presumably now had once they cracked Sarge's encrypted copy—but the computer core, as well. There must be data there the pirates didn't want them to access.

The message wasn't all, though. They'd left something else on the screen, but the log-in window blocked her visual. Kat hesitated before reaching out to the touchpad, looking to Scotch for permission.

"Well, it's not like they're going to sabotage the thing when they want something from us." Still, before stepping out of her way, he tore open the hand wipe and sanitized the keypad and any other part of the tablet she might touch. He then pulled off the protective gloves over the soiled hand wipe and dumped it all in the trash chute by the door.

Kat stepped forward and called up the digital keypad. As she typed her code, the log-in window closed, revealing someone had switched her wallpaper to an image file of Sarge asleep on a beach somewhere, looking like nothing so much as a relaxing tourist... except for the torn fatigues and zip strips around his wrists, just visible behind his back. Kat tried to get as much data as possible, but whoever had set this had some tech-savvy because the electronic footprints had been erased.

"What the hell?" Kat whipped around until she could see Scotch's face. For some reason, he looked gut-kicked, his eyes locked on the screen of her tablet computer. "How long were we out?"

"You've been out for two hours. We estimate Sarge has been missing for a little longer than that."

"Two hours?!" Well, that explained the shake-up call in medbay.

Scotch nodded, concern, exhaustion, and something else shading his expression. "You got the lightest dose. Those bunked furthest from the main vent came out of it first. Those closest are mostly still down. One or two went under hard."

He looked grim. "I was the only one not hit."

Of course, he'd been in medbay... arguing his sanity. "When you entered the barracks, the lingering gas triggered the atmospheric sensors in the corridor, which hadn't been tampered with. That alerted Environmental."

Kat's chest muscles tightened as she processed what Scotch said.

She looked back at the image, and her nerves jangled uncomfortably, trying to remember something still hidden in the foggy recesses of her memory.

One thing remained clear, the *Cromwell's* ranks weren't the only ones compromised. The bunkrooms required an assigned identchip to enter. Only Sarge, Scotch, and Zaga—the team leader for Beta Squad—could enter any of the quarters. Someone had serious tech skills to get past those sensors *and* hack into *her* system.

Kat moved her fingers over the keyboard. In part, she searched her system for malware the pirates may have left behind, but she also used the motions to disguise a few hand signals. Every team had its own code, a secret way to communicate in the field. She flashed their sign for 'infiltrator' and then briefly glanced up to catch Scotch's eye. The tech sergeant's grimace deepened. Kat made another slight gesture signifying 'fake' and nodded at the image still on her screen. At that one, Scotch looked both relieved and confused.

"Figures," Kat muttered aloud. "We're stuck here breathing in canned air, and Sarge lands on the perfect beach somewhere, working on his tan."

Scotch ran his left hand through his hair, scratching his ear along the way. The message masked: Play along.

"Someone's gonna pay."

Kat nodded, then pointed at the coordinates. "Any idea where that is?"

Scotch's expression remained grim. "Not a clue."

They didn't even know if the pirates actually had Sarge or if this engineered image was completely bogus. Hell, they didn't even know if the pirates were the only players in this game. Kat swore heatedly as she shut the system down. "There is no way they could have left the ship, right?"

"Nope. Seriously unlikely."

Kat smiled a nasty smile. She could tell just by the feel of it.

"Then I guess it's time for some hide-and-seek."

Scotch nodded. His eyes looked hard, but his expression had gone so neutral it was scary. Kat shivered. He reached out and brushed her jaw. Odd for him to do, but she got the message and activated her bonejack.

"Go on, you," he said to her. "Now that you're decent head back to medbay and check on the rest of the team. Make sure everyone reports to the new crew quarters, Deck 20, Corridor Alpha-15, Compartment 1428," he instructed her aloud. But over the bonejack, he continued, *It's 1630 hours right now. Prep the team for search and rescue no later than 1730. Anyone asks, we're making up the scheduled live-fire exercise.*

What about you? she asked by the same means, then vocalized for the benefit of the guards and anyone else listening, "Aye, tech sergeant, Deck 20, Corridor Alpha-15, Compartment 1428, acknowledged."

Her jaw buzzed as Scotch continued over the 'jack, *I was cleared for entry in here so I could inspect the barracks for any other... surprises and disable them. I best get to that and see what else I can learn about our 'friends.'.*

He grinned as she left, reminding Kat of her earlier smile.

Scotch forced himself to turn away rather than watch Kat heading off to medbay. He bit back a groan and scrubbed his hand over his face and up through his hair. Then, shaking his head and cursing himself for a fool, he got back to work. First, he turned to the guards, uncomfortable inspecting the place so intently with strangers at his back.

"Gentlemen, dismissed," he ordered. "I will be here a while. No need for all of us to keep watch. Go take a break while I finish up. I'll let you know when I'm ready to leave."

One merely said, "Thank you, sir," as he headed out the hatch. The other started to protest before Scotch cut him off.

"In case you didn't recognize it, corporal, that was an order."

"Yes, sergeant," the man said, not looking happy about it, though his tone remained neutral. Scotch not only watched him leave, but he followed him to the hatch and locked it, not wanting to be disturbed.

In truth, Scotch had already inspected the common areas and most of the quarters in minute detail. Sarge's quarters first, of course, on discovering it had been tossed. But then, he had been looking mostly for signs of tampering and sabotage. The first search turned up nothing, but he had no choice. He had to do it all again.

He moved quickly and methodically, not leaving things scattered but not bothering with precision when putting them away. Sarge's quarters and the one Kat shared with three other team members were the only places left to search. At this point, he'd started to hope there was nothing to find, but he would fully execute this duty, formality or not, needing to rejoin his team with no doubt in his mind that he could trust them.

As Scotch had already gone over Sarge's bunk in fine detail, he returned to Kat's quarters. First, he headed to the very back of the compartment. Moving from left to right, he examined the storage lockers and their contents, running his hands along the insides and looking for any fixtures or fittings that looked like they had been recently removed or manipulated. Emptying equipment bags and inspecting those contents. A metal disk popped free as he repacked Dalton's high-tech weapons gear, but it appeared to be no more than a factory stamp, so he dropped it back in the bag and went on with his search. Other than a bit of dust, he didn't find a thing.

He then moved to the most overt spaces with the same exacting efforts... the bunks, the cubicles, the footlockers... Above, below, and in between each surface. The same. Heck, he even lay on his back and crawled beneath the bunks but came across nothing more than an inspector's seal. But then, as he shimmied out from under the bunk opposite Kat's, he realized something. He reached up and ran his finger over the impression. At first, he'd thought the detail had been stamped on the metal frame. A closer inspection revealed a separate disk bonded to the surface. Frowning, he rolled across the aisle, ending face up halfway beneath Kat's bunk. He reached up again in the same spot.

The one with no seal.

Just to be certain, he moved further under and searched the whole frame, running his hand over every inch of the surface. In the spot he would expect a seal to be, the surface seemed rougher and faintly tacky, like the remnants of an adhesive resistant to being removed. Scotch rolled back out and got to his feet to examine the underside of the top bunks as well. In each case—save for Kat's—the inspector had placed their mark in the same location. So, who had removed Kat's, and why? Scotch recalled seeing similar seals throughout his search, mostly on furniture and large pieces of equipment. He hadn't thought anything of them... until now.

In his search, he'd encountered such a disk where, given his current knowledge, he would not have expected one to be.

Moving back to the storage lockers, Scotch hauled out Dalton's kit. As the team's weapons specialist, she had specialized gear in keeping with her MOS. Nothing had seemed out of order on his first inspection, but this time he emptied it all out and went millimeter by millimeter. Finally, on the butt of one of her box-like calibration tools, or whatever it was, he found what he'd hoped not to find. A hollowed-out recess an inch long and half an inch deep and wide. In the area surrounding the depression, the housing had the same faintly gummy texture as the underside of Kat's bunk.

Setting the tool to the side, Scotch searched the bag, going as far as to flip it over and shake it out. More dust, making him cough, but also a metallic *ping* as something struck the deck. He dropped the bag and squatted down, reaching for the now-familiar disk. Settling on his heels, he turned the seal over. It definitely matched those beneath the bunks. He turned it again and examined the backside. Traces of adhesive remained but not clean. More like how tape looked when removed too many times: grimy and knurled where the glue clumped together and pulled away from the surface. He took up the tool in his other hand and laid the disk over the hollow. Not only did the adhesive stick, but the disk looked as if it had always been there.

But what did that prove?

He placed his evidence aside on Kat's bunk and sifted through the rest of the tools and debris on the floor emptied from Dalton's kit. Eventually, he found it. What he hadn't wanted to find. A microcomm etched with a Legion insignia. Seeing it tore him up. No betrayal hurt worse than one dealt by the hand of your family, and for him, the Devils were family. Part of him felt that betrayal like a wound bleeding out his heart's blood. Part of him felt a failure, certain he'd let down Sarge and the rest of the Devils by not identifying this threat sooner.

He closed his fist around the device as if he would crush it, but it just creased his palm. Growling, he shoved it into his pocket. Still not knowing who to trust among the command staff, he'd have to hold onto it for now.

Leaving everything where it lay, he headed for their new quarters, activating his squad band as he went.

CHAPTER 10

WE LOST CAMPBELL. | *WHERE'S DALTON?*

Kat and Scotch both spoke over the squad band at the same time. Her emotions in turmoil, Kat barely felt the ripple along her jaw. She fell silent and waited for Scotch to go on.

What?! By his tone, Scotch clearly wanted to have heard her wrong.

Kat repeated herself. *We lost Campbell.*

Silence. *I'll be right there.*

Five minutes later, Scotch stalked into the common room of the temporary barracks. He headed right for where she and the team waited. Even in the midst of battle, she'd never seen a more intent expression on his face.

Kat's teeth ground together, and she swallowed hard, feeling the ripple of tense muscles all the way to her feet. As he approached, she reached into her pocket and pulled out its contents. By the time he stopped in front of her, her fingers had uncurled to reveal the all-too-familiar sight of a compressed carbon cube—Campbell's physical remains, by the etching.

"Airman, report."

Kat complied, her voice flat and neutral only by rigid control. "According to the report registered by the med-tech on duty, at 0400 hours, Warrant Officer Armand Campbell succumbed to complications triggered by a delayed reaction to the foreign substance inhaled into his system."

By the time she finished reporting, her voice had acquired a hard edge, and Scotch's complexion had gone from white to deep red, his expression both uncharacteristic and disturbing. Kat had no doubt she wore a similar one.

"Where. Is. Dalton?" Scotch's voice vibrated with cold, quiet rage.

Kat's breath caught. What had he found in his search? His fingers flickered in the sign she'd used earlier. 'Infiltrator.'

Her grip tightened on the cube. She felt conflicted... confused. Betrayal always hit hard, but dealt by someone you'd fought life-and-death beside... someone who had saved you... It took an effort for Kat to keep her expression blank. "Corporal Dalton is unaccounted for."

There was only one place Dalton would head: the *Teufel*. Where the backup data on the *Cromwell* had been secured. They had to assume she had Sarge, who had the code to the shielded compartment where they'd hidden the intel. All of which meant, other than the actual encryption code, the traitor had everything she needed in one tidy package, including her method of escape. They had to catch up with her before she managed to launch. The *Teufel* wouldn't be easy for Dalton to pilot on her own—pray, God, she was on her own—but not impossible.

If that happened, Sarge was as good as cubed.

Apparently, Scotch had a similar thought.

He nodded at Campbell's remains.

"Keep that safe for now, Kittie," he said. "Sarge'll need it in a while."

He then turned to the assembled team, his stance and expression a warning to each and every one of them: disloyalty would be met with extreme prejudice. If there were any other traitors among them, they had to be pissing themselves on the inside.

Kat immediately nixed that thought. If she started doubting the rest of her teammates, they were doomed. If they lost cohesion, they lost their edge. The key was to be alert, not suspicious. She blanked her mind of any misgiving and focused on Scotch.

"I have reason to believe Dalton has engaged in subversive actions and even now has secured our commander against his will. To what end, I cannot say, but at this point, I can't tell who to trust outside of this room, so we have to deal with this ourselves and ask forgiveness later," he said. "So, grab your weapons and follow me, or get the hell out of my way."

Kat, gauss rifle in hand, moved in lockstep with him as he went out the hatch heading for the docking bay.

They didn't storm the transport.

Kat had to admit, it would have felt good, but it also would have backed Dalton into a corner. Not that that wasn't where they wanted her... they just didn't want her to realize it. Instead, they stopped one level above and gathered in a huddle.

"Tivo, Truitt, Kramer... you're going EVA. I need you to institute a security lockdown of the docking collar and disable the release mechanism. You make our transport a permanent part of the *Cromwell* if you have to, understood?"

"Acknowledged, sir," they answered, their tone low and intent, their responses in perfect unison.

Scotch sent the team on their way with a jerk of his head. Silently, they hurried down the corridor, moving fast, but maintaining noise disciple with the skill of men long trained in the art of combat. He then turned to Beta Squad, with a charged look at Zaga, their squad leader. At his brief nod, Scotch continued. "Miki, requisition a transport in case we need to pursue. Zaga, take Colonel, Kopecky, Danzer, Hemry, Ike, and Truck and set up a covert perimeter around the *Teufel*'s berth in case Dalton attempts to flee.

"Kat, you're with me," he said, motioning her to follow him back to the lift. "Leave your weapon here."

"Yes, Tech... *what?!*"

He pivoted and gave her a hard look. "Leave. The weapon. Here. You and I are the diversion so the rest of the team can execute their missions. We don't know what we're going to find in there. Going in armed could put Sarge at risk."

Kat's grip tightened on her rifle. Her teeth clenched at just the thought of going in not loaded for bear.

"You're a pain in my ass," she ground out. Thrusting the weapon into Kramer's hands, she accepted his pistol in return, shoving it into the waist-band of her pants at her back as she stalked after Scotch. "So, let's hear the plan."

"We go in like we're following instructions, then we keep Dalton talking so the others can do their jobs. If we have a chance, we take her down."

They saw no one in sight as they exited the lift and made their way across the docking bay, not even the watch. Kat kept alert, her eyes roving across the bay, searching for movement. As they drew closer, the *Teufel* appeared still in lock-down.

Kat cast a questioning glance sideways toward Scotch as he entered his security code. She remained silent, and ready to follow his lead, not wanting to set him off. He looked pissed and clearly ready for a fight. She could see it in the glimmer that darkened his hazel eyes to hardened bronze. The only outward sign that gave any hint to his current disposition. Didn't matter, though... Any adversary near enough to tell was already shit out of luck.

The two of them boarded the transport as if this were a standard pre-mission inspection. Scotch went in first. Ducking through the airlock portion of the vessel, Kat nearly ran up his ass. She could feel the tension pulsing off of him.

"Hey, what gives?" she asked, stepping around him and into the crew compartment of the transport. She thought she heard a sound from the load compartment and started to move in that direction when Scotch snapped out a sharp "no!" His hand came down on her arm. He started to draw her back, but suddenly the pull eased, though his grip did not. Kat glanced over her shoulder at him.

What she saw hit her like a kick in the gut by a steel-toed combat boot. The edge of her lip curled instantly, and she scowled. Her hand brushed over the pocket holding the cube. It looked more likely that poor Dalton wasn't unaccounted for after all, though Kat would have to scan the embedded identchip to be positive. Disturbing to think that the medbay staff might have been infiltrated.

Very deliberately, Kat reached up and lifted Scotch's hand from her shoulder so she could slowly pivot all the way around. As she did so, she activated her squad band and tried to send a warning to the rest of the team. No response. She bit back a curse. The traitor must have engaged a blocker.

"Welcome back, Campbell," she spoke in tones of hardened steel to the man standing behind and to the left of Scotch. "What happened? Did Hell throw you out for giving Devils a bad name?"

Scotch's eyes narrowed. Message received. Not that he could do much with the knowledge. Turned out he had a pistol to his head. If Campbell hadn't been a dead man before, he certainly would be soon.

"You know, Alexander, that mouth of yours is about the only smart thing about you," Campbell responded. "You have two choices," the traitor told her, "Secure Sergeant Daniels, or I'll take him out."

Like the latter wasn't going to happen at some point anyway. Kat looked down at the zip restraints Campbell held out, but she didn't move to take them.

Scotch snarled and made as if to turn.

...Until the pistol slammed upside his head. At the same time, Campbell used his free hand to jerk Scotch off balance. "Don't even try it, Daniels... I need her. You're just insurance."

Kat liked the sound of that. Not the part about Scotch, but the little slip that told her Campbell either didn't have the goods or couldn't access them. Otherwise, he wouldn't need her either, not if he had Sarge. She kept her satisfaction off her face when the traitor turned his attention back to her.

"Just to be clear: you play nice, Alexander, and Scotch here doesn't bleed," Campbell said. Kat heard an unspoken 'yet' in there somewhere. "We want the data, all of it, and the encryption codes. Now get him zipped before I make it a non-issue. Then you're going to behave and help me find the stash, or I start target practice..."

Snatching the zip-ties, Kat started to circle the two of them. Campbell's pistol clicked as he thumbed the hammer back.

"Like I didn't get the same training you did... do it from there. Just reach your arms around him, and make it good and secure."

"Yeah?" Kat's lip lifted in a sneer. "Well... I must have been absent the day they trained us to sell out." Probably not smart to bait him, but it did give her a few moments to think before committing to an action she'd likely regret. Campbell didn't even twitch, though his eyes went flat like a killer preparing to... well... kill. He pressed the muzzle harder against Scotch's temple.

Kat had no choice but to comply. Her only weapons were her combat knife and the borrowed pistol. Drawing either would be too visible. Campbell would have time to fire before she brought either to bear. Her hand-to-hand training wasn't much use at the moment either, given that Scotch stood between her and the enemy. She had to hope an opportunity would come clear. Or at least that they could stall Campbell long enough for the Devils to close in...

Tension turned Scotch's body harder than granite. Even with him cooperating—albeit unwillingly—Kat had to press herself obscenely close before she could secure his wrists behind him. As she did, something hard shoved into her gut. She let her eyes drift up slowly as if trying not to focus on this forced intimacy and met Scotch's eye. His gaze hooded, and every muscle went taut, but he remained absolutely still.

Except for his hips. He deliberately shifted them forward, his eyes never leaving hers. She gasped. A second ago, she would have thought the two of them couldn't get any closer—short of stripping off their clothes and making a concerted effort to occupy the same space—but just that subtle press made it clear that something other than his anatomy poked her. Like the hilt of a combat knife. Then, not so subtle, Scotch deliberately teetered, as if off-balance, like when Campbell had jerked him back earlier.

Kat kept her eyes on Scotch, catching the minute shift of his gaze toward the traitor. She drew a deep breath and let her eyes drift closed, then slowly brought them open again, in silent acknowledgment.

Resting her left hand on Scotch's chest as she drew her right back around to his side, Kat allowed a look of calculated vulnerability to flit across her features. Seemingly in response, Scotch dropped his chin, as if in defeat, but more importantly, taking his head out of alignment with the barrel of Campbell's pistol.

For a fraction of a moment, Kat hesitated as visions of Scotch with the top of his head blown out short-circuited her nerves. And then his jaw flexed. Static-like tingles traveled along her bonejack, but no words. She didn't need them. She understood completely.

A crash came from the load compartment as if something heavy fell to the deck. Kat couldn't have arranged a better distraction if she'd tried. For just a second, Campbell's attention wavered. Not knowing if either of them would see the outside of the transport ever again, Kat shoved Scotch into the traitor with her left hand even as she drew out his combat knife with the other. The two of them tumbled to the deck. The pistol fired once, a suppressed round. The bullet lodged somewhere in the bulkhead. A scream ricocheted through the transport as Kat dove down on top of the others. Something hard crunched beneath her knee, and the squad band hummed back to life.

Kat remained focused on her target. She lunged forward, her left hand locking on Campbell's gun, shoving it down and away before he could fire again. Her right hand brought the combat knife to bear, letting momentum carry the blade down through Campbell's eye and into his brain. As she yanked the blade out, his body spasmed, jerking and thudding against the deck until everyone and everything seemed coated with the traitor's blood.

Scrambling back into a crouch, with the knife still in hand, Kat yelled and lunged again as someone came at her from the shadows of the load compartment. A solid kick from that direction numbed her wrist and hand.

"Stand down, Alexander," the approaching figure ordered, stumbling into the crew compartment. The gravelly voice sounded unfamiliar, but when Kat turned, she recognized the battered face.

"Well, I'll be damned," Scotch said, straining to look around from where he lay twisted on the deck.

Kat swore, and her legs buckled as the adrenaline ran out. By reflex, she caught the bulkhead, remaining upright, only to have the state of the compartment—and her person—catch her gaze. As she stared at her blood-soaked fatigues, it occurred to her she'd killed a man close up enough to see the light go out of his eyes... what remained of them... and to wear the evidence of her deed. Her first legitimate close-combat kill.

And it was a member of her team. Training kicked in, and she shut down the tremors that began to shake her before they could become uncontrolled.

She'd have to deal with this, but not now.

Over the restored squad band, Kat heard Scotch give the Devils orders to abort their missions and head back to quarters. She noted that he didn't mention any particulars, including that they had liberated Sarge. The man himself stood over them, swaying slightly. His neck and the whole right side of his face bore a mass of bruises, and a sloppy field dressing wrapped his left arm from wrist to elbow. His hands were bound in front of him, though Kat suspected they hadn't started out that way. Fresh blood stood out bright on the gauze and what looked like a smudge of bootblack darkened his sleeve. She noticed pronounced lines around his mouth, and pain left his eyes glazed. Beneath that, Kat spied the deep, sharp pinch of recent betrayal.

He toed Campbell's body. "Thanks for taking out the trash." Sarge's voice sounded odd, but then, what else should she expect with a solid band of deep purple bruises coloring his neck?

Kat grinned up at him, then raised the combat knife with a nod toward his restraints. He held out his hands, and she wiped the blade clean on Campbell's shirt before using the blade to snap Sarge's zip ties. Then, as she looked up into his face, she faltered, her grin fading away. Kat didn't know what to make of her commander's grim expression. She opened her mouth, not even sure what to say, when Scotch started grumbling from the deck.

"Hey, how about undoing your handiwork?"

When she saw he'd arched his neck and back to look over at her, Kat's grin returned, though a pale reflection of what it had been before.

"I don't know... this kind of works for me." Scotch's eyebrow shot up until she continued, "Reminds me of hog-tyin' with PawPaw."

Though she taunted him, Kat turned to free his wrists, only to jerk back in confusion as Scotch gasped. His gaze flared with shock and betrayal.

"Kat!" he cried out, but it was too late. She tried to pivot away, but something sharp pierced her left shoulder.

An icy burn invaded her body, and numbness radiated toward her spine, swiftly robbing her of all sensation in its wake. She couldn't tell if she dropped the combat knife before she slumped across Scotch, but as the drug knocked her out, she prayed she had, or one of them was dead.

CHAPTER 11

Each time his console pinged, John Cryson tensed and immediately closed the window he was working on to access the incoming message. Each time, he faced disappointment. He closed the feed on another supply report. Nothing that couldn't be dealt with later. Not a good idea to attempt administrivia with his mind this distracted, anyway. Not with an operative overdue. Not with *this* operative overdue.

"Where the hell are you, Christine?" he muttered beneath his breath, spinning his chair to stare up at the Legion banner. He hadn't intended to provide another generation to bear that particular yolk. Children had never been on his long-term plan.

Then came Franscine Dalton. A case of shore leave with consequences. Not that Cryson had known. Christine wasn't supposed to either, he gathered, but she had learned of him by hacking her mother's personal log as a precocious tween. All but his name.

That she didn't discover until the conclusion of Franscine's hard, protracted death. According to his daughter, a virus ate her mother's brain. In the end, there had been little sense and no control. Secrets both real and imagined came tumbling free in a jumble, including his name, only sorted out after Franscine's passing. His daughter hunted him down, satisfying her longing for the father she had romanticized into a hero long before she'd know who he actually was.

He hadn't turned his back on the unexpected when she'd shown up, all grown and combat-trained to boot. Of course... it stung that the enemy had trained her, but hey, his benefit, their expense. How could he argue with that?

He hadn't rejected the opportunity presented by a loyal operative already inserted into the AeroCom ranks, but why did it have to be his daughter? True, even after five years, he had yet to grow used to even thinking of himself as a father, but he found the role meant more to him than he ever would have expected. Not that he'd done any amount of actual parenting—hell, she'd been twenty when they'd first met—but a well of pride bubbled somewhere inside of him nonetheless. His Christine wasn't just a fierce warrior, but frighteningly intelligent, canny even.

Over the years, she had fed them intel, some tech, and she had even altered data on her end, to the Legion's advantage, never once even coming close to getting caught. While not their only operative, she had proven herself most effective. Enough that his superiors were quite pleased with both of them. They would be less so if they knew the particulars of their relationship. Only three people knew he had a daughter... well, two, now with her mother dead.

Ping.

Cryson jumped at the incoming message, swearing as he noted it wasn't her.

"What?" he snarled at the ensign on the other end of the comm, one of the tech crew he had working on the data Petrov had retrieved.

The man paled but did not flinch. "We have completed our review of the data from the Groom Experimental Complex."

"And...?" Cryson prompted when the man fell silent.

"It's not there."

"What do you mean, it's not there?"

"The drive contained relatively little data. Either the operative did not get everything, or someone initiated a data dump before the retrieval."

Cryson took a deep, measured breath, working to control his temper. "Are you certain?"

"None of the file signatures on the drive is more than a week old," the ensign reported. "Though... it does look like some of the files may be reinstalled backups of older data... Nothing on the *Cromwell*, though."

"Keep checking. Flag anything of potential use, regardless of the nature."

"Yes, sir."

Closing the connection, Cryson sat back in his chair and considered the situation.

He had not wanted to doubt Petrov. God knew Cryson himself had experienced how quickly an operation could go to shit, but this repeated failure hinted at either incompetence or sedition. Either had to be dealt with swiftly before those in command called Cryson's own commitment into question.

Time to have a chat with his *friend* Petrov.

First, Cryson reengaged his comm.

"Security. How can I help you, sir?"

Cryson sat forward, his tone controlled. "What have you found?"

The man looked a bit confused.

"Petrov's quarters," Cryson hissed, his agitation slipping through the cracks in his composure.

"Nothing, sir. The compartment was clean, his terminal as well. We found no sign of subversion."

"And what about his person? Was he searched when he was taken to Detention?"

"Yes, sir. I conducted the search myself. Lieutenant Petrov had nothing of a questionable nature on his person."

"Do we have the results of the Inquiry?"

"Still pending, sir."

A tension headache pulsed across Cryson's temple. He would have preferred conclusive evidence. Either Petrov was compromised and very skilled at hiding it, or he was clean, and his failures were the product of shitty luck and bad options. Time to find out which.

"Meet me in Detention with a security detachment."

"Yes, sir."

Cryson killed the connection and spun his chair, only to check himself, reining in his temper until he regained control. An interrogation required focus. He could not afford an emotional distraction. He needed to remember this was not about personal betrayal.

Sitting back, he locked his gaze on the Legion banner. They had been fighting for their rightful place for so long. Men and women easily lost faith in a cause they had only inherited. In a dream passed down at a grandfather's knee. But they could not afford to think as individuals when they were born soldiers. Without the hope of someday claiming Demeter, they were a people without a place, without a goal, drifting aimlessly among the stars. Their dedication must remain unwavering, or the Legion would cease to be and leave each of them at the mercy of the universe.

He could not allow doubt or disloyalty to take root among his ranks.

Climbing to his feet, Captain John Cryson marched with determined strides through the narrow corridors of the *Destrier*. He closed his mind to the battered bulkheads and dripping pipes, the stale air and faint lived-in odor that only the top-of-the-line ships avoided, and focused on the equally distasteful task ahead of him.

As he approached Detention, the security chief and his detail fell in line. Cryson recognized at least one of the men as having lost family on the *Viper*. He almost said something but remained silent. If he could not trust those beneath him to do their duty properly, he had no call to be in command.

The four of them passed through the security airlock and headed for the second cell on the right. Rather than a normal slide hatch, these compartments sealed with a manual bolt in addition to an electronic lock. Cryson's jaw felt like it would crack under its own clenched force as he waited for the security chief to key in his code and disengage the bolt. Then, per protocol, the man stepped aside and allowed Cryson to precede him.

Petrov stood across the room, his posture both ready and wary. The bruise along his jaw where Cryson had decked him had begun to yellow and green around the edges, but a few new ones stood out reddish-purple at his right temple and the edge of his collar.

"Time to talk," Cryson said as the men quickly moved to secure the prisoner. He fought, but not for long, gaining fresh bruises, no doubt, including a nasty blow to the gut that doubled him over.

"Enough," Cryson commanded.

Petrov gasped for breath but straightened to attention right along with those restraining him. Their gazes locked, and Cryson, through strength of will, did not flinch away. He sneered in disdain at the look of accusation in the other man's gaze. The gall, when clearly Petrov had much more to answer for than just a few bruises.

Cryson turned and left the cell, calling over his shoulder, "Bring him to the interrogation room."

They left him sprawled face down on the deck of his cell. For a long moment, Anton just lay there, too numb to feel betrayed, wondering how things had spiraled so badly out of control. At each turn, he had made the best choice he could of an array of bad options, but never would he have imagined those decisions would bring him to this. He may not have shared the fervor that drove some of his fellow Legionnaires, but he had ever been loyal to the cause and John Cryson.

Had been.

But they had broken him, right along with his faith and any number of ribs. He bit back most of a groan, but part of it escaped as he attempted to push himself up from the floor. A rustling sound filtered through the vent between his cell and the one to the right of it.

"You okay?" Sally called out after a moment.

Anton told himself not to answer. Not to give them any more cause to doubt him, but at that thought, he gave a strangled laugh—not much more than a single bark—before sucking in a gasp at the sharp, shooting pain in his chest.

Ah, fuck it, he thought. No reason to be rude at this point. Cryson and the rest had already condemned him as a traitor. And anyway, he didn't much care what they thought. Even if he should be exonerated, he was done. Trust had been broken, and it would not be mended.

The only person on the ship he gave a damn about anymore wanted to talk.

"I'm alive," he finally answered, just barely lifting his head so his words weren't muffled against the deck. "Does that count as okay?"

"Depends. You likely to stay that way?"

Smothering another groan, he pulled himself closer to their shared wall. If he propped himself up, Anton could just see her through the ventilation slats. She had her head turned his way, her brow furrowed in concern. As he dipped a little lower for a better angle, he tried not to think about the grim reason the vents were there to begin with, particularly in light of her question.

"I expect so," he said, adding in his thoughts alone, *For better or worse.*

Sally seemed satisfied with that. Or at least, she lay back on her bunk staring at the ceiling, arms folded beneath her head and her left leg cocked up at the knee like she lounged on a prairie somewhere staring up at the stars. He wished. She hadn't done a thing to deserve being locked up. His choices had put them in these cells. Not an ideal situation, but better than the alternative. Shaking off the guilt that thought raised, Anton cleared his throat and went for some lighter conversation.

"So... Mustang... they call you that because you're a cowgirl?"

He watched as she looked toward their shared wall, her expression a tiny bit pitying, a tiny bit amused. "I'kin tell you're not from an AeroCom tradition."

Anton grimaced, though she couldn't see him from where she sat. Heck, he could barely see her. "What's that supposed to mean?"

"Well, the term's about two centuries old, a carry-over from the early days of the American Armed Forces, but AeroCom still uses the phrase." He heard Sally chuckle and wished a cell wall didn't muffle the deep, rich sound. "Anyway, a 'mustang' is a commissioned officer who started in enlisted service... of course, it's not like I'm the only one ever, but being a Texan named Sally, I guess I got hit with a double whammy, and the name stuck."

A vague memory surfaced in Anton's mind from his youth... beneath the stars, his great uncle crooning to calm him as they hid out in the wilds of Demeter. "Isn't there a song—"

"Not if you're smart there isn't."

And with that, Anton felt the conversation flounder. He leaned his head against the wall and heaved a silent sigh. Had he done her a favor by rescuing her? He hadn't considered what would happen to her after that, not until the captain had chewed him a new asshole.

As if she read his mind, Sally murmured, "Thank you, by the way, for saving my life." She paused, and he returned his eye to the slat. "'Course, would have been better if you hadn't put it at risk, to begin with, but I do appreciate you didn't leave me there to die."

Then Anton watched her roll back over and drape an arm across her eyes because prisoners weren't given the courtesy of a dark room. It seemed he hadn't done right by anyone lately. Anton slumped to the floor and lay there. Even if he'd had the energy to move to his bunk, he felt too low to bother.

CHAPTER 12

KAT WOKE ON A SURGE OF NAUSEA, HER HEAD THUDDING LIKE A DRUM AND HER body one large ache. A rush of sound registered, shouts and feet pounding the deck, drawing closer. She startled, her body jerking when she groaned and it echoed beside her, in more masculine tones.

"What the hell...?" Scotch muttered by her ear. Kat rolled her head and opened her eyes, her gaze lingering on his bruised temple before darting away to scan their surroundings. Her brow dipped in confusion. What were they doing laying together on the docking bay floor beside the *Teufel's* empty berth?

Wait... *empty?*

Gritting her teeth, she rolled away from Scotch and pushed to her feet, her fatigues moving as stiff as her body. She glanced down and gasped. Dried blood covered her clothes.

Scotch stood up beside her, fatigues not quite as bloody. As their condition registered, so did the scent of blood, causing Kat's nausea to surge once more. Willpower alone held it back.

"What the hell happened?" Scotch repeated.

Before Kat could respond—as if she had anything to say—the deck crew reached them, milling about and bombarding them with questions neither could answer. The airmen parted as a member of the command staff pushed through, expression stern. His collar bore a gold oak leaf and his name tape read 'HENDERSON.'

"Return to your duties," Major Henderson ordered those looking on before turning to Scotch. "Explain yourself, tech sergeant."

"I'm sorry, sir. I have no explanation," Scotch responded, his tone respectful. Those unfamiliar with him were likely deceived into believing him calm. Kat knew better. "One moment, Corporal Alexander and I were inspecting our assigned shuttle craft..." he pivoted slightly and gestured behind him. "...the next, we woke up here, with no knowledge of what happened in between."

The major turned to Kat. "Is that true, corporal?"

Kat straightened her stance and nodded. "I'm afraid so, sir."

Henderson's eyes narrowed and he looked them over closely. Kat fought to keep her stance and her expression neutral. Beside her, she could feel Scotch radiating tension. Neither of them moved.

"Follow me," he ordered as he headed across the deck.

They trooped down the *Cromwell*'s corridors in silence the whole way to medbay. Henderson approached the head corpsman on duty. He had a quiet word with the man and then turned to Kat and Scotch. "Once your injuries have been seen to, report for assessment."

With quick efficiency, the medbay crew separated the two of them, placing them in different triage units.

"Please remove your uniform and place it in this bag," the corpsman instructed.

For just a moment, Kat hesitated as warnings went off in her head. The worry took root that this could go badly for them. Careful to keep her motions relaxed and compliant, Kat stripped. Feeling something in her pocket as she did so, she managed to extract her exabyte drive and hide it in her palm before handing over her uniform. She then accepted a gown in exchange, all without a word. As the corpsman left, Kat donned her gown and moved her boots out of the way, slipping the drive inside. Then she sat on the exam table, going over the situation in her head. It didn't take long.

One moment, she and Scotch had been on a rescue run, trying to intercept the subversives who had captured Sarge. The next, they were sprawled unconscious in front of the *Teufel's* empty berth, drawing a crowd. That was it. That was all she could remember. Part of her started to panic.

Scotch? Her jaw rippled faintly, but she heard nothing in return.

Grimacing, she fidgeted, wishing all of this were over already. She ached and even after taking off her soiled clothes there remained enough residue on her skin to make her gag.

Eventually, someone came in to take her vitals and an unsettling array of biological samples, then someone else entered to clean her up, examine her right wrist—which bore a bad bruise—and inspected her for other injuries, of which there were none.

"You're free to go, corporal," the corpsman said, handing her a new set of fatigues.

Kat wondered a moment if she'd misunderstood, until she heard Scotch call from just outside her unit: "Move it, Alexander! The brass is waiting."

In the end, there was nothing they could tell command. According to medbay, the compound used to knock them out messed with their short-term memories. Grudgingly, they'd been dismissed.

As they entered the common room unexpectedly, Kat caught murmurs among the team. *Why did we abort? Why are we waiting? Who's really calling the shots? Where there's one traitor, could there be more?* Not everyone spoke, but they all listened.

Kat frowned, worry creasing her brow. Their questions were understandable, but if it didn't stop here and now, those doubts could easily spread, breaking down team cohesion.

Save for the cold, hard glint in his eye, Kat would have wondered if Scotch had heard them at all. That is, until Tech Sergeant Jackson Daniels strode through the common room like Patton taking the podium. Shoulders back, arms swinging in precise rhythm with his legs, footsteps echoing on the metal deck, everything about him screamed perfect military-grade posture. His fierce countenance exuded the hard edge of command.

Their own expressions wary, the Devils separated before him, giving him a clear path. Scotch entered Sarge's quarters without a word or a glance to anyone.

Kat considered the wisdom of following, but before she could step forward, he returned. Facing the team, he held something high—Brockmann's carbon cube. It seemed quite small in his large hand. At the sight of it, Kat frowned, her hand reflexively going to the pocket of her fatigues, only to find it empty, except for the exabyte drive.

Of course, it was. These weren't even her fatigues. Still, unease filled her belly, and some fragment of memory struggled to find its way through the fog, only to vanish as it thickened. After a long pause, Scotch slowly turned, being sure to face each member of the unit head-on, capturing their gazes and staring hard until their eyes dropped.

"This..." His low voice vibrated from a clenched jaw, forcing silence as all attempted to hear. "This is your comrade. Brockmann," —At his words, Kat's frown deepened, knowing in her gut that the sight of the cube had triggered whatever memory eluded her— "fallen, cubed. She isn't alone. We are down four of our unit, either lost..." Scotch raised the cube a little higher. "Or gone... This unit has been betrayed by those pretending allegiance with us, even as Corporal Alexander and I were betrayed when we confronted the enemy."

He paused, his fierce expression not once wavering, his head never dropping, lest it be taken as a sign of fault. "We failed in our efforts," Scotch went on, his words colored with honest regret. "The pirates took the day... If you want to take it back, consider this... do you want to risk adding more cubes to the tribute box because we went off after them, half-cocked and without authorization? Do you really believe unsupported and unprepared will do the job? Do you really, *truly* think we can accomplish *anything* with division in the ranks?"

With that, he challenged them, waiting for his words to permeate the mind of each soldier listening. Then, with careful calculation, he allowed the barest of curls to roll his lip. "*If* you did, I would be ashamed to call you Devils right now."

Any last mutterings died off, and outraged expressions went stony as the men and women of the 142nd Mobile stilled and listened. He lowered his arm and took Brockmann's cube in his other hand, holding it out so each of them saw the vow marks they'd etched into its surface.

"I don't believe any of that. I believe in *you*." Here he spoke his words low, with power and strength anchoring them. "I have contacted General Drovak. He will be arriving within a matter of days with support to evaluate our ranks and the *Cromwell's* crew," Scotch continued as he slid the cube back into his pocket. "He will have our full cooperation in this. We will assist in all ways possible until we are cleared for duty."

Kat nearly flinched herself. This Scotch unnerved her. No light-hearted humor, no easy grin. Just grim determination. His intense gaze trailed over each of them. "This will be done with all due haste so that we can gain clearance to hunt down those pirates. Understood?" Every airman present indicated assent.

Everyone else had retired to their bunks, but Scotch found himself too worked up to sack out. Instead, he headed for the commander's quarters to return Brockmann's cube to the tribute box. As Scotch closed the footlocker, a tone sounded over his private frequency, followed by an unfamiliar voice.

Technical Sergeant Daniels, you are to report immediately to Colonel Corbin's quarters, D10CdZeta3Cp110, do you acknowledge?

Scotch's jaw flexed in annoyance as another surge of adrenaline shot through his system. At this rate, he would never catch some sleep. *Aye, acknowledged.*

As he left the compartment and entered the common room, he encountered Zaga.

"You too?"

Zaga nodded with a grimace, and Scotch's gut muscles clenched. There was only one reason to summon both of them right now: to assign temporary command of the team. From the look on his face, Zaga figured the same thing.

Scotch blew out a slow breath. "Okay, then. Let's get this over with."

They headed out together in silence. Scotch wasn't sure how he wanted this to play out. Zaga was a good leader. A bit stronger on strategy but not quite as confident in his own decisions. Still, Scotch would have no problem following him—and providing support—if that is what Command had decided.

And if they decided Scotch should assume command, he would damn well lead.

Both outcomes left him just a bit anxious. Not because he didn't believe either of them could handle it, but because it indicated that the higher-ups did not expect Sarge to be recovered... or restored. That didn't sit well with Scotch. Not at all.

"Hey... Daniels, you plan on stopping or just walking out the door? I'm thinking you might not enjoy that first step..."

Scotch grinned as Zaga pulled him up short. He had been so deep in thought he hadn't even realized they'd reached their destination. Scotch faced his teammate and ran a quick visual inspection, finding nothing out of order. Zaga returned the favor. They exchanged nods, pivoted, and Scotch presented his identchip to the sensor next to the hatch. At the hail from inside, he opened it and entered, leaving Zaga to close it behind him.

They moved to stand side by side at attention.

"Tech Sergeants Daniels and Asturrizaga reporting, sir."

Colonel Corbin pushed to his feet at their entrance, his expression grim and his gaze searching. Scotch wanted to shake off the feel of his look but resisted. Beside him, Zaga tensed as if sensing a threat.

The colonel leaned forward and pushed something small and metallic across his desk.

"Sergeant Jackson, care to explain how you came by this?"

Startled, Scotch looked down and almost reached for the object, flinching back as he recognized the Legion emblem etched into its surface. He blinked and shook his head.

"I'm sorry, sir. I'm not quite sure what you mean."

"That," Corbin said, his finger jabbing toward the object, "fell out of your pocket when you and Corporal Alexander were discovered unconscious on the docking bay deck."

"That is not mine... sir," Scotch started to say, only to shake his head again as if to clear it. He frowned as fragments of memories bubbled up. "After the attack on the Devils' barracks, I had orders to search the quarters. I found that among Sergeant Dalton's belongings. The aforementioned incident occurred before I could report."

The colonel's gaze narrowed, and the corners of his mouth dipped down, but he said nothing. For a long, taut moment, silence ruled the compartment. Then Corbin picked up the microcomm and locked it away. He nodded once, as if he'd made a decision, and the tension broke.

"At ease, sergeants." Colonel Corbin said, then gestured to his left, where another airman stood. "I would like to introduce you to your new acting commander, Master Sergeant Tim Ryan."

For the second time since he'd entered Corbin's office, the bottom fell out of Scotch's gut.

Aching like she'd been the guest of dishonor at a blanket party, Kat gave up on resting. She grabbed her kit and a spare tank top and shorts from her cubby and left her bunk, shuffling across the common room to the hygiene facilities. The common room appeared empty, except for Truck and Kramer, who looked like they'd zonked out watching a vid. Or so she believed until she reached the hatch and groaned. First, one of them snickered, then the other, continuing in a feedback loop. The wiseasses had slapped on a sign that read, "Shit. Shower. And _Shave_." Just to get a rise out of them, she ripped it down and tossed the crumpled wad their way, sending them into a fit of all-out laughter.

"Real classy, guys," she called over her shoulder as she went through the hatch. "But I don't like either of you enough to shave right now."

She could still hear their laughter as the hatch closed, one of them making kissy sounds back at her, the other pretending to cry inconsolably before dissolving into laughter once more. Kat grinned and shook her head. Immature as it might seem, she had to admit that the silly shit they all pulled to blow off steam kept the team sane.

Stowing her kit in the changing area, she stripped down and tossed her clothes in the laundry chute before stepping over to one of the fully enclosed shower stalls. She would never get used to this. One of the weirdest things she ever encountered at a military installation—with the exception of some of her teammates. The stalls weren't there for privacy or modesty but containment and reclamation. Turning to the keypad, she presented her identchip to the sensor, then keyed in her selection. Today, with the way she ached, she burned almost a month's worth of vice credits on a hot-water shower. Hell, what she really wanted was a long soak in a full bath, but there weren't enough v.c.'s on the ship to cover that. She would settle quite happily for the shower, though. And she better enjoy it too, because it would be ion showers from here on out after this.

Climbing in and closing the door, she leaned against the wall and waited for the stream and steam. When it kicked in, she groaned again, really glad the guys couldn't hear her this time as the sound nearly made *her* blush. For ten of her fifteen-minute allotment, she stood there and just let the cycling water fall, get filtered through the system, heated, and fall once more, her muscles loosening enough that she no longer felt like a bag of knots. She nearly fell asleep right there, even standing up, except a sudden rap sounded on the stall door.

And just like that, every muscle tightened up again.

"You asshole!" she bellowed, not even caring if Drovak himself stood out there.

Shoving the stall door open, she came out ready for a fight, only to stop abruptly at the sight of Scotch standing there, the tips of his ears bright pink but his face looking like someone kicked his puppy. Without a word, he reached out, grabbed her towel, and handed it to her before turning and heading back out to the common room.

"What the hell?" Though she'd had five minutes left, the stream cut off once the door opened, so Kat dried herself and got dressed before stalking after Scotch, ready to take her lost vice credits out of his hide.

She stopped abruptly at the sight of the full team sitting around the conference table across the room. Scotch stood at the head of the table, waiting, Zaga beside him.

Well... crap. Without a word or even a look, Kat took the closest empty chair.

With a nod, Scotch locked gazes with each one of them, making his way around the table. "Thank you. This will take just a moment of your time.

"This meeting is to inform you that in the absence of Master Sergeant Kevin Daire, Command has assigned Master Sergeant Timothy Ryan as acting commander of the 142nd Mobile Special Operations Team, effective immediately.

"Any questions?"

"What the hell?" someone murmured.

As all eyes turned her way, Kat's ears grew hot as she realized that someone was her.

She grimaced, and everyone chuckled. Well, everyone except for Scotch. The worry and tension rose from him in acrid, near-visible waves reaching her from even the length of the table.

"This is a command decision, and you will all accord Sergeant Ryan the same respect you would Sergeant Daire."

"But what if we get deployed? What the hell does Ryan know about special ops?" Kopecky asked, his lip curled.

"All operations are on hold until General Drovak arrives. Once he is here, Zaga and I will request an appeal. Until then, Ryan receives our full support. Am I understood?"

"Yes, sir," they all responded, subdued but in unison.

Without another word, Scotch pivoted and disappeared into his quarters.

Zaga sighed. "Dismissed."

CHAPTER 13

THE COMM ALERT SOUNDED DURING CRYSON'S SLEEP CYCLE. HE WANTED TO snap and snarl at the ensign on the other end, but that was hardly fair when he had left the order to be notified when this particular message came in, *whenever* it came in.

"Sir, we've been hailed by an AeroCom transport claiming to be with the Legion. The pilot issued all the correct passcodes."

"Did they identify themselves?"

The comm went silent a moment. "He said to tell you..." —again, silence as if the corporal checked to make sure he got it right— "He said... the judas goat approaches."

He? Cryson tensed at that.

"What is his ETA?"

"Two standard hours." The corporal hesitated again. "Sir, there's more."

"Well, out with it then!" Cryson snapped.

"The transport... it's the *Teufel*."

Fuck! How stupid could the pilot be? Or was he just oblivious? Operative or not, after the destruction of the *Viper*, the man risked his life piloting that vessel anywhere near the *Destrier*.

"Does anyone else know that?"

"No, sir."

"Keep it that way. Instruct the pilot not to dock until ordered and to maintain radio silence until contacted. Once you deliver the message, report to my quarters."

"Yes, sir."

Popping into the head, Cryson rinsed the sleep from his face and slapped on a stim patch before changing into a uniform. Then he hailed the mess and had them send up espresso and something to eat. When he was good and ready, he entered his private office and prepared to meet his latest headache.

A rap on the hatch interrupted his thoughts.

"Come in."

The ensign entered. By chance or not, Cryson recognized him as the same messenger who had initially reported the destruction of the *Viper*. He nodded and beckoned the young man forward. The ensign stopped three feet from where Cryson sat. He stood straight and proud and attentive, not yet jaded by the hard life of a Legionnaire. Refreshing and a pity all at once. "What is your name, ensign?"

"Jean Patrick Denning, sir."

"Well, Ensign Denning, I have two very important tasks for you. First, keep your mouth shut about everything I am about to share with you. Can you do that?"

The soldier stared at him, his eyes widening as they darted to the Legion banner hanging on the wall and back again. He swallowed hard before responding, "Yessir!"

"Very good, soldier," Cryson softened his voice, encouraged by the fervor in Denning's response. "I don't know who is piloting that vessel, but we can't have the crew rain down vengeance before I find out why they're here. I need you to clear the docking bay on my orders, then contact that transport and have them connect to the farthest starboard docking module, then shut it down until I instruct otherwise. No one is to know the *Teufel* is docking."

"Understood, sir."

"Once he is on board, bring the pilot directly to my quarters, then stand by outside with security until I determine the situation."

Kat didn't wait gracefully any better than Scotch did, especially with the Devils' fate in question. Bad enough to have command of the team go to someone other than one of the squad leaders; even worse for it to be someone outside their ranks. As Kopecky pointed out, Ryan didn't have the training or experience to command a special operations team, and every one of the Devils knew it. He sure as hell didn't understand the men and women of the team and how they worked. How then were they supposed to trust him with their lives? Their only hope to overturn the assignment was to appeal it with General Drovak.

And so, spit-and-polished in their dress uniforms, Tech Sergeants Jackson Daniels and Zack Asturrizaga and Corporal Katrion Alexander were among the first to enter the docking bay to meet the man with the power to restore order to the 142nd and unleash them from their enforced downtime. Master Sergeant Ryan had been... unavailable.

A warning klaxon sounded, and all hangar personnel scrambled for the far end of the docking bay. Scotch, Zaga, and Kat followed as the depressurization barrier lowered, segmenting the deck into two halves. The external hull panels retracted, revealing the *Venture* positioned outside.

Perhaps the incoming ship had locks incompatible with the external docking collars, or perhaps those commanding her elected to make a point, but they prepared for a deck landing. Using maneuvering thrusters, the transport nosed in and touched down in the designated zone, venting billowing clouds of exhaust, mostly harmless water vapor absorbed by the *Cromwell*'s internal filtration system. Almost before the retractable hull panels of the docking area slid back into place, the *Venture* activated its own rear hatches, which folded to the sides until the whole aft section of the craft lay open, revealing a hard-edged military force in all its splendor. From the transport's armored depths, two companies of peacekeeper forces in dark blue battledress steadily disembarked.

The three Devils re-entered the docking bay as soon as the secure klaxon sounded. They came to a halt outside the demarcation line indicating the clear landing perimeter and watched the procession. As the five hundred peacekeepers formed ranks alongside the docked vessel, the external command-deck access hatch cycled open, revealing General Drovak, a bulldog of a man—complete with jowls—with hair so white it was nearly translucent, and his aide, a captain with a thick brush of startling, metallic silver hair despite his clearly youthful face. The docking crew scrambled to wheel the stair platform in place to allow both to descend.

The aide stepped forward before Drovak could exit the hatch, blocking the general's path. The younger man took stock of the area before stepping aside and giving his superior a sharp nod.

Odd. Very odd. Kat shivered and tensed.

* Anyone else feeling kind of judged?* she murmured to Scotch over her bonejack on his private frequency. Scotch just gave her a repressive look as he strode forward to meet the general. Kat and Zaga followed right in step, though Kat nearly fell out of sync, zapped by a peculiar jot of static as she moved across the deck plates. All three of them stopped and saluted once they were a couple of feet away.

"Tech Sergeants. Corporal," General Drovak acknowledged them. "I hear you've had a bit of excitement recently." His eyes settled on Kat. She couldn't read his expression. No doubt, he knew exactly who she was, having acquainted himself with the details of her file and the reports of said recent excitement.

"A little, sir," Scotch responded. "Nothing we couldn't handle."

The general laughed, as he was meant to, then gave them each a little nod. "Thank you for ensuring we had a proper greeting, now if you will excuse us..."

"Sir, please, if we could have just a moment?" Scotch said, stepping forward. Both Kat and Zaga moved to support positions at Scotch's back, one to either shoulder, and stood silently at attention.

Drovak frowned slightly, but he did stop.

"General, our team has been assigned an acting commander with no combat or special ops training," Scotch said, keeping his tone discrete. "Respectfully, we are concerned at the impact this could have on our combat effectiveness and our safety in the field."

The general's frown deepened. "I hear your concerns, sergeant, but I am afraid in light of recent events, this assignment must stand. The decision comes from further up the chain of command."

Kat felt Scotch tense as if against a blow, but his voice held no evidence of it as he nodded and said, "Understood, sir."

"I have no doubt the Devils will overcome these challenges and distinguish themselves as always, should the situation arise," the general said, his gaze alighted on each of them but seemingly lingered on Kat more intently. She chaffed beneath his gaze. Something about the general put her on edge, but she couldn't figure that out any more than she knew what he thought.

Kat tried hard to rein back her discomfort before she physically reacted. She must have done a piss-poor job gauging by the faint smirk on the aide's face. Still, Drovak didn't even blink. Maybe the other guy was just more observant.

"...Swarovski will accompany you to the crew quarters," the general was saying as Kat forced her attention back to where it belonged, knowing she'd missed something and hoping fervently it wouldn't come back to bite her. "He'll gather a sitrep from the rest of your unit while I meet with Colonel Corbin to sort out this mess." Drovak's expression settled into grim and steely lines as he headed for the lieutenant that had just appeared at the hangar bay doors. The man bore the *Cromwell's* command staff markings on his uniform and looked faintly annoyed.

The officers beside Kat shared an understandable air of disapproval. Colonel Corbin should have been here to meet the general himself... on time.

As the junior officer hurried toward them, moving deeper into the docking bay, he jolted like Kat had earlier, as if he received the mother of all static shocks. A peculiar look crossed his face, something between alarm and confusion, and then his features went oddly slack. His steps followed suit, turning jerky, then faltering. In short order, the man crumbled to the deck.

As a combat medic, Zaga moved into action first. Along with a handful of the docking bay personnel, Kat surged forward to help. Before Zaga could touch the man, peacekeepers detached from the newly arrived forces. As they closed in around the fallen man, edging Zaga aside, Drovak glanced in their direction, exchanging a veiled look, presumably with Swarovski, before tipping a subtle nod toward the exit. As the general turned away, Swarovski called out, "Stand down, Sergeant Asturrizaga. Corporal Alexander."

Kat frowned, her eyes going to the fallen airman before meeting the aide's gaze. "Excuse me, sir, but that man needs help."

Swarovski nodded, to all appearances unfazed.

"And he's receiving it." Then he gestured toward the exit. "Shall we?"

Kat was torn. She wanted to dislike him for his high-handedness alone—officer and general's aide aside—but she just couldn't do it. Between Captain Swarovski's pleasant, soothing voice and his calm demeanor, her offense just slid away. This man was absolutely nothing like Kat would have expected, and she found herself liking him for it. For some inexplicable reason. Damn him.

Even as she thought that, amusement lit Swarovski's gaze and a faint smile flitted across his lips. Again, he gestured, along with a slight gentlemanly bow that reminded her a bit of PawPaw when he hauled out his Sunday manners. Confused, Kat shook her head and moved toward the exit.

As the four of them headed for the Devils' quarters, Kat's knotted muscles slowly unwound their tension. No matter what shitstorm they had been through or what lay ahead, Kat finally sensed progressive steps had been taken to sort it all out. She felt relieved knowing that shortly General Drovak's aide—and by extension, the general himself—would know everything they did about the current situation and be in a position to do something about it.

Kat almost grinned as Scotch inserted himself between her and Swarovski, though his overt positioning surprised her. Great... a whole other potential shitstorm.

"Let's get this done," Scotch growled.

On that, they all agreed.

A pilot in an AeroCom uniform came through the hatch, blindsiding Cryson. For a single beat, Cryson felt nothing, then rage following swiftly after. The soldier stopped in the middle of his quarters. Despite the yellowish-green bruises marring his face and neck, the man emanated a hell of a lot more military bearing than anyone else on the *Destrier* ever had... except, perhaps, Petrov. That alone made Cryson hate him even more. His bearing made it seem like the man stood in judgment over all of them, though his very presence here signified a betrayal that carried a death sentence under most military tribunals.

Cryson hadn't expected this particular messenger. He had never met the man, but he sure as hell recognized the bastard.

"Sergeant Daire," Cryson snarled as he rose to circle the two-fold traitor, stopping within snapping distance of his face. "Care to explain why you felt the need to destroy my frigate and slaughter thirty of my men?"

Daire didn't even blink, let alone flinch. In a rasping voice, he said, "They weren't supposed to be there, and they wouldn't back off. I took the only course of action I could to preserve my cover and complete my mission."

"Not good enough!" Cryson muttered through clenched teeth as his fist shot out. The sergeant brought up his arm to deflect even as his other hand grabbed Cryson's wrist in a restraining grip.

"I am *not* one of your men. I am *not* under your command. I have successfully executed my mission to the best of my ability. We can either make the exchange I agreed to, or you can fuck off and tell your superiors *you* sacrificed the intel they're after to take a little vengeance out of *my* hide."

Cryson snatched his arm out of the man's hold.

"Where is it?"

Daire rolled his lip and gave Cryson a look he longed to smash flat.

"I'm desperate, not stupid. I don't hand you anything until I get what I was promised."

"Why are *you* even here?"

"Dalton's dead."

Cryson locked down tight, refusing to betray his shock. His contained rage rattled his insides. "Explain!"

"I wasn't the only operative. Another attempted to intercept the intel I had secured. I don't know who he answered to. He used gas to knock out my team so he could search our quarters. Dalton never woke up."

"And what intel do you believe you secured?"

The AeroCom sergeant's jaw flexed, and he swallowed as if something bitter filled his mouth. "The complete specs and plans for the McCormick-class attack vessel Cromwell, as well as the evidence implicating the Legion in the attempt to steal said data... oh, and a cryobag containing the body of the operative who tried to intercept all that. You'll find the body in the transport I arrived in, if it means anything to you."

The traitor would never know exactly how much it did.

Then, using only two fingers, the man reached into his pocket with slow, precise motions. Cryson tensed but did not move against him. He watched closely as Daire pulled something small and black from his pocket, holding it out flat on his palm.

"I also managed to secure Dalton's remains in case she has family out there waiting for her to come home."

Cryson's knees nearly buckled, and a single sharp hiss escaped him. Stiffening his stance, he reached out and accepted the small black cube.

"I couldn't retrieve her things without notice."

The rage surged up through every cell in Cryson's body as his hand closed over the cube. What the hell did he want with a bunch of things he'd never even set eyes on before? What he wanted was his daughter standing before him, hale and whole. Not in a fucking compressed cube in his fist. He couldn't even take satisfaction in killing the one responsible, though he took eminent pleasure in knowing he was dead.

Cryson's tone did not reveal one hint of his inner turmoil as he called out, "Denning!"

The hatch opened at his raised voice, and the two security personnel he'd ordered came in, followed by the ensign. Senior Corporals Dell'Aquila and Jenner flanked Daire before he could react. Not that the man was stupid enough to resist.

"Where is the intel?" Cryson asked again.

"Where's my son?" Daire countered.

For a long moment, they glared at one another, two fathers in torment with nothing to be done to lift the pain. Not that either of them would admit it. Not that either of them would concede. Without a blink, Cryson snarled at the traitor as he addressed his men.

"Take this man to Detention," he ordered the guards, then he turned to the ensign. "Denning, summon a work crew and follow me. We're going to search his shuttle."

In the end, the search took four hours and eight men. They did everything but take the shuttle apart before they found what they were looking for. Not that it had done them one bit of good. Cryson had the crew install a beacon, ensure the craft was still flight-capable, then shut it down until they could refit it for Legion use.

The files were useless in their current state, according to the computer tech on his monitor. Cryson hadn't expected anything less. Unfortunately, their efforts to secure the code from Sergeant Daire had so far been unsuccessful.

"How long before you can read them?" Cryson asked, his words rife with frustration.

The tech shrugged. "They're encrypted. Without the code key, who knows how long it will take? We could get lucky. Or we could roll a one."

Cryson scowled, then cocked his head at the nonsensical comment before responding in a low, controlled tone, "Then you better get working on it and improve our odds."

He cut the connection. Spinning his chair around, he shoved to his feet and paced the limited space. Every hour that passed increased the risk that Hirobon or some other concern would succeed where the Legion so far had failed. They could not allow that to happen. One way or the other, he needed to secure the *Cromwell* before they lost any hope of advantage, and the Teutonic Knights and their *objective* be damned.

Cryson would not let his daughter's death be in vain.

Pivoting back to his console, he called up a secure interstellar comm link and engaged encryption.

"Take the ship, now."

CHAPTER 14

THE SUDDEN BLARE OF A KLAXON YANKED KAT OUT OF SLUMBER. SHE JERKED upright and, by well-trained reflex, scrambled into her gear and to her feet in two minutes flat. The cabin lights came on dim, alternating with red warning flashes, giving the compartment a surreal nightmare vibe. By the strobing light, she could see her cabin mates not far behind her, both of them focused and intent. As Kat loaded her 10mm Phoenix pistol with frangible rounds safe to use aboard ship, the deck plates shuddered beneath her.

"What the hell?" Sergeant Kamilla Danzer swore as she grabbed the empty bunk above her for balance, pushing her pale blonde hair out of her eyes.

"Just get your shit together and fall out," muttered Warrant Officer Miki Mata. "We're not going to learn anything in here."

"Miki's right, Danzer, let's go," Kat said as she holstered her weapon.

As they hurried out into the common room, a faint smell of ozone, like a hot wire, wafted in through the vents. Kat's fingers tingled with the impulse to yank on a breather, reminded of the sleep gas that had targeted their former quarters. Sergeant Ryan stood in front of the hatch with Scotch beside him, a combat kit strapped to his back.

Kat fell into the second row of assembly next to True while Miki assumed a position to her other side. It took more effort than it should have for Kat to keep her attention focused on their new acting commander instead of Scotch. Assigned by Colonel Corbin, Kat didn't know or trust Ryan. Not that she wouldn't serve under him to the best of her training, but she held a lot more confidence in her teammate, and right now, every taut muscle from Scotch's forehead to his toes made her wonder why they were all standing here and not already moving out. Like a good airman, she remained silent and attentive. It wasn't her place to question Ryan's command. No matter how much she wanted to.

Not for the first time, she felt Sarge's absence and hoped with everything within her that he would be restored to them soon.

"The *Cromwell* has sustained damage from coordinated attacks by subversives attempting to seize control of the ship," Sergeant Ryan began once all the team had assembled, bringing Kat's attention back to the here and now. "Command is assessing the damage and what intel may have been compromised. The perpetrators have fled in appropriated AeroCom shuttles headed for Demeter, and we are being deployed in pursuit. This is an intercept mission. You have five minutes to gather your kit, fall into formation behind Sergeant Daniels, and meet me in the hangar bay. Dismissed."

As the team hustled to comply, the thrill of pending action rippled deep in Kat's bones, followed by a hunger for retribution in her belly. But, in the back of her brain, she wondered how AeroCom's flagship had been so easily infiltrated. Hell, how the *Devils* had been so easily infiltrated! And what other subversives remained to be ferreted out...?

"Move your slow-as-shit asses!" Scotch bellowed. "I'm not your mama waiting at this hatch to hand you your lunch box! Grab your gear. Column of twos. Fall in!"

A different kind of thrill ran through Kat as Scotch's familiar leadership reminded the Devils who they were, an elite and efficient team of special operatives. Why he had not been promoted to lead the 142nd Mobile SOT, she would never understand. Kat ducked into her cabin and snagged her kit, already packed and stowed beneath her bunk. She shrugged it on and joined the formation next to Kopecky, who stood behind Miki and Tivo. In short order, True, Danzer, and the rest of the team formed up behind Kat with a couple of minutes to spare.

Pivoting to face the hatch, Scotch ordered, "Atten-HUT! Secure packs!"

At his command, they each reached out and gripped the pack of the airman in front of them then tugged on it hard, confirming it was properly secured, a throwback to AeroCom's Air Force roots, though these weren't parachutes, and they weren't about to jump out into space. Still, tradition endured, and Kat had to admit it didn't hurt to make sure you weren't going to lose any of your gear. Of course, she could have done without True formed up behind her. He tugged vigorously and held on just a bit longer than he needed to. Kat knew if she looked behind her, his gaze would still be all too hopeful. So, she didn't.

"Sir, packs secure, sir!" they called out with one voice.

Scotch barked, "Move out!" then he led the double column of airmen down the wide corridor toward the troop-transport lift, setting the pace at double time. Kat noticed the klaxon had been terminated, as had the red warning flashes, but the compartment hatches they passed were in lockdown mode. An understandable precaution... It only made sense to restrict movement under the circumstances.

Pushing the thought away, Kat focused on the mission before her. It felt damned good to be taking action at last. But as they moved through the corridor, her nostrils flared and her gut clenched in protest as she picked up a faint and somehow familiar odor. On alert, she scanned the area around them but saw no sign of threat. And still, her nerves continued to *ping* like radar.

Scotch, do you smell something? she sent over his private frequency.

The enemy's fear?

Kat almost laughed. Almost. But her growing tension wouldn't let her.

I'm serious.

So am I. But I get what you mean. There's something on the air I can't identify, but Environmental hasn't sent up any alerts, and we have orders.

Something isn't right.

What part of orders do you not understand, corporal?

Sorry, sir, Kat responded more out of reflex than anything. She had a bad habit of forgetting Scotch ranked her.

Report it to Command and keep hoofing it. We have traitors to catch.

Kat did as instructed but remained alert, her gaze sweeping her surroundings and her right hand resting on the grip of her Phoenix 10mm. A second smell joined the first. As the new smell grew stronger, so did Kat's tension until it was all she could do to leave her pistol holstered.

Ozone... she smelled ozone again... and fried synthetics...

Just as the realization kicked in, Kat spun as muffled shouts sounded from a compartment to her right. Even as she noted the hatch was not in lockdown mode, it suddenly swung inward. Combatants streamed through the opening bearing an assortment of weapons, both issued and improvised. No doubt, they hadn't loaded theirs with frangible rounds.

Ambush! she broadcast over the squad band as commotions rose from key points along the column. Others echoed her cry. She shifted into a combat stance and drew her pistol, crouching to present the smallest target while maintaining maneuverability. Moving evasively, she fired on the closest attacker.

As the rounds flew, chatter lit up the squad band.

Medic! Rear column, right! Medic!

Command, we are under fire. I repeat, under fire. Subversives engaged, D20:CdAlpha15.

Acknowledged. Reinforcements are on the way.

Disabling shots if possible, kill shots if necessary!

And above it all, the red flashing lights strobed as the klaxon blared.

With a grimace, Kat filtered it all out. *Aim, fire, move. Aim, fire, move. Aim, fire, move.* A bullet grazed her arm, just creasing her sleeve, but her shot took down her target. She continued firing until she emptied her weapon, then ducked behind a support strut to reload.

Kat! Look out! In the chaos, she couldn't identify the voice, but her head snapped up to see a subversive approaching from the head of the column take clear aim at her chest from close range. Kat dove away from her position but could feel the shooter track her trajectory. The sound of the actual shot firing blended seamlessly into the cacophony of combat. Though she couldn't hear it, she felt her chest muscles clench in anticipation as her body hit the deck, but she felt no impact.

Kat! This time, the voice was Scotch's. She didn't know what stunned her more, the depth of anguish in that one word, or the answering sensation deep in her gut. His pain tore through her worse than any round. She silenced her squad band before the distraction got her killed.

As she rolled up facing the direction of the threat, she snapped her pistol closed and brought it to bear just in time to see Sergeant Oren Truitt place himself between her and the subversive taking aim at her for a second shot. Moments later, True jerked and crumpled to his knees, the back of his kit spotted with blood, the only evidence his gear had absorbed a kill shot from the wrong direction. In the sudden silence, a single shot rang true before Oren and his weapon fell to the deck, the enemy tumbling right after.

"No!" Kat screamed aloud, her nose burning with the sharp, smoky odor of spent ordnance. Teeth clenched, she raised her now-loaded weapon and scanned the zone for another target, rotating full circle, but the rest of the subversives were either dead or fled.

She remained so focused that she barely noticed the faint tingle up her jaw as her squad band re-engaged on its own. Well, with outside help, anyway.

Corporal Alexander. Kat nearly jumped at the sudden low, lethal growl over what she hoped was her private frequency. *If you ever shut down you're 'band in combat again, I will hand you your ass fifty ways to Sunday. Am I completely understood?*

She holstered her weapon and slowly pivoted. It took all her effort not to flinch away from Scotch as she had never seen him before, his every muscle tauter than a twisted wire, his expression blank save for the fury smoldering in his gaze. "Ever," he bit off aloud, just inches from her face.

Kat gave him a sharp nod, for the first time *ever,* afraid to speak in his presence.

He nodded back, then jerked his gaze away, his eyes briefly closing only to snap open once more. She wouldn't have noticed the way he worked his jaw to loosen the muscles if she hadn't been so close. He took a distancing step back and scanned the hazy corridor, his gaze locking on the makeshift triage just past what would have been the end of the column.

"Corpsman, report."

At Scotch's command, the man seemingly in charge of the wounded straightened and turned. Beneath the smoke residue and blood, Kat was startled to recognize him as Corpsman Kane, the medical personnel who'd delivered Brockmann's remains forever ago, before Kat had reason to question anyone's loyalties.

"Sir, mostly superficial injuries, already treated on-site," Kane answered, his expression neutral... numb. "Two seriously wounded, Sergeants Jamal Kramer and Danny Mack, currently being transported to the medbay." And here he looked down, hiding signs of pain medical personnel are taught to hide. "One fatality, Sergeant Oren Truitt, awaiting transport to the morgue."

The tension in Scotch's jaw ratcheted up again.

"Thank you, Corpsman. Please proceed."

Kane glanced at Kat's arm. "Here, just let me take care of that..."

Kat blinked, confused, having all but forgotten the graze on her arm, realizing its stinging only after the corpsman tugged her around to clean and patch it up. She murmured her thanks, but Kane had already returned to the wounded.

Beside her, Scotch turned and took two strides toward the nearest open compartment. The last one Kat had passed when the attackers struck. Along his way, Scotch delivered a solid kick to the traitorous corpse in his path, sending the dead weight sliding out of his way, smearing blood across the deck. Kat had never seen Scotch like this before, but she also would never forget that the wiseass he showed the world hid a powerful titan. With healthy caution and no little respect, she moved up behind him to peer into the compartment that had hidden the subversives.

Past his shoulder, Kat glimpsed what appeared to be a smoldering crewman sprawled on the compartment deck. A scorch mark in the outline of his shoe showing where he had stood, and muddy fluid spread out from him in a sluggish puddle in mimicry of the blood out in the corridor. It reminded her of the stuff that had come from pseudo-Ghei's body back when this mess had all started.

"I don't see any tasers around, do you?" Kat murmured.

That startled a chuckle from Scotch, but he remained otherwise silent as he stepped into the compartment and crouched beside the, for lack of a better word, body. He didn't touch it but traced the air above the areas of open 'skin.' Kat watched him closely and wondered what pieces he was cobbling together. Finally, he pivoted and met her gaze. She watched his nostrils flare as he drew a deep breath through his nose.

"Two smells," he said after a moment. "First one's the same as when you fried Ghei."

Kat nodded, surprised she hadn't realized it sooner, totally unsurprised at how it had put her on edge even before she found herself in the middle of a firefight.

"The other one, though..." He frowned and fell silent.

"The other one..." Kat prompted.

Scotch's brow furrowed. "Well, call me crazy, but it smells like the exhaust that came off the *Venture* when she docked."

Someone cleared their throat in the doorway, sending both Kat and Scotch back into full combat mode, spinning around with their weapons in their grip without even a thought in between. Even so, Scotch had the presence of mind to place his hand on the barrel of Kat's pistol directing it down.

"Kind of a dumbass move to startle two operatives right after a battle, don't you think?" Scotch muttered at the security member standing in the door.

The man ignored his words, just stepping to the side with a clear gesture. "Excuse me, sir, but I'm going to have to insist both of you vacate the compartment and return to quarters. Captain Swarovski will contact you there with further instructions."

For a moment, Kat wondered if hers would need to be the restraining hand this time as the man's curt tone rubbed up against what had to be Scotch's last nerve. He straightened and somehow seemed to broaden at the same time, projecting alpha vibes like Kat had never seen him do before. She started to step forward when Scotch just gave the man a dismissive look and brushed past him.

"Dayum..." Kat murmured beneath her breath as she followed.

"Gather your gear and form up!" Scotch called out to the members of the 142nd. Kat scrambled around his bulk and fell in beside Tivo in column formation. "Back to barracks!"

They retraced their steps without a further word, moving a bit slower to accommodate those wounded in the encounter.

Swarovski waited for them in the common room. He sat silently to the side in the same chair Kat had occupied another lifetime ago when True and Campbell had dueled with makeshift pool cues over a point of 'honor.' She nearly heaved at the memory. In surreal detachment, she realized both men were dead now, only one of them a hero. Well, to her, anyway. Kat swiftly compartmentalized that thought. She'd haul it out later when functioning wasn't a priority. On impulse, she silently murmured the bedtime prayer for Truitt in St. Sue's memory and vowed to learn a proper memorial prayer when the universe wasn't going to shit around her.

Turning her attention back to Swarovski, Kat nearly did a double-take as the situation dipped back down into surreal. The lieutenant sat there, petting a small bundle of fur in his lap. Said furball looked up at Kat with big yellow-green eyes. A mask of brown-and-black stripes framed its tiny white muzzle. The young cat met her gaze and gave a silent meow. Kat's head slowly tilted to the side as she attempted to resolve the sight before her with the chaos of the last hour.

"A Parr scout assigned to me for training," Swarovski answered the question she hadn't asked. "Given the... situation... I was hesitant to leave Spec in my quarters."

Kat drew a deep breath and nodded, like any of that made sense to her right now. She had heard of Parr scouts, though, genetically modified cats linked to a human handler via a PsiComm neural net. The technology had originally been developed by Dr. Ty McPherren for human modification. If Kat remembered correctly, the controversial procedure had been abandoned when one of the subjects was later discovered to have been pregnant during the time of testing. The experimental mods had translated to the child with unpredictable—and uncontrolled—effects, creating a new subspecies of augmented humans, dubbed Ty'Pherreins. The early generations of Tys had been unstable, but they had adapted and acquired control by the third and fourth generations, their mental traits remaining dormant until puberty. They bred true with each other for light eyes, pale hair, and powerful psionics.

Jonathan Parr later adapted the technique for the scout program.

This was the first time Kat had ever, well, met a Parr, she supposed. The results had apparently been more satisfactory with feline subjects.

The cat meowed a second time, again silently. The sight so tugged her heart that Kat almost made the sound for him. Only the impulse nearly shook a hysterical giggle from her, so she throttled that down and just stood there, not knowing what else to do, bumping like a reed in the water as the others moved past her. Except for one. She felt Scotch's solid presence stop at her back, his hand coming to rest on her shoulder.

"Go on, Kittie Kat," he murmured low and gentle. "Clean yourself up and eat some grub."

Then Kat noticed what she'd missed before. Behind Swarovski, on their battered conference table, someone had laid out a buffet-style spread that had to have come from the officers' mess, clearly courtesy of General Drovak. Kat hadn't smelled a bit of it over the stench of blood and spent ordnance burned into her sinuses. Likely the others couldn't either, but just the same, they had already lined up and were filling their plates. At a nudge from Scotch, Kat joined them, ignoring the food and stimulant beverages on the table to grab a mug of sugar-laden tea to rebalance her shocked system and stave off an adrenaline crash.

That was the plan, anyway.

As she settled in a chair far across the room from Swarovski, Scotch headed her way with two plates of food in his hands. Kat groaned. Too worn out to argue, she accepted the smaller of the two. Nothing outrageous. Just a mound of pasta and protein. Though, it did look like a higher grade of tank meat than they served in the General Mess. Scotch had brought her high-energy fare in a much more modest portion than filled his own plate, she noticed as he settled in the chair beside her and methodically began to consume his meal. When she just watched him, he frowned and gestured to what he'd brought her.

"Eat, *now*, while you have the chance. Once they have the intel they need, they'll send us right back out again. No knowing how soon that will be."

Kat knew he was right. She didn't like it, but she knew. Didn't mean she could bring herself to eat.

"Are you going to force me to make that an order?"

Knowing he wouldn't let up, Kat followed his example, methodically emptying her plate without tasting one blessed bite of it. Probably just as well... less likely to come back up that way. As she shoveled in the food, she focused on the rough, worn texture of the chair beneath her, the cool, smooth metal of the utensils in her hand, the murmur of those around her as the others decompressed in their own way, losing herself in the tactile data, so she didn't have to think.

As the eating slowed and the chatter increased, Kat noticed Swarovski lift Spec from his lap and place him on the ground before standing. The catling tilted his head back and peered at his handler a moment, then stretched, his stubby little front legs extended before him, and his back arched. When he straightened, the Parr scout made right for Kat as Swarovski started walking the room, stopping briefly to speak with the other members of the team. Kat groaned as Spec settled at her feet, tail curled prettily and tucked against his side. Slow and steady, the cat looked up at her and silently meowed.

Scotch chuckled beside her. "Go on, airman," he murmured.

Kat had no clue which of them he spoke to, but Spec gathered his haunches beneath himself, crouched there a moment, then gave his butt a little wiggle before jumping to the arm of her chair. Not wanting to hurt his dignity, Kat pressed her lips tight against the laugh that wanted to burst out.

Another silent meow.

Didn't matter. Kat got the message. With a weary smile, she handed Scotch her mostly empty plate and sat still as the cat jumped into her lap, where he curled up and began to purr. By sheer impulse, Kat dropped her hand and stroked Spec's fur, the softness of it immediately uncoiling a measure of the tension knotting her belly.

Scotch chuckled again and may have muttered 'lucky cat' as he rose to his feet and walked away with their plates. He moved clear across the room before Kat heard his parting comment over her private frequency. No doubt, he planned it that way.

Lord, have mercy, I'd dearly love to hear you make that sound...

Before Kat could respond—as if she even knew what she would say—Swarovski cleared his throat.

"Your attention, please."

The room fell silent, and all eyes turned toward the lieutenant.

"Thank you. And thank you for your service today... and your sacrifice. Beyond the injuries and casualties sustained by your team, your acting commander, Sergeant Ryan, was injured in a separate encounter at the docking bay. In light of these events and the delay they caused, your mission has been postponed. The subversives that managed to get clear of the *Cromwell* have moved beyond sensor range, and those captured are being interrogated in an attempt to determine where the others have fled. Once we have a further course of action, you will receive new orders. In the meantime, tend to your wounded and recover.

"If you should discover any relevant information, report it to Sergeant Daniels immediately." With that last statement, Swarovski nodded toward Scotch. Probably a good thing, as none of them thought of him as Sergeant Daniels with any regularity. "Again, thank you. I will leave you to your rest."

Once he finished speaking, the hatch opened, and a detail of airmen bearing catering corps markings filed in. They headed toward the now-demolished buffet, clearing up the mess and departing in short order. As they left, Kat noticed what looked like an armed escort waiting in the corridor.

Swarovski nodded farewell, then turned toward the outer hatch, pausing as Spec hopped from her lap and scampered after him. Kat watched Swarovski bend down to scoop the cat up and deposit him on his right shoulder, where his uniform seemed extra padded. As they left, Kat stood up and headed for her bunk, trying to ignore two things: how cold her lap now felt and Scotch's earlier wisecrack.

CHAPTER 15

WHEN CORPSMAN KANE ENTERED THE DEVILS' BARRACKS WITH TRUE'S remains and personal effects, it hit Kat like a sudden jolt from a live wire. They all knew it was coming, but it still took her by surprise. The last time Kane had crossed their threshold, it had been to deliver Brockmann. This time, as he handed Oren Truitt's cubed remains to Scotch, Kat wanted to scream. Though True had been just a friend...

No. She hadn't held any romantic feelings toward him, but she could no longer think of True as *just* anything. If it hadn't been for his sacrifice, she would have been the one cubed. Kat stepped forward, already drawing her combat knife. Scotch nodded solemnly. With understanding in his gaze, he handed her the cube.

Kat wanted to say something. *Needed* to say something. But what?

She thought again of Brockmann. *St. Sue*, saying a prayer for the fallen.

Kat's lips started to move without her conscious thought behind them. Low and steady, reverent. "Yea, though I walk through the Valley of the shadow of Death, I shall fear no evil..." and then her memory failed. She didn't falter. She just fell silent, frustration bringing angry tears to her eyes as she searched her brain for the correct words.

Only, into the awkward silence, Scotch chuckled deep and low before raising his deep voice. "...because I am the meanest motherfucker in the Valley..." he finished for her, and she wanted to yell at him. She wanted to give him hell because nothing felt more inappropriate for Oren Truitt, one of the most awkward and decent and sweetest guys she had ever met or served with. But then she stopped as a series of images flashed across her memory. Moments she hadn't even realized had registered on her thoughts. *True's fierce expression as he called out her name in warning. His sure grip as he brought up his pistol. His steady aim as he took out the enemy, despite the fatal hit he had taken. The unwavering way he'd stood between her and Death.*

However True had been in the downtime, in his honest heart, that wasn't all he had been.

Sergeant Oren Truitt had been a warrior, elite and exemplary, full of courage and honor and steel.

Looking at the other Devils before her, they held the same conviction.

Without another word, Kat raised her blade to his compressed-carbon cube and etched the first line. In silence, the rest of the Devils followed suit until Scotch made the final cut and handed back the cube.

Kat closed her fingers around it and silently swore by everything within her that True would have vengeance.

"You know," Scotch said, breaking the silence. "He didn't get his handle for being loyal, though he certainly was that..."

Looking up, Kat took the lure. "How'd he get it?"

"There was not one thing that man aimed at that he didn't hit. And I will tell you... we certainly put him to the test. Distance, size, orbital velocity... none of that made a difference. Crack shot every time," Scotch told her, starting up a round of reminiscing meant to blot out the horror of their friend's ending. As he guided her to a chair, others settled around them, while a few disappeared into their quarters, only to return with enough alcohol to drink away a month's worth of vice credits, along with glasses for everyone.

Kat looked around for Corpsman Kane, wanting to thank him, and invite him to have a drink, but at some point, he must have ducked out, leaving the bag containing True's personal effects on the table closest to the door.

Turning back, Kat set the cube in a temporary place of honor and accepted the glass Scotch handed her, settling in to pay tribute to her friend as the Devils told tales well into the night.

Gaze lowered and head bowed, Yuki-ko transversed the hallways of Hirobon's headquarters with slow, gliding steps, ever mindful of impressions. Since the age of five—when her mother's spirit entered the land of darkness—Yuki-ko had learned to carefully choreograph her every move, holding her place by rigid discipline. Serenity and control her best-honed weapons in the corporate landscape where she had been raised.

Always before, she had conducted herself to her father's expectations. This was the first time she had failed him, causing him and Hirobon to lose face before all their corporate holdings, but worst of all, before their competitors.

Entering her chambers at last, even here she did not relax her pose. Without glancing, she ran a hand over a control panel beside the door. One touch locked the chamber. A second touch transformed the lighting to a softly dappled shadow-and-light reminiscent of the sun's rays dancing through layers of thick cherry blossoms. A third touch and the soothing song of the *uguisu*—the Japanese bush warbler—caressed her ears, easing the tension of her most recent audience with her father.

Closing her eyes, Yuki leaned against the door and, by long practice, released the tension born of his continued disappointment in her. For once, she deserved his judgment. Ever dutiful, Yuki-ko had failed her father in only two things: her gender and delivering the data on the *Cromwell*. On only one of those points could she redeem herself. She need only figure out how, a task not well assisted by her current agitation.

One deep, slow breath after the next, she commanded her spirit to relax. Only after the sharp pain between her brows eased to its ever-present ache did she straighten and, with more gliding steps, move to the low meditation table at the center of the chamber. With the precision of an oft-repeated ceremony, she turned to the side and indulged in her sole rebellion, lighting a waiting stick of incense, releasing the soothing scent of lotus flower into the chamber. As soon as the embers glowed, she covered the stick with a permeable plastic shield, allowing only the scent to circulate. Open flames—even only embers—were not allowed in the oxygen-rich atmosphere of the station. She could have used the station's scent generators, as her father did, but she felt the technology dishonored the tradition.

Turning back to the mediation table, Yuki knelt upon the cushion built into the deck and gently pressed the first of three buttons on the side of the table. Light blossomed along the far edge, familiar features limned in a soft glow, the muted colors vibrant in Yuki-ko's memory. She bowed low to the holographic images of her *o-kaa-san*—mother—and *sobo*—grandmother. In her heart, she never stopped longing for their presence, while in her mind, she held only relief they had been spared the burden of false honor to which her father clung.

With ruthless control, Yuki-ko smothered the child of that thought. This was not the place for the tension of such musings.

The honoring of her ancestors observed, Yuki-ko turned her gaze to the table before her. Truly a feat of engineering to behold. Within the clear thick polymer of its surface lay the microcosm of her grandmother's Zen garden. Perfection reproduced in every minute detail, from the shrubs and mossy stones to the pond and the glistening white sand, all surrounding an elegant bonsai trained by her mother Kazuy's hand. One could note a light breeze swaying the reeds that grew from the pond if one peered closely. Once, she would swear, the garden had even cast a gentle rain. Real rain, not a projection, regulated by the table, though Yuki-ko could not explain the workings of the technology. Understanding was not required for appreciation.

She opened a compartment in the table's base and removed a seemingly simple bamboo wand. Taking a centering breath, she drew the wand across the table's surface, watching the 'waves' form below as if she drew a rake through the sand. The wand contained microsensors corresponding to sensors in the base of the table. Not traditional, but sand was as restricted as flame in an environment sustained by sensitive equipment, where gravity could not always be guaranteed.

Yuki-ko continued to work her wand, emptying her thoughts and embracing Zen. With each pass, she released her tension as her grandmother had taught her long ago, her spirit cradled by the peace of *Sobo's* garden. As she began her third pass through the sand, circling stone and water and moss, a chime sounded, breaking the calm fostered by the songbird's music.

"Fuzaken na yo!" Even as the curse left her lips, Yuki-ko felt shame fill her being, displacing the calm she had achieved. Raising a silent plea to her mother and grandmother for forgiveness, Yuki-ko drew composure and serenity around herself like armor, carefully put away her precious wand, and composed her expression before rising and moving to her work surface, tucked away behind a sliding screen in the corner of the room. Pressing the controls built into the desktop, Yuki-ko restored the room to its neutral aspect before sitting at her console and answering the comm. An image of a bald man appeared, a familiar *gaikokujin*—foreigner—working for Hirobon interests among the Legion forces. His name was Larry Dell'Aquila, and he held loyalty only to himself. Too fond of women and drink and comfortable ways, and unconcerned with anyone's causes, even his own. A cunning man without honor but much greed. She trusted him no further than the moment he received his compensation. But she would be unwise not to use him. Such men were the only means her people had of infiltrating a group as distinct as the Legion.

"Speak," Yuki-ko instructed him.

He sneered. "What am I, a dog?"

"If you have nothing to tell me, you waste my time," she answered coolly, reaching to disengage the connection. This man annoyed her, and not merely because he had disturbed her meditation.

"Whatever, but I thought you'd like to know that the Legion is a step ahead of you... and you're a step further back than you thought you were."

Yuki-ko leaned forward, her features just as expressionless, but her eyes narrowing. "Explain yourself."

"Ah... we're getting ahead of things. I don't believe we've discussed my finder's fee."

With a few taps on the keys before her, Yuki-ko called up her... discretionary fund, entered the standard figure, and hit send.

Dell'Aquila looked down as something chimed on his end. When he looked up, his pale blue eyes shone bright and calculating. He gave a slight nod and stroked his salt-and-pepper goatee. "Nice..." he said, drawing out the word. "But not enough."

"Excuse me?"

"No... not nearly enough. Not when I'm about to hand you the big prize. Not when I have intel you *need* to know."

Yuki-ko went still, her expression neutral but the lines of her body taut.

"Please, explain," she asked, her tone more polite at that moment than the spirit she held within her. Dell'Aquila pointedly looked down and raised one eyebrow.

Pressing her lips thin, Yuki-ko tapped sharply on a few more keys, all the while calculating exactly how to reveal her inside source to his compatriots without exposing herself.

As a second chime sounded over the comm, the man broke into a smug smile, making Yuki-ko long for a single moment in his presence with her katana in her hand. He reminded her of nothing so much as a malevolent Buddha.

"Explain, now," she commanded.

The smile disappeared, replaced by a sneer.

"Cryson has the data on the *Cromwell*," he told her, followed by a long and manipulative pause.

"And?" Yuki-ko prompted, her patience exhausted by this petty man.

"Annnd... the body of one of your Ronin. An AeroCom pilot named Campbell."

The blood drained from Yuki-ko's face until her entire body felt like ice, yet still, she maintained composure. "You are ill-informed. A Ronin has no master."

"Whatever you tell yourself," Dell'Aquila said with a smirk. "Either way, he did your bidding. Now Campbell's dead, and you are screwed..." The man paused like the opportunistic pig he was. "Unless..."

"Do not play games with me. Name your price."

His figure was immaterial. The rest of his lewd demands cemented her desire to end his petty existence in the most satisfying manner... and by satisfying, she fully intended painful. Perhaps she was, in fact, too much her father's daughter, but she owed no honor to an honorless man.

Yuki-ko nodded and lowered her gaze, staring at the console through thick, dark lashes. "Leave the body, but send me the data, and I swear to free you from your service to the Legion."

"And the rest?"

"Send me the data," she responded before cutting the connection, leaving him to make what he would of her answer.

Ready to kill, Cryson marched into Detention and straight to the cell holding Sergeant Daire. "Open this," he snapped at the guard, stalking inside when the man complied. Part of him noted the sorry state of the AeroCom traitor, fresh bruises and contusions, the careful way he held himself, speaking of possible fractures. Some of the crew must have discovered who he was.

Cryson restrained himself from adding to Daire's tally of injuries, but only just barely. For now.

"What the hell are you trying to pull?" he snarled, thrusting out the cube, the upward-facing surface revealing carefully etched writing: *Warrant Officer Armand Campbell.*

Daire slowly dropped his gaze as if even that small effort pained him.

"Not pulling a thing. That is her. If you don't believe me, check the body in my shuttle. *That* was Campbell."

Cryson nodded to one of the guards milling in the corridor. Straightening, the man pivoted and left to carry out the unspoken order. Satisfied, Cryson turned back to Daire. "Why would this say Campbell, then?"

"I can't say for sure," Daire answered with just a hint of a shrug. "She was found in his quarters. If I had to guess, she fooled the sensor into believing she was Campbell to gain access. Why, I couldn't say." He nodded at the cube. "Easy enough to confirm if you scan the chip embedded in there. I am sure you'll find confirmation if you dig deep enough."

"Sure, because you placed it there?"

Despite his status and his current state, the man had the nerve to roll his eyes. "What the hell would that accomplish? You wanted the data. I secured the data."

Fed up beyond measure, Cryson lunged for the man, slamming him against the bulkhead and pinning him there, taking pleasure in Daire's sharp gasp and the faint sound of broken bones grinding. "Give me the encryption code."

Daire smirked, though signs of pain limned his lips. "Do you truly believe you found the real files? I told you, I'm not that stupid. You've found the evidence against the Legion, but the rest of the data won't do you a damned bit of good, even with the code."

Growling in frustration, Cryson slammed Daire again before letting go and whirling away. "See what you can get out of him," he growled as he passed the guards.

"Hey, Cryson... where's my son?" Daire's taunt followed Cryson out of the Detention Block.

Hell.

As much as he didn't trust Daire, Cryson needed to know. On the way back to his quarters, he stopped by Medical.

"I need a scan of this," he ordered, handing over the cube.

The orderly looked confused. "Sir?"

"That contains an AeroCom radio frequency tag. I need a scan of the data it contains."

"Yes, sir... but..."

"But what?" he said, working hard to keep the growl from his voice.

"I can scan it, but I can't read it. That'll take one of the com specialists."

"Just do it!" Cryson ordered through clenched teeth. "Now! The same for the body being sent up from the docking module. Report to me immediately with the findings."

"Yes, sir!"

Cryson stalked to his quarters, too fed up to deal with anything more.

As he entered, a priority message alert flashed on his console.

He stopped still just inside the hatch. Closing it behind him—along with his eyes—he just stood there a moment, forcing himself to breathe deep and slow. Once he had regained control, he crossed the deck and sat before his console, keying in the security code to unlock the message:

<<Acquisition Failed. Operatives Compromised. Inbound.>>

"Fuck!"

CHAPTER 16

K AT WOKE THE NEXT 'MORNING' WITH HER HAND RESTING ON TRUE'S CUBE, and her slightly pounding head burrowed beneath her pillow. Groaning, she pulled herself into a tight ball, leaving the cube sitting on the edge of her bunk, gleaming faintly in the slowly brightening light, in silent recrimination. She burrowed even deeper as the sound of Scotch's voice rose out in the common room.

"Mornin', ladies..." He drew out the words, the faintest hint of his southern drawl flitting through them as he addressed the whole team. "Or should I say afternoon? Get your butts out of those bunks! Physical Training in thirty minutes, Deck 15, Corridor Gamma-7, Compartment 276."

A chorus of good-natured insults rose in response, followed by the sounds of every Devil scrambling from their bunks. Kat was no exception. Snaking her hand out, she grabbed Truitt's cube and shoved it beneath her pillow. She then checked the pocket of her fatigues to make sure the backup drive was still in place—always on her person until she figured out what the hell to do with it. Finally, she swung her feet to the deck and pushed herself upright, groaning under her breath.

The next two hours disappeared in a haze. Eventually, Kat's muscles loosened and limbered but nowhere near peak efficiency. With each leaden step and push-up, she regretted overindulging the night before, tribute or not. Unwinding was one thing, but each of them had a responsibility to maintain combat readiness. Lives could depend on their physical fitness and not just their own.

Scotch pushed them for another solid hour before showing some mercy. "Hit the showers and get some chow," he ordered, sounding way too energized. "The rest of the afternoon is your own."

Exhausted, Kat took the fastest ion shower she could manage and still slough off the stink. As a nod to breakfast, she grabbed a protein bar from the supply in the locker room on her way out, fully intending to crawl back into her bunk for the rest of her free time.

As she joined a loose herd of her teammates heading back to quarters, they passed Scotch leaning next to the corridor hatch, his sweat-dampened tee shirt and shorts clinging to his body. Forcing her gaze away, Kat gnawed on her bar and locked her eyes on Miki's back.

"Don't forget to hydrate, people," Scotch called out, giving her a pointed look as he held out a water bulb in front of her until she glanced his way and grudgingly took it.

A dull throb already pulsed at her temple, a sure sign of dehydration; from last night's drinking or this morning's workout, it didn't matter which. Only a fool disregarded the signs.

Kat popped the seal on the bulb and slowly sipped at the contents, as much to ignore Scotch falling into step beside her as to pace herself. She was only a little annoyed at how he always looked out for her. With anyone else, she'd feel a burning need to prove she could handle herself. With Scotch, there was no point. When he got a notion of what she needed, he carried it through with determination, not disrespect.

Not that he showed her preferential treatment. Team was family. He looked out for them all. It just seemed that, well recently, he watched out for her a touch more than he had before.

Kat must have zoned. Scotch gave her a nudge with his shoulder, guiding her through the hatch into the common room. Pressing another bulb into her hand, he pointed her in the direction of her bunk. Mortification set in. Standing straight and setting her jaw, Kat pulled away. She was stronger than this. She'd been taking care of herself her entire life, and she was certainly capable of continuing that now.

They stopped in the middle of the common room.

Kat met his gaze with a determination of her own, only to falter at what she saw. Or thought she saw. There, then gone. The faintest echo of the hope and doubt and vulnerability she'd seen in Truitt's eyes when he tried to ask her out after they'd brought Brockmann home. Kat blinked and looked again.

This time she saw only an open expression of pride.

In confusion, she stepped back, and the moment broke. Scotch gave her a nod before moving past her to his own quarters, murmuring privately over her bonejack, *Drink up, Kittie Kat, then get some rest. You'll feel better.*

In the end, sleep would not come.

Kat lay there with a washcloth draped over her eyes to shield against the light, drawing deep, slow breaths and letting them out just as slowly. With each breath, her muscles loosened, and her mind cleared, but she could not achieve deeper respite. Rather than fight it, she let her mind wander where it would, letting it decompress in the rare moment of stillness.

So much had happened so quickly. Her thoughts felt scattered in the resulting whirlwind, reduced to reactive reflex when the situation called for careful deliberation. In this moment, she was content simply to breathe, too tired to concern herself with more.

She wasn't one to meditate, but out on the prairie, beneath the stars and surrounded by lowing cattle... PawPaw had taught her the value of emptying her thoughts and giving the universe a chance to fill the space with what mattered.

After what could have been hours... or only minutes... Kat tucked her washcloth in a cubby built into the bunk and slowly sat up, swinging her feet to the deck. She slid her hand beneath her pillow and brought out Truitt's cube. She couldn't remember how she'd ended up with it, but she knew what she needed to do.

Climbing to her feet, she went looking for Scotch.

She found him by himself in the common room, drinking the bootblack AeroCom called coffee. He wore such a hangdog expression she almost offered up one of her remaining vice credits so he could have the real thing.

Then he opened his mouth.

"Did you drink?"

Kat rolled her eyes. She had, but she'd be damned if she was going to encourage his mother-henning. Sitting across from him, she ignored his question and set the carbon cube on the table.

"Didn't Sarge have a tribute box where he kept these safe?"

Scotch's expression grew somber as he nodded, his hand reaching out to trace the marks newly etched into the cube's surface. "Last night, you were upset, worried he wouldn't... know anyone inside, so we let you hold on to it."

Inwardly, Kat groaned and reached for a water bulb from the rack. She hadn't realized she'd gotten *that* smashed. Scotch went on, true to form.

"We figured we owed him one last night in bed with a sexy lady."

At his words, Kat flinched, suddenly overwhelmed by a flashback of True's hopeful expression when he'd asked her out, followed by an intense flood of guilt and remorse. Snatching up the cube, she headed toward the quarters Scotch shared with Zaga, the other tech sergeant on the team. She couldn't imagine Scotch would have put Sarge's stuff anywhere else when Ryan took over his quarters.

"Coming?" she growled over her shoulder.

It took just a stride or two for Scotch to catch up.

When he rounded in front of her and blocked her path, Kat snapped. She brought her clenched fists up, slamming them against his chest. He didn't stop her. Again, she hit, this time harder, flinching as the corner of True's cube scored him, leaving a thin ribbon of blood beading his neck. As she swung again, he caught her hands and held them in a firm but careful grip.

"Why are you such a pain?" she asked, her teeth clenched and tears streaming down her face. "Always cracking jokes. Always being a wiseass."

Scotch got real quiet for a moment, his gaze dropping. It looked like he might not answer. Then he hunched down, forcing her to look at him. The serious look in his usually mischievous eyes stunned her.

"My Pop told me when I signed up, 'When the shit hits the fan, you can laugh, or you can cry. You choose.' I will choose to laugh every damn time because that will put more fear in the hearts of those sons of bitches than anything else I could do.

"Now... what's got you so torn up?" he asked, dropping his voice low enough only she could hear, even though they were alone.

Her tears welled even more, and when she tried to speak, her jaw shook.

"Shhhh... shhhh..." Scotch murmured, his expression turning bleak as he drew her close. "It's okay... I'm sorry. I didn't realize..."

Frantically, Kat shook her head, pushing back out of his grip.

"N-no! No..." she managed, still shaking. She smacked his chest again, this time with her empty hand, palm flat, suddenly desperate for him to understand that he'd misunderstood. "I... I said *no*, and I meant it... and he died for me anyway."

Scotch's eyes widened as he caught her meaning. He held her gaze and slowly, gently drew her back in. A tremor ran through her body, and she tilted her head back, afraid to lose his eyes, but Scotch folded her in his arms and dropped the tenderest of kisses atop her head.

She had no idea where it came from, but Kat muttered a swift "Hell, no!"

Truitt's cube fell from her grip as she grabbed onto Scotch's shirt and yanked herself up the length of him, lean, muscular thighs anchoring her around his waist so she could finally give in, pressing her lips to his in a kiss salty and sweet and satisfying. Not to mention hotter than sin.

When Scotch moaned and brought his arms up to support her, Kat stiffened, suddenly and instantly aware of what she'd done. She tried to scrabble away, but he wouldn't let her.

"Oh, hell, *yeah!*" he murmured back, holding tight so she couldn't shimmy down again. "And I dearly *did* love hearing you make that sound..."

He kissed her once more, this time taking charge—not one thing sweet about it—before groaning and carefully setting her on her feet. Before she could do more than stiffen her spine, he left through the outer hatch, his gait a little stiffer than usual.

Not quite sure what happened... or what it meant... Kat carefully knelt to pick up True's cube. Brushing it off with a silent apology, she returned to her bunk.

Cryson sat before his console, just staring at the monitor, knowing he needed to report but unable to formulate the words. Idly, his fingers played over the touchpad in no particular order, leaving a senseless trail across the message window. While he watched, the letters vanished as a new window popped up displaying a familiar cross. Before he could react, an external source took over his system.

"Your attack on the *Cromwell* has threatened our whole operation," the Teutonic Knight said without preamble.

"How the hell are you accessing my console?"

"How the hell did you survive this long?"

Cryson grimaced. What were they, ten? He didn't bother answering. He also didn't bother asking how the Knight knew about the thwarted attack. It didn't matter at this point. Cryson fully expected to lose his command over this, but he would be damned if he would lose his self-respect kowtowing to this power-trip junkie.

"You were expressly ordered more than once to desist in your efforts to obtain the *Cromwell.*"

"Consider it field testing for your precious synthetics."

"They failed."

Cryson smirked. "Not surprised. They're clearly not ready yet. Better to know now, right?"

"*Why* did they fail? I want a full report on what happened."

"As soon as I debrief my operatives. Now, are we done here? I have work to do."

Cryson would swear the colors on the monitor darkened like a thundercloud as he waited for the Knight to answer, but that could just be his outlook on life readjusting.

"We are close to securing the objective. Be prepared for extraction."

With a grimace, Cryson nodded, but the link had already disconnected.

At some point, exhaustion must have defeated Kat's efforts to stay up, waiting for Scotch to return. She woke to the muffled sounds of laughter and hatches opening and closing. Scrambling to her feet, she grabbed Truitt's cube and headed for the common room.

Someone had set up the makeshift pool table in the far corner, where they held team meetings. A few members of the team lounged nearby, waiting for their turn, carbon-fiber rods leaning beside them. Truck and Tivo looked her way, but Colonel stayed focused on his shot. Truck waved her over in silent invitation. When she shook her head, he nodded and went back to the game.

Kat saw no sign of Scotch. Looking toward his quarters, she sighed, then looked down at the cube before straightening her shoulders and pushing herself forward. True deserved better than this. Time to find the tribute box and see him safe inside. Even so, Kat's strides slowed the closer she got to Scotch's hatch. Once she stood before it, she couldn't bring herself to knock—present her identchip to the hatch sensor. Rather visceral memories of earlier tugged her off balance.

"Everything okay, Kat?"

Pivoting, Kat found herself face to face with Zaga. Literally. Of Peruvian descent, he stood her height, but half again her build, all muscle.

"Uh, yeah, I just..." she grimaced as she floundered, holding up True's remains. "Just looking for the tribute box."

The tech sergeant's expression sobered. He might lead Beta Squad, but all of them were Devils. He tilted his head toward the hatch. "C'mon. Sarge's things are in here."

She followed him inside, tension buzzing like an electrostatic charge down her limbs. Zaga went past the bunks to the built-in storage lockers at the back. Just as in the compartment Kat shared, there were four bunks, two to a side, with room beneath the bottom bunks for two sets of footlockers. Which one belongs to Scotch? she wondered. Her gaze did not linger, though her thoughts briefly did before she yanked them back to the task at hand. An extra footlocker took up space at Zaga's feet.

With a slight frown, Kat looked around as if there were anything else she might have missed.

Zaga retrieved whatever he was after, then turned. "What's wrong?"

"Where are the rest of Sarge's things?"

"Rest? That's it." Zaga nodded to the footlocker at his feet.

The tension returned with a particularly sharp zap. Kat had not thought this through. She wanted to set True to rest, but she hadn't considered that that meant going into Sarge's personal gear.

"Listen, I have to go. Just make sure the hatch closes when you leave, okay?"

Kat nodded as Zaga moved past her but remained where she stood until he left. Bad enough to intrude, without showing the world. At least, that was what she told herself as she tried to unstick her feet from the deck. Was she doing the right thing? Or should she just leave the cube on top? Kat recoiled at that thought. A teammate's remains were sacred, not to be left unsecured, unprotected.

Shaking her shoulders to loosen them up, she moved forward and knelt in front of the footlocker. It appeared unlocked. She slid the toggles to each side, popping the fasteners, and raised the lid. Carefully lifting out the inset drawer of precisely folded spare uniforms and kit, Kat set it aside, turning back to the personal effects and equipment revealed beneath. She had hoped that the box would be close to the top, easy to access without having to disturb Sarge's privacy too much. No such luck. Gingerly, she removed the surface objects. A small white Bible. A bundle of letters. A sad, worn shell of a bear, gutted of its stuffing, but clearly once well-loved and abused.

She frowned as she picked up the bear, expecting limp fabric and nothing more. Instead, some inner content held the folded shape stiff, crackling as she gripped it.

"Care to explain how you got in here, corporal?"

At the sudden voice, Kat pivoted and dropped the memory of a bear as she spied Scotch in the hatchway. He stood there, stiff and looming, like a statue of some Greek general poised for battle. Hurt and pissed off, she nearly gave him one. Until she looked into his eyes and saw her own doubt and confusion and... something else she wasn't ready to recognize reflected there.

The common room went silent behind him, the soft murmurs of those out there trailing off expectantly. Kat would be damned if she gave everyone a show. Schooling her expression into a semblance of calm, she reached into her pocket and pulled out the cube. "Tech Sergeant Asturrizaga let me in to add Sergeant Truitt's remains to the tribute box."

For a moment, it looked like Scotch might push for the fight, then he blew out a massive sigh and let his head drop briefly to his chest.

"You are such a friggin' pain in my ass," he muttered as he stepped into the compartment and let the hatch close behind him, giving them privacy from their bored and nosy team.

"Feeling's mutual," she grumbled back, not completely clear herself on which feelings she referred to, those spoken or unspoken. Not ready to explore that thought, she turned back around and reached into the footlocker for the simple aluminum box revealed at the bottom. She felt the deck plates vibrate beneath her as Scotch came closer. At least, she told herself it was the deck plates. Annoyed, she wrestled her focus back to the task. As she drew the tribute box out, Scotch settled on the bunk to her right, close behind her, and just watched. It took effort not to jump as he leaned over her shoulder, but all he did was scoop up the little white Bible. She tried to tune out the rustling of pages coming from behind her, her lips pressing thin with annoyance.

Achieving a measure of calm, Kat set the box before her and slowly opened the lid. Her hand trailed over the cubes already there, the cool, slick surfaces marred only by the etched names and ranks of the fallen, and—in the case of those lost in battle—the hashmarks left by the surviving members of the team. She only recognized one of the names. Kat's touch lingered on Sue's cube in silent remembrance.

When Kat reached for Truitt's cube and started to place him inside, Scotch's hand settled on her shoulder, causing her to hesitate.

She glanced back, her brow furrowed, but he was not looking at her.

With his head bowed and his hand still on her shoulder, Scotch recited the 23rd Psalm the right way this time, reading from Sarge's Bible. His deep, low voice resonated within her, filling Kat with warmth, the reverence in his tone moving her. Kat lowered her head and let the words settle on her heart like a soothing rain.

As the passage ended, they both remained silent, steeped in the rare and fleeting moment of peace. Kat nearly protested when Scotch gently squeezed her shoulder and let go. Nearly. Turning back to the open box before her, she rubbed her thumb across the surface of Truitt's cube in a final goodbye, then placed it next to Brockmann's, settling it into low grooves that locked it in place. Kat then closed the lid and returned the box and Sarge's personal effects to the footlocker, startling a little as Scotch held out the Bible to her. When she picked up the soft, limp form of the gutted bear, she frowned, confused as it draped over her hand as it hadn't done before.

"What's wrong, Kat?"

"Shh..." She clenched her fingers around the bear, only then realizing it no longer crackled. Dropping her eyes to the ground, she frantically searched for the source.

"Kat..."

In her relief, she ignored him as she found what she searched for in the shadow of his bunk. A scattering of loose pages. What appeared to be printouts of private communiqués and a bundle of official orders, creased and crumpled and partially torn. As she gathered them up, intent on putting everything back as it was, she swayed as she caught a few glaring... damning words, any remnant of her earlier peace vanishing as the words' relevance registered.

"What the hell?"

The pages trembled as she held them out to Scotch, her lips numb as she uttered the words aloud, anger and betrayal burning in her gut. "...in return for your service to the *Legion*..."

The pages bore the name of Kevin Daire.

Scotch's gaze roiled and flashed like the mother of all hurricanes at sea, but his hand remained calm and steady as he took the papers from her. Kat wanted to snatch them back by the time he skimmed the documents for the third time in silence, his expression darkening with each pass.

Kat's thoughts ricocheted as she waited for him to finish. All this time, they believed they fought pirates, and it was the stinking Legion. Suddenly all of the seemingly separate... and even conflicting data started to synch up. What if Ghei had attempted to pick out a word and not a name? While Kat still didn't trust Colonel Corbin, Legion fit the pattern as well. A rogue military force, little more than mercenaries with a hereditary obsession with bringing the planet Demeter under their sovereign rule. But it couldn't be just them. Some other power had to be at play. Campbell and Sarge had been against one another, not working for the same side... or so it seemed. Trying to work out the tangle of intrigue put Kat on edge. She fidgeted as she waited for Scotch to finish until her patience ran out. "Well?"

He looked up and locked eyes with her. Kat almost gasped at the briefest glimpse of disillusionment and uncertainty staring back before he shrouded his gaze. Still silent, he held out the papers. Her brow furrowed hard as she glared at them, her sense of honor shaken to its foundation.

Reading them felt wrong, disloyal. An invasion of privacy, but what allegiance did they owe to a traitor?

None.

With the memory of the recent take-over attempt sharp in her mind, Kat took the papers back and skimmed them just as closely, part of her regretting the decision with each new blow of betrayal they revealed. The more she read, the more she remembered. Kat gasped as the hazy memories billowed up like muck from the bottom of her thoughts, coming clearer as they surfaced: *Scotch held at gunpoint. Campbell alive and well and holding the gun. Campbell dead on the deck with a combat knife Kat had wielded protruding from his eye. Sarge bound and bloody. Sarge betraying them both, drugging them and dumping them, before stealing the* Teufel *and the specs for the* Cromwell...

First Campbell, then Sarge... and—like a sucker punch—according to a note scribbled on one of the pages, Dalton as well. But Scotch had already discovered that, hadn't he? Kat's thoughts swirled with the chaos of a maelstrom, but one thing remained clear: It became harder and harder to have faith in the fidelity of their brotherhood. Three Devils gone bad, two others dead. An attempted insurrection on board... Kat had no idea who to trust anymore.

But then she reached the papers at the bottom of the stack, not in much better condition than the others, and confusion unsettled her even further. Orders. AeroCom orders instructing Master Sergeant Kevin Daire to infiltrate the Legion. Orders issued by General Drovak. The issue date corresponded with just before they'd discharged Kat to the Groom facility. She looked back through the Legion documents and, though they listed no date, based on some of the content and the condition of the pages, they felt... older.

Which did she believe: Betrayal... or Duty? Her loyal heart screamed *Duty*.

She looked up to find Scotch watching her intently. Before she could say a word, he snapped to his feet and reached for the papers, which she readily relinquished.

"Come on," he ordered, his tone devoid of emotion. "We need to have a talk with General Drovak."

They climbed the decks and walked the utilitarian corridors in silence until they reached the block of compartments assigned to General Drovak and his entourage. Along the way, they passed work crews on repair duty, and Kat's steps faltered. This was the first tangible evidence of the take-over attempt she had seen outside of their own engagement with the enemy. That thought alone shook her more than the sight of scorch marks on the deck and bullet holes in the bulkhead. Never would she have expected to refer to fellow AeroCom airmen as the enemy.

Of course, the moment they chose insurrection, they ceased to be AeroCom airmen.

Swift as she could, Kat shut down that thread of thought, not liking how close to home that blow might hit. Squaring her shoulders and resuming her pace, Kat brought herself back into line with Scotch just as he halted before compartment 203. She took a step back to stand behind his right shoulder as he 'knocked' by presenting his identchip to the sensor beside the hatch.

Almost immediately, the hatch swung inward. Swarovski stood in the opening, Spec balanced on his padded shoulder perch. The little cat—*Parr scout,* Kat corrected herself—meowed a silent greeting, raising his paw toward her.

Any other time, Kat would have expected to hear a subvocal quip over her private frequency, but their business here was of a most serious nature. It would have to be when Scotch forwent an opportunity to joke.

"Please, come in," Swarovski greeted them, stepping aside to clear the way before pivoting and gesturing for them to follow. Kat's eyes widened a bit as the aide led them into an interior chamber very much like their own quarters, save for the scale and the office décor. On the side closest to the hatch, 'glass'-fronted bookshelves lined the bulkhead. The far side of the double-wide compartment held standard storage lockers, only less beat up. Beside the lockers sat a long conference table with a digital screen built into the bulkhead just beyond and smaller consoles inset into the table's surface before each seat. But none of that held Kat's eye.

In clear pride of place, in the middle of the compartment stood an antique wooden desk anchored to the deck by padded clamps. PawPaw would have lusted after that desk. Polished mahogany, brass fittings, neat, enclosed compartments of correspondence. A discrete comm with a neodymium base adhered to a metal plate bonded to the corner of the desk was the only concession to tech. Kat caught a faint whiff of beeswax and turpentine, just like she'd used polishing PawPaw's cherished heirlooms back home.

In sharp contrast to the stark surroundings and utilitarian chairs anchored before it, the desk should have looked out of place, but somehow, the gleaming wood lent the compartment a dignified air. Kat resisted the impulse to run her hand over the polished surface.

Scotch cleared his throat, and Kat reined in her mental wandering.

"If you'll have a seat," Swarovski directed. "General Drovak will be with you shortly."

As he turned to leave, the Parr jumped from his shoulder and padded across the room. Kat grimaced and tried to shoo him away, but as before, he stopped in front of her and looked up with wide, tawny eyes.

Give in, corporal, Scotch murmured to her alone. *There ain't no resisting that level of cute.* Before he even finished the comment, the little furball had already leapt to her lap and settled in, this time occupying himself by rolling on his back to capture his tail. Kat resisted the urge to brace Spec against his more energetic lunges, not wanting to offend the fierce little beast. His antics, for the briefest of moments, unwound her tension just a touch.

With a faint smile, Swarovski glanced back. "Can I bring either of you something to drink?"

"This isn't a social visit, sir," Scotch answered, no hint of amusement in his voice. The papers rustled in his grip.

Swarovski nodded, unruffled. "I know, but the offer still stands."

Kat remained silent, following Scotch's lead.

With a final nod, Swarovski returned to the outer compartment just as the general came striding in. Drovak waved them down before they could shoot to attention. Settling behind his desk, he eyed them closely before leaning forward and activating the comm on the desk.

"Yes, sir?" Swarovski's voice rose through the speaker.

"Coffee, black."

"Right away, sir."

Then Drovak gave them a considering look. "Sergeant, corporal, how can I help you?"

Back ramrod straight, Scotch leaned forward and laid the papers on Drovak's desk, the official orders on top. He said nothing, and neither did Kat. The general drew the papers to him and flipped them around, skimming through them in silence. When he was done, he sat back, his posture more at ease than Kat expected.

"Again, how can I help you?"

Kat found it difficult to remain silent, but Scotch held the higher rank.

"We're in the dark here, general," he answered. "And it's getting my team killed. Our commander is... missing, there have been repeated attacks on this ship from without and within, and frankly, our resources are being underutilized."

Just barely, Kat managed not to gasp. Or she thought she did. When she looked down to compose herself, Spec looked up at her as if perhaps she hadn't been as successful as she thought. Abruptly, she straightened again, but neither Scotch nor General Drovak had shifted their gazes toward her. She did not slump in relief. Outwardly.

Slowly, Drovak nodded. "I cannot argue with you there, sergeant, even were I inclined to. In the eyes of most major powers in this solar system, the *Cromwell* is a prize. Whether the vessel herself or just the intelligence of her construction. Command is aware of this, but awareness is not enough to identify all the parties in play. We have had to employ their tactics. That can cloud the waters until it is difficult to tell friend from foe."

"Not so difficult when they're shooting at you, sir."

The general grimaced. He shifted forward until his silver bristle gleamed in the light from above. "I am afraid our deception has worked against us in an unanticipated manner."

Kat felt Scotch tense before he likewise leaned in. "Deception?"

Before the general could respond—if he even intended to—the hatch opened, and a rich, complex aroma wafted in just ahead of Swarovski. Kat inhaled deeply, her mouth watering as she savored the scent of a blend that far exceeded the quality of any roast she had ever enjoyed, even that served from her mother's elite Capitol Hill coffee service.

"Deception?" Scotch repeated, his tone dangerously neutral. Kat immediately forgot about the coffee. Or told herself to, anyway, though she continued to breathe deep.

The general did not respond, his attention turned to his aide. "Thank you, captain. Please, set it down and have a seat. It will keep."

As Swarovski took the chair to her right, Spec jumped ship and curled up in his trainer's lap. Kat hardly noticed as the general leaned forward, his arms on the desk and his fingers laced, as his sharp gaze tangled with Scotch's.

"Yes, deception," he responded as if their conversation hadn't been interrupted. "It goes without saying that no aspect of this discussion is to leave this chamber."

"Yes, sir," both she and Scotch responded in unison.

"Very well. The *Cromwell* is a failure. A very well-sold failure. Advanced, but not as effective as it should be in the manner claimed."

This time Kat had no doubt she'd gasped aloud. By his expression, Scotch felt just as stunned.

"Excuse me, sir?"

"Sergeant, exactly how effective could a cutting-edge prototype be when everyone knows about it?"

The general arched a brow and watched them expectantly as if waiting for them to catch on.

"You leaked the details..." Kat murmured. "You wanted them to know about it, so you created the buzz."

Drovak looked pleased. "Well, not me personally... but yes, we facilitated the revelation of certain classified aspects of the McCormick design. No better way to discover the sleepers in your ranks than to lure them out with an irresistible prize. Besides, it gave the opposition something harmless to focus on."

Scotch surged to his feet. "Harmless?!" The single word vibrated with tension steeped in barely harnessed anger.

"Sergeant Daniels," the general addressed him, his voice level but sharp. "Resume your seat, now. My words were perhaps ill-chosen in light of recent events but accurate nonetheless. We are less at risk from them acquiring failed design specs than we are from their ability to deceive our senses and infiltrate our ranks with constructs... *composites* that mimic trusted members of those ranks to near perfection.

"Which reminds me..." Kat stiffened as the general turned his bright blue gaze upon her. "Our most sincere thanks, *Sergeant* Alexander. Your encounter with the Ghei composite provided vital intel that helped us to devise a preliminary means to neutralize that threat."

"Well, at least something besides bruises came out of all of that," Kat uttered the wiseass comment before she realized it, startling a laugh from everyone but herself. Then what the general had said sank in. "E-excuse me, sir?"

General Drovak gave her a nod, a look of pride on his face that made no sense to her. "You heard me correctly. Effective immediately, you are promoted to the rank of sergeant for exemplary service in the field." He turned toward Swarovski. "Captain, if you would...?"

Swarovski rose and moved to one of the storage lockers on the far wall, the Parr balanced in the crook of his right arm. Unhindered by his burden, he opened the one closest to the hatch and drew out a black velvet box. He then closed the locker and returned to hand the box to General Drovak, who stood and came around the desk.

"Sergeant Alexander, Sergeant Daniels, please stand."

Stunned, Kat turned her gaze to Scotch. His expression had softened and warmed, and on him, the deep look of pride felt authentic. "Come on, sergeant, get to your feet."

Together they stood and faced the general, who held out the box to Scotch. "Would you like the honors?"

"Thank you, sir." Straightening his shoulders, Scotch accepted the insignia.

Kat turned and stood at attention before him, trying not to grin like a goofball at this longed-for advancement. Scotch's eyes twinkled as they met hers, but he swapped out her rank emblems with an air of ceremony, saluting her when he was done, despite his higher rank, acknowledging her new promotion per the Devils' tradition. Kat returned it with equal precision, only to drop all dignity and hug him, laughing like crazy. He gave her a quick squeeze but then stepped back, forcing a return to decorum that Kat shouldn't have abandoned.

"Sorry," she murmured to the room at large, but her smile remained in place.

"Congratulations, Sergeant Alexander," General Drovak said, offering her his hand. "My apologies for the delay. I had meant to take care of this as soon as I came on board," he said as they shook. "But other... matters intervened."

That's when Kat's smile receded as she realized what the general had done.

This was her prize... but their distraction. Her joy in the moment faded just a touch. She had no doubt the promotion was authentic, but the timing seemed suspect. The brass usually indulged in more pomp and circumstance for such presentations.

"Thank you, general," she said as she met his gaze, her own determined. "But with all due respect, we need to know what we're up against, and we need to know now. This is more than just the Legion trying to gain an advantage."

For the long silent moment that followed, fraught with enough tension her toes nearly dug into the deck, Kat had no doubt she was about to be busted all the way down to private.

The general's lips briefly turned down before flattening out into a line. He nodded sharply. "It is always more than just the Legion. Hirobon... the Dominion... the Teutonic Knights... I could keep going, but what would that accomplish? The others are just more subtle in their efforts. Less desperate...

"We'll keep an eye on those who are left, but I don't expect they will try anything now that their presence is overt."

"You know that there are more, and you're doing nothing about it?" Kat asked, incredulous.

"Sergeant Alexander, no military or government in all of history has ever been free and clear of enemy operatives among their ranks. The key is knowing who they are and how and when to use their efforts against them."

A soft *hmph* came across her 'jack, but other than that, Scotch remained silent.

Kat had to ask, though, too used to betrayal at this point to assume the answer... "General, are any of those operatives Devils?"

Though she'd directed her question to Drovak, Swarovski cleared his throat. She turned to him expectantly.

"I can personally assure you that every remaining member of the Devils is loyal to the team and AeroCom," the aide answered.

Though part of her remained skeptical, Kat sensed his conviction, his sincerity. She wanted to believe.

She also realized she still had intel she hadn't reported, the memories clouded by whatever Sarge had drugged them with when he'd made his escape. Turning back to the general, she came to attention. "General Drovak, sir. I have more to report. Details I've just recently remembered."

His gaze sharpened, and he sat forward. "Proceed..."

"When Sergeant Daniels and I boarded the *Teufel* to search for Sergeant Daire, it was under the belief that he had been taken hostage by Sergeant Dalton, who was unaccounted for. However, once inside, we were ambushed by Warrant Officer Campbell." Here Kat hesitated, overwhelmed by flashes of memory from that encounter.

"And?"

Kat mentally shook free of the visceral images and continued. "Sir, we had been informed by medbay that Campbell died as a result of the earlier gas attack. I had believed I had his cube in my pocket."

The general's brow furrowed. "Do you have that cube now?"

She shook her head. "It was gone when I regained consciousness. I did not fully remember these occurrences until I discovered those." Kat pointed at the papers that had brought them to this audience before locking her eyes forward, just past the general's head. "I can assure you that he is now most definitely dead. The blood on our uniforms was his. During the course of the encounter, Campbell threatened Sergeant Daniels's life and forced me to restrain him. Using Sergeant Daniels's combat knife, I neutralized the threat. At the time, it did occur to me that the cube might actually be Sergeant Dalton's remains."

Drovak gave a little huff, then turned his gaze on Scotch. "Are you able to corroborate any of this?"

"I'm sorry, sir, I am afraid my memories are still a bit blurred from the encounter."

"Swarovski," the general barked, startling the Parr but not the lieutenant.

"Yes, sir?"

"Secure a copy of the medbay scans from Campbell's records. Confirm Sergeant Alexander's theory, if possible, and see if you can determine the root of the discrepancy. We need to make sure the medical staff has not been compromised."

"Right away, sir." And Swarovski left, taking the cat with him.

Once they were gone, an awkward silence settled over the room.

"Anything else?" the general asked.

Kat made every effort not to fidget, acutely aware of the exabyte drive still in her pocket.

"Sir, were they supposed to get the data?" she asked, her hand snaking into her pocket to finger the backup. "Because the original files are gone, all of them. What we retrieved from the black box... what we retrieved from the rock-ship... Other than this"—she pulled the drive from her pocket, sensing Scotch tense as she did so—"all we have left are our personal accounts of the events, and the set of coordinates the subversives left on my computer, presuming those are even worth anything."

Rather than answer, the general held his hand out for the drive, which Kat reluctantly relinquished. "And what," he asked, "is this?"

Kat could not discern from his tone how her report had been received.

"A backup of the data retrieved from the auxiliary black box from the Groom Experimental Complex," Kat answered. "All of the research data, plus the security data from the station itself, including the drive signature of every vessel to leave or approach the complex up to the moment of transmission."

At that, the general quirked a brow but made no further comment, simply collecting the papers and the chip and locking them away in his desk. Kat wanted to protest. She nearly did, except for Scotch's single sharp *no* sounding over her private frequency.

"Thank you both for bringing all of this to my attention," the general said as he stood, turning to Scotch. "Dismissed."

They both turned to leave, only to stop as the general addressed Kat.

"Sergeant Alexander, if I could have a moment." It wasn't a question.

Puzzled, Kat stopped and pivoted back, sparing a glance over her shoulder as Scotch left the general's quarters. Her teammate looked back just once, enough for Kat to tell he wasn't happy about the conversation. He glared back at her with more anger than she had ever seen him direct her way. She straightened her shoulders and looked away as Swarovski closed the hatch but Scotch still got in the last word.

We will discuss this later, sergeant.

Unaware of the exchange, the general waited until the hatch closed before redirecting his attention back to her. "Thank you for waiting. Please, sit. Coffee?"

As much as she had lusted after it earlier, the thought of it now burned her gut. Kat shook her head and watched as the general poured his own cup.

"Full disclosure, I know your mother," General Drovak continued, diving right in as Kat took the indicated seat, his bright blue eyes watching her closely while giving nothing away.

Nodding, Kat sat ramrod straight, saying nothing, though she cursed a blue streak inside, already anticipating where this was headed. Was this why he'd given her the promotion? As a token concession before he took it all away? It wouldn't be the first time Mother managed to interfere, or surely the last. Of course, none of this would matter once Scotch was done with Kat. If he reported she'd acted independent of orders, she'd be out, Mother's work done for her.

Kat's brain scrambled to come up with the beginning of plan C. She was running out of good-guy militaries to join. But she had too much principle to go mercenary. And certainly not the Legion, as so many others seemed to have done. It took all her focus to suppress a grimace.

Maybe if she'd been paying better attention, the general wouldn't have blindsided her.

"But I knew your father first," he continued, throwing Kat even more off-kilter as he gave her a knowing smirk. It was no secret the efforts Congresswoman Laine Alexander had taken to roadblock her daughter's military career.

Kat straightened her posture even further. "I hadn't known that, sir."

"Used to have coffee together every Wednesday afternoon when I was assigned as a congressional liaison." Those blue eyes crinkled. "Just born, and he was already insanely proud of you. He would be even more so now. I was saddened at his passing."

Maybe it was the informal nature of their current conversation, but Kat wasn't quick enough to temper her response. "Murder, don't you mean?" She had never known her father. She'd barely been one when he'd died. Killed by angry protesters over a failed proposition he had supported. She dropped a rock over that emotional hole before she fell in. It had taken her years of therapy as a child to subdue her rage—though all truth told, PawPaw had more to do with straightening her sullen self out—but the incident still had the power to light her up like a ten-second fuse if she wasn't careful. Never a good thing, especially not when talking to a superior.

Drovak nodded in concession before straightening, his bearing transforming in an instant. "Precisely. Which brings us to the case in point."

Certain she couldn't have heard right, Kat cocked her head, eyes narrowing in confusion. "Excuse me, sir?"

"Other than my family," the general confided, his body leaning forward and his gaze intent and unwavering, "there are few individuals in this universe that I know better than I know you."

Every fiber in Kat's body went still, her hindbrain acutely aware of the closed hatch behind her, with Scotch on the far side. Though she tried to hide her discomfort, General Drovak grimaced and shook his head. "Not that I would ever disrespect your father's memory like that, or my oath as your superior, but do I look like I am even remotely interested in chasing after young women a third my age, and at least as well-trained in combat as I am, if not better?"

"No, sir," Kat answered, doing her best to shake her nerves. "But then, Ghei didn't look all that artificial either."

That startled a bark of laughter from the general, breaking the tension. "Point well taken, airman." Then his expression sobered again. "After your father's death, I made a vow to myself to look after you. Out of respect for your mother, however, I was forced to do so from a distance. The relevant point being, I trust you implicitly. You are as honorable as your father and as determined as your mother. You are intelligent, observant, and thanks to that grandfather of yours, your word means more to you than your next breath. You have values that mean something to you. Sadly, that cannot be said for everyone in our ranks."

Kat felt a twinge of guilt, glad the general hadn't been privy to her earlier conversation with Scotch. Not sure how to respond, if the general even meant her to, she merely nodded in acknowledgment and waited for him to go on.

"I have a problem." The grimace returned. "I need to trust in those beneath my command, even when I know, in at least some cases, my faith is misplaced. Though we have identified a good percentage of those with divided loyalties, even I am not so arrogant or foolish to believe we've discovered them all. Unless they are dumb-fuck stupid, any remaining subversives will be ever-vigilant around anyone with rank above them..."

"...but who's to say they won't get sloppy in front of the noob...?" Kat finished for him, fully confident in where he was going with this. "That's why I was bumped to the GEC, wasn't it, sir?"

General Drovak didn't answer directly, but he did look pleased with her deduction. "I need you to be alert. I'm not asking you to spy on anyone, but we cannot afford another situation like the one with the *Alexi* or the recent attempt to take over this ship."

"Sir, may I ask a question?" At his nod, Kat continued. "What happened to the *Alexi*? Scotch said the *Cromwell* just disabled it, but I've heard it was lost, with all hands aboard."

He gave her a long, considering look. Long enough for her to regret her question.

She didn't doubt he would answer, but she was no longer certain she wanted to hear.

Drovak must have found whatever he had been looking for in her expression. "The hows and whys make little difference. What is important is preventing a repeat of the outcome. Understood?"

Kat straightened her posture once more. "Yes, sir."

"Very well, sergeant, you are dismissed."

She wondered how long it would take to get used to that.

"Thank you, sir." Kat stood and pivoted, heading toward the hatch, but what the general had said nagged at her, and she turned back. She was pushing it, but she had to know. "Sir, if I may..."

"Proceed..." the general said with a nod.

Kat struggled with the words, not wanting to ask but needing to. "Please, sir, was Sergeant Daire one of those cases?"

For a moment, the general remained silent. Finally, he straightened, then held her gaze. "Sergeant Daire is under my orders. As far as this command is concerned, he is MIA, and we will work to restore him to our ranks."

Kat couldn't help but notice that the general's eye had briefly flickered away, then back again. No more than a flutter. Less than a second of hesitation, followed by an unswerving gaze, but it unsettled her, instilling the faintest shadow of a doubt. Kat shrugged it off. If there was anything she knew in her gut, it was her faith in Sarge. She nodded and took the general at his word.

He nodded back, then tilted his head toward the hatch. "Please send in Captain Swarovski on your way out."

"Yes, sir," she answered. "Thank you, sir," she added, though she doubted the general heard her.

As she reached for the hatch, it swung open, and Swarovski again stood to the side, making room for her to pass. Kat noticed Scotch had waited for her. He stood by the outer hatch, deceptively relaxed at parade rest, but his clenched jaw bore a hard white line.

Though Swarovski's gaze remained neutral as she passed, Kat had never before felt so fully seen, though she couldn't explain what that meant, even to herself. As she walked by, he gave her the subtlest of winks.

Honest to God, Scotch looked about to explode as he saw the exchange. He straightened and stepped forward, his face bright red and every muscle now as taut as his jaw. Before he had a chance to prove her right, she hustled him through the hatch and back toward the Devils' quarters.

Of all that had happened lately, this encounter was, perhaps, the most unsettling.

CHAPTER 17

STANDING AT THE OBSERVATION PORTAL FACING THE STARBOARD DOCKING module, Cryson glowered out at the AeroCom shuttle *Teufel*. The devil icon on its hull seemed to laugh back at him. As advantageous as the opportunity had seemed when Christine had presented it to him, he should have realized everything would go to hell the moment he recruited a Devil.

Daire hadn't lied. At least, not about the cube. Or the body.

This operation had cost Cryson his daughter and his second in command, not to mention valuable resources and strategic operatives. If he wasn't careful, it could mean his career, as well. They needed to crack the encryption on that data... and hope to God it wasn't another deception.

As Cryson pivoted away to head for the command deck, an alert tone sounded over his comm badge. Swearing beneath his breath, he headed for the nearest systems terminal and keyed in his security code. A commlink opened as soon as his code cleared, showing a grim-faced sergeant wearing unit markings for the detachment assigned to the Legion's covert outpost down on Demeter. The name tape on his uniform read 'COLE.'

"Sergeant Cole, report."

"Sir," he answered, torquing his body to the side to give a clear view behind him. "I believe these are yours."

Cryson's erstwhile hidden operatives milled in the atrium behind the beleaguered sergeant, battered and bruised and in some cases slightly charred, all of them in some variation of AeroCom uniform. Well, at least at first glance, they weren't easily identified as Legion. But what the hell were they doing *there*? That was no simple base, interchangeable for any other. The Legion and their allies would be dealt a serious blow were that location compromised. By sheer will, Cryson restrained himself from any apparent outburst.

"What would you like me to do with them, sir?" the sergeant asked when Cryson didn't respond.

With careful, controlled breaths, Cryson answered, "I want to speak to whoever seems in charge of them. Have everyone assessed for injuries, then bunk the rest down in the barracks for now."

"Yes, sir," Cole acknowledged. "Please hold the link."

As the screen went blank, Cryson looked around to see who was in the immediate area. He spied Dell'Aquila and Jenner patrolling the zone. Other than that, there was just the docking crew going about their duties. None of them seemed to pay him any attention. Even so, too many moved about the docking bay for Cryson's comfort. He logged out of the terminal and moved to the dockmaster's office, sending the man out with a glance. Once the hatch closed behind him, Cryson keyed in his security code. The secure comm window opened immediately. He didn't recognize the woman on the screen, a slender blonde with slate grey eyes, but that wasn't unusual. The Legion-issued microcomms were audio- or text-based communication only, and most of the time, Christine had been his point of contact.

"Agent Jan Orwell, reporting, sir." He recognized the name. It belonged to a more-than-competent operative known for her calm head and decisive action. A bit of his tension eased.

"What the hell are you doing there, Orwell?" he demanded. "You were to report back to the *Destrier*."

"We had no choice, sir. The vessels we appropriated were berthed in the maintenance bay. They barely got us down to the planet. We were careful making our way to the outpost, breaking up into groups of no more than two or three."

Cryson nodded. "And what went wrong on the *Cromwell*?" he asked, his tone strained even to his own ears.

"Somehow, they neutralized the synthetic operatives. All at once, they shorted out in the middle of the offensive. We were left without control of key systems integral to the mission's success."

"Damn it!" Cryson swore, slamming his hand down on the dockmaster's desk. He found exactly zero satisfaction in being right about the synthetics, though... his mind already saw a way to turn their failure to his advantage, drawing attention away from other, less easily explained shortfalls of the operation.

"Are any of our operatives still on the *Cromwell*?"

Orwell nodded, her expression grim. "Those who were captured, and the dead or wounded."

"I mean, are there any operatives uncompromised?"

"A few, sir. Those who were not in a position to engage when the attack went down."

"Good. Send me a full report, along with any intel you were able to secure, and then hold your position."

"Yes, sir," Orwell said. "Right away, sir. Sending it now."

Cryson was impressed. Too bad the Legion didn't have more like Orwell. He was about the close the link when she spoke up, halting his hand in mid-motion.

"Sir, we were able to secure one of the defunct synthetics. It's hidden with the shuttles."

It took all of Cryson's effort not to grin like a half-mad fool. "Well done, Orwell. I will be in touch with further instructions. Tell no one you have that synthetic."

"Yes, sir."

He ended the connection, and though he could in no way see the vessel from where he stood, he turned in the direction of the *Teufel*, his key to getting down to the planet and retrieving those operatives—and the synthetic—with the Allied Forces none the wiser.

His outlook marginally improved, Cryson left the docking bay and headed for the command deck. Time to set course for Demeter.

Scotch didn't make it as far as the team quarters. They passed the PT room on the return route, and he pointed Kat inside, knowing what he had to say couldn't be said where the team or anyone else might overhear. When she started to protest, he gave her a warning look, too upset to trust himself to speak. She fell silent, for once not even snapping a comeback. He'd like to think it was out of wisdom, but her recent actions made him wonder for once if she had any.

He checked to make sure the compartment was empty then began to pace, not even sure where to start.

Kat stood at attention where she'd stopped.

Smart girl... sometimes, he thought, his exasperation getting the better of him. He needed a moment to cool down or at least get his thoughts under control.

It took a little longer than that.

"What the hell, Kat?!" he finally snapped. "What in the ever-loving hell were you thinking? Copying sensitive data? Seriously? No part of you thought maybe that was a bad idea?"

When she started to respond, he shook his head.

"No. Don't even. You need to listen to me and listen to me good. I am not talking to you as a ranking officer. I am talking to you as someone who... cares, and you better be damned glad about that too. Do you understand? Stop doing things I could have to bust you for at some point." Despite his assurance, she avoided looking at him, her gaze forward and her posture precise. Silently, she nodded.

Scotch huffed out a sigh and ran his hand over the blond bristle atop his head. He expected to encounter sweat, but his brow remained dry. She had him so on edge, anger fighting with concern. He didn't know what the future held for them. Wouldn't let himself even consider it right now. But he knew for sure he damn well wanted her at his back. Only, if she kept making such rash decisions, she'd get herself booted for real. He had to get her to see that.

"You are a good operative, an effective operative, but if you keep going rogue, it's going to catch up to you. Stop acting like you're *not* part of a team. That the rules don't apply to you. It's not all on you to make this come out right. For God's sake, trust us..."

At that, she scowled and dropped her military posture.

"Excuse me?"

Scotch didn't miss the dangerous hint of twang to her words. Part of him delighted as her eyes snapped fire, but the rest of him needed to know common sense was sinking through.

"I know... I know... there's been a lot of broken trust around here, but you heard Swarovski, not one of the remaining Devils is anything but loyal to their oath and the team. To each other. To *you*.

"Kat, please, listen to me," he said, gently gripping her shoulders as he ducked down to meet her gaze evenly. She felt like a coil wound tight under pressure, but he continued on. "You can't keep letting instinct over-rule protocol. Sarge cut the Devils a lot of latitude, but I know he already talked to you about this. Your independent action is getting out of hand.

"Besides, he is gone... and he might not be coming back. After everything that has happened, Command can't let anything slide. They can't afford to overlook breaches of conduct in the aftermath of an attempted coup. Disobeying Ghei... hiding your injuries... burning a copy of sensitive data... Turning off your comm in a combat situation... Things like that could force them to discipline you, even discharge you. Or worse. To maintain order, they have to judge you on the action, not the outcome."

Her gaze dropped to where he held her, and Scotch relaxed his grip, hardly realizing how it had tightened. In the end, he let go altogether and took a step back.

"I hear you," she said softly, locking gazes with him, and he could tell by what he saw there that she did, but then she smirked and tilted her head, giving him a devil of a look. "But I prefer maverick to rogue..."

One laugh escaped him before he grew serious again. "I mean it, Kat. Following every instinct even when it breaks protocol could end the career you've fought so hard for..."

She looked away, for the briefest moment appearing vulnerable, before squaring her shoulders and nodding. "I know. I will do better," she promised, and he saw in her eyes that she believed what she said. But could he?

Without another word, she turned and left him standing in the middle of the empty PT room.

Wound tight and questioning her own decisions, Kat wandered the corridors and decks of the *Cromwell*, trying to wrestle her thoughts back into order. PawPaw would have been ashamed of her. Well... not *her*, but the choices she'd made. He'd raised her to be independent, not reckless. As much as she hated to admit it, she'd given Scotch valid reason to call her out. She'd let her own judgment override protocol. Willfully.

So far, she had been lucky.

No more tempting fate. No more bucking the chain of command.

Now, if only the situation with Scotch was as readily sorted... except she didn't know what that meant, for either of them. And from his conflicted responses, she didn't think he did either. AeroCom did not forbid personal relationships among the ranks—within certain strict guidelines—but neither did they encourage them, at least not those of a more serious nature. Dalliances blew off steam. Commitments created opportunities for what Command considered conflicts of interest.

Divided loyalties were not conducive to military efficiency.

Blowing out a breath in frustration, Kat couldn't blame Scotch for acting as grumpy as a bear with a thorn in his paw even before she gave him more cause. She tucked all those messy thoughts away and looked around her, searching for the corridor marker that would tell her where she was. Instead, she saw Spec bounding toward her. In the distance, Swarovski followed.

"Are you two stalking me?" she asked as the captain drew closer, only half-joking.

Swarovski's eyes twinkled as they met hers, but only on the surface. Beneath, they seemed more intent. He gave a shrug and gestured down at the Parr, who now sat prim and proper at Kat's feet waiting to be acknowledged, his tail—as always—prettily curled against him. "Speaking for myself, no..."

Shaking her head, Kat squatted down so Spec could sniff her hand and decide for himself if he wanted a scritch. With a solemn gaze, the scout sniffed, then slowly rubbed against her fingers, melting Kat's heart. When she ruffled the fur behind his ears, his purr filled the corridor. Oh, she was going to miss this little guy when he and his handler moved on.

"Trainer..."

Kat's brow furrowed. It sounded like he was correcting her, though she hadn't said anything. "Sorry?"

"Training exercise," Swarovski answered, nodding at the Parr scout again.

She would swear that hadn't been what he said the first time. But then, her attention had been on the cat... Kat turned her gaze on Spec again and gave a sudden laugh. Blinded by his cuteness, she hadn't noticed the tiny military-grade harness he wore. She wished she remembered more about the scout program. The Devils could use another hellcat.

Kat rose easily to an upright position. "Sorry to have disrupted. I'll leave you two..."

She halted mid-conversation as an alert tone sounded over her private frequency, sending a ripple up her bonejack.

Sergeant Alexander, report to crew quarters.

Kat frowned. She didn't recognize the voice. Private frequencies weren't common knowledge. Unless she gave it to someone, the only people that would have it would be her team and Command. Sergeant Ryan, perhaps? It had to be. Shit! With more urgency, Kat looked up, searching once more for the corridor marking: *D12:CdEpsilon.*

Swarovski got her attention, gesturing the way he had come. "That way... right, two over, and three down. You'll recognize how to get back from there."

Nodding her thanks, Kat headed off at a jog, halfway down the corridor before it occurred to her to wonder how he'd known what she'd needed. She stopped and pivoted, her gaze locking in on his lean frame and premature silver hair... no, not premature, *natural* silver hair.

"Ty'Pherrein," Kat murmured half to herself as she met Swarovski's wary but hopeful gaze, recalling the epithet garnered by the engineered race literally born out of Dr. McPherren's technique. He had the light-colored eyes and silver hair characteristic of the Tys. And, clearly, he had their psionic abilities as well.

Kat had known that AeroCom worked in cooperation with the Dominion—who had given shelter to the Tys when they fled persecution— she just hadn't made the connection when Swarovski arrived as Drovak's aide. As likable and honorable as the captain seemed, Kat couldn't help but wonder how much of that impression was... influenced. At the very least, she had no doubt he'd used his abilities to vet the team—first when he'd come to their quarters to debrief them and again after the attempted coup. While she found comfort in knowing she could trust her remaining teammates, Kat felt uneasy with anyone being privy to her inner thoughts and feelings... or whatever it was Swarovski picked up on.

Even from meters away, she noticed his expression change, going from wary but hopeful to guarded, though there was no way he should have been able to hear her. The bright sparkle in his gaze dimmed as he straightened his shoulders and gave her a brief nod before turning and striding away, Spec padding at his heels. If she had to identify his look, it would be one of resignation. Kat's heart ached to acknowledge that, guilt a bitter taste at the back of her throat for causing the change in his demeanor. She took a step toward him, only to stop abruptly as the earlier tone repeated across her bonejack, reminding her of her orders. With a heavy heart, she turned back the way she'd been heading, moving double time.

CHAPTER 18

CAPTAIN TY'RIAN SWAROVSKI WANDERED THE CORRIDORS OF THE *CROMWELL* using his psionics to avoid crossing paths with others, moving further and further from the active sectors of the ship.

He had spent his entire life hiding what he was from everyone except for those he had grown to wish didn't already know. He'd been told it was so they would not take advantage of his... unique abilities. Clearly, they meant others, for those who had raised him showed no compunction themselves. As an adult, he had come to value the secrecy more as a defense against the distrust, and even fear, from those who did not understand the nature of his kind or their evolution.

The pain of seeing Kat's dawning realization had been nothing compared to that of her frantic thoughts spearing him from even meters away, though he'd kept his mind to himself. While he did not yet properly know her, he mourned what he expected was the loss of any future friendship they had been likely to share. He could not blame Kat. Few details about the Ty'Pherrein race were general knowledge. Intentionally. How else could they live in peace? But there was no avoiding the fact that the earliest generations had been dangerously... unstable. And such damaging facts had a way of circulating when little else did, creating boogie men of those in any way associated with the madness.

"Damn!" Ty'rian cursed aloud, both at the unchangeable truth of his and every other Ty's existence, and at the realization that he had wandered farther than he'd intended, his security clearance opening pathways otherwise locked off in the mothballed portions of the ship.

With a sigh, he looked down at the patient Parr sitting at his feet. Spec looked up at him with solemn eyes, and Ty'rian only then realized the soft, ongoing mantra murmuring through his thoughts.

It be okay. You see. Kat likes us, Spec repeated now that he had his trainer's full attention.

A fleeting smile crossed Ty'rian's lips, and he knelt closer to the cat, rubbing his head and under the edge of his harness, where he knew Spec itched.

Okay, now. Let's go eat. Everything be great then.

"If you say so. Hop up. We'll get there quicker."

All aboard the monkeytruck! WooWoo!

Ty'rian laughed hard enough he shook, earning him an annoyed look from Spec, who waited to leap to his perch.

With the Parr in place, Ty'rian pushed to his feet and turned around, facing the hatch leading back toward the active sectors of the ship. As he passed through, he felt Spec tense and shift on his shoulder away from the right. Ty pivoted as well, but it was too late.

The last thing he felt as the hypo-spray took effect was Spec pushing off and dashing away, his fading thoughts frantic.

Kat entered the common room out of breath, out of sorts, and quite confused. She looked around for a reason for her summons, but all she saw were the members of her team hanging out or prepping for their next duty shift. As each of them noticed her, they snapped a salute in recognition of her new promotion. Distracted, Kat almost didn't notice, barely sketching a return salute of her own.

"Hey, what's up, Kat?"

She turned toward Danzer, who came out of the head, pulling a tee shirt down over her skivvies. Kat frowned and looked around again. "I don't know. Was Sergeant Ryan looking for me for something?"

"Not that I know of," Danzer responded, turning toward where Colonel, Truck, and Tivo sat bullshitting. "Any of you see Joe Navy around?"

"Nope. Probably off rereading his field manual," one of them called out while the others laughed and goofed off, mimicking Ryan's by-the-book demeanor.

Danzer grinned and shook her head. "Better cut that out before he hears you."

That just set them off more, ramping up their pantomime.

Kat just moved on past, too on edge to participate in the banter. She had a bad feeling. Crossing to Scotch's quarters, she shrugged her identchip past the sensor. After a moment, the hatch opened. Scotch leaned against the hatch collar, relaxed and half asleep.

"Hey there, Kittie Kat," Scotch greeted her, almost losing her name in a yawn. "Everything okay?"

"I don't know..."

He straightened, coming more alert as he wiped the sleep from his eyes. Not saying anything, he stepped to the side, waiting for her to enter. Muffled catcalls rose out in the common room as the hatch slid closed behind her. Kat barely noticed.

Scotch gestured to the tidy bunk across from his rumpled one. "Talk to me."

Kat didn't even know where to start. Once she settled, Scotch sat facing her on his bunk—and if that wasn't a sight to distract her. She hadn't noticed until then that he wore nothing but a tee shirt and boxers.

"He's a Ty."

Scotch frowned at her, his head slightly tilted in confusion.

"Swarovski is Ty'Pherrein."

"Yeah, I noticed. He's also a decent guy, and he's on our side. What's wrong?"

Kat had no answer beyond her own discomfort. "I don't know. It's just... I thought I knew who he was, and then he wasn't..."

Scotch just gave her a look that said, come on. "I'm pretty sure he's still just Swarovski. Who did you think he was?"

"I don't know. I know it doesn't make sense. I'm just out of sorts with everything happening."

"Listen, Kat," Scotch said, leaning forward and capturing her gaze. "There is enough bullshit out here on the ass-end of the galaxy without borrowing more. Judge people based on what they do, not what they are. Assuming you have call to judge them at all."

Kat shifted on the bunk, uncomfortable and feeling called out, but rightly so. Not for the first time, Scotch echoed PawPaw's wisdom. Her grandfather would have been so disappointed in her at that moment.

"I know... it's just... it's a lot all at once."

"Don't worry. You've got this. Just get out of your own head for a while. You have good instincts, so trust them."

She dropped her gaze, feeling ashamed, and found her hands fidgeting with the bottom of her shirt. When she looked up, she caught heat simmering in Scotch's gaze as he watched her. He gave her the faintest of smiles and shrugged unrepentantly.

Kat turned her head away and forced her hands to still, folding them flat in her lap. "And then I received orders to report to crew quarters, but when I got here, no one could explain."

Scotch shook his head and shrugged again. "Wasn't me. I would have ordered you to *my* quarters..." he said, spreading his hands and waggling his brows, hamming it up.

She laughed as he meant her to, and her cheeks went a little warm as she realized she wouldn't have minded orders like that. But as laughter from outside spiked and then faded to a murmur, her gaze went to the hatch.

"Hey, relax. You are wound too tight," Scotch said, his words a mix of soothing and concerned. As he spoke, he swung his legs up onto his bunk and scooted back until he butted up against the wall. "Come here and finish my nap with me."

Her belly clenched at his innocent-seeming suggestion, and her gaze turned to the hatch, then back again, her lower lip caught between her teeth.

"Nap," he repeated, drawing out the word. He then patted the bunk in front of him and waved his hand toward where she sat. "Here or there, wherever makes you more comfortable, but do something before you burst a blood vessel."

With that, he placed his head on the pillow and closed his eyes, only a faint tension in his muscles giving away that he waited for her to decide. Taking a deep breath, Kat rose and crossed the narrow aisle between the bunks. She turned and lay down fully clothed in the space he'd left for her. For a moment, they both lay still and taut, then Scotch slowly released his breath in a hum of contentment and relaxed, folding himself around her like a blanket.

Kat didn't intend to sleep, but as she relaxed into Scotch's warmth, he took her along with him.

Worn down and fed up, Cryson pretended attentiveness as his superiors dressed him down for the most recent in a line of epic failures beyond his control. After half an hour, he didn't even bother to pretend. When they were finally done, he straightened in his chair and, with all sincerity, vowed to do better.

As he disconnected, a familiar and hated symbol appeared on his monitor.

"The target has been acquired. Send immediate transport for retrieval on this heading. Our operative will guide the pilot to the ship."

Cryson's pulse throbbed at his temple, and his jaw ached from clenching. Didn't the Knights—or this one, anyway—have anything better to do than pester him? With so much going on, he had forgotten about that blasted objective, though his superiors had backed up the order. Not that Cryson had tried that hard to remember. Then what the Knight had said registered.

"Noted," he acknowledged, but the icon had already vanished as the commlink closed. *Damn it. I'm a soldier. A patriot. Not a flunky.*

In the back of his brain, a part of him suggested 'pawn' might be more appropriate.

Cryson willfully ignored it as he called up a comm link to the base. Sergeant Cole answered promptly.

"What can I do for you, sir?"

"Get me Scout DeVeaux and Agent Orwell. I have a mission for them."

As the *Destrier* rocketed toward Demeter, Senior Corporal Lawrence Dell'Aquila slipped away from the command deck in the middle of a security briefing, muttering something to the soldier next to him about the relief room. The guy barely noticed, which suited Larry just fine. With Captain Cryson at the conn and most of the crew preparing for the operation, no one paid attention to him. Not that they would think to question security. He hurried through the ship as if on task—which he most definitely was, just not one the captain would endorse.

He ducked into one of the security closets located throughout the ship. Locking the hatch behind him, he accessed the terminal, entering the chief's identcode. First, he initiated prelaunch on the shuttle *Fidèle*, his ride out of this shithole. Then he deactivated the cameras and key security systems shipwide, setting up alerts of his own on the corridors leading to the captain's quarters and the Detention Block. Before he shut the system down, he cleared the security footage cache for the last hour and lifted Lieutenant Petrov's security code.

On his way out, Larry raided the weapons locker, grabbing several pistols and spare pulse packs and clips of frangible rounds, secreting them about his person.

Then, heading to the captain's quarters, he used the pilfered code to enter, hard locking the hatch once he slipped inside. Other than the luxury of space, the compartment wasn't much different than the common crew quarters. Larry shook his head. What a waste of rank.

Knowing he didn't have much time, even with the measures he had taken, he hurried across the room to the computer terminal. Using hacking skills gained on a true pirate vessel before he signed on with the Legion, he easily accessed the drive, grinning like crazy as he hijacked the captain's direct access to the decryption servers and located the *Cromwell's* data files.

Of course, Larry hadn't gotten where he was without being burned before. As a precaution against any impulse Yuki-ko might have to swindle him of his well-earn finder's fee, Larry wrapped the files in another layer of encryption, one that would devour itself—and its contents—should anyone try to decrypt the file without the code. Then, with the package poised and ready, he opened an interstellar comm link and reached out to the lovely Yuki-ko, the prettiest piranha he ever did see.

"Do you have the files?" she demanded the moment the connection engaged.

"Well, hello to you too," Larry greeted her, slowly shaking his head back and forth in admonition just to see the way her eyes narrowed, and her lips went thin and prim. He truly enjoyed pissing her off when she couldn't do a thing about it, but not too much. She was his means of shaking loose of the Legion. He had signed on for the money, not the cause. Only there had been way too much of the latter and not enough of the former.

"Do you have the files?"

He lifted his eyebrows and gave her a slight smile as he anchored a data link to their comm signal and made a show of sending her what she was after. Once he saw the faintest glimmer of sly satisfaction in her gaze, he cleared his throat.

"And my payment?" he prompted.

"You have already been well compensated."

"Ms. Fujitsu, you disappoint me. It is bad business to renege on an agreement."

Though her posture was and always had been painfully erect, she seemed to straighten even further, her face expressionless but her gaze cold. "This is not what I would call business."

"You know, you're right. A businessman would have gotten payment before sending the goods," Larry said, nothing sly about his satisfaction. "This... this is thievery, and a thief knows there is no such thing as honor."

Yuki-ko's gaze narrowed once more. "Your point, Mr. Dell'Aquila?"

Larry smiled and leaned forward. "My point is, when you decide you want access to those files, send my payment, because if you try and decrypt them on your own... let's just say you can kiss your precious data goodbye."

And, with that, he lifted his right hand and waved with a wiggle of his fingers, even as he cut the connection. Then, dropping his carefree façade, he scrambled, all too aware that exchange had taken too much time.

He quickly downloaded the *Cromwell* data to his own yottabyte cube then shut the system down, not bothering to erase his... well, Petrov's footprint. For good measure, he also copied everything from Cryson's personal terminal, including several encoded data blocks. Who knew what they contained, and in the end, who cared? Larry was nothing if not mindful of potential gain in all things. He had long ago learned there was always a market for information. And he might just need it if Yuki-ko held out too long.

Leaving everything the way it was as a final flip-off to the good captain, Larry pocketed the cube and hurried to Detention to arrange his distraction.

Kat woke to a fierce and frantic little kitty landing on her chest and the sound of a throat clearing somewhere nearby.

"What the...?"

"Woman, is that all you know how to say?" Scotch murmured in her ear.

Kat's gaze snapped up and back, tracking on his voice. Her brow dipped in a puzzled frown before she remembered their shared nap.

"What did I miss?" she asked, reaching for the Parr to lift him off so she could sit up. Spec resisted, apparently quite determined. With his grip, she expected to have claws tangled in her fatigues, but when she glanced down, she gasped, again locking gazes with Scotch.

He just laughed. "Yeah, shocked me too."

"He... he's got hands!" She looked back down to where Spec held on tightly to her shirt, his paws more like those of a loris monkey or a raccoon. "How did we not notice he has hands?" Her voice must have risen. Again, she heard a throat clear and looked over toward the hatch. General Drovak lifted his hand in greeting while Sergeant Ryan looked about ready to have a fit behind him.

"Mittens," the general answered as he came over and deftly lifted the little Parr away, holding him securely in his arms despite Spec's efforts to get down again. "Scouts are more effective if they're able to masquerade as plain ol' cats when they need to.

"Now, if you'll join us outside...?" Drovak said, his expression grim. "We have a situation."

Kat nearly tumbled from the bunk in her haste to sit up, only Scotch held her steady.

"Right away, sir," he responded.

With a nod, the officers returned to the common room, the hatch closing behind them.

"Oh, shit! Oh, shit!" Kat muttered as she stood to tug her rumpled clothes back in order.

Scotch just shook his head and climbed around her, snagging his fatigues on the way out of the bunk. "Come on, Kat, focus. You can freak out later that the CO caught us *sleeping*."

Kat swatted at him as he moved past her, but again, he was right.

"Come on, sergeant. Get a move on."

Together, they left the compartment and joined the rest of the team around the conference table. In sharp contrast to earlier, not one of the Devils heckled them. General Drovak and Master Sergeant Ryan stood at parade rest waiting beside the mission board at the head of the table.

Shit... what happened while we were sleeping? Kat murmured over Scotch's private frequency.

Butt in chair, airman, and we'll find out.

Kat slid into an open seat next to Miki while Scotch rounded the table and sat beside his fellow squad leader, Zaga. As Kat turned her attention to the waiting officers, a now-familiar weight jumped to her lap. The Parr trembled and leaned into her. Keeping her attention at the head of the table, Kat petted Spec until he calmed, then settled. She couldn't help but notice the look of approval the general sent her way.

As acting commander, Ryan stepped forward, the tablet linked to the message board in his hands. "Sometime between 1800 and 1930 universal standard time, subversives abducted Captain Ty'rian Swarovski and extracted him from the *Cromwell*. Their purpose is unknown."

Kat gasped and sat forward, earning herself an annoyed squeak from the Parr.

All eyes turned to her.

"You have something to add, Sergeant Alexander?" Ryan asked, his annoyance clear.

"I saw Captain Swarovski this evening, sir. About 1900 UST, amidship, Deck 12, Corridor Epsilon. He said he was putting Scout Spec through a training exercise."

"Where was he heading?"

Kat's earlier guilt crept out of hiding, now with an added twist. "I don't know. I received a summons to return to crew quarters. He... he told me how to get back and then proceeded aft."

Nodding, Ryan turned back to the mission board. But that wasn't it. Kat straightened and spoke again, shrugging off her guilt to speak with confidence. "Sir, permission to speak?"

"What is it, Alexander?"

"Sergeant Ryan, when I reached quarters, no one here had summoned me."

Drovak and Ryan exchanged looks. Ryan's expression turned neutral as he glanced back in Kat's direction. "Thank you, sergeant. Now, to continue...

"Based on intel recovered after the subversive attack, we believe they have taken him, here—" Ryan tapped the tablet, and a series of images filled the mission board. "A former AeroCom testing facility located in the remote mountain region on Demeter."

He tapped again, and a diagram of the compound followed the photographs. "The main structure consists of three levels above ground, and three levels below ground, with additional support buildings. AeroCom records indicate that all usable resources, including defenses, were stripped when the building was decommissioned.

"We have received confirmation from our Dominion allies that Legion forces have commandeered the derelict installation for a base of operations. However, we have no information as to their intent or how long they have been entrenched.

"As of 2000 UST, the *Cromwell* moved into geosynchronous orbit above Demeter. Effective immediately, the 142nd Mobile Special Operations Team will deploy in a search-and-rescue operation.

"Our orders are to infiltrate that base and retrieve Captain Swarovski. As the situation allows, we are to gather intel on the Legion presence there."

Kat fought back a wince. She couldn't help wondering what Colonel Corbin had been thinking to put this clueless asshat in charge of a Special Ops Team. Did Ryan seriously think he was prepared to participate in a SAR operation? All of them had received exhaustive training to equip them for such missions. Ryan, on the other hand, clearly had never served outside of a non-combat setting.

"Any questions?"

Zaga raised his hand.

"Yes, airman?" Ryan asked.

"What is to be done about the Legion forces?"

General Drovak stepped forward. "If I may, Sergeant Ryan?"

"By all means, sir." Ryan fell back to parade rest.

Drovak took a moment and met the gaze of every Devil as if to acknowledge them and ensure all focus was on him. Kat swore he even included Spec. She knew for a fact his eyes subtly crinkled as he locked with her, which would have felt a bit weird, save for their recent conversation. To imagine, she had a fairy god general. As he came full circle, the general nodded, clearly pleased with what he saw.

"Our top priority is Captain Swarovski's retrieval," he said. "Failure in this would seriously damage AeroCom's alliance with the Dominion. Let me be very clear... failure is not an option."

Tension ran like a current through the team at his words.

The general continued, "As for the now-Legion facility, all other action will be dependent on your findings after insertion. Both peacekeeper companies will be ready for deployment upon your report, as will an assault wing of Valkyrie fighters from the nearest AeroCom base. We will either rout them out or bomb them to hell once you've extracted the captain."

He then stepped back and relinquished the floor to Sergeant Ryan.

"The transport is waiting at berth M0221. Warrant Officer Mata will pilot the insertion. You have ten minutes to gear up. Understood?"

"Sir, yes, SIR!" the Devils responded. Ryan looked unaware of the subtle tone of derision in their voices.

"Dismissed."

As General Drovak moved to depart, Kat stepped forward.

"Excuse me, general..." she said, attempting to hand over the Parr, only to discover he'd latched on to her blouse once more.

General Drovak's brow slightly furrowed as he turned to her. "Ah... yes. Scout Spec has been assigned to the 142nd for this mission, sergeant." He pointed to a small pile of gear by the hatch. "The Parr can explain the gear to you. His crate is already aboard the shuttle."

Before she could say anything else, the general had turned and gone, the hatch closing behind him.

"Kat, get moving!" Scotch called from across the common room, jarring her out of her shock.

Setting the now-cooperative Parr next to his gear, Kat scrambled for her bunk, stripping out of her fatigues and shimmying into her light armor—a ballistic mesh black suit with attached metal-infused ceramic plates—quicker than she ever had before, detaching her helmet completely for transport. She then grabbed her kit, making sure her tablet and field tools were inside, and left her bunk. When she reentered the common room, she stumbled to a stop in formation.

Sergeant Ryan stood by the corridor hatch, frowning down at the Parr Scout, who sat beside him totally unfazed, now ready and waiting in his own set of bad-ass cat armor, complete with clawed gauntlets and a miniature PacsComp helmet that left his muzzle clear but covered everything else.

"Cool, we have a new mascot!" Kopecky joked as he fell in beside her. "Does he do tricks?"

"Knock it off, Pecker! That scout is a valuable asset and trained just as hard as you to be here," Kat snapped, offended on the Parr's behalf.

"Children, quit squabbling," Scotch murmured as he and Zaga moved past them to take position beside the acting commander. When he reached the front, Scotch murmured something to Sergeant Ryan before taking his place beside him.

"Sergeant Alexander," the acting commander called out. With a nervous rumble in her gut, Kat stepped forward, coming to attention before Ryan.

"Yes, sir?"

"Alexander, you are hereby assigned as handler for the Parr Scout Spec, acknowledged?"

Kat's eyes widened, and her thoughts scrambled. What the hell did she know about being a scout handler? Scotch was going to pay dearly for this one. She had no doubt it had been his suggestion.

"I said, acknowledged?"

"Yes, sir. Thank you, sir." Despite her nerves, Kat almost laughed as she heard a happy chirp and Spec's suddenly increased weight settled against her calf. He totally threw her, though, when a soft, almost child-like voice came over the squad band, followed by a light tug on her calf armor plate.

Kat...

Startled, Kat looked down. She hadn't known the Parr could talk. Or think at her, anyway, facilitated by the PacsComp. Even in his power armor, Spec seemed so small. Almost smaller than the padded perch he held up to her. With his help, she managed to put it on over her left shoulder, marveling at the design that left her range of movement unimpeded but provided sufficient purchase for an armored cat to ride.

Once she had it in place, Spec tugged her armor again. *Down.*

Kat knelt, and the Parr leapt to her shoulder by route of her bent knee, staggering her only slightly. Even in his armor, he didn't weigh much more than her rifle, but it would take a little adjusting. She had barely straightened—pleased as the cat shifted to compensate—when Ryan snapped, "Form up and move out!"

High tension ran through each of them as they traveled the corridor again in columns of two, like friggin' green recruits, with Sergeant Ryan leading the march. This time they transited the distance to the docking bay without incident, but the remembrance of the time before haunted them.

As the Legion Courir-class stealth transport entered Demeter's troposphere, DeVeaux fought the stick hard. Nothing to do with reentry, nothing to do with meteorological conditions or technical malfunctions... Just a half-crazed gene-mod that was supposed to be friggin' unconscious wrestling her for control!

"Put him under, already," she snarled. "Before he takes us all out!"

"I am trying!" Agent Jan Orwell shouted from the cargo compartment. "But his metabolism just keeps processing through."

"Then triple-dose him so I can at least land this thing instead of crashing."

A long moment of silence followed, then suddenly the transport jerked into a near-roll as the force DeVeaux fought abruptly withdrew. She quickly corrected as Orwell stumbled back into the flight chamber, her face stark white and her entire front dark and glistening with blood, though there had been no sound of a fall.

"*Merde!* What happened to you?"

For a moment, Orwell said nothing as she tried to stem the blood flowing from her nose. Then softly, in a voice that trembled, she said, "The Ty."

"How? He could not hit you. What is wrong? What did this?"

"With his..." Orwell's words slurred, and her face grew even paler. "With his min—"

A sudden gush of blood spattered the compartment as the woman's eyes and head both rolled back, and her body crumpled to the deck.

DeVeaux muttered every curse she knew in French and otherwise. She could not leave the stick, and given the volume of blood, she suspected doing so, even if she could, was pointless. And still she muttered curses, frightened shitless that the monster's metabolism would free him from the sedative once more before she could get clear.

Recklessly increasing speed, the Legion scout skimmed down a different mountain a few miles from the base, carefully following the coordinates provided. Her hands shook as she came in for a rough landing, the meaty smell of fresh blood flooding her nostrils along with the pong of piss and shit now rising from Orwell's body.

DeVeaux sobbed with relief as the transport collided with some give, then stopped. She sat there, sweat trickling down her brow, only to panic and swipe at her forehead, imagining runnels of blood. Her ears strained to pick up any sound of movement from the back, but she heard nothing. When she finally rose, she squeezed her eyes closed tight, not wanting the horror burnt into her brain. Somehow, she found her way to the external hatch without falling or doing serious damage.

Stumbling out into the twilight, her eyes now open to search the terrain, she called out, "Where the hell are you? Come take him. I'm done with this."

Brightness flared before her, lighting the mouth of a tunnel sloping down beneath the root of the mountain. A man sat behind the wheel of a motorized cart just within the entrance, his face in shadow with the light at his back. As he powered forward, DeVeaux recognized him as one of the civilians working at the base. The ones that always made her uncomfortable. Tonight's mission reinforced her desire to remain uninformed and uninvolved. In fact, all she wanted at the moment was to climb into her Corsair and wing away.

She threw her hand in the air, turning her back on the man and the shuttle as she walked off into the forest roughly headed in the direction of the base.

She left a trail of bloody footprints.

CHAPTER 19

ABOARD THE COMBAT TRANSPORT 57-DELTA, THE REMAINING MEMBERS of the 142nd Mobile SOT sat grim and silent as they approached the planet Demeter, following the coordinates Command had given them. What would they encounter when they landed? A trap? Another SNAFU? Or Sarge's redemption? Kat just didn't know.

In the drive compartment, Miki was at the stick. Next to her, Sergeant Ryan had the conn. Though everyone on the mission had been vetted, Kat still had a hard time trusting Ryan. He was one of those regulation officers, all spit and polish, expecting everything by the book. Out in the field, stuff happened. Would he be ready to handle shifting situations? The sergeant lacked special ops training. Hell, he lacked genuine combat experience. PawPaw would have called him a pogue, a strictly rear-echelon officer.

Kat forced those doubts away and did her best to clear her mind and take advantage of the opportunity to rest when she felt an odd tremor through the bulkhead next to her. When it didn't repeat, she discounted it as normal turbulence until Mata swore, sort of.

"*Aaw*, Chris on a crutch!"

The soft-pedaled curse was so unexpected, Kat chuckled, but her amusement was short-lived as what seemed like a whole battalion of klaxons sounded. Warning alerts flashed on Miki's console, their garish light pulsing through the crew compartment. Kat considered getting up to check on Spec—locked down in his crate in the cargo compartment—when the transport shimmied and shook with more violence than any of them had ever experienced before in a craft presumably still in one piece.

"Mata, report!" Sergeant Ryan ordered.

Miki remained silent, busy fighting the stick. Kat didn't blame her. What was Ryan thinking to distract the pilot from her effort to regain control of the ship?

Next to Kat, Scotch released his seat restraint and started to rise in automatic reaction to the emergency.

Kat tugged him back down by his arm. Scotch settled next to her, but his attention remained fixed on those in the drive compartment. He scowled until he resembled PawPaw's bulldog, Rufus, though she expected Scotch's expression did not hide a sloppy sweet pup waiting for an excuse to roll over and have his belly rubbed, the way Rufus's did.

Down, boy, she murmured across the 'jack. *He's supposed to be big dawg here. Remember, that's part of what got us out of the dock.*

Scotch responded with a sub-vocal growl that rattled Kat's jaw. Unless they were on the squad band, no one else heard a thing. Kat fought down a laugh. *What? You gonna start pissin' next? This is the* acting commander's *show. Behave so we can take care of these Legionnaires. Then you won't have to deal with Ryan,* she reminded him over the private band. *Now strap back in while you still can.* She held her breath as she waited for him to listen.

Scotch looked ready to implode, his gaze never leaving the back of Ryan's head.

Buckle up, airman, Kat tried again, keeping her mental tone low and even. Not an order, just one airman looking out for another. This time he listened. He ranked her, but she knew he trusted her, which couldn't be said for Ryan. As Scotch locked down, she heard him order the rest of the Devils to do the same. Ryan should have given that order, but he still hadn't. What had Corbin been thinking? He might be a master sergeant, but she suspected Ryan had no idea how to command in a crisis.

As their flight grew more erratic, Kat released her crash harness from its compartment and slid her arms into the straps, securing everything together firmly over her armor-plated chest. A sudden bead of sweat escaped her comm hood and ran down her forehead. Enough red lights flashed on the cockpit console to cause an epileptic fit in someone not even prone to them. Each time the ship shuddered, Kat shivered and tensed, regretting that she'd stowed her helmet for the flight.

"Mother-lovin' son of a female dog!" Mata's knuckles stood out white, the tendons prominent in both hands and wrists. Despite the pilot's clear efforts, the stick shimmied and shook in time with the ship, yanked about by unseen atmospheric forces. It was a testament to Miki's skill that they still flew at all, let alone in a semblance of the proper orientation. Not that Ryan had any clue of that.

"What is the malfunction, pilot?"

Miki spared him one scathing look. "Good question, how about you tell me?"

"Leave her alone to do her job," Scotch snapped.

Suddenly, the tortured shriek of rending metal filled the transport, followed by a loud *pop*. Heavy, oily smoke billowed through the transport before it jerked, held its place a moment, and then plummeted faster. Gasps filled the crew compartment, followed by Ryan's cries of pain as his limbs banged about. Kat clutched her harness tight and kept her legs and body braced against her seat as best as she could. And yet, she still managed a glancing blow alongside her temple when the ship jerked and took her skull with it, bouncing her off the bulkhead.

"Ah! Crap!" Jags of light momentarily shot across Kat's vision. Past them, she saw Ryan, secured only by the standard strap across his hip, finally struggling with his harness. He didn't have a chance of securing it. His body slammed about with the force of the rough descent, his head leaving bloody smudges on the drive compartment wall. Kat winced as the man's right wrist bent in ways a wrist wasn't meant to. From the pilot's seat, Mata growled as Ryan bumped the control for the already struggling stabilizers.

She started to snap at him but stopped mid-word, her eyes locking on the monitor in front of her. The one that displayed images from the external sensors...

"*Fuck.*"

From the woman who didn't swear without sanitizing the phrases, that said it all.

No one said a word, but Kat noticed Scotch tense further before forcing his body lax.

"Brace for impact!" he ordered. Everyone complied, except for Ryan. Kat was pretty certain the last blow had knocked their acting commander unconscious.

The transport shuddered with even more violence. Mata redoubled her fight with the stick. Kat saw her muscles trembling. Moments later, the vessel's forward momentum briefly slowed after a hard, jarring impact. Instinctively, Kat ducked toward Scotch as much as her harness and armor allowed. The hull by her head crushed in, just barely missing her, as a high-powered stream of freezing wind invaded the compartment through a breach no bigger than the tip of her pinkie. A jagged edge of metal caught Kat's cheek as the side of the ship crumpled around her. The smell of burning electronics mingled with the sharp tang of blood. Kat barely resisted the urge to shuck the harness and bolt from her seat, away from the questionable hull section. Good way to end up with more than a goose egg on the side of her head.

"Mata, do what you have to do, but get us on the ground in one piece, stat!" Scotch barked.

The pilot stabilized the transport somewhat, if not slowed it. What remained of the ship bobbed and dipped, shaken like a child's snow globe, but Mata managed to keep it flying relatively straight and at a reasonable angle of descent... for the most part.

Another jarring impact trampled that thought, this time on the opposite side of the craft. They dipped to the right, the transport threatening to go into a spiral. In the drive compartment, Mata made up for years of almost-curses. Sparks flew out of the control console, and half the warning lights went dark as the electronics malfunctioned, dimming the eerie, hellish glow limning the smoke. The pilot wrestled with the controls and mostly won until something toward the back of the transport exploded.

A different *pop* followed as the fire suppression system released its chemical foam, smothering the impending blaze before it could begin. Somewhere near the wreckage, Ike screamed. More shudders ran through the bulkhead as if the shuttle strafed a mountaintop.

"This is it, folks," Mata bellowed.

They zoomed down at what felt like a headfirst, ninety-degree angle. Then, impact. A great, jarring crash, followed by a sudden slide sideways. Briefly, tortured steel shrieked, and rock smashed. They didn't roll, but near enough, Kat figured she now knew what a dime stopped on its edge felt like—well, if it could feel. The collision and sudden stop sent her and everyone else slamming into their harness straps, and in some instances, the bulkhead. Kat gasped as the impact snatched away her breath. Her head snapped to the side, colliding with the edge of the deformed hull where she'd already hit it before. The muffled groans of her fellow Devils filled the shuttle, cut by the faint hiss of escaping steam, as the crew compartment went dark.

Anton Petrov had no idea how long he'd been lost in a fog. At some point, he'd made it to the bunk but had drifted ever since, aware only of the hard slab of what some generously called foam beneath him and the full-body, bone-deep aches he could no longer pinpoint. He slid out of his stupor quickly at the sound of the security bolts on his cell door retracting. By the time the hatch opened, he was on his feet and ready for whatever they threw at him.

Or maybe not.

His brain locked up at the sight of a Legion security officer named Dell'Aquila half-supporting what was left of an AeroCom sergeant. Someone had worked him over. He moved under his own effort but seemed to need the assist. Or did he? Something about the way he held himself made Anton wonder.

"Good, you're upright," Dell'Aquila said. "This man has a shuttle docked on the farthest starboard module. If you're smart, you'll take him and get out of here."

"Doesn't sound very smart to me," Anton said, slowly shaking his head. He was fully aware of his precarious position. The captain and members of the crew already doubted his loyalty. Fleeing would only confirm their mistaken opinion.

The man grinned like an evil little cherub. "Now there is where you would be wrong. Someone has spread the word that you're a traitor, and all the data files on the *Cromwell* that this guy stole for us have just been swiped. As I managed to... obtain *your* security codes, I wouldn't want to be you when the captain finds out."

"You set me up to take the blame?" Anton ground out, clenching his fists.

"Well yeah, but to be fair, if you get to that ship, it won't really matter, will it?"

Anton's eyes narrowed as he carefully considered the man. "You son of a bitch! Why even bother letting us out?"

The guy laughed and gave him the side-eye, a smirk still on his lips. "If they're looking for you, they're not likely to notice me, now, are they? Yet, it gives us both an equal chance to get away." As he spoke, the Legionnaire stepped out from under the sergeant's arm, leaving the man to lean against the hatch. "Make up your mind now, 'cause I'm leaving, and it won't be long before they notice this one's gone from his cell. I'll even lead you to the shuttle."

Anton turned to the other man. "Are you on board with this?"

AeroCom straightened and pushed away from the wall supporting him. "I'd say I'm done here." Anton had to respect his grit, but did he want to take responsibility for the walking wounded? He considered leaving the stranger to his fate, horrified to find he'd descended to that level. And he still didn't know what to do. His whole life had been the Legion. Nothing aboard the *Destrier* or in the Legion held Anton's loyalty anymore. He did care about one thing, however... He pointed to the cell next to his. "Let her out, and we're gone."

Dell'Aquila nodded. "Done."

Anton's gaze locked with AeroCom's. He noticed a glimmer of respect in the man's eyes that he had rarely seen before. It felt good to realize that respect was for him.

A weight Anton hadn't yet acknowledged lifted from his chest. If nothing else, all of this would be worth it, just to get Sally free and safely away. His soul bore enough black marks from his time with the Legion without adding one more.

Kat woke up disoriented, struggling with conflicting impulses to grab for both her head and her gauss rifle. A groan rasped its way up from her battered chest. A strong hand reached out to brace her, pressing her gently against the back of her flight chair as the other hand released the clasp on the offending straps of her harness.

"What did I tell you about not usin' up what's left of those lives, Kittie Kat?" Scotch grumbled, catching her as she slumped forward.

"Still got some left," she mumbled back. "What happened?"

"Looks like sabota—" he started to answer only to cut off as the shuttle shifted, then settled.

Kat strangled a groan as she slid partway out of her oddly angled seat, the motion abruptly halted. Jags of light cut across her vision once more as her arm and shoulder screamed for a brief, intense moment under the weight of her body as the damaged hull pinned her in place. Her ballistic suit caught on the jagged metal and tore, then her shoulder followed as the draw of gravity on her body popped her free.

There was no helping it. She screamed.

"Whoa... careful there. I got you," Scotch murmured, his lips brushing the top of her head as she indulged in some cursing of her own. With a *thunk*, Zaga knelt beside her with the medkit. Kat gritted her teeth as he swabbed her various wounds with alcohol, stitched up her shoulder, then smeared on antiseptic cream. She nearly flinched away but Scotch wouldn't let her move, bracing her for Zaga's treatment. The cream must have been part analgesic because the pain faded to a dull ache by the time he applied the bandages. Zaga snapped a cryopack to activate it, then slid it through the rip in Kat's suit to lie directly on her bandaged shoulder. Several overlapping strips of duct tape secured the ceramic plate and everything under it in place. Good thing they were trained to fire their weapon with either arm.

Kat nodded her thanks as Zaga hurried over to help the other wounded. Moans and curses and quite a few clangs and bangs sounded all around her. She suspected the latter was someone stripping the transport of anything usable.

"Come on, let's get you outside." Scotch carefully drew her close-fitting comm hood over her bandaged head and helped her to her feet, not letting go as she staggered on the sloped deck. Until that moment, she hadn't quite noticed the chill in the air. The cold only intensified as they made their way to the external hatch, which someone had blown out with det cord. She had to assume the deformation surrounding the exit resulted from the crash and not the demolitions.

"If you wanted a new door, all you had to do was ask." The wiseass comment slipped past her lips before she realized it.

Next to her, Scotch snorted. "I do believe I'm an influence on you, Kittie."

She remained alert enough to notice he didn't say good or bad.

They both fell silent as they cleared the wreckage. Uncontrolled landings were nothing new to Kat. Between training simulations and participating in emergency aid efforts, the corps made sure all its airmen were intimately familiar with the reality of a crash site. This was her first time as one of those crashed. She could have done without the new insight. Her stomach tightened as she took in the wounded being tended on the slope around her. Ryan looked to be the worst. His face was barely recognizable beneath the bruises and contusions, but his chest rose and fell in steady breaths. Beyond him, Mata and Ike lay stretched out on bedrolls. The injured looked pretty banged up but not critical. Where were the others? Where was Spec? Kat spun a little too quickly, swaying as she searched for the rest of her teammates.

"Hey, watch it. You've met your quota of injuries for a while," Scotch muttered as he steadied her. "Don't worry... they're all okay. Better than you, except for Miki and Ike."

Not that she doubted him, but Kat didn't stop searching until she saw each of the Devils for herself, moving efficiently about the makeshift camp getting shit done before the light faded, helping with the other injured, or joining in the teardown of the transport. Toward the rear of the crash, Tivo and Kopecky scrambled to suppress the growing fires. Just the kind of beacon they didn't want any unfriendlies to spy. Even as Kat watched, they put out the flames and worked to disperse the dark plumes of acrid, polymer-scented smoke.

She turned to Scotch, worry furrowing her brow. "Where is Spec?"

"He's opted to stay in his crate for now," Scotch answered, pointing over by Miki and the wounded. "The crash rattled him."

Still staggering slightly, Kat turned a circle, viewing the scarred landscape around them. They had clipped a mountain on their way down. Dislodged rocks, bushes, and bits of transport littered the valley 57-Delta had plowed into. Her eyes traveled up. Okay... crevice, because those were steep mountains, and she stood in no gently rolling basin but a narrow, inhospitable wedge between two towering, tree-covered peaks.

Kat cursed.

"That about sums it up," Scotch spoke in hushed tones, as if not wanting to disturb the wounded being tended around them. "Tivo's extracted the locator beacon and the comm system. Once everyone's patched, and we've divvied up everything usable from the transport, we're humping out of here. We need someplace a little more hospitable and a lot less obvious.

"I sent Pecker and Truck to scout the terrain earlier," he continued. "There are overhangs a little further down. They cut deep into the mountainside. Too open to call them caves, but they offer cover and some protection from whatever this planet calls weather. In the morning, the rest of us will relocate camp."

CHAPTER 20

THEIR NEW CAMP EPITOMIZED COLD COMFORT. NO FIRE, NO TENT OR BEDROLL, and Kat's ration bar wasn't even a memory; she'd been that exhausted when she forced it down. And, thanks to the less-than-hospitable temperature of the planet, they couldn't even shuck their protective light armor to get comfortable. Kat couldn't complain, though. They were alive and far enough from the wreckage of their transport that the enemy shouldn't stumble on them anytime soon. Presuming there was even an enemy out there looking. Though they had crashed fairly near their target coordinates, she spied no sign of activity, covert or otherwise. Kat wondered if they hadn't been sent off on a snipe hunt.

Her head throbbed, and her cheek burned beneath the bandage covering the gash she'd gotten in the crash. Various other parts of her body ached with exhaustion. Time to get horizontal. Though they had reached the promised overhangs, Kat preferred to sleep out under the stars. With Spec as her power-armored shadow, she moved just outside the shelter next to a large rock she'd noticed earlier. It marked the only square of reasonably level ground that didn't have a crap-ton of rocks poking out of it, not that she would have felt them in her equally uncomfortable armor. Even Spec had opted to stay suited up.

With a sigh, Kat dropped her pack, and they both lay down to rest, while under the lip of the mountain the other members of the mission team did the same. Or most of them, anyway. In a pitiful imitation of the real thing, someone meowed above her and to the right. The sound of intentionally dislodged pebbles followed, pinging down the slope. Kat chuckled softly as the Parr grumbled beside her, whether at the disturbance or Scotch's poor rendition, she couldn't say.

"You better have milk and cookies with you," she called out in hushed tones, so spent she didn't have the focus needed to speak over her bonejack.

A faint chuckle whispered on the air as Scotch squatted beside her, eyes and teeth gleaming faintly through his open visor. The rest of him faded into the dark as the chameleon circuit on his armor shifted slowly in patterns of black and dark grey, mimicking the shadows cast by the moon. "How about a bedtime story, instead?" He spoke low enough the words barely carried to her ear. Something in his tone sounded ever so slightly suggestive, but that could have just been her imagination.

Kat growled, too tired and sore to smack him.

Another chuckle. "I brought you a present." Scotch held up a couple of analgesic patches between two fingers.

Now, if that wasn't motivation to move her sorry ass. Kat winced as she reached for the numbing agent. She couldn't make out Scotch's expression in the dark, but he gently pushed her arm back down. Dropping one knee to the ground, he leaned forward and tugged open her armor enough to slide a patch onto her shoulder, where she needed it most. The relief wasn't instantaneous but close enough. Kat's sigh wobbled slightly as she settled back, marginally more comfortable. Scotch gripped her good shoulder in understanding as he tucked the spare patch into the utility pocket on her forearm.

He then lowered himself to the ground next to her, leaning against the large rock that sheltered the place where she'd sacked out. For a couple of moments, he remained silent. His head slowly panned from side to side, and his muscles subtly tensed. In this mode, he could be on his feet and engaged in combat quicker than the downward sweep of a blink. All the members of the 142nd Mobile SOT could. Well... when they weren't all banged to hell.

"What are you doing out here?" Kat asked, shifted her head, pillowed on her gear.

"Guard duty. Now hush and go to sleep."

They had secured the camp and the surrounding landscape—the team wouldn't be bedding down otherwise—but thanks to the crash and injuries sustained by Sergeant Ryan, command fell to Scotch, and Kat knew how on edge that left him. Not that Scotch wasn't always hyperaware in the field, whether officially in charge or not, but the added responsibility kicked his natural impulses into overdrive.

"So, what's this about a bedtime story?" Kat asked once the tension in his shoulders eased. She knew better than to take him literally. He used such banter to defuse the edginess. Being alert was good. Being jumpy reduced combat effectiveness in high-stress situations. No, Scotch had come by to give her an update.

"Ryan's pretty banged up... severe concussion, broken wrist, a couple of deep contusions. He's stable for now, but Zaga's going to have to watch him close." Scotch said softly enough he might as well have been talking over the 'jack.

While Kat didn't wish their acting commander ill, she found it difficult to empathize with the man's injuries. His poor choices on the shuttle now put their mission—and the Devils—at risk. She shunted the thought away as Scotch went on.

"Miki's not so bad off. She jammed her knee in the crash, though. Those two are the worst of the injured." Out in the dark, something chittered, probably a Denebian, the pony-sized ant-like creatures that inhabited Demeter's mountainous regions. Scotch fell silent, scanning the terrain once more, his body taut and alert. Kat tensed beside him, ready to move at his signal.

For a few long moments, only night sounds broke the silence. She had no way of knowing if they were normal, all-is-well sounds or if they represented a warning the Devils should heed. Scotch must have decided there was no immediate threat because he resumed speaking.

"Ike is operating at half-capacity, semi-mobile, but not much use if it comes to heavy fighting. The rest of us are banged up but functional."

Functional, huh? She hoped Scotch was right. Kat reached up and ran her fingers lightly over her temple. A heavy, ridged scab bisected a lump the size of a baby's fist. It had the feel of a future interesting scar. Her first... or second, depending on how the cut on her cheek healed up... and she hadn't even gotten them in combat. Talk about embarrassing. The analgesic patch had done its job, leaving her with dull thumps in her head and shoulder rather than the sharp throbs of earlier, but she didn't feel up to par. And yet, thanks to her training, no matter how she felt at the moment, if a threat engaged their team, she *would* fight with all she had and more, regardless of her existing injuries.

"So, we're staying put a while?" she asked.

She felt Scotch nod. "Some of us."

Kat had a feeling she was about to regret her *functional* status.

"Get some rest, Kittie Kat," Scotch drawled. "You're gonna need it."

Like Anton had believed escape would be that easy. The entire time they'd slipped through the ship, he'd been waiting for his recently crappy luck to kick in. Instead of waiting, he should have bugged out in the other direction.

He, Sally, and... damn, he still didn't even know the man's name... AeroCom sheltered in a maintenance corridor just fifty feet from the promised shuttle. Dell'Aquila had taken off, easily blending in with the crew. Anton cursed the man, watching as he broke off and headed down the causeway to another berth.

"Hey, Petrov, head in the game," Sally prodded him as she and Aero-Com charged the weapons Dell'Aquila had tossed at them, unloaded, before he ditched them.

"We were never expected to reach that shuttle," he told her, still wondering how he could be such a fool as to put any amount of faith in what a Legionnaire said. "*This* is his diversion."

Sally shook her head, impatience twitching her right cheek as her nimble hands continued to move over her pistol sure and fast. "So? I've spent my life defying expectations, now load up and get ready because I damn well ain't giving up this close to freedom."

He looked toward AeroCom, who had finished charging his weapon and had picked up Anton's.

"You heard the lady," the man said as he handed over the ready weapon, grip first.

Shaking off his despondency, Anton accepted the weapon and moved to the mouth of the corridor. An alarm sounded overhead, loud and shrill, and someone had cleared the docking bay. Two more security details had arrived, but the men spread out, searching the bay instead of heading right for their position. Maybe the situation wasn't as hopeless as it seemed. Dell'Aquila must have disabled the security sensors.

Anton looked toward the others. "Get ready to move."

They nodded back as they moved into position behind him.

"Now!" he whispered as he crept slowly out of the corridor, keeping his profile low and his pistol at the ready. "Low and fast. Get down that causeway!"

He heard them scramble away behind him, but he didn't look. Their movement had caught security's eye and shots fragmented around him. Anton ducked and moved and returned fire with careful precision, all too aware of how little ammo he had. Soon he'd be throwing the gun at them. Only, finally, at his back, Sally called out, "Clear!" just before slugs started splitting the air above his head.

At a low crouch, he turned and ran. *Nearly there. Nearly there.* He kept repeating that in his head as previously injured muscles screamed, and a sharp, hot pain lanced his ribs. *Nearly there. Nearly—* A fireball pierced his leg, and Anton tumbled hard and to the right, slamming into the bulkhead a meter from safety. A volley of weapon's fire exchanged overhead. Anton rolled, bracing his weapon on his good thigh, returning fire.

"G-go," he forced out between clenched teeth. "Just toss me your weapon and go. I'll hold them." Anton didn't even know if she heard him. He kept on firing.

"Like hell, you stupid sonofabitch," Sally muttered as she grabbed him by the shoulders and dragged him to safety, shots coming from behind her, pinning security down.

"Thanks, AeroCom," Anton said, impressed by the man's fierce focus and steady aim.

"Daire, Sergeant Kevin Daire," the soldier corrected Anton as they reached the cover of the causeway. He then lowered his weapon and took over Anton's weight. "I got him, Lieutenant Tanner. Go fire the shuttle up." Then Daire heaved him up over his shoulders and ran.

Spiraling eagerly down into darkness, Anton retreated hard from the pain.

There is a very important difference between flying a ship and being a pilot. It is more than just skill. It is soul, an innate awareness that leads to craft and pilot maneuvering with precision, without hesitation or conscious thought, each reading the other with complete clarity. Sergeant Kevin Daire could fly a ship, and he expected the Legionnaire could too. Sally Tanner, however, *was* a pilot. Hell, Sally Tanner had to be the best damn pilot AeroCom had ever lifted to space, or Kevin was no judge of skill. She handled the *Teufel* like she'd always been at the stick.

After stabilizing the Legionnaire, Kevin checked the man's safety straps, then released his own feet from the boot docks holding them in place on the deck. He let his legs drift upward as he pulled himself toward the drive compartment to assume the conn. Out of habit, of course, seeing as Tanner ranked him. He pivoted down into the command chair anyway.

"Ma'am, it is an honor to watch you fly."

"Enjoy it while you can," she said, her gaze intent on the control screens. "Legion fighters have just taken up pursuit, and this bird has no talons."

Weapons. Kevin pushed off from his seat and arrowed back to the load compartment, dodging miscellaneous gear Cryson's men had left scattered after their search.

"Hey! Where you goin'?" Tanner called out.

"To fit you out with some talons," he yelled back as he grabbed a set of neodymium-soles from an equipment locker and fitted them over his boots. Once he could move upright and stand stable, he grabbed what he needed to refit the *Teufel* with cannons, relieved the Legion hadn't yet stripped the shuttle of useable gear. He struggled with the tension cap from the two-stage weapons port on the starboard side but finally cleared it. Sliding in a cannon auto-mount, he jacked the controls into the system and replaced the tension cap. A brief jolt and mechanical whir indicated the external seal retracted on reconnect. Moving quickly, he repeated the process on the leeward side before unstrapping his feet from the magnetic soles and arrowing back to the drive compartment. As he slid into the command chair, he activated the console before him. First, he engaged what minimal shielding they possessed as glancing blows shook the shuttle. Then, with no allies to worry about, he set the cannons to autofire and sat back to watch the show.

Sally gave a Texas-style whistle as she continued to bob and weave through the vacuum of space, dodging enemy fire.

"Where are we going, besides out of here?" she asked.

"I don't know. Give me a minute." Kevin called up the comm system and engaged an encrypted link. His fingers danced over the keys as he entered his security code and reported their situation. Within moments he had a promise of reinforcements and a set of coordinates, but not the ones he'd expected.

He plugged them into the system.

"Demeter."

Kat couldn't do it. She just couldn't do it. Sitting there on the side of a mountain, doing nothing but waiting to be rescued, about drove her mad. Despite the bitter cold, she hefted up the comm and, along with her ever-present feline shadow, marched out to the clearest spot she could find outside their camp, climbing slightly higher in the hope of getting some kind of signal. She sat there in the bright sun and buffeting wind and sent up random hails for what seemed like hours. Might even have been. It took long enough that Spec tired of tossing random pebbles in the air to pounce at and curled up beside her.

It took long enough she almost didn't realize when she received an answering hail, faint and crackly as it was, and nearly kept on sending.

"...repeat...read you, and have locked on your signal...ETA extraction, one hour from mark."

She wanted to whoop and holler the whole way down the mountain. Well, to the camp, anyway. But she restrained herself. *We have contact! ETA one hour!*

Good, Scotch interjected. *Get your butt down here and ready your gear before your ride gets here.*

Excuse me?

You heard me, Scotch answered, cutting the connection.

Kat stalked down that mountain, across the uneven terrain, and up under the overhang to confront him in person. "You are not leaving me here! I am more than ready and able to kick someone's ass up to and including yours! There is no way I'm sitting this one out."

"There's our little HellKat," Scotch chuckled. He then turned and gestured over Zaga. "Check her out," he requested, his tone immediately all business as he stepped to the side to give Zaga room for the medkit. As he opened the kit and started pulling out items, Scotch locked gazes with her. Kat worked hard not to give ground.

"If he clears you for combat, you can go. Otherwise, you will be on that transport if I have to hog-tie you myself."

Kat jutted her jaw but said nothing, well aware that was the best she was going to get. She turned away from Scotch as Zaga started giving her instructions. *Bend. Lift. Walk a straight line. Rub your head and pat your belly at the same time. Put your right foot in...*

Zaga almost had her on that last one, but she caught the gleam of unvoiced laughter in his eyes when she glared at him. He gave her the once-over as best he could on the side of a mountain, in armor. When he was done, he turned to Scotch and nodded. "Good to go, chief."

Chief? That was new...

Scotch quirked his lip and shook his head, looking equally annoyed and relieved at the assessment. Heaving a sigh, he waved Kat toward her gear, and then he sighed again as he took a closer look at her, his gaze lingering on her damaged shoulder. Kat fidgeted as he frowned.

"You and Miki about the same size?"

Kat frowned back, not sure where he was going with this. "Yeah... or close enough."

"Good, go swap armor with her," he ordered. "You're not fighting anyone like that."

CHAPTER 21

CAPTAIN JOHN CRYSON FOUGHT AN OVERWHELMING SENSE OF IMPENDING doom. Not just for this shit-show of a mission, but his very career. Was he to lose everything that mattered? With each failed objective, surely his superiors began to question his command, his dedication. Or even his loyalty. Through no fault of his own.

He clenched his fists as in his mind's eye, Anton's spectre gave him a pointed look.

"Status report?" Cryson snapped, banishing the phantom.

"The shuttle continues to evade," said the ensign monitoring the pursuit of the *Teufel*. "They are returning fire, sir. Three Esprit fighters with minimal damage, one destroyed in the initial exchange."

"Destroyed?!" Cryson sat forward, gripping the arms of his command chair. "That is a transport shuttle, ensign. What the hell are you talking about? We searched that craft down to the rivets. There was no sign of active armaments short of debris lasers."

"The dispatched fightwing commander reports returning cannon fire."

Though none of the crew had looked away from their tasks, Cryson was conscious of the attentive air that hung over the command deck at the report. He fought the urge to snarl.

It is one shuttle. One damn shuttle. And three... insignificant *prisoners,* Cryson thought, his teeth grinding as frustration clawed at his gut. Though he might thirst for immediate retribution, he couldn't justify it. The fighters were too valuable a resource to risk them getting payback. Besides, the Legion still had the data. It was only a matter of time before they cracked the encryption to uncover all the *Cromwell's* secrets. That should satisfy Command.

"Recall the fighters," Cryson ordered as he stood from his chair and crossed the deck to the hatch. "I'll be in my quarters. I want a full report when the fightwing returns. Direct incoming messages to my terminal."

"Yes, sir."

The first thing Cryson saw as he entered his quarters was the glow of his terminal. Someone had been there. He moved to the desk, his hands shaking. Fighting to get himself under control, he accessed the decryption servers. His head fell forward, and his knees nearly gave way. For a long moment, he stood there, his hands braced on the desktop and his head hanging as he took deep, settling breaths. Whatever else happened, he wasn't completely screwed. The files were still there.

His relief was fleeting. He called up the system logs. Tension returned as he scanned the list of files copied—including the *Cromwell* data—ratcheting up, transforming as his eyes hit an outgoing message log to Hirobon, complete with a fucking datalink.

Petrov's security code tagged each instance of betrayal.

It was too late to resume pursuit of the shuttle, but his former lieutenant would pay, eventually. In the meantime, Cryson sent an encrypted message to his operative at Hirobon, instructing him to intercept the files.

In a manner only military bureaucracy could manage or understand, one hour became ten.

Finally, in the frigid twilight before dawn, Kat and the rest of the assault force stood on the mountainside beneath the fading stars as a Valkyrie-class interceptor dropped out of orbit like a bright silver arrow. They watched as the pilot came in at a steep angle and then flattened out. Gimbaling six clusters of aerospike engines to achieve VTOL, the ship hovered above the clearing before their camp. All Kat could make out through the craft's canopy was a shock of bright red hair.

"This is Scarlet Jay of the Morrigans," the pilot hailed them over the comm, her husky voice relaxed. "Who's ready to get off of this rock?"

Before they could respond, the craft bobbed slightly before correcting as the integrated 20mm cannons powered up and changed angle with a low, smooth hum.

"Incoming!" Scarlet Jay barked from the cockpit as she suddenly fired the engines, sending her craft higher in the atmo until it was barely visible. "The signal is confirmed as Legion frequency."

Kat searched the sky. All she could see was a bright pinpoint as a ship above the horizon reflected the sun. It bounced and zipped as it evaded the air-to-air missiles Scarlet Jay fired its way.

"Be right back," Scarlet Jay sent over the comm, her voice hardened and intent. At the same time as her message came through, a familiar ripple ran along Kat's jaw. Sarge's voice came over her bonejack, issuing an urgent order to stand down. He must have broadcast that over the squad band because every Devil turned as one and lunged for the comm. Scotch reached it first.

"Scarlet Jay, this is Sergeant Daniels of the 142nd Mobile SOT, desist. Desist. Incoming is an AeroCom vessel! I repeat, incoming is an AeroCom vessel."

Kat forgot to breathe, her lips tingling as her gaze tracked the sky, waiting for a sign the message reached its target before the missiles did.

The comm crackled.

"Acknowledged. Scarlet Jay on a return course."

As the interceptor veered off in a silver arc across the horizon, the dot in the sky drew closer until the *Teufel* came into view. Cheers went up from the Devils, or most of them, anyway. Kat grinned over at Scotch only to find his expression solemn.

Everything okay? she sent over his private frequency.

It seemed he might not answer, then in a guarded tone quite unlike the Scotch she knew, he replied, *We'll see.*

The comm crackled again, and Kat jumped at the unexpected but familiar voice that spoke. "Mustang Sally here. The *Teufel* is coming in. We have one for medivac. I'm aiming for an outcrop an estimated thirty meters below your position. Do you copy?"

Scotch lifted the mic. "Acknowledged, Mustang Sally." Then, lowering the mic, he turned to Zaga. "You and O'Connor head down to meet them. Take your kit and one of the sling stretchers just in case." As they hiked down the incline, Scotch turned to those clustered around the comm.

"We don't have time for this, people. Get the wounded staged for retrieval. Stat."

By the time Scarlet Jay's interceptor hovered once more before their camp, Miki, Ryan, and Ike had been lined up at the lip of the overhang. The pilot carefully positioned her craft so the cargo hatch opened within three feet of the rocky surface, the engine clusters stirring up six columns of dust. A lean, muscular woman of Asian descent crouched at the ready on the edge of the load compartment, her chin-length ebony hair whipping about her face.

Scarlet Jay's voice came over the comm. "Raven will assist you with the onload."

"Acknowledged," Scotch said into the mic. Then with a grimace, he added, "We have one more incoming."

"I'll hold position for as long as I can."

Disengaging the mic, Scotch motioned Kat over.

"Get these three loaded, then you and the team gear up. I'm heading downrange to assess the situation."

"Yes, sir."

Scotch ducked beneath their sheltering overhang and pawed through the gear the wounded would not need for the upcoming op. He came away with a delta-eight assault weapon, a suit of light armor, a PacsComp-enabled helmet, and an ammo can of RADEF flechette SSC cartridges, some of the gear Ike's and some Ryan's. Turning to where the wounded were being staged, Scotch asked, "Mind if we borrow these?"

"Go for it," Ike called back. Ryan wasn't in any condition to respond.

Slinging the armor and rifle over his shoulder and hefting the rest, Scotch scurried down the mountain toward the trees, intercepting Zaga and O'Connor as they hiked up, someone suspended between them. Kat watched as they all stopped and spoke briefly before continuing their respective ways. She jerked as a tingle ran up her jaw. *Didn't your momma teach you it's not polite to stare?* Scotch said, his tone stern, with an undercurrent of amusement.

With a grimace, Kat turned back to the waiting wounded. *Mother would have a fit if she heard you call her momma.*

With a laugh, Scotch fired back, *Duly noted... for future reference.*

Kat stumbled at his words, feeling just a bit queasy at the thought of Scotch meeting her mother. One a force of chaos, the other a force of control. She couldn't think of one scenario where such an encounter would come out positive for any of them. Of course, who was to say she and Scotch would survive long enough to test that assumption?

On that cheery note, she headed for the group of airmen by the cargo hatch, including Zaga, O'Connor, and their erstwhile burden, now perched on the edge of the hovering deck. They stepped back as the woman called Raven helped him move further in so the hatch could close.

The interceptor had already lifted off and rocketed away before Kat realized what she'd seen just before that.

Scotch, she sent over his private frequency. *Where did the Legion officer come from?*

We have to have a long talk when we get back if you don't know that by now. It might even include diagrams and a hands-on demonstration.

She had to remind herself being a wiseass was how he diffused his tension.

Seriously, Scotch.

I'll explain when you get down here.

He disconnected before she could push him further.

Ty'rian woke up with bile laced with a heavy chemical taste spewing up his throat. Coughing and gagging, he tried to turn to spit to the side, only to find his head locked into place, strapped into what felt like some over-engineered halo brace bracketing his head, shoulders, and chest. He struggled to breathe, his body bucking against more restraints.

"Ah, ah, ah... Careful there," a voice murmured from nearby. "You'll hurt yourself."

Something *whirr*ed nearby, like well-oiled gears shifting, and suddenly whatever he was bound to tilted forward, allowing the spittle to stream from his mouth. Though it could not move, his head spun.

It wasn't until a blur approached his face and the edge of a cup brushed his mouth that Ty'rian realized he couldn't see. He couldn't turn his head away, but he refused to drink.

"What have you done?" he snarled, the words weak but full of venom.

"Don't worry. It will wear off."

Not exactly an answer, though clearly, a prisoner had no right to those.

Ty'rian closed his eyes and tried to focus, his mind reaching for what he wanted to know. And finding nothing. Nothing at all.

"What have you done?!" he yelled, only to gag on more bile as his body revolted against mental efforts that had always been natural for him. "What have you done?" he murmured again, weaker than before.

"Have you heard of enzyme inhibitors?" The voice remained matter-of-fact. "I'm afraid one was necessary for both of our safety."

Panic gripped Ty'rian even harder until he sat there, both numb and frantic, his head spinning like a whirlwind. He did not answer, but then he wasn't expected to. While Ty'rian was no scientist, he understood enough to know how his own body—and mind—worked, and the modifications he'd inherited from the first of Dr. McPherren's test subjects and down through three more generations were dependent on an enzyme structure to create the node that gave Ty'Pherreins their unique mental abilities.

His captors had, in effect, crippled him.

Tears streamed down his face uncontrolled as, for the first time since puberty, Ty'rian was locked within his own mind.

It feels good to move, Kat thought as they humped it down the mountain, *aches and all.* It wasn't easy—what combat operation ever was, in armor and helmet and gear?—but the challenge and the activity loosened her up, and anticipation warmed her blood. It was time to rain down retribution on the Legion, and Kat definitely wanted a piece of that. For True, for Brockmann, for the Devils themselves. But more than that, for the innocents dragged into the middle of this power play, the people of Demeter whose lives were in constant conflict because the Legion wanted to reclaim past glory.

Head in the game, Kat, Kopecky's voice came over her 'jack, apparently her back-up minder with Scotch gone ahead.

With a grimace, Kat turned her attention to the terrain before she took another slide down the mountain, or worse... turtled like a newbie. Kopecky was right to call her out. Between the slope and the rocks and massive old-growth trees dotting the mountainside, now was not the time to lose focus.

As they reached the tree line the *Teufel* came into sight, perched expertly on an outcrop just big enough to hold it. Every single one of the Devils gave a subvocal cheer over the squad band, almost as if they had planned it. But as Sarge and Scotch exited the shuttle to watch the team approach, the rest of the Devils took their cheers vocal, not privy to the intel she and Scotch had previously uncovered. Kat's gut twinged at the sight. Sarge looked beat to hell. He wore the spare light armor, sans helmet. The more the cheers continued, the more Kat felt herself withdraw from the celebration.

Sarge gave them a stern look and the cheers silenced. *Are you on an op or a picnic? File inside, and let's go kick some ass!*

Kat resisted the urge to frown. She paused at the edge of the outcropping while all the others surged past her to slap Sarge on the back. She stayed apart, hesitant to join in the elation felt by the rest of the Devils. As the team filed past him into the shuttle, Sarge looked her way, smiling as he noted the new rank, snapping a salute.

And who's this? Sarge asked, his gaze locking on Spec, perched on Kat's shoulder.

Parr Scout Spec, sir, Kat answered, but at the same time, Scotch chimed in over the squad band, *HellKitty!*

No! Stop it, Scotch, you'll give him a complex!

Sarge laughed at their usual banter, then sobered. *Are you coming, sergeant?*

Kat sobered, though she hadn't been that far from it, to begin with.

I guess that depends, sir.

On?

If you are on our side or the Legion's.

She watched closely—as he had with her not so long ago—for any change in his expression, any sign of deception, but he remained open, without even offense coloring his gaze.

Our side, every time, airman.

The fervor in his words was unmistakable. Kat chose to trust her gut and her commander. The particulars didn't matter unless he decided to share them, and she had to admit, now wasn't the time. She gave him a nod and a heartfelt salute.

He returned them and waved her aboard.

She noticed scorch marks on the hull as she approached the hatch, one just barely creasing the hull art. She reached out, brushing her fingers across the devil, still here, but not unscathed... pretty much like the Devils themselves.

Kat gasped as she passed through the airlock, dismayed at the state of the shuttle's interior. It looked like it had been tossed, gear all over the place, infrastructure disassembled. Scotch leaned against the bulkhead between the crew and load compartments. His expression looked as grim as she felt. Kat stepped to the side as Sarge cleared his throat behind her. He moved past her but sat in the crew compartment with the rest of the team instead of making his way to the drive compartment.

"Sir?" Scotch said, looking toward the command chair.

"It's your operation, Daniels," he answered. "I'm headed for a date with medbay once we drop your sorry asses."

Scotch grinned at Sarge's ribbing, then moved forward to assume the conn, while Kat took the space beside Sarge on the bench, Spec crowding in beside her.

"Lock down," Scotch called over his shoulder, and the team strapped in with their safety harnesses.

"All secure," Sarge called forward.

"Lifting off," Sally responded.

The sound of her warm Texas twang made Kat smile—a little reminder of home and all the reasons Kat had joined AeroCom.

As the *Teufel* lifted off and dipped down to skim the mountain, Kat settled back as best she could in full kit and helmet and bearded the dragon. *You promised to explain...* she sent over Scotch's private frequency.

Well, it's not like we don't have a little time. Scotch acknowledged. *A while back, the Legion tried to recruit Sarge, claiming they knew where his son was.*

Son? Kat hadn't even known Sarge had been married, let alone a father. It did explain the bearskin, though.

Yeah. Anyway, Sarge reported it to Drovak, who decided to take advantage of the situation. Like Drovak said, the Cromwell *isn't everything it was supposed to be. Still a damned effective ship but hyped up from here to Earth and back again. On purpose. AeroCom wants everyone focused on the* Cromwell, *so they aren't poking into anything else.*

Games. All of this hell and heartache had been about *mind games?* Kat fumed. She had had enough manipulation from her mother without the military joining the fun.

Sarge was ordered to 'turn,' not just to feed the Legion intel Command wanted them to know, but to dig up information on the composites.

And me? she snapped. *Was I ever going to be told how I was being used? You know... before they were forced to? Was Brockmann, and True, and all the other Devils?*

Come on, Kat, it's the military. When have they ever told anyone more than they felt was absolutely need-to-know?

Did you need to know?

That hung between them for a long moment.

Only about your purpose on the GEC, and I wasn't told that until we were on our way to retrieve you, Scotch responded. *The rest Sarge explained before you got here.*

Me, or the composite?

Be fair, Kat, we didn't know Ghei was a composite until we arrived!

When Sarge shifted beside her and gave her a look, Kat took a couple of hard, fast breaths and got herself under control, releasing the tension that had caused her to stiffen. Scotch was right. She wasn't being fair about any of it. Tensions ran high, and she'd let them get the better of her. It wasn't like this was her first tour. She'd known what she was signing up for. And whatever mixed feelings she had about that, a combat op was not the place to explore them.

Do you believe him? she asked, though she already knew the answer. After all, Scotch boarded the shuttle. She'd made that call herself, but she'd feel a hell of a lot better about it if she wasn't the only one.

I do, but even if I'd had a doubt, Drovak confirmed it all over interstellar comm.

That drove a cynical laugh out of Kat. *Of course, Drovak.*

The two of them fell silent, tensing as the shuttle dipped and banked and occasionally brushed against some element of the landscape they could not see. All in all, quite representative of life in the military. Kat reminded herself she had no cause to complain, given how relentlessly she'd pursued her career.

They couldn't fly all the way to their objective. Not without betraying their approach to the enemy, but they came within five klicks of the coordinates. With mad skills that had Kat shaking her head in awe, Mustang Sally landed the shuttle on top of the trees as steady as if it were tarmac, deploying balancing struts to distribute the weight evenly across the sturdy limbs and trunks. Quickly, the recovery team lowered themselves into the canopy, Spec leaving Kat's shoulder to leap directly into the boughs.

Call me, Sally quipped as she raised the struts and rocketed away to return Sarge to the *Cromwell.*

As the shuttle flew away, Scotch spoke over the squad band, *Engage your chameleon circuits and settle in, folks. We head out at dusk.*

Kat selected a sturdy branch and rigged a sling for herself, as did the rest of the recon team, spreading themselves around the crown of a forest giant massive enough to accommodate all of them. The branches, in the end, looked festooned with the most peculiar cocoons. She looked around for Spec and spied him curled comfortably nearby in the fork of the tree.

As they got settled, Scotch made his way from limb to limb, checking on everyone. When she looked up, she discovered him perched above her sling, hanging down to leer in at her. *Need help tucking in?* he asked.

You are weird.

May be, darlin', but you... are fine! He blew her a kiss—or maybe not, it was hard to tell in the gloaming—then he scampered like a monkey to his nearby sling and rolled right in. Kat's silent laughter set her gently swaying until she drifted off to sleep.

Yuki-ko glared at her screen, rubbing at the tension creasing her brow. She trembled as the twenty-seventh copy of the file Dell'Aquila sent her ate itself as had the twenty-six before, the fragments of the code fluttering like ash before her eyes. As they slowly faded away, the mercenary's crass laughter echoed in her memory.

She opened up the twenty-eighth copy, vowing to exact her vengeance on Dell'Aquila—and John Cryson—if it took her until her dying day.

CHAPTER 22

DUSK BENEATH THE CANOPY HUNG AS DARK AS MIDNIGHT UNDER A MOONLESS sky. In the deep shadows, all around Kat, silent warriors unfolded from their cocoons, lethal and predatory. With their helmets on, rifles slung, and camouflage engaged, they looked alien in the landscape. Of course, if she weren't in similar gear, she wouldn't be able to see them at all. But through her helmet display, they showed like ten fireflies scattered through the branches, each represented by a florescent green triangle and a three-letter reference code designating their names. Spec bounced from limb to limb between them, clearly excited to be on his first mission. He registered on Kat's HUD as a small green double-triangle designated SPC.

They attached rappelling lines and prepared to descend in silence. Only Kat didn't know what to do. She messaged Scotch, the PacsComp automatically translating the squad band to text. *<How do I get Spec down? – ADR>*

She waited for his response to scroll across her HUD. *<Ask him. – SCT>*

Real helpful! she thought. But what if it was? Kat looked down at the Parr. Feeling foolish, she sent to the scout, *<What do I do? – ADR>*

<Down – SPC>

It took Kat a moment—and a tug on her leg armor—for her to realize that was his answer. She squatted down on the broad tree branch, and the Parr approached. Rearing back on his haunches, he flipped back his armored gauntlets and did something with his belly armor, unfolding two plates like segmented wings with grips on the ends.

<Closer – SPC> he sent, and Kat leaned forward. Balancing carefully, Spec climbed her armor until he rested on her chest and reached out to fold the grips on his extensions until they clamped onto her chest plate, locking him tight. Then he looked up at her.

<Down – SPC>

With a silent laugh and a cat hugging her chest, Kat rappelled to the forest floor, rejoining her team.

<Kat, you and the Parr take point. Everyone else, spread out and stay alert. This is a covert mission. We do not engage unless we have no choice. Acknowledged? – SCT>

The entire team, including Spec, responded in the affirmative.

As Kat started out, a smaller window appeared to the left side of her head's up display showing her what the Parr saw as he ranged slightly ahead and much lower. At first, she found it disorienting as the scout jumped and climbed over obstacles, but she adjusted.

They moved like shadows through the forest, climbing over and around the giant root system, the marker for their objective coordinates shifting as they advanced, pausing only to avoid detection as enemy patrols intersected their path. As they moved deeper into the trees, about three klicks off their objective, Spec sent a message across the mission feed.

<Movement, left, twelve meters ahead. Is not a patrol. I smell blood – SPC>

<Danzer, Hemry, break off and investigate. Everyone else, hold position – SCT>

<Acknowledged – DZR – HRY>

Kat watched through Spec's feed as the two moved forward. Something must have alerted the target because it shifted away from them and increased speed.

<Target breaking right – SPC>

<Intercept! No kill shots, secure target! – SCT>

The order went out to the whole team.

Kat brought her rifle to the ready and advanced toward the target, vaulting over the roots and high-stepping over obstacles reminding her of the grueling PT Scotch had put them through not too long ago.

She would have to thank him, eventually.

The team markers on her HUD all advanced, converging on the target's position. Being point, Kat was closest. As she landed on the far side of an arching root, her knees flexing to absorb the impact, a pistol fired, sending her slamming into the root behind her. The ceramic plate over her right shoulder shattered, but the ballistic mesh held. Kat smothered a scream as the wound from the crash tore open at the impact. Ignoring the pain, she switched her rifle to her other hand and pushed to her feet, continuing her pursuit of the target, a woman in a Legion pilot's uniform armed with nothing more than a fucking pistol. What the hell was she even doing in the middle of the forest?!

<Alexander, report! – SCT>

<Later. Busy – ADR>

The team icons continued to advance, nearly encircling the target, but Kat didn't care. This one was hers. She vaulted and climbed and ducked for another fifty meters before she cornered the woman again. As the Legionnaire brought up her pistol, Kat watched the Parr inset on her HUD as Spec leapt from the cover of another arching root and swiped at the woman's gun, sending the pistol flying into the underbrush as furrows of blood welled up across the back of her hand.

"Stand down," Kat ordered, aiming her rifle but holding fire. <Spec, to me – ADR>

The woman stood there, her raised hands trembling and her eyes wild as she watched the blood run down her wrist. The Legionnaire seemed ready to pass out, but she just swallowed hard and looked away, glaring at Kat and her weapon.

Kat held aim until the others came on scene.

Scotch and Zaga came right to Kat's side, alerted by the PacsComp biometrics that she required a medic. Truck and Kopecky secured the prisoner while Danzer retrieved her weapon, which Spec was batting around like a snake he really, really wanted to kill. The rest of the team set up a perimeter.

<What happened? – SCT>

<She was waiting for me when I came over one of the roots. It's nothing. The stitches just tore – ADR>

Scotch looked to Zaga for confirmation. The medic nodded as he opened her black suit and repaired the damage, slipping an analgesic patch in before reapplying the bandage. When he closed her suit back up, he sent <A bit of fresh bruising from the impact, but no new damage, aside from the tearing. Move it – ZGA>

Kat complied, rotating her shoulder and raising and lowering her arm at every angle, wincing only slightly as the repair tugged.

<Shoulder your weapon – SCT>

Again, Kat complied, bringing the butt of her rifle to her left shoulder.

He shook his head. <Dominant side – SCT>

Kat shot Scotch a glare she was glad he couldn't see as she switched sides. There was a reason they'd been trained to ambidextrous fire. At first, her arm trembled with the weight of the rifle, gradually holding steady as the patch took effect.

Scotch nodded. <Report if that gets worse – SCT>

<Yes, sir – ADR>

<Now, let's see what we've got – SCT>

He turned and headed for the prisoner. Kat started to follow, only to discover Spec anchoring her foot, licking the blood off his claws like any other cat. Her attempt to move tumbled him. He looked up at her and gave a silent meow.

<Hey! – SPC> he sent, as he righted himself.

<Sorry – ADR>

Kat moved past him and headed for Scotch's side, arriving as Zaga finished patching up the woman's hand, better treatment than the Legion would have given them, were the situation reversed. When Zaga stepped back, Truck and Kopecky zip-tied her hands behind her while Scotch began the interrogation.

Question after question—from her name to the reason the Legion invaded Allied territory—the woman ignored him, staring straight ahead, her expression blank, occasionally broken by a contemptuous sneer. She had been trained well to resist interrogation.

The longer they stood there, the more Kat realized Spec continued to thrash his tail in growing agitation.

<What's wrong? – ADR>

<Smells. Smells like Ty'rian! – SPC>

For a moment, Kat didn't know who the Parr meant, then she accessed the briefing via the PacsComp. Ty'rian was Captain Swarovski's name.

<Scotch, ask her where the Ty'Pherrein is – ADR>

He stilled a moment, then repeated the question aloud.

Kat watched the Legionnaire closely. The moment 'Ty' left Scotch's lips, the woman freaked. Her gaze darted to her left, and just as quickly, she yanked her arms free from her guards' grip and ran the other way, her eyes wide and her face deathly pale, muttering in rapid-fire French. Hemry and Kramer easily caught her, but she thrashed and bucked until Kat wondered would she hurt herself or them. They ended the threat by knocking her legs from under her and sitting her between the knobs of two high roots.

<Zaga, sedate her – SCT>

The medic drew a hypospray from his kit and knelt beside the woman, pressing the injector to her neck. After a moment, her struggling stopped, and her head nodded forward.

<Hemry, Kramer, keep guard over her – SCT>

Scotch then turned to the rest of them, his gaze locking on Kat.

<Talk to me – SCT>

Kat looked down at the Parr and then back up, holding Scotch's gaze. *<Scout Spec smells Captain Swarovski on the prisoner. When you asked her where he was, she looked toward the mountains... that way – ADR>* Kat pointed to her right, about forty-five degrees off from their coordinates.

<Are you sure? – SCT>

<Sure that's where she looked? Yeah. Sure that's where he is? Not really, but we have a scout that can follow scents, and she was clearly with Swarovski. All Spec needs to do is sniff her – ADR>

Scotch nodded and looked from Devil to Devil as if checking his resources, his gaze ending on Spec. *<Well, HellKitty, get sniffing – SCT>*

<Yes, sir! – SPC>

Spec darted forward, his nose twitching from one end of the Legionnaire to the other. He pinched a piece of her uniform where it touched her skin and looked up at Kat. *<Cut, please – SPC>*

Kat pulled out her combat knife and cut a swatch, holding it out to the Parr.

<Thanks – SPC>

He folded back his gauntlet and accepted the scrap, sniffing it deep before twisting to put it in a utility pocket on his back. Then, after he restored his gauntlet and had another sniff at the prisoner's boots—which Kat just realized were caked with blood—Spec darted off.

<Hey! Wait... – ADR>

Scotch shook his head and waved her back when Kat would have followed. *<Let him get a head start. He has to find the trail. Huddle up. We can track him via PacsComp – SCT>*

<Yes, sir – ADR> But Kat's gaze followed the direction the Parr disappeared. She frowned and sent a separate message. *<Spec, was it his? The blood? – ADR>*

<Nope – SPC>

Relieved, Kat turned her attention back to the huddle.

<Tivo, send a message to Command requesting extraction of the prisoner. Maybe they'll have better luck getting something out of her. Hemry, Kramer, you remain here, stand guard until extraction – SCT>

<Yes, sir – VEE>

<Acknowledged – HRY – KMR>

Nodding, Scotch looked over the remaining team. *<Well, what are you waiting for? We have a man to rescue! – SCT>*

CHAPTER 23

TENSION CRACKLED ON THE COMMAND DECK OF THE *DESTRIER* AS THEY approached the planet Demeter, stopping just beyond the range of both the Allied tracking satellites and the Hirobon outpost. They just sat there with no further course of action. All of the crew avoided Cryson's gaze as they went about their duties or pretended to.

"Scan for other vessels," he ordered, contemplating the viewscreen as he tried to formulate a plan. The operatives were on the planet, as was the defunct synthetic. The *Teufel* was gone—damn, Anton and Daire both—but Cryson needed to retrieve those assets.

"One Shonin-class freighter on vector for departure," one of the crew reported. "Two private yachts locked in stable orbit..."

Cryson frowned, wanting to believe but distrustful that neither the Dominion nor AeroCom seemed to have craft in orbit around this contested planet. Of course, both of them had more than enough defensive vessels flight-ready on the ground. Still...

"Keep scanning," he said.

A message pinged on the monitor beside his command chair. He glanced over and bit off a curse at the sight of the cross icon. Text scrolled across his screen. *<We have a problem. Your pilot crashed a Legion craft right outside our secure entrance, in plain sight. Then walked away.>*

A sigh escaped him, and John Cryson began to wonder for the first time if any legacy was worth such aggravation. *<Was the prisoner delivered intact?>*

<Not the point.>

He could do nothing. No longer caring about the Knights' machinations, and beyond hope in regard to his career, Cryson typed back, *<I'll get back to you.>* and ended the connection.

"Sir, we have what looks like a Legion craft on sensors fleeing the Hirobon station with Senshi-class fighters in pursuit," the scanning operator reported. "The beacon has been recoded, but the hull designation matches our manifest, it's the shuttle *Fidèle*."

"What?!" Cryson turned to his monitor and called up an interstellar link to Yuki-ko, his only contact at Hirobon.

"Captain Cryson, I do not have the time for you."

"Why are you pursuing one of my vessels?" he demanded, fully aware she wanted to tell him, or she would never have answered.

"To pay Larry Dell'Aquila back for the worthless data he stole from you," she murmured with a slight bow. "You are welcome."

Cryson went very still, now staring at a blank screen. His blood pounded in his veins, and rancor took root in his heart.

"Why was I not informed that crew and craft were missing?" he demanded.

No one answered. Perhaps wisely.

"Sir, your orders?"

"Pursue that craft. Take fire when in range."

"Sir?"

"I said, fire when in range!"

The *Destrier* came about and breached the safe margin, passing within scanning range. Cryson no longer cared what vessels were nearby or what satellites registered their presence, as long as he could deal retribution for just one betrayal.

As they drew closer to the fleeing shuttle and the gunner staged the rockets, a sudden blast shot past their hull. The *Destrier* shuddered in its wake.

"What was that?" Cryson growled, his gaze snapping to the scanning operator.

"I don't know, sir. Sensors pick up nothing."

"Continue to pursue that vessel."

As the crew scrambled to correct course, another blast fired past their hull, this one closer.

A hail came across the comm.

"This is AeroCom vessel *Cromwell*. You are in violation of restricted space. If you do not depart Demeter orbit, our next charge will be a disabling blow, and we will confiscate your vessel."

Cryson was very nearly ready to let them have it. Nearly.

The helmsman turned toward him, his expression uncertain. "Sir?"

Through clenched teeth, Cryson snarled, "Retreat."

He continued to watch the disappearing shuttle until it was no more than a dot lost among the stars. The irony did not elude him that the shuttle's name meant 'Faithful.'

The remainder of the recovery team crouched beside what appeared to be a seamless mountain. After following a trail of blood and fears, they discovered a gash in the landscape where velocity met immovable force. Kat saw no sign of the craft that left the scar, but she was beyond certain the rust-colored footprints leading away from it belonged to the Legion pilot they'd left in the forest.

<*Has he discovered anything? – SCT*>

Kat turned to her team leader. <*Trail ends... or rather starts here – ADR*>

<*Spread out, everyone, find me a direction to go in – SCT*>

They combed the area in the middle of Demeter's moonless night. Kat and Spec crisscrossed the area spreading out from the site of the crash. They discovered no tracks, but the Parr kept making grumbling noises that the PacsComp struggled to translate.

<*Spec, what's wrong? – ADR*>

He turned to look at her and gave a silent, petulant meow, his little muzzle looking distinctly frownish. <*Stink. Blech – SPC*>

Kat moved to where he crouched down, expanding the sensor readings on her HUD, looking for any sign of what the Parr referred to. Nothing registered for what seemed like forever, then, suddenly, a flash of red. And another.

<*Scotch! I have something – ADR*>

The team converged on her position.

<*What is it? – SCT*>

<*Atmospheric analysis picks up faint traces of fuel along this path – ADR*> She gestured to the ground before her and carried through to where jagged boulders jutted up from the base of the mountain. <*Spec says it stinks – ADR*>

<*Remind me to requisition Spec a tuna when we get back – SCT*>

Spec started to purr, which the PacsComp didn't have nearly as much trouble with.

<*Okay, people, we have a direction now find me the door! – SCT*>

In the end, it was nothing but an optical illusion. A ramp led to a shiny metal door that reflected the surrounding outcrop, blending into the mountain.

<*Seriously? – ADR*>

Zaga came up beside her as Kat scanned the area surrounding area for sensors or traps.

<Not like they get much traffic up here – ZGA>

<Help me find the control box. They might be cocky, but I doubt they're stupid. There's no way getting in is this easy – ADR>

<I have electrical activity over here – VEE>

Kat made her way over to Tivo. Setting down her kit, she extracted her tools and her tablet. Then, going on the hunch that their adversary was, in fact, too full of themselves to bother being tricky, she reached out and pushed down on the area where Tivo pointed. It took a few tries, but she found the correct point. A seam of rock depressed and slid away, revealing the controls for the retractable door.

<Do we have anything on warning sensors? – ADR>

<Ten located and disabled, scans show no sign of similar signatures in the zone – OCR>

Kat waved her thanks in O'Connor's direction and turned back to dissecting the panel before her.

<Come on, Kat, we're burning cover – SCT>

She looked up to spy the lightening sky way overhead, not even close to touching where they huddled, but still. *<Al... most... There! – ADR>*

Without a sound or even a vibration, the doors retracted, and light poured out the tunnel.

<Crap! – ADR>

Kat turned back to the panel and accessed the screen, looking for a way to turn off the sudden beacon lighting up the mountainside. With a few hurried adjustments, darkness resumed.

<Good job, Alexander – SCT>

<Thank you, sir – ADR>

<Listen up, Zaga, Danzer, Tivo, O'Connor, you hold position here. Do not let anyone leave, enter, or close that door, understood? – SCT>

They all nodded.

<Everyone else, with me. Kat and Spec have point. I'm tail end. Move it! – SCT>

In the pitch black of the tunnel, Kat switched her PacsComp to active infrared, as did the rest of the recovery team, all save for Spec. They made their way in silence, creeping downward for about thirty feet before leveling off. And then it seemed they walked halfway through the mountain that never ended. Kat continued to scan for the electronic signature that betrayed the sensors outside but encountered nothing. Even so, the hair at her nape bristled beneath her helmet. By her PacsComp, they'd gone another a little over one klick when she would swear she heard shuffling somewhere in the darkness. Before her, Spec had gone belly to the ground, his head scanning back and forth as he crept forward.

<Hey, Scotch... – ADR>

And the PacsComp cut off, reduced to internal functions.

Bright light flared all around them, and blaring klaxons echoed off the walls as a half-dozen soldiers piled from alcoves along the tunnel. Kat's eyes squeezed shut at the influx of light. There was nothing she could do about the sound but ignore it. She took aim on the afterglow emblazoned in silhouette on her vision, but did not fire, forcing her eyes into a squint to make sure she targeted the other side. Her eyes burned, but Kat saw clearly enough to aim and fire as she took evasive action. Using one of the alcoves they had not noticed in the dark as cover, she took careful aim not to add to the ricochets bouncing from the tile walls, nearly deafened by the echo of gunfire punctuated by cries of the wounded. She fired two shots in quick succession, wincing as the rifle kicked against her shoulder. As one enemy fell dead and the other spun away with blood blossoming from his upper arm, Kat crouched down to take stock, dodging back from enemy fire. She came up hard against something metal. Pivoting, she spied a utility cart stored at the back of the alcove, plugged in to charge, but nothing else. Turning back to the tunnel, she peered out once more.

Truck had taken cover in an alcove on the far side, back toward the way they'd come, and Kopecky huddled against the same wall, caught in the middle between them, a bright red gash in his ballistic mesh and shattered ceramics littering the ground. Scotch stood over him. Both had their weapons raised, fending off assault. There was no sign of Spec.

Kat switched her rifle to her other hand and slammed the weapon from three-round-burst into full-auto, chewing up the remaining men, keeping her aim down the center and away from the walls.

The silence echoed as the gunfire died away.

Scotch immediately dropped and took a knee beside Kopecky, using his combat knife to tear the ballistic mesh further.

"Kat! Truck! Get over here!" he bellowed, being stealthy no longer a concern. "Quick!"

They scrambled from their cover and converged. The metallic tang of fresh blood flooded Kat's sensors.

"Here, take this." Scotch thrust his knife toward Kat, not even looking to confirm she had it before he bent once more to tear the strip he'd started from Kopecky's black suit. When he was done, he took the knife back. "Truck, watch for incoming. Kat, I need you to press down right here."

She leaned where he pointed just at the juncture of Kopecky's thigh, briefly stemming the growing crimson pool. Once she was in place, Scotch cut away the rest of the armor from the thigh down, sawing at the ballistic mesh until black suit and plates fell away, leaving blood-soaked flesh. Looping the strip of fabric just above the wound and tying it off, Scotch then pulled a splint from the first aid kit tucked among the various explosives in his kit and cinched the tourniquet tight.

He then turned to Truck. "That's not going to help for long. You have to get him out to Zaga."

"I'll run all the way," he answered.

"No! Wait..." Kat stood and ran back toward her alcove. She scurried around the cart and confirmed it had a charge. Then, yanking out the plug, she climbed in and fiddled with the controls, finding them not much different from the carts PawPaw used on the ranch. Carefully, she backed out and drove to her team, leaving the cart running but shifting into park and hopping out.

"Come on, let's get him in the back."

"Good. Now get him out of here," Scotch said, turning to her.

"Sorry, but you may need me," Kat answered, gesturing toward her kit. "Besides, I have to find my scout."

Scotch looked like he wanted to argue, but there was no time, and Kat knew it.

"Go! Get him out of here!" Scotch growled at Truck. Turning back to Kat, he nodded in the direction of their objective and headed out at a clip.

Kat quickly followed, pausing only once as she passed an enemy body. Spying an id badge, she snatched it up, sliding it into a utility pocket as she continued running.

Little by little, Ty'rian's captor deactivated the enzyme inhibitors, forcing him to drink a foul substance to regain the tiniest sliver of his true self. Not too much. Just enough that he could play lab rat for the bastard's tests.

And if that wasn't rich. He had been snatched to improve the operation of the very composites he'd helped to neutralize.

"I don't know what you expect to accomplish," he muttered after exhaustive scans and pokes and prods and not a little mental torture. "It's not like any of us will ever do this voluntarily, and the results are hardly worth it impeded."

His captor turned and glared at him. "Looks like you might be ready for a bit of rebalancing," he snapped, moving from the computer to the beaker containing the enzyme inhibitor.

No longer desperate enough to be compliant, Ty'rian locked his jaw tight, the extent of his possible rebellion while restrained in his neuroscanner-slash-personal cage. When the man reached to pry open Ty'rian's jaw, he released long enough to grind down on the fingers, hatred in his eyes and the man's blood on his lips, daring him to lash out at the very thing he required intact.

Swallowing a scream, the man wrenched his hand away and instead snatched Ty'rian's finger, yanking it back further and further, leverage in their battle of wills. A loud snap filled the lab as Ty'rian refused to yield, abruptly drowned out by an alarm, as was his strangled scream.

As the pain-fueled adrenaline coursed through his blood the effects of the compound loosened. Ty'rian's vision cleared and the shutters blocking his mental abilities gave just the slightest beneath his continued efforts to break free.

His tormentor snarled and Ty'rian returned his glare only just noticing the emblems at the man's collar. Ty'rian stiffened as he recognized the symbol of the infamous Teutonic Knights, well aware of their machinations. He renewed his struggle with increased vigor.

"Clearly, we no longer have time for this," the Knight growled as he reached for a large-bore syringe on the counter behind him. "I'll just have to collect some samples and grow my own psionics. Shouldn't take long with our advancements in progenesis..."

Ty'rian went dead-still, his eyes blazing, every dark and painful memory from his childhood being raised in a lab bubbling up to fuel his rage. He said nothing. Did nothing, outwardly, but with all his focus he threw his will against the barrier locking him inside his own mind. For the first time ever, with his conscious thought, he willed harm to another person.

The syringe fell to the floor, shattering.

So did the Knight.

The going was much quicker with the tunnel brightly lit, though Kat could have done without the continuing klaxon. When they reached the end, they found a frustrated Parr slashing at a set of utilitarian double doors. Spec spun and crouched, hissing until he realized it was them. He shook his head as if to clear it, but the link to the PacsComp remained inactive.

Unable to communicate, he bounded over and pressed hard against Kat's leg, meowing up at her over and over without sound until her heart nearly broke for him. Kneeling, she patted his platform, holding steady until he gained his perch.

As she straightened, she noticed Scotch had set C4 charges all around the entrance of the tunnel. He then lifted his rifle high, ready to strike the doors in an effort to bust them open. She gripped his arm, stopping the blow. "Let's try this first... we might want those doors to work later," she quipped, holding up the id she'd grabbed.

"Wiseass," he murmured as she swiped the badge across the sensor beside the door.

Instantly, the klaxon cut off as the door buzzed open.

Before either of them could move, Spec squeaked the loudest sound Kat had ever heard from him and leapt from her shoulder, kicking her back with his force.

"What the hell...?"

Scotch just shot her one of his looks and ran after the cat, their triangular icons bouncing off into the distance, turning right.

<Oh! The PacsComp link is back online! – ADR>

<Goodie, now move your ass. This Parr is linked to you, which means I'm running blind – SCT>

Kat followed the icons, weapon at the ready, the path twisting and turning back on itself like a maze. In the distance, she heard shouting and the sound of many feet pounding the floor. She ignored it, as she'd been trained, other than to gauge them distant enough to disregard.

As she traversed the subterranean maze, she passed open door after open door. Some rooms contained labs or server banks, while others held what looked like the high-tech equivalent of medieval torture chambers, with chairs and restraints similar to the one used to restrain Ghei and what looked like the production mold used to create the synthetics. All the rooms appeared hastily abandoned.

<They just fled. They didn't even try to defend... – ADR>

<Not surprising. The Teutonic Knights aren't known for military conquests. They'd rather manipulate behind the scenes... conquer from within. Now move your ass already! – SCT>

Despite Scotch's urgency, Kat gave in to the temptation to dart into several of the rooms looking for what intel she could grab—computer data, photographs... anything, only the place had been stripped clean, nothing but empty file draws and gaps in the computer towers where drives had been ejected. Cursing, Kat gave up, as Scotch's aggravated urgings continued to scroll down her display.

Good thing she had the PacsComp signal to follow, or Kat would have been hopelessly lost, the hidden base a veritable warren, twisting and turning beneath the mountain. She finally caught up as Scotch and Spec held position beside a nondescript door, one of the few still closed.

Spec looked back at her.

<OPEN! – SPC>

Before she could override the electronic lock, Scotch stood back and kicked in the door. They both froze at the sight of Swarovski half-strapped into some bizarre contraption, working to rip off his restraints one-handed. Dried blood covered the bottom half of his face, and at his feet lay a body in what used to be a white lab coat.

"What did they do?" Kat said, moving forward to help him, except Scotch threw out his arm to stop her. Only then did she realize Spec cowered at her feet.

"Rig it all to blow," the Ty growled, his eyes half-crazed and his words rife with menace. "Now!" At his yell, all the straps tore away, leaving him unbound.

He hadn't used his hands.

Slowly, Scotch passed Kat his weapon and swung his pack down, flipping it open to reveal a few remaining charges. "Okay, *captain*, okay," he said in a soft murmur, low and soothing, "just let me know what you want gone."

"All of it!"

"No problem, I got you. Just point me to the right things, okay?"

"Wait!" Kat grabbed Scotch's shoulder. "We need that intel... they've taken everything else!"

"NO!" the Ty roared, lunging forward until he crouched between them and the computer banks, his expression frantic to the point of being nearly unhinged.

"That data is our best opportunity to counter the composites!" she argued. "Destroying it here won't take it away from the enemy. It only robs us of the chance to defuse their advantage."

Swarovski snarled, and Kat fought not to retreat in atavistic response.

Suddenly, Spec darted in front of her, rearing on his haunches with titanium-clawed gauntlets poised to strike his trainer. Over the PacsComp, Kat heard his sounds of distress, but the Parr did not waiver in her defense.

A shudder coursed through Swarovski's body, and a measure of clarity returned to his gaze. His eyes dropped and darted to the computers as he straightened and backed away, but his teeth and his hands clenched as if to do so he fought every instinct for self-preservation.

He gave her a stiff nod. Even so, she looked toward Scotch for approval before approaching the nearest terminal.

"No."

Kat drew breath to argue again, but Scotch cut her off.

"I said, *no*. If the captain feels this strongly, there is a reason. There are other ways." He waited for her to nod, however reluctantly. "Now fall back to the corridor."

"But..."

"Now!"

Kat backed up slowly until she cleared the door.

<Now hold position while I take care of this. Acknowledged? – SCT>

<Acknowledged – ADR>

<I tell you to go, you go! – SCT>

Kat remained silent, but he didn't push her. She strained to listen. The distant movement she'd heard earlier had faded. Her grip tightened on her rifle, and her teeth clenched. "Scotch..." she said aloud.

<Not. Now! – SCT>

"Scotch," she repeated urgently, "we've got to go! Now!"

He hurried to the door and poked his head out, spying the thickening smoke.

"Shit!"

She watched as he ducked back into the room, rushing to his kit and grabbing the charges. He slapped one on every computer or storage device in sight and turned to Swarovski.

"Done. Now let's go home."

"Go," Swarovski ordered. "Just go, while you still can."

"Can't do it. We have orders to bring you home."

"Just go," he repeated, tears streaming down his face as he raked his fingers through his hair despite several being broken, his gaze tormented.

For a moment, Kat expected to die in a pool of her own blood like the man crumpled at Swarovski's feet when a squeak rose from below her. Spec suddenly bounded into the room and passed Scotch before either of them could react. The Parr came to rest at the Ty'Pherrein's feet, squeaking frantically and tugging at his trainer's leg. At his *friend's* leg.

"Come on," Kat said softly, edging out of the door and toward the way out. "Let's get Spec home."

Despite their conflict moments ago, Swarovski looked up at her as if that was the first he'd noticed her. He then looked down at his feet. Grabbing the cat, he ran, Kat and Scotch close behind him. They barely made it to the tunnel when something exploded behind them, and dust and debris billowed down the corridor.

"Go! Go! Go!" Scotch ordered, but Kat stopped at the first alcove, then the second, then the third, until she found what she searched for. This time she took less care, zipping out of the alcove and down the tunnel, barely slowing for Scotch and Swarovski to pile on. Then she pushed the cart to its recommended limit and beyond as the tunnel crumbled behind them, and the mountain tried its best to fall on their heads.

Kat didn't even stop to wonder if the other end of the tunnel would be open. She powered through, the cart going briefly airborne on exit as it zoomed up the ramp.

As she skidded to a halt, she heard so much cheering and applause she expected someone to hand her a trophy next.

Now that's what I call bringing down the house, HellKat. Dayum! Scotch said over her private frequency. Kat's bark of laughter contained just a touch of manic edge as she half-heartedly swatted him.

EPILOGUE

THE LAST THING KAT EXPECTED TO SEE WHEN THEY CALLED FOR EXTRACTION was the *Teufel* setting down her struts. But there she was. Weary and spent, Kat still had enough energy to grin.

"Come on, kids," she called out to the Devils sprawled out on the bones of the mountain, "time to go home."

Not one of them complained.

As she hauled herself up and gathered her gear, she startled at hearing Sarge's voice over her bonejack. *Well done, sergeant.*

She spun around to find him waiting at the hatch, waving the team inside.

"Well, come on," he called out. "Command's got a surprise for you."

Scotch, what is he talking about?

How should I know? he muttered back. * Ask him.*

Kat didn't, though, not too sure she was up for any more surprises, personally. Instead, she helped load the wounded—walking and otherwise—then plopped herself on a bench in the crew compartment. Spec moved to sit at her feet with his suit still on but his helmet back. He looked up at her, then over to Swarovski and back again, seeming conflicted. She reached down to scritch behind his ear, then nodded toward Ty'rian. Spec leaned into her touch a moment, and she heard him purr. When she sat back, he pivoted and sauntered over to his former trainer, leaping to the bench beside him. The sight made Kat smile. Then, like any good operative, she settled into a light rest, rousing only to gather her gear and disembark with the rest of her team.

Once she exited the hatch, she instantly came awake, her mouth opening in awe and her eyes darting everywhere, finally settling on General Drovak, waiting with a delegation to greet them, much as she and Scotch and Zaga had done for him not so long ago.

Only... this was *not* the *Cromwell*.

"Welcome to the *Cypher*, the true flagship of the AeroCom fleet and your new base of operations," General Drovak said, his chest puffed out like a rooster as he ushered the Devils aboard.

Kat looked around in wonder at the clean lines and state-of-the-art equipment. The *Cromwell* had been impressive enough, but against this ship, it looked rough-edged and almost unfinished. But all of that faded as if nothing in her thoughts at the sight of the man that stepped from behind the general.

"PawPaw!" she yelled as she hurled herself across the deck and into his arms, glad she'd swapped out her armor for fatigues. "What... How are you here?!"

He laughed and hugged her tight, filling her with such joy she barely felt the pain as he squeezed her shoulder. Or maybe not. PawPaw ran his sharp gaze over her, taking in her current state. Then he stepped back enough to speak face to face.

No one else would have likely caught it, but Kat noticed his gaze briefly flicker in Drovak's direction before he responded, "I called in a few favors. And it appears I've agreed to temporarily come out of retirement. Probably best not to tell your mother."

Before Kat could respond to that, PawPaw's expression lost a measure of its softness, and his gaze shifted past her shoulder. "Besides, I need to have a conversation with Tech Sergeant Daniels."

At his words, Kat tensed, resisting the urge to glare at General Drovak. What the hell had he told PawPaw that brought him clear across the universe? All she and Scotch had between them was banter, one kiss, and a nap. Neither of them had any time to sort out their intentions or desires. Not that it was anyone's business.

As tension coiled up her spine, she felt Scotch come up behind her. Soothing sounds rippled up her bonejack, followed by Scotch's classic irreverence. *No need to get your fur up, Kittie. It's just a talk.*

Then aloud, he said, "I'm at your disposal, sir."

PawPaw gave a curt nod. "This way."

When Kat moved to follow, PapPaw turned and fixed her with a stern look. "*I* will be having private words with Sergeant Daniels. *You*, young lady, will get yourself down to medical and have that shoulder looked at. Now skedaddle."

No one had the gall to laugh, though Kat knew they wanted to. She ignored them and just nodded. No argument she might make would hold water with Clark Matisse when he'd set his mind. Even so, it killed her to walk away without a few choice words of her own. She loved PawPaw dearly, but he had a bad habit of still seeing her as the wide-eyed little girl he'd taken in all those years ago. That had to stop.

Anton Petrov looked up into a hard flashback as the door of his cell slid open to reveal a man in an AeroCom uniform... only this time, both man and uniform were in a much better state of repair. With a ghost of a smile tugging at his lips, Anton raised a hand in greeting.

Nodding, the man stepped further into the room.

"I don't have long, but there's something I wanted to say." He fell silent a moment, a haunted look passing across his eyes. Anton waited patiently. After all, he had no plans for the next dozen years or so.

"Thank you." The words were clearly heartfelt, if perplexing.

Anton's brow furrowed. "For what?"

Letting out a deep breath, AeroCom... *Sergeant Daire* looked down a moment as if gathering himself, before straightening and meeting Anton's gaze. "For letting me see what he might have looked like if he hadn't died in my arms."

Anton's eyes widened as he realized the sergeant referred to the footage they had shown him of his 'son,' back when they'd recrui... pushed him to flip sides. "You knew... You knew we lied to you."

Kevin gave a short laugh. "That's okay. I lied back... hard."

"I'm glad," Anton told him with a rueful grin. "It's good to know there are people out there that can't be bought."

They both fell silent long enough that Anton resisted the urge to fidget. Finally, Daire nodded and took a step back toward the hatch.

"I really hope you find your feet"—he looked around at the stark walls of Anton's new cell—"after you're done with all of this." Another taut pause as if Daire measured the wisdom of what he was about to say. "Maybe... maybe I could help you..."

Anton shook his head hard, not bothering to mention that Daire's higher-ups had already tried pressuring him to turn... *consultant* on matters of the Legion. Then it occurred to him that this might be their alternate approach. He didn't want to believe that, but he couldn't afford not to. He put a bit of steel in his voice as he said, "Let me be very clear, just in case it's relevant here. I am done with all of this."

"Fair enough, but consider this, there is a difference between military and mercenary."

Anton respected Daire, so he resisted the urge to laugh.

Not much of one, he thought, while aloud, only faintly mocking, he said, "Yeah, one had funding."

"And the other has honor," Daire countered, turning Anton's cynical quip back on him.

Looking down at the fading bruises on his knuckles, Anton shook his head slowly this time, weary. "Wherever I land after this, it will have nothing to do with any armed forces."

"Wherever you land, I wish you well."

The words rang with honest intent, and Daire's gaze held nothing but goodwill and a glimmer of pride, no matter how hard or deep Anton searched. Before the silence once more grew awkward, the sergeant turned around and left, the hatch closing behind him.

A couple of hours had passed by the time the corpsman and psych finished with Kat. Finally, weary and no little annoyed, she made her way to the Devils' new quarters, aided by Spec, who she'd discovered waiting patiently outside medbay. Without the Parr's help, she would have just found a quiet corner to curl up in until someone found her, she felt that tired. The only thing that kept her going were the words PawPaw had had with Scotch. And the ones she intended to have with *him*...

When Spec indicated the correct hatch, Kat hesitated. He bumped her leg, and his too-cute voice came over her bonejack, *Open.*

Maybe she imagined it, but he sounded even more tired than she was. Reaching out, she pushed the hatch open. The sounds of laughter and pool balls cracking together drifted out into the corridor. Kat squared her shoulders and stepped inside. The layout and standard-issue furnishings were much the same as those they had been assigned on the *Cromwell*, if perhaps a bit more clean-lined. Their gear must have already been transferred because Pecker and Truck played on the same makeshift pool table they'd had on the decoy ship. The rest of the team sprawled throughout the common room, some eating, others napping. A few watched the guys play pool.

Scotch sat on a couch in the middle of it all, his gaze locked on the hatch. On her. His body seemed relaxed, but the look he gave her sharpened as she came in. One hand patted the cushion beside him. The other held two ounces of what looked like rich amber whiskey, the glass frosted with condensation. She resisted the urge to lick her lower lip, remembering with a bittersweet twinge the last time they'd shared a drink.

"Hey, you survived," she said, only half joking.

Scotch grinned and nodded, then patted the cushion again. Breathing deep, Kat gave in and sat beside him.

"So... what did he say?"

"After long and detailed discussion," Scotch told her, his expression serious but with an amused glint to his eye. "I have been given permission to court you proper, as time and circumstances allow. And, should I ever even think of hurting you and doing you wrong, a certain rancher will personally bust me down to private, starting with my legs..."

With a subvocal growl, Kat moved to stand. Time to find PawPaw and remind him she'd learned how to adult a long friggin' time ago.

Scotch chuckled and drew his arm around her, locking her in place beside him. He brushed his lips across the top of her head. "Relax, Kittie. He's had his words, but it's always been your say. Whatever happens here—or doesn't—you set the pace. I'm in no rush."

Releasing her tension on an unsteady breath as tingles ran straight to her toes, Kat reached over and snagged his glass.

ABOUT THE AUTHOR

AWARD-WINNING AUTHOR, EDITOR, AND PUBLISHER DANIELLE ACKLEY-MCPHAIL has worked both sides of the publishing industry for longer than she cares to admit. In 2014 she joined forces with husband Mike McPhail and friend Greg Schauer to form her own publishing house, eSpec Books (www.especbooks.com).

Her published works include seven novels, *Yesterday's Dreams, Tomorrow's Memories, Today's Promise, The Halfling's Court, The Redcaps' Queen, Daire's Devils,* and *Baba Ali and the Clockwork Djinn,* written with Day Al-Mohamed. She is also the author of the solo collections *Eternal Wanderings, A Legacy of Stars, Consigned to the Sea, Flash in the Can, Transcendence, Between Darkness and Light, The Fox's Fire, The Kindly One,* and the non-fiction writers' guides *The Literary Handyman, More Tips from the Handyman,* and *LH: Build-A-Book Workshop.* She is the senior editor of the *Bad-Ass Faeries* anthology series, *Gaslight & Grimm, Side of Good/Side of Evil, After Punk,* and *Footprints in the Stars.* Her short stories are included in numerous other anthologies and collections.

In addition to her literary acclaim, she crafts and sells original costume horns under the moniker The Hornie Lady Custom Costume Horns, and homemade flavor-infused candied ginger under the brand of Ginger KICK! at literary conventions, on commission, and wholesale.

Danielle lives in New Jersey with her husband and fellow writer, Mike McPhail, and four extremely spoiled cats.

ALLIED SUPPORT TROOPS

Accelerator Ray
Alf Shupe
Andrew J Clark IV
Andrew Timson
Anita Morris
Anonymous
Anton Kukal
Bill Kohn
Bjorn Hasseler
Brad Jurn
Brendan Lonehawk
Brian Walker
Brooks Moses
Budding Dan
Carol Gyzander
Chand Svare Ghei
Christopher J. Burke
Craig "Stevo" Stephenson
Curtis and Maryrita Steinhour
Dale A Russell
Danielle Ackley-McPhail
Dave Hermann
David Lee Summers
David Sherman
David Stolarz
Ed Ellis
Elmi

Ergo Ojasoo
Evan L
Gary Phillips
Howard J. Bampton
Hrvoje Bukša
Ian Harvey
IdleDice
Isaac 'Will It Work' Dansicker
Ixias
Jacen Leonard
Jack Campbell
Jakub Narębski
Jason Rhine
Jennifer L. Pierce
Jeremy Audet
Jim Gotaas
JoanneBB
Joe M.
Joel Jefferson
John Fallon
John Idlor
John L. French
John T. Sapienza, Jr.
Jonathan Mendonca
Josh McGinnis
Joshua C. Chadd
Keith Hall

Keith Tracton
Keith West, Future Potentate
  of the Solar System
Kelly Pierce
Ken "Merlyn" Mencher
Ken Warner
Kerry aka Trouble
KJSP
L.E. Custodio
LetoTheTooth
Linda Pierce
maileguy
Marc "mad" W.
Mari Hersh-Tudor
Mark Newman
Marvin Langenberg
Matt & Ellie A
Mike Maurer
Mike Skolnik
Morgan Campbell
Morgan Hazelwood
ND Gray
Norman Jaffe
Otter Libris
P Anne Stevenson

Pepita Hogg-Sonnenberg
Peter D Engebos
pjk
Pook
Raphael Yedwab
Rob Steinberger
Robert C Flipse
Robert Claney
Sam Lubell
Sam Tomaino
Scott Schaper
Sergey Kochergan
Shervyn
Sheryl R. Hayes
Steph Parker
Stephen Ballentine
Steve Perry
Svend Andersen
Tasha Turner
Thomas Karwacki
Tina M Noe Good
Ty Drago
Vee Luvian
Will McDermott
Yakira Heistand

CPSIA information can be obtained
at www.ICGtesting.com
Printed in the USA
LVHW010250260122
709187LV00002B/80

9 781949 691795